The Native Born
Or
The Rajah's People

by

I. A. R. Wylie

Double 9
BOOKS

The Native Born
Or
The Rajah's People
by I. A. R. Wylie

ISBN: 978-93-59956-66-4

Published by

DOUBLE 9 BOOKS
2/13-B, Ansari Road
Daryaganj, New Delhi – 110002
info@double9books.com
www.double9books.com
Tel. 011-40042856

ABOUT THE AUTHOR

Ida Alexa Ross Wylie (16 March 1885 – 4 November 1959), who wrote under the pen name I.A.R. Wylie, was an Australian-British-American novelist, screenwriter, short story writer, poet, and supporter of women's right to vote. Her works were praised by the literary and journalism establishments of her time, and she was known around the world for them. More than thirty of her books and short stories were turned into movies between 1915 and 1953. One of these was Keeper of the Flame (1942), which starred Spencer Tracy and Katharine Hepburn and was directed by George Cukor. Wylie's mother was an English farmer named Ida Millicent Ross (1855–1890), and her father was Alexander Coghill Wylie (1852–1910). She was born Ida Alexa Ross Wylie in Melbourne, Australia, on March 16, 1885. The father of I.A.R. Wylie, Alec Wylie, was from Glasgow, Scotland. He was in debt most of his life and was often on the run from debtors. So, sometime in the 1880s, after failing to become an MP, he left the UK for Australia. But not before his first wife divorced him in 1883 for cheating and violence, getting custody of their two children and asking her sister Christine to marry him, which she turned down. He quickly married Ida Ross, the daughter of a farmer in Australia. I.A.R. Wylie, their first child, was born in Melbourne, Australia, in 1885. She was named after her parents, Ida Ross and Alec Wylie.

CONTENTS

PREFACE

In earlier days a preface to a novel with no direct historical source always seemed to me somewhat out of place, since I believed that the author could be indebted solely to his own imagination. I have learned, however, that even in a novel *pur sang* it is possible to owe much to others, and I now take the opportunity which the despised preface offers to pay my debt— inadequately it is true—to Mr. Hughes Massie, whose enthusiastic help in the launching of this, my first serious literary effort, I shall always hold in grateful remembrance.

I. A. R. W.

May 9th, 1910

BOOK I

CHAPTER I
WHICH IS A PROLOGUE

The woman lying huddled on the couch turned her face to the wall and covered it with her hands in a burst of uncontrollable horror.

"Oh, that dreadful light!" she moaned. "If it would only go out! It will send me mad. Oh, if it would only go out—only go out!"

Her companion made no immediate answer. She stood by the wall, her shoulders slightly hunched, her hands clasped before her in an attitude of fixed, sullen defiance. What her features expressed it was impossible to tell, since they were hidden by the deep shadow in which she had taken up her position. The rest of the apartment was lit with a grey, ghostly light, the reflection from the courtyard, in part visible through the open doorway, and which lay bathed in all the brilliancy of a full Indian moon.

"When the light goes out, it will mean that the end has come," she said at last. "Do you know that, Christine?"

"Yes, I know it," the other answered piteously; "but that's what I want—the end. I am not afraid to die. I know Harry will be there. He will not let it be too hard for me. It's the suspense I can not bear. The suspense is worse than death. I have died a dozen times tonight, and suffered as I am sure God will not let us suffer."

Margaret Caruthers bent over the cowering figure with the sympathy which education provides when the heart fails to perform its office. There was, indeed, little tenderness in the hand which passed lightly over Christine Stafford's feverish forehead.

"You give God credit for a good deal," she said indifferently. "If the light troubles you, shall I shut the door?"

Christine sprang half upright.

"No!" she cried sharply. "No! I should still see it. Even when I cover my face—so—I can still see it flickering. And then there is the darkness, and in the darkness, faces—little John's face. Oh, my little fellow, what will become of you!" She began to cry softly, but no longer with fear. Love and pity had struggled up out of the chaos of her despair, rising above even the mighty instinct of self-preservation. Margaret's hand ceased from its mechanical act of consolation.

"Be thankful that he is not here," she said.

"I am thankful—but the thought of him makes death harder. It will hurt him so."

"No one is indispensable in this world."

Christine turned her haggard, tear-stained face to the moonlight.

"How hard you are!" she said wonderingly. "You, too, have your little girl to think of, but even with the end so close—even knowing that we shall never see our loved ones again—you are still hard."

"I have no loved ones, and life has taught me to be hard. Why should death soften me?" was the cold answer. Both women relapsed into silence. Always strangers to each other, a common danger had not served to break down the barrier between them. Christine now lay quiet and calm, her hands clasped, her lips moving slightly, as though in prayer. Her companion had resumed her former position against the wall, her eyes fixed on the open doorway, beyond which the grey lake of moonlight spread itself into the shadow of the walls. In the distance a single point of fire flickered uneasily, winking like an evil, threatening eye. So long as it winked at them, so long their lives were safe. With its extermination they knew must come their own. Hitherto, save for the murmur of the two voices, a profound hush had weighed ominously in the heavy air. Now suddenly a cry went up, pitched on a high note and descending by semitones, like a dying wind, into a moan. It was caught up instantly and repeated so close that it seemed to the two women to have sprung from the very ground beneath their feet. Christine started up.

"Oh, my God!" she muttered. "Oh, my God!" She was trembling from head to foot, but the other gave no sign of either fear or interest. There followed a brief pause, in which the imagination might have conjured up unseen forces gathering themselves together for a final onslaught. It came at last, like a cry, suddenly, amidst a wild outburst of yells, screams, and the intermittent crack of revolvers fired at close quarters. Pandemonium had been let loose on the other side of the silver lake, but the silver lake itself remained placid and untroubled. Only the red eye winked more vigorously, as though its warning had become more imperative.

Christine Stafford clung to a pair of unresponsive hands, which yielded with an almost speaking reluctance to her embrace.

"You think there is no hope?" she pleaded. "None? You know what Harry said. If the regiment got back in time—"

"The regiment will not get back in time," Margaret Caruthers interrupted. "There are ten men guarding the gate against Heaven knows how many thousand. Do you expect a miracle? No, no. We are a people who dance best at the edge of a crater, and if a few, like ourselves, get swallowed up now and again, it can not be helped. It is the penalty."

"If only Harry would come!" Christine moaned, heedless of this cold philosophy. "But he will keep his promise, won't he? He won't let us fall into those cruel hands? You remember what happened at Calcutta—"

"Hush! Don't frighten yourself and me!" exclaimed Margaret impatiently. "Does it comfort you to hold my hand? Well, hold it, then. How strange you are! I thought you weren't afraid."

"I shan't be when the time comes—but it's so very lonely. Don't you feel it? Are you made of stone?"

Margaret Caruthers set her teeth hard.

"I would to God I were!" she said. All at once she wrenched her hand free and pointed with it. Her arm, stretched out into the light, had a curious, ghostly effect. "Look!" she cried.

The red eye winked rapidly in succession, once, twice, three times, and then closed—this time for ever. An instant later two dark spots darted out into the brightly lighted space and came at headlong pace toward them. Christine sprang to her feet, and the two women clung to each other, obeying for that one moment the instinct which can bind devil to saint. But it was an English voice which greeted them from the now darkened doorway.

"It's all over!" Steven Caruthers said, entering with his companion and slamming the door sharply to. "We have five minutes more. Mackay has promised to keep them off just so long. Stafford, see to your wife!" He spoke brutally, in a voice choked with dust and pain. The room was now in pitch darkness. Harry Stafford felt his way across, his arms outstretched.

"Christine!" he called.

She came to him at once, with a step as firm and steady as a man's.

"Harry!" she cried, her voice ringing with an almost incredulous joy. "Oh, my darling!"

He caught her to him and felt how calm her pulse had become.

"Are you afraid, my wife?"

"Not now. I am so happy!"

He knew, strange though it seemed, that this was true and natural, because her love was stronger than life or the fear of death.

"Do you trust me absolutely, Christine?"

"Absolutely!"

"Give me both your hands—in my one hand—so. Kiss me, sweetheart."

In the same instant that his lips touched hers he lifted his right disengaged hand, and something icy-cold brushed past her temple. She clung to him.

"Not yet, Harry! Not yet! Oh, don't think I don't understand. I do, and I am glad. If things had gone differently the time must have come when one of us would have been left lonely. Now, we are going together. What does it matter if it is a little sooner than we hoped? Only, not yet—just one minute! We have time. Do not let us waste it. Let us kneel down and say 'Our Father,' and then—for little John—" Her voice broke. "Afterward— when you think fit, husband, I shall be ready."

He put his arm about her, and they knelt down side by side at the little couch. Christine prayed aloud, and he followed her, his deeper voice hushed to a whisper.

The two other occupants of the room did not heed them. They, too, had found each other. At her husband's entrance Margaret Caruthers had crept back to the wall and had remained there motionless, not answering to his sharp, imperative call. He groped around the room, and when at length his hands touched her face, both drew back as one total stranger from another.

"Why did you not answer?" he asked hoarsely. "Are you not aware that any moment may be our last?"

"Yes," she said.

"I have something I wish to say to you, Margaret, before the time comes."

"I am listening."

"I wish to say if at any period in our unfortunate married life I have done you wrong, I am sorry."

She made no answer.

"I ask your forgiveness."

"I forgive you."

The sound of firing outside had grown fainter, the shrieks louder, more exultant, mingling like an unearthly savage chorus with the hushed voices By the couch.

—"Thy will be done—" prayed Christine valiantly.

Margaret Caruthers lifted her head and laughed.

"Don't laugh!" her husband burst out. "Pray now, if you have ever prayed in your life. You have need of prayers." He lifted his arm as he spoke; but, as though she guessed his intention, she sprang out of his reach.

"No!" she said, in a voice concentrated with passion. "I am not going to die like that. Stafford can shoot his wife down like a piece of blind cattle if he thinks fit—but not you. I won't die by your hand, Steven. I hate you too much."

"Hush!" he exclaimed. "The account between us is settled."

"Do you think I can begin to love you just because we are both about to die?"

"You are my wife," he answered, grasping her by the wrists. "There are things worse than death, and from them I shall shield you, whether you will or not."

"Is it not enough that you have taken my life once?" she retorted.

"What do you mean? How dare you say that!"

"I say it because it is true. I have never lived—never. You killed me years ago—all that was best in me. Save your soul from a second murder."

"If you live, do you know what may lie before you?"

"You talk of things 'worse than death.' What shame, what misery could be worse than the years spent at your side?"

"You are mad, Margaret. I shall pay no attention to you. I must save you against your will."

All through the hurried dialogue neither had spoken above a whisper. Even in that moment they obeyed the habit of a lifetime, hiding hatred and bitterness beneath a mask of apparent calm. Without a sound, but with a frantic strength, Margaret wrenched herself free.

"Leave me to my own fate!" she demanded, in the same passionate undertone.

"You have ceased to be responsible for me."

He made one last effort to hold her. In the same instant the firing ceased altogether. There followed the roar and crash of bursting timber, the pattering of naked feet, the fanatic yells drawing every second nearer.

"Margaret!" he cried wildly, holding out his revolver in the darkness. "If not at my hands, then at your own. Save yourself — "

"I shall save myself, have no fear!" she answered, with a bitter, terrible laugh.

From the couch Christine Stafford's voice rose peacefully:

"Lord, into Thy hands I commend my spirit!"

Another voice answered, "Amen!" There was the report of a revolver and a sudden, startling stillness. It lasted only a breathing space. Furious shoulders hurled themselves against the frail, weakly barred door. It cracked, bulged inward, with a bursting, tearing sound, yielded. The moonlight flooded into the little room, throwing up into bold relief the three upright figures and the little heap that knelt motionless by the couch.

The crowd of savage faces hesitated, faltering an instant before the sahibs who yesterday had been their lords and masters. Then the sahibs fired. It was all that was needed. The room filled. There was one stifled groan — no more than that. No cry for mercy, no whining.

Little by little the room emptied again. The cries and bloodthirsty screams of triumphant vengeance died slowly in the distance, the grey moonlight resumed its peaceful sovereignty. Only here and there were dark stains its silver could not wash away.

CHAPTER II
THE DANCING IS RESUMED.

"Oh, I love India—adore it, simply!" Mrs. Cary exclaimed, in the tone of a person who, usually self-controlled, finds himself overwhelmed by the force of his own enthusiasm. "There is something so mystic, so enthralling about it, don't you think? I always feel as though I were wandering through a chapter of the *Arabian Nights* full of gorgeous princes, wicked robbers, genii, or whatever you call them. Isn't it so with you, Mrs. Carmichael?"

Her hostess, a thin, alert little woman with a bony, weather-beaten face, cast an anxious glance at the rest of her guests scattered about the garden.

"There aren't any robbers about here—except my cook," she said prosaically. "My husband wouldn't allow such a thing in his department, and in mine he is no good at all. As for the princes, we don't see anything of the only one this region boasts of. He may be gorgeous, but I really can not say for certain."

"Ah!" said Mrs. Cary, with a placid smile. "You have been in fairyland too long, dear Mrs. Carmichael. That's what's the matter with you. You are beginning to look upon it as a very ordinary, everyday place. If you only knew what it is to come to it with a virgin heart and mind-thirsting for impressions, as it were. That is how we feel, do we not, Beatrice?" She half turned to the girl standing at her side, as though seeking to draw her into the conversation.

"It is indeed new for *me*," the latter answered shortly, and with slight emphasis on the personal pronoun.

"I was about to remark that this is scarcely your first visit to India," Mrs. Carmichael put in. "I understood that your late husband had a government appointment somewhere in the South?"

Mrs. Cary's heavy face flushed, though whether with heat or annoyance it was not easy to judge.

"Of course—a very excellent appointment, too—but the place and the people!" She became confidential and her voice sank, though beyond her daughter there was no one within hearing. "Between you and me, Mrs.

Carmichael, the people were *dreadful*. You know, I am not snobbish—indeed I must confess to quite democratic tendencies, which my family always greatly deplores—but I really couldn't stand the people. I had to go back to England with Beatrice. The place was filled with subordinate railway officials. Don't you hate subordinates, dear Mrs. Carmichael?"

Mrs. Carmichael stared, during which process her eyes happened to fall on Beatrice Cary's half-averted face. She was surprised to find that the somewhat thin lips were smiling—though not agreeably.

"I really don't know what you mean by 'subordinates,'" Mrs. Carmichael said, in her uncompromising way. "Most people are subordinates at some time or other. My husband was a lieutenant once. I don't remember objecting to him. At any rate," she continued hastily, as though to cut the conversation short, "I hope you will like the people here."

"I'm sure I shall. A military circle is always so delightful. That is what I said to Beatrice when I felt that I must revisit the scene of my girlish days. 'We must go somewhere where there is military.' Of course, we might have gone to Simla—I have influential friends there, you know—but I wanted my girl to see a real bit of genuine India, and Simla is *so* modern. Really a great pity, I think. I am so passionately fond of color and picturesqueness— comfort is nothing to me. As my husband used to say, 'Oh, Mary, you are always putting your artistic feelings before material necessities.' Poor fellow, he used to miss his creature comforts sometimes, I fear."

Her laugh, painfully resembling a giggle, interrupted her own garrulity, which was finally put to an end by a fresh arrival. A slight, daintily-clad figure had detached itself from a group of guests and came running toward them. Mrs. Carmichael's deeply lined, somewhat severe face lighted up.

"That is my husband's ward, Lois Caruthers," she said. "She has been with me all her life, practically. As you are so fond of genuine India, you must let her show you over the place. She knows all the dirtiest, and I suppose most interesting corners, with their exact history."

"Delightful!" murmured Mrs. Cary, with a gracious nod of her plumed headgear. Nevertheless, she studied the small figure and animated features of the new-comer with a critical severity not altogether in accordance with her next remark, uttered, apparently under pressure of the same irresistible enthusiasm, in an audible side whisper: "What a sweet face—so piquant!"

An adjective is a pliable weapon, and, in the hands of a woman, can be made to mean anything under the sun. Mrs. Cary's "piquant"—pronounced in a manner that was neither French nor English, but a startling mixture of both—had a background to it of charitable patronage. It was meant, without doubt, to be a varnished edition of "plain," perhaps even "ugly," though Lois Caruthers deserved neither insinuation. Possibly too small in build, she was yet graceful, and there was a lithe, elastic energy in her movements which drew attention to her even among more imposing figures. Possibly, also, she was too dark for the English ideal. Her black hair and large brown eyes, together with the unrelieved pallor of her complexion, gave her appearance something that was exotic but not unpleasing. *Enfin,* as most people admitted, she had her charm; and her moods, which ranged from the most light-hearted gaiety to the deepest gravity, could be equally irresistible. She was light-hearted enough now, however, as she smiled from one to the other, including mother and daughter in her friendly greeting, though as yet both were strangers to her.

"I have come to fetch you, Aunt Harriet," she said, addressing Mrs. Carmichael. "Mr. Travers has got some great scheme on hand which he will only disclose in your presence. We are all gasping with curiosity. Will you please come?"

Mrs. Carmichael nodded.

"I will come at once," she said. "I'm sure it's only one of Mr. Travers' breakneck schemes, but they are always amusing to listen to. Lois, come and be introduced. My adopted niece—Mrs. Cary—Miss Cary."

They shook hands.

"Lois, when there is time, I want you to do the honors of Marut. Miss Cary especially has as yet seen nothing, and there is a great deal of interest. You know—" turning to her visitors—"Marut is supposed to have been the hotbed of the last rising."

"Indeed!" murmured Mrs. Cary vaguely. "How delightful!"

Lois Caruthers laughed, not without a shadow of bitterness.

"It was hardly delightful at the time, I should imagine," she observed. "But what there is to see I shall be very glad to show you. Will any day suit you?"

"Oh, yes, any day," Beatrice Cary assented, speaking almost for the first time. "I have nothing to do here from morning to night."

"That will soon change," Lois said, walking by her side. "I am always busy, either playing tennis, or riding, or getting up some entertainment. The difficulty is to find time to rest."

"You must be a very much sought-after person," Beatrice observed, in the tone of a person who is making a graceful compliment. The hint of irony, however, was unmistakable.

"I am not more sought after than any one else," Lois returned, unruffled. "Every one has to help in the work of frivolity."

"I shall be rather out of it, then," Beatrice said coolly. "I am not amusing."

"It is quite sufficient to be willing, good-natured and good-humored," Lois answered.

They had by this time reached the group under the trees, where Mrs. Carmichael and her companion had already arrived, under the escort of a tall, stoutly built man, who was talking and apparently explaining with great vigor. As Lois entered the circle, he glanced up and smiled at her, revealing a handsome, cheerful face, singularly fresh-colored in comparison with the deep tan of the other men.

"That is Mr. Travers," Lois explained. "He is a bank director or something in Madras, and has been on a long business visit north. He is awfully clever and popular, and gets up everything."

"Rich, I suppose?"

Lois glanced up at her companion. The beautiful profile and the tone of the remark seemed incongruous.

"I don't know," she said rather abruptly. "He has four polo ponies. Nobody else has more than two."

"Do you calculate wealth by polo ponies, then?"

Lois laughed.

"Yes, we do pretty well," she said—"that is, when we bother about such things at all. Most people are poor, and if they aren't, they have to live beyond their income, so it comes to the same in the end."

"Everybody looks cheerful enough," Beatrice Cary observed. "I always thought poverty and worry went together."

"Who is that talking about poverty and worry?" asked a voice behind them. "Is it you, Miss Caruthers? If so, I shall arraign you as a disturber of the peace. Who wants to be bothered with the memory of his empty purse on such a lovely day?"

Lois turned with a smile to the new-comer.

"No, I am innocent, Captain Stafford," she said. "It was Miss Cary who brought up the terms you object to."

"Well, won't you introduce me, then, so that I can express my displeasure direct to the culprit?"

The ceremony of introduction was gone through, on Beatrice Cary's side with a sudden change of manner. Hitherto cold, indifferent, slightly supercilious, she now relaxed into a gentleness that was almost appealing.

"This is a new world for me," she said, looking up into Captain Stafford's amused face, "and I have so many questions to ask that I am afraid of turning into a mark of interrogation, or—as you said—a disturber of the peace."

"You won't ask questions long," he answered, with a wise shake of the head. "Nobody does. Wherever English people go they take their whole paraphernalia with them; and you will find that, with a few superficial differences, Marut is no more or less than a snug little English suburb. A little more freedom of intercourse—a little less Philistinism, perhaps—but the foundations are the same. As to India itself, one soon learns to forget all about it."

He then turned to Lois, who was intent on watching Mr. Travers.

"You weren't on the race-course this morning," he said in an undertone. "I missed you. Why did you not come?"

"I couldn't," she said. "There was too much to be done. We are rather short of servants just now, for reasons—well, that, according to you, ought not to be mentioned on a fine day."

He laughed, but not as he had hitherto done. There was another tone in his voice, warmer, more confidential. It attracted Beatrice Cary's attention, and she looked curiously from Lois to the man beside her. About thirty-five, with a passably good figure, irregular, if honest, features, and an expression usually somewhat grave, he made no pretensions to any exterior advantage. He could apparently be gay, as now, but his gaiety did not conceal the fact that it was unusual. Altogether, he had nothing about him which appealed to her, but Beatrice Cary was inclined to resent Lois' obvious intimacy with him as something which accentuated her own isolation.

"Can you make out what Mr. Travers is saying?" Lois asked, turning suddenly to her. "I can't hear a word, and I'm sure it's awfully interesting. Captain Stafford, do you know?"

"I can guess," he answered, half smiling. "When Travers has a suggestion to make, it usually means that some one has to stump up."

There was a general laugh. Travers looked around.

"Some one has accused me falsely," he declared. "I have a prophetic sense of injury."

"On the contrary, that is what I am suffering from," Stafford retorted. "Since hearing that you have a new scheme, I have been hastily reckoning how many weeks' leave I shall have to sacrifice to pay for it."

Travers shook his head.

"As usual—wrong, my dear Captain," he said. "My scheme has two parts. The first part is known to you all, though for the benefit of weak memories, I will repeat it. Ladies and gentlemen, in this Station we have the honor of being protected from the malice of the aborigine by two noble regiments. We count, moreover, at least thirty of the fair sex and forty miscellaneous persons, such as miserable civilians like myself, and children. Hitherto, we have been content to meet at odd times and odd places. When hospitality has run dry, we have resorted to a shed-like structure dignified with the name of club. Personally, I call it a disgrace, which should at once be rectified."

"I have already contributed my mite!" protested a young subaltern from the British regiment.

"I know; so has everybody. With strenuous efforts I have collected the sum of five hundred rupees. That won't do. We require at least four times that sum. Consequently, we must have a patron."

"The second part of your programme concerns the patron, then?" Captain Webb inquired, with an aspect of considerable relief. "Not yourself, by any chance?"

"Certainly not. If I had any noble inclinations of that sort I should have discovered them a long time ago. No, I content myself with taking the part of a fairy godmother."

"I'm afraid I don't follow," Stafford put in. "What is the fairy godmother going to do for us? Produce a club-house, a patron, or a cucumber?"

"A patron, and one, my dear fellow, whom I should have entirely overlooked had it not been for you."

"For me!"

"It was you who made the discovery that the present Rajah is not, as we thought, an imbecilic youth, but a man of many parts and splendidly adapted to our requirements."

"I protest!" broke in Stafford, with unusual earnestness. "It was by pure chance that, in an audience with the Maharajah Scindia, the late regent of Marut, I got to hear that his whilom ward was both intelligent and cultured. I believe it was a slip on his part, and, seeing that Rajah Nehal Singh has shunned all English intercourse, I can not see that there is any likelihood of his adapting himself or his purse to your plans."

"Oh, bosh!" exclaimed Travers impatiently. "You are too cautious, Stafford. Other rajahs interest themselves in social matters—why not this one? He is fabulously rich, I understand, and a little gentle handling should easily bring him around."

There was a chorus of bravos, in which only one or two did not join. One was Colonel Carmichael, who stood a little apart, pulling his thin grey moustache in the nervous, anxious way peculiar to him, his kindly face overshadowed.

"On principle," he began, after the first applause had died down, "I am against the suggestion. Of course, I have no deciding voice in the matter, but I confess that the idea has not my approval. I know very well that, as you say, other native princes have proved themselves useful and valuable acquisitions to English society. In some cases it may be well enough, though in no case does it seem to me right to accept hospitality from a man to whom we only grant an apparent equality. In this particular case I consider the idea—well, repulsive."

"May I ask why, Colonel?" Travers asked sharply.

"By all means. Because less than a quarter of a century ago the father of the man from whom you are seeking gifts slaughtered by treachery hundreds of our own people."

An uncomfortable, uneasy silence followed. Captain Stafford and Lois exchanged a quick glance of understanding.

"I know of at least two people who will agree with me," continued the Colonel, who had intercepted and possibly anticipated the glance.

"You are right, Colonel," Stafford said. "I bear no malice, and any idea of revenge seems to me foolish. As far as I know, the present Rajah is all that can be desired, but I protest against a suggestion—and what is worse, a practice, which must inevitably lower our dignity in the eyes of those we are supposed to govern."

The awkward silence continued for a moment, no one caring to express a contrary opinion, though a contrary opinion undoubtedly existed.

Beatrice looked up at Captain Webb, who happened to be standing at her side. Her acquaintance with him dated only from an hour back, but an uncontrollable irritation made her voice her opinions to him.

"I think all that sort of thing rather overstrained and unnecessary," she said. "Your chief business is to get the best out of life, and quixotic people who worry about the means are rather a nuisance, don't you think?"

Captain Webb's bored features lighted up with a faint amusement.

"O, Lor', you mustn't say that sort of thing to me, Miss Cary!" he said in a subdued aside. "Superior officer, you know! If you want an index to my feelings, study my countenance." He pretended to smother a gigantic yawn, and Beatrice's cool, unchecked laughter broke the constraint.

Travers look around with a return of his old good-humor.

"Well," he said, "I have two votes against my plans, but, with due respect to those two, who are, perhaps, unduly influenced by unfortunate circumstances, I feel that it is only just that the others should be given a voice in the matter. Do you agree, Colonel?"

Colonel Carmichael had by this time regained his placid, gentle manner.

"Certainly," he agreed, without hesitation.

"Hands up, then, for letting Rajah Nehal Singh go his way in peace!"

Three hands went up—Colonel Carmichael's, Stafford's and Lois'. Beatrice glanced at the latter with a smile that expressed what it was meant to express—a supercilious amusement. Her indifference was rapidly taking another and more decided character.

"Hands up for drawing the bashful youth into Circe's circle!" called Travers, now thoroughly elated. A forest of hands went up. Captain Webb and his bosom comrade, Captain Saunders, who, for diplomatic reasons had remained neutral, exchanged grins. "You see," Travers said, turning with deferential politeness to the Colonel, "the day is against you."

"The Old Guard dies, but never surrenders!" quoted the Colonel good-humoredly.

"The next question is, on whose shoulders shall the task of beguilement fall?" Travers went on, glancing at Stafford. "I suppose you, O, wise young judge—?"

"It is out of the question," Stafford answered at once. "I consider I have done enough damage already."

"What about your serpent's tongue, Travers?" suggested Webb. "When I think of the follies you have tempted me to commit, I feel that you should be unanimously elected."

Travers bowed his acknowledgments with mock gravity.

"Since there are no other candidates, I accept the onerous task," he said, "but I can not go about it single-handed. The serpent's tongue may be mine, but I lack, I fear, the grace and personal charm necessary for complete conquest. I need the help of Circe, herself." His bright, bird-like eye passed over the laughing group, resting on Lois an instant with an expression of woebegone regret. Beatrice Cary was the next in line, and his search went no farther than her flushed, eager face. "Ah!" he exclaimed, "I have found the enchantress herself! Miss— —" He hesitated, for an instant unaccountably shaken out of his debonair self-possession. Webb sprang to the rescue with a formal introduction, and Travers proceeded, if not entirely with his old equanimity. "I beg your pardon, Miss Cary," he apologized. "Your face is, strangely enough, so familiar to me that I took you for an old acquaintance— perhaps, indeed, you are, if in our modern days Circe finds it necessary to travel incognito."

Beatrice joined in the general amusement, her unusually large and beautiful eyes bright with elation.

"May I claim your assistance?" Travers went on. "Instinct tells me that we shall be irresistible."

"Willingly," Beatrice responded, "though I can not imagine how I can help you."

"Leave that to me," he said, offering her his arm. "My plans are Napoleonic in their depth and magnitude. If you will allow me to unfold them to you before the dancing begins— ?"

She smiled her assent, and walked at his side toward the Colonel's bungalow. On their way they passed Mrs. Cary, who, strangely enough, did not respond to the half-triumphant glance which her daughter cast at her. She turned hastily aside.

"Mr. Travers is no doubt— " she began, in a confidential undertone; but her companion, Mrs. Carmichael, had taken the opportunity and vanished.

The light-hearted, superficial discussion, with its scarcely felt undercurrent of tragic reminiscence, had lasted through the swift sunset, and already dusk was beginning to throw its long shadows over the gaily dressed figures that streamed up toward the bungalow.

On the outskirts of the garden lights were springing up in quick succession, thanks to the industry of Mrs. Carmichael, who hurried from one Chinese lantern to the other, breathless but determined. The task was doubtless an ignominious one for an Anglo-Indian lady of position, but Mrs. Carmichael, who acted as a sort of counterbalance to her husband's extravagant hospitality, cared not at all. England, half-pay and all its attendant horrors, loomed in the near future, and economy had to be practised somehow.

Of the late group only Lois and John Stafford remained. They had not spoken, but, as though obeying a mutual understanding, both remained quietly waiting till they were alone.

"Shall we walk about a little?" he asked at last. "I missed our morning ride so much. It has put my whole day out of joint, and I want something to put it straight again. Do you mind, or would you rather dance? I see they have begun."

"No," she said. "I would rather be quiet for a few minutes. Somehow I have lost the taste for that sort of thing to-night."

"I also," he responded.

They walked silently side by side along the well-kept path, each immersed in his own thoughts and soothed by the knowledge that their friendship had reached a height where silence is permitted—becomes even the purest form of expression. At the bottom of the compound they reached a large, low-built building, evidently once a dwelling-place, overgrown with wild plants and half in ruins, whose dim outlines stood out against the darkening background of trees and sky. The door stood open, and must indeed have stood open for many years, for the broken hinges were rusty and seemed to be clinging to the torn woodwork only by the strength of undisturbed custom.

Stafford came to a halt.

"That is where—" he began, and then abruptly left his sentence unfinished.

"Yes," she said, "it is here. I don't think, as long as we live in India, that my guardian will ever have it touched. He calls it the Memorial. My father was his greatest friend, and the terrible fact that he came too late to save him has saddened his whole life."

Stafford looked down at her. The light from a lantern which Mrs. Carmichael, with great dexterity, had fixed among some overhanging branches, fell on the dark features, now composed and thoughtful. She met his glance in silence, with large eyes that had taken into their depths something of the surrounding shadow. He had never felt so strongly before the peculiarity of her fascination—perhaps because he had never seen her in a setting which seemed so entirely a part of herself. The distant music, the hum of voices, and that strange charm which permeates an Indian nightfall—above all, the ruined bungalow with its shattered door and silent memories—these things, with their sharp contrasts of laughter and tragedy, had formed themselves into a background which belonged to her, so that she and they seemed inseparable.

"Oh, Lois, little girl!" Stafford said gently. "I have always thought of you as standing alone, different from everything and everybody, a stranger from another world, irresistible, incomprehensible. I have just understood that you are part and parcel of it all, child of the sun and flowers and mysteries and wonders. It is I who am the stranger!"

"Hush!" she said, in a voice of curious pain. "Hush! Let us go back. We must dance—whether we will or not."

He followed her without protest. The very rustle of her muslin skirts over the fallen leaves made for his ears a new and fantastic music.

Close behind them wandered the two captains, Webb and Saunders, arm in arm. At the entrance to Colonel Carmichael's Memorial Webb stopped, and, striking a match against the door, proceeded to light his cigar. The tiny flame lit up for an instant the languid patrician features.

"A cigar is one's only comfort in a dull affair like this," he remarked, as they resumed their leisurely promenade. "Awful wine, wasn't it?"

"Awful. The Colonel is beginning to put on the curb—or his lady. It's the same thing."

"It will be better when the club comes into existence," said Webb, blowing consolatory clouds of smoke into the quiet air.

"It is to be hoped so. Spunky devil, that Travers. Wonder how he means to do the trick. He knows how to pick out a pretty partner, anyhow."

"That Cary girl? Yes. Wait till the heat has dried her up, though. She'll be a scarecrow, like the rest of them. By the way, what were her people?"

"Heaven knows—something in the D.P.W., I believe. The mother was dressed in the queerest kit."

"I heard her talking about 'the gentlemen,'" remarked Webb, laughing, as they went up the steps of the bungalow together.

The Memorial was once more left to its shadows and silence. At the edge of the compound a group of natives peered through the fencing, watching and listening. Their dark faces expressed neither hatred nor admiration, nor sorrow, nor pleasure—at most, a dull wonder.

When they were tired of watching, they passed noiselessly on their way.

CHAPTER III
NEHAL SINGH

The Royal apartment was prepared for the suffocating midday heat. Heavy hangings had been pulled across the door which led on to the balcony, and only at one small aperture the sunshine ventured to pierce through and dance its golden reflection hither and thither over the marble floor. The rest was hidden in the semi-obscurity of a starlit night, which, like a transparent veil, half conceals and half reveals an untold richness and splendor.

At either side slender Moorish pillars rose to the lofty ceiling, and from their capitals winking points of light shimmered through the shadows. Fantastic designs sprang into sudden prominence on the walls, shifting with the shifting of the sunshine, and at the far end, raised by steps from the level of the floor, stood a throne, alone marked out against the darkness by its bejeweled splendor. Of other furniture there was no trace. To the left a divan formed of silken cushions had been built up for temporary use, and on this, stretched full length on his side, lay an old man whose furrowed visage appeared doubly dark and sinister beneath the dead white of his turban. His head was half supported on a pillow, and thus at his ease he watched with unblinking, unflagging attention the tall, slight figure by the doorway.

It was the Rajah himself who had let in the one point of daylight. It fell full upon his face and set into a brilliant blaze the single diamond on the nervous, muscular hand which held the curtain aside. Apparently he had forgotten his companion, and indeed everything save the scene on which his eyes rested. Beneath the balcony, like steps to a mighty altar, broad and beautiful terraces descended in stately gradations to a paradise of rare exotic flowers, whose heavy perfume came drifting up on the calm air to the very windows of the palace. This lovely chaos extended for about a mile and then ended abruptly. As though cultivated nature had suddenly broken loose from her artificial bounds, a dark jungle-forest rose up side by side with the flowers and well-kept walks, and like a black stain spread itself into the distance, swallowing up hill and valley until the eye lost itself in the haze of the horizon. Within a few hundred yards of the palace a ruined

Hindu temple lifted its dome and crumbling towers into the intense blue of the sky. And on garden, jungle, and temple alike the scorching midday sun blazed down with pitiless impartiality.

For an hour the Rajah had remained watching the unchanging scene, scarcely for an instant shifting his own position. One hand rested on his hip, the other held back the curtain and supported him in a half-leaning attitude of dreamy indolence. Against the intensified darkness of the room behind him his features stood out with the distinctness of a finely cut cameo. A man of about twenty-five years, he yet seemed younger, thanks, perhaps, to his expression, which was extraordinarily untroubled.

Thought, poetic and philosophic, but never tempestuous, sat in the dark, well-shaped eyes and high, intellectual forehead. Humor, sorrow, care, anxiety and doubt, the children of a strenuous life, had left his face singularly unscarred with their characteristic lines. For the rest, beyond that he was unusually fair, he represented in bearing and in feature a Hindu prince of high caste and noble lineage. Between him and the old man upon the divan there was no apparent resemblance. The latter was considerably darker, and lacked both the refinement of feature and dignity of expression which distinguished the younger man. Nevertheless, when he spoke it was in the tone of familiarity, almost of paternal authority.

"Art thou not weary, my son?" he asked abruptly. "For an hour thou hast neither moved nor spoken. Tell me with what thy thoughts are concerned. I would fain know, and thy face has told me nothing."

Nehal Singh let the curtain fall back into its place, and the yellow patch of sunshine upon the marble faded. He looked at his companion steadfastly, but with eyes that saw nothing.

"My thoughts!" he repeated, in a low, musical voice. "My thoughts are valueless. They are like caged birds which have beaten their wings against the bars of their cage and now sit on their golden perches and dream of the world beyond." He laughed gently. "No, my father. You, who have seen the world, would mock at them as dim, unreal reflections of a reality which you have touched and handled. For me they are beautiful enough."

The old man lifted himself on his elbow.

"Thinkest thou never of thyself?" he asked. "In thy dreams hast thou never seen thine own form rise at the call of thy waiting people?"

"My waiting people!" Nehal Singh repeated, with a smile and a faint lifting of the eyebrows. "No people wait for me, my father. So much I have learned. I bear a title, a tract of land acknowledges my rule—but a people! No, like my title, like my power, like myself, so is the people that thou sayest await me—a dream, my father, a dream!" He spoke gravely, without sadness, the same gentle, wistful smile playing about his lips.

The other sank back with a groan.

"The All-Highest pity me!" he exclaimed bitterly. "A child of blood and battle, without energy, without ambition!"

Nehal Singh, who had paced forward to the foot of the throne, turned and looked back.

"Ambition I have had," he answered, "energy I have had. Like my thoughts, they have beaten themselves weary against the bars of their cage. What would you have me do?" He strode back to the door, and, pulling aside the curtain, let the full dazzling sunshine pour in upon them. "See out there!" he cried. "Is it not a sight to bring peace to the soul of the poet and the dreamer? But for the warrior? Can he draw his sword against flowers and trees?"

The old man smiled coldly, but not without satisfaction.

"There is a world that awaiteth thee beyond," he said.

"A world of which I know nothing."

"The time cometh."

Nehal Singh studied the wrinkled face with a new intentness.

"Hitherto thou hast always held a barrier between the world and me," he said. "When the call to the Durbar came, it was thou who bade me say I was ill. When the Feringhi sought my presence, it was thou who held fast my door, first with one excuse, then with another. And now? I do not understand thee."

Behar Asor struggled up into a sitting posture, his features rendered more malignant by a glow of fierce triumph.

"Ay, the barrier has been there!" he cried. "It is I who have held it erect all these years when they thought me dead and powerless. It is I who have kept thee spotless and undefiled, Nehal Singh, thou alone of all thy race and of all thy caste! The shadow of the Unbeliever has never crossed thy man's face, his food thy lips, nor has his hand touched thy man's hand. Thou art the chosen of Brahma, and when the hour striketh and the Holy War proclaimed from east to west and from north to south, then it shall be *thy* sword—"

Nehal Singh held up his hand with a gesture of command.

"Thou also art a dreamer," he said firmly. "Thy heart is full of an old hatred and an old injury. My heart is free from both. Seest thou, my father, there were years when thy words called up some echo in me. Thou toldest me of the Feringhi, of the bloody battles thou foughtest against them because they had wronged thee; how, after Fortune had smiled faintly, thou wert driven into exile, and I, thy son, bereft of all save pomp and title, placed upon thy empty throne. These things made my blood boil. In those days I thought and planned for the great hour when I should seek revenge for thee and for myself. That is all past."

"Why all past?" Behar Asor demanded.

"Because the truth drifted in to me from the outer world. I saw that everywhere there was peace such as my land, even after thy account, has rarely known. Law and order reigned where there had been plundering and devastation, prosperity where there had been endless famine. More than this, I saw that in every conflict, whether between beast and beast or man and man, it was always the strongest and wisest that conquered. The triumph of the fool and weakling is but a short one, nor is the rule of crime and wickedness of long duration. Why, then, should I throw myself against a people who have brought my people prosperity, and who have proved themselves in peace and war our masters in courage and wisdom?"

Behar Asor struggled up, galvanized by a storm of passion which shook his fragile frame from head to foot.

"Thou art still no more than an ignorant boy," he exclaimed. "What knowest thou of these things?"

"I have read of Englishmen whose deeds outrival the legends of Krishna," Nehal Singh answered thoughtfully. "They fought in your time, my father. Thou knowest them better than I."

The old man ground his teeth together.

"They are dead." There was a reluctant admiration in his tone.

"Nevertheless, their sons live."

"The sons inherit not always the courage of their fathers," Behar Asor answered, with a bitter significance.

Nehal Singh had wandered back to the throne, as though drawn thither by some irresistible attraction, and stood there motionless, his arms folded across his breast.

"Do not blame me," he said at last. "No man can go against himself. Were it in my power, I would do thy will. As it is, without cause or reason I can not draw my sword against men whose fathers have made my heart beat with sympathy and admiration."

Behar Asor sank back in an attitude of absolute despair.

"I am accursed!" he said.

With a smothered sigh, Nehal Singh mounted the steps and seated himself. In his attitude also there was a hopelessness—not indeed the hopelessness of a man whose plans are thwarted, but of one who is keenly conscious that he has no plans, no goal, no purpose. As he sat there, his fine head thrown back against the white ivory, his eyes half closed, his fingers loosely clasping the golden peacocks' heads which formed the arms of his throne, there was, as he had said, something dreamlike and unreal about his whole person, intensified perhaps by the dim atmosphere and shadowy splendor of his surroundings.

Behar Asor had ceased to watch him, but lay motionless, with his face covered by the white mantle which he wore about his shoulders. The first storm of angry disappointment over, he had relapsed into a passive oriental acceptance of the inevitable, which did not, however, exclude an undercurrent of bitter brooding and contempt.

Some time passed before either of the two men spoke. At last Behar Asor lifted his head and glanced quickly sidewise at the figure seated on the throne. Nehal Singh's eyes were now entirely closed and seemed to sleep. Such a proceeding would have been excusable enough in the suffocating heat, but the sight drove the old man into a fresh paroxysm of indignation.

"Sleepest thou, Nehal Singh?" he demanded, in a harsh, rasping voice. "Is it not sufficient that thou hast failed thy destiny, but in the same hour thou must close thine eyes and dream, like a child on whose shoulders rest no duty, no responsibility? Awake! I have more to say to thee."

Nehal Singh looked up.

"I have not slept," he said gravely, "though, as to what concerns duty and responsibility, I might well have done so, for I have neither the one nor the other. Speak, I pray thee. I listen."

Behar Asor remained silent a moment, biting his forefinger. There was something in the action strongly reminiscent of a cunning, treacherous animal.

"Thou hast laughed at thine own power," he said at last, "though I have sworn to thee that, as in my time, so today, the swords that sleep in a hundred thousand sheaths would awake at thy word. They sleep because thou sleepest. Well—thou hast willed to sleep. I can not force thee, and mine own hand has grown too feeble. But since thou hast chosen peace, remember this, that it can last only with thy lifetime. So long thy people will be patient. Afterward—" He shrugged his shoulders significantly.

"Thou hast more to tell me," Nehal Singh said.

"If thou wilt keep peace in thy land, see to it that thou hast children who will carry it on for thee after thou hast passed into the shadow," Behar answered. "Hitherto thou hast led a strange and lonely life, preparing as I willed for the destiny thou hast cast aside. Take now unto thee a companion—a wife."

As though clumsy, untutored fingers which had until now tortured some fine instrument had suddenly, perhaps by chance, perhaps by instinct, struck a pure harmonious chord, Nehal Singh rose to his feet, his weary dreamer's face transfigured with a new light and new energy.

"A wife!" he said under his breath. "A woman! I know nothing of women. In all my life I have seen but two—my mother and a nautch-girl— who cringed to me. I should not like my wife to cringe to me. Are there not such as could be my companion, my comrade? Or are they all servile slaves?"

Behar Asor laughed shortly and contemptuously.

"They are our inferiors," he said, "hence they can not be more than companions for our idle hours. But you will have idle hours enough, and there would be many who would call themselves blessed to share themselves with thee. A great alliance—"

Nehal Singh interrupted him with the old gesture of authority.

"Thou hast said enough, my father," he said. "I will think upon it. Until then—leave me my peace."

With a slow, meditative step he went back to the curtained doorway and, pulling aside the hangings, went out on to the balcony. It was four o'clock, and already the heat of the day had broken. Long rays of sunlight struck eastward across the garden and touched with their faded golden fingers the topmost turrets of the temple. In the distance the shadows of the jungle had advanced and, like the waves of a rising tide, seemed to swallow up, step by step, the brightness of the prospect. Nehal Singh descended the winding stair that led to the first terrace. Thence three paths stretched themselves before him. He chose the central one, and with bowed head passed between the high, half-wild, half-cultivated borders of plants and shrubs. A faint evening breeze breathed its intangible perfume against his cheek, and he looked up smiling.

"A woman!" he murmured dreamily. "A woman!"

CHAPTER IV
CIRCE

The dominion over which Rajah Nehal Singh exercised his partial authority was a tract of unfruitful land extending over about two hundred square miles and sparely inhabited by a branch of the Aryan race which through countless generations had kept itself curiously aloof from its neighbors. The greater number were Hindus of the strictest type, and perhaps owing to their natural conservatism they had succeeded in keeping their religion comparatively free from the abuses and distortions which it was forced to undergo in other regions. Up to the year 18—the state had been to all practical purposes independent. Its poverty and unusual integral cohesion made it at once a dangerous enemy and an undesirable dependent, which it was tacitly agreed to let alone until such time when action should become imperative. That time had come under the reign of Behar Asor— then Behar Singh. This prince, who, his followers declared, could trace his descent from Brahma himself, unexpectedly, after he had been living in hand-in-glove friendship with his European neighbors, proclaimed a Holy War, massacred all foreigners within his reach, and for eighteen long months succeeded, by means of a species of guerrilla warfare, in keeping the invading armies at bay. Partly owing to the unflagging determination of the English troops, partly owing also to the intense hatred with which he was regarded by all Mohammedans, he was eventually overcome, though he himself was never captured. It was believed that he died while fleeing through the vast jungles with which his land was overgrown, and this idea was strengthened by the fact that, though a large reward for his capture was offered, nothing further had ever been heard of him.

From that time the land came under the more or less direct control of the Government. As a concession to the population, Behar Singh's one-year-old son was placed upon the throne under a native regency, but English regiments were stationed at the chief towns, and a political agent resided at the capital. Neither the regiments nor the political agent, however, found any work for their hands to do. A calm, as unexpected as it was complete, seemed to descend upon the whole country, and the officers who had taken up their posts with a loaded revolver in each hand, figuratively speaking, began very quickly to relapse instead into pig-sticking, polo and cards.

The climate was moderate, the vegetation beautiful if unprofitable, and the sport excellent. Thus it came about that a danger spot on the map of the Indian Empire became a European paradise, and that to be ordered to Marut was to become an object of envious congratulations. Not, as Mr. Archibald Travers had with justice complained, that the reigning prince, as in other states, took any part in the general gaiety or in any way enhanced the agreeableness of his capital. As far as was known, no European eyes had ever lighted on him since his childhood. Under one excuse and another he had been kept persistently in the background, his place being taken first by the regent and then by succeeding ministers, until it was generally supposed that the young Rajah was either afflicted with some loathsome disease or mentally deficient, probabilities which the Government, with unpleasant recollections of Behar Singh's too great intelligence, accepted with unusual readiness. There were no causes for suspicion. The Rajah never left the precincts of his palace garden, a piece of land whose cultivation had cost untold sums, and which, together with the Hindu temple, was supposed to stand as the eighth wonder of the world. Fabulous stories were told of the beauty and rarity of the vegetation, and of the value of the jewels which were supposed to decorate the temple and royal apartments. As there was no opportunity of confirming or refuting the statements, they were allowed to grow unhindered.

It was in this small sphere that Nehal Singh spent his childhood, his youth and early manhood. Of the outer world he had seen nothing, though he had read much, his education extending over all European history and penetrating deep into that of his own country. Nevertheless, the picture his mind had formed had little in common with the reality—it was too overshadowed by his own character. As a blind man may be able, through hearsay, to describe his surroundings detail by detail and yet at the bottom be possessed by an entirely false conception, so Nehal Singh, to all appearances well instructed, was in reality as ignorant as a child. The heroes whose figures peopled his imagination were too heroic, the villains too evil, and both heroes and villains were either physically beautiful or hideous, according to their characters.

He had no comrade against whose practical experience he might have rubbed this distorted picture into a more truthful likeness. His only companions had been his native instructors and the priests—men separated from him by a gulf of years and a curious lack of sympathy which he had in vain striven to overcome. Thus he had been intensely lonely, more lonely than he knew, though some dawning realization crept over him on this particular evening as he passed through the temple gates. For a moment he stood with his hands crossed over his breast, absorbed in prayer to Brahma, the Creator, in whose presence he was about to stand. In such an hour, amidst the absolute stillness, under the stupendous shadows of the walls, which had, unchanging, seen generation after generation of worshipers drift from their altars into the deeper shades of Patala, the young prince felt the wings of divine spirits brush close past him, bearing his prayer on unseen hands to the very ear of the golden-faced Trinity who, from his earliest years, had seemed to look down upon him with solemn kindness.

This evening, more perhaps than ever before, every fiber in him vibrated beneath the touch of the holy charm, and the prayer which passed soundlessly over his lips came from a soul that worshiped in fiery earnestness and truth. A minute passed as he stood there, then, removing his shoes, he stepped over the threshold and walked forward between the gigantic granite columns which supported what was left of the dome-shaped roof. There was no altar, no jewel, no figure cut in the hard stone that was not known to him with all their mysterious significance. Here had been spent all his leisure hours; here had been dreamed his wildest dreams; beneath this column he had seen as in a vision how Vishnu took nine times human form and a tenth time came, according to the Holy Writings, with a winged horse of spotless white, and crowned as conqueror.

To-day these things pressed down upon him with all the weight of a tremendous reality. With beating heart he entered at last into the Holy of Holies and stood before the god's high altar, visible only to those of purest caste. His head was once more bowed. He did not venture to look up at the golden figure whose ruby eyes, he knew, stared straight through his soul into every corner of the world and beyond into Eternity. His belief, pure, unsoiled from contact with the world, was a power that had gone out into the darkness and conjured thence the spirits that shrank back from the cold prayer of the half-believer. They stood before him now—these wonderful spirits. He believed surely that, should he dare to raise his eyes, he would see them, definite yet formless, arising glorious out of the cloud of golden reflection from Brahma's threefold forehead.

Thus he prayed, not kneeling, since the god cared only for his soul:

"Oh, Lord Brahma, Creator, hear me! Thou who madest me knowest whither I came and whither I go; but I, who am as the wind that bloweth as thou listeth, as a flower that springeth up in the night and unseen fadeth in the midday heat, I know not thy purpose nor the end for which I am. Lord Brahma, teach me, for my soul panteth after knowledge. Show me the path which I must tread, for I am weary with dreams. Teach me to serve my people—be it hand in hand with the Stranger and his gods, be it alone. Teach me to act, and that right soon; for my childhood days are spent and my man's arm heavy with idleness. Send me forth—but not alone—not alone, Lord Brahma, for I am heart-sick of loneliness. Give me my comrade, my comrade who shall be more to me than—"

He stopped and, obeying an impulse stronger than himself, lifted his face to the idol. It had vanished. In its place stood a woman.

At another and cooler moment, with a mind filled with other thoughts, with a heart untroubled by new and all-powerful emotions, he would have known her, if only from hearsay, for what she was. But with that passionate prayer upon his lips, she was for him the answer, a divine recognition of his need and of his lately recognized loneliness.

Tall, slender, with a pale, transparent complexion, touched like a young rose with the faintest color, dark, grave eyes and hair that seemed a part of the obscured god, whose pure lines, though foreign, harmonized in every detail with the classic beauty of her surroundings, she stood and watched him, as he watched her, in perfect silence.

"Lakshmi!" he murmured at last; and, as though the one word had broken a charm which held them both paralyzed, she smiled, and the smile lit up the Madonna face and made it as human as it had seemed divine.

"Forgive me," she began, speaking in English, "I am afraid I have disturbed you, but—" She paused, apparently confused by the directness of his gaze. The faint pink upon her cheek deepened.

"Who are you?" he demanded in his own tongue.

Her look of non-comprehension steadied him, at least outwardly, though it did not check the fierce, painful beating of his pulses. He repeated the question in pure though hesitating English.

"I am an Englishwoman," she answered at once, "and have lost my way. For hours—it seems hours, at any rate—I have been wandering hither and thither, trying to find my party, with whom I was enjoying an excursion. By some chance I came across this temple, and hoped to meet some one who might help me. You see, I am a stranger in this part of the world. I—I hope I have done no wrong?"

She looked at him pleadingly, but he ignored her question. It never occurred to him to doubt her explanation, or wonder at the unlikeliness of the chance which should have led her through the intricate paths to this hallowed spot.

"You are English?" he echoed. The fever in his blood was subsiding, but, like some great crisis, it was leaving him changed. It had swept him out of the world of languorous, enchanted dreams into a world of not less enchanted reality.

"I fear I am presumptuous," she began again; "but are you not the Rajah? If so, I am certain you must be very, very angry. For the Rajah—so I have been told—does not love the English."

She smiled again, meeting his unwavering gaze with a frank good-humor which for him was more wonderful even than her beauty. No woman—and for that matter, no man—had ever dared to look him in the eyes with such a laughing, fearless challenge.

"Yes, I am the Rajah," he answered. Then, after a pause, he added with great simplicity, "You are very beautiful."

She laughed outright, and the laugh, which rang like the peal of a silver bell through the vaulted chamber, filled him with a sudden sense of her danger. She stood with her back turned indifferently on the golden image, an Unbeliever whose shod feet were defiling the sacred precincts, an object, then, for hatred and revenge—not for him, truly. In his eyes she was still an emissary from Brahma, and thus in herself half sacred; but he knew well enough that such would not be the opinion of the few fierce priests who worshiped in the temple.

"You are not safe here," he said, with an energy which was new to him. "Come!"

He led her hurriedly out of the sanctuary into the great entrance hall. There he slackened speed and waited until she reached his side.

"For a foreigner it is not safe to enter the temple," he explained. "Had any one but myself found you, I could not answer for the consequences."

"They would have harmed me?"

"It is possible."

"That would have been terrible!" she said, glancing at him with eyes that expressed rather a daring courage than fear.

"Most terrible," he assented earnestly.

"Yet—you also, Your Highness, you have also the same reasons for anger. My intrusion, innocent though it was, must have been equally offensive to you."

"No," he said. "That is quite different."

He offered no further explanation, and together they passed out of the two immense gopuras into the evening sunshine.

"I will bring you to the gates which lead on to the highroad," he went on. "Thence one of my servants will conduct you back to the town, where I trust you will find your friends."

"You are most good," she answered gratefully.

They walked side by side between the high walls of cypress and palm. The path was a narrow one, and once his hand brushed lightly against hers. The touch sent a flood of fire through his young veins. He drew back with a courtesy which surprised himself. He had never been taught that courtesy toward a woman could ever be required of him. Of women he had heard little save that they were inferior, in intellect and judgment no more than slaves, and his curiosity had at once been satiated. He sought things above him—those beneath him excited no more than indifference. But this woman was neither an inferior nor a slave. Her free, erect carriage, steadfast, fearless eyes proclaimed the equal. So much his instinct taught him in those brief moments, and his eager curiosity concerning her grew and deepened. Every now and again his gaze sought her face, drinking in with an almost passionate thirst the fine detail of her profile, compared to which his dreams were poor and lifeless. Once it chanced that she also glanced at him, and that they looked at each other for less than a breathing space full in the eyes.

"I fear you are angry, Your Highness," she said earnestly. "I must have offended against your laws even more than I know."

"Why do you think I am angry?" he asked.

"You have scarcely spoken."

"Forgive me! That is no sign of anger. I am still overcome with the strangeness of it all. You are the first English person I have ever met."

She stood still, with an exclamation of surprise.

"Is that possible? I thought all Indian princes mixed with English people. Many, indeed, go to England to be educated—"

"So I have heard," he broke in, with a faint haughtiness. "I am not one of them."

"Yet you speak the language so perfectly!" she said.

A gleam of naive pleasure shone out of his dark eyes.

"I am glad you think so. My—one of my ministers taught me."

They walked on again. Here and there she stopped to look at some curious plant—always a little in advance of him—so that he had opportunity to study the hundred things about her which confirmed his wondering, increasing admiration. Slight as she was, there was yet a gracefully controlled strength in every movement. In his own mind, poor as it necessarily was in comparisons, he compared her to a young doe he had once startled from its resting-place. There was the same fragile beauty, the same grace, the same high-strung energy. In nothing was she like the women painted for him by his father's hand—things for idle, sensuous pleasure, never for serious action.

Plunged in a happy confusion of thought, he had once more relapsed into silence, from which she startled him with a question evidently connected with their previous conversation.

"And so you have lived all your life in this lovely garden?" she said, looking up at him with a grave wonder in her eyes.

"All my life," he answered.

"You have never seen anything of the world?"

"Never." He felt the pity in her tone, and added, with a shamefacedness curiously in contrast with his former hauteur: "But I have read much."

"That is not the same thing," she returned. "No book could make you understand how wonderful and beautiful things are."

He looked at her, and for a second time their eyes met.

"You are right," he said. "Hitherto I have thought myself all-wise. I have studied hard, and I believed there was nothing I did not know. Now I see that there are wonders in the world of which I have never even dreamed."

Her glance wavered beneath the undisguised admiration in his eyes and voice. Then she asked gently:

"Now that you have seen, will you not leave your hermitage? Surely it is wrong to shut one's heart against the world in which one lives. There is so much work to be done, so much to learn, and you have been granted power and wealth, Your Highness. The call upon your help is greater than upon others."

His brows knitted.

"Do you hate us so?" she asked.

"Hate you?" he repeated wonderingly. "Why should I hate you?"

"Yet, from your tone, I judged that you had kept seclusion because intercourse with my country-people meant defilement," she said boldly.

A flush crept up under his dark skin.

"Those are things I can not explain," he said; "but they have nothing to do with hatred. I have heard much of the English heroes. Their deeds of daring and self-sacrifice have filled my heart with love and veneration. I know that they are the greatest and noblest people of the earth. I love great and noble people. I do not hate them."

"I am glad," she said.

They had reached the gates which opened out on to the highroad, and as though by mutual consent both came to a standstill.

"Your Highness has been most good to me," she went on. "I can find my way perfectly now. I am only puzzled to know how I should ever have lost it so much as to have wandered into your garden."

"Some sentry must have slept," he remarked grimly.

"But you will not punish any one?"

"Whoever it was, he was only the servant of destiny, like us all," he said. "No harm shall come to him." He paused, and then added with a slight effort: "One of the sentries shall accompany you."

"No, no," she answered energetically. "That is not necessary. I would rather go alone."

He pointed upward to the sky, whose blue was deepening into the violet shades of night.

"It will be dark before you reach your destination," he said. "Are you not afraid?"

She laughed merrily.

"Of what should I be afraid? There are no maneaters about here, as I understand. As for men, I am prepared to encounter at least six of them. Look!" She drew from the bosom of her dress a small revolver of exquisite workmanship, and held it out to him. "It has all six chambers loaded," she added.

He took the weapon, pretending to examine it; but his pulses had recommenced their painful beating, and he saw nothing but her face.

"Are all Englishwomen so brave and beautiful?"

This time she did not laugh at the simplicity of the question.

"Come and see," she answered boldly. He said nothing, and she went on: "At any rate, I must go now. My people will be very anxious, and I have so much to tell them. They will envy me the privilege I have enjoyed of seeing your wonderful gardens. I shall tell them how kind you have been to a foolish wanderer."

"If the gardens please you, they are always open to you," he said.

She shook her head sadly.

"I am afraid it is not possible. You see, I could not come alone. Propriety will forgive me this once, because it was an accident—a second time, and my reputation would be gone for ever." She held out her hand frankly. "So it must be good-by for ever!"

An instant he hesitated, torn between a deep ingrained principle and desire. Then he took the small hand in his own.

"It will not be good-by for ever," he said. "We shall meet again."

"I should be glad. We have been quite good friends, haven't we? But you see, you will be in a garden into which I may not enter, and I in a world which for you is forbidden ground. I am afraid there is no hope."

"Nevertheless, we shall meet again," he repeated.

"Why are you so certain?"

He smiled dreamily.

"Nothing in this world happens without purpose," he answered. "So much my books and eyes have taught me. We do not drift aimlessly into each other's lives. We are borne on the breast of a strong current which flows out of the river of Fate, and whether we meet for good or evil is according to the will of God. But of one thing I am sure: it must be for good or evil."

For a moment she said nothing. Her face was turned away from him, and when at last she spoke, her voice had lost something of its daring certainty.

"I hope, then, our meeting is for our good," she said.

"I feel that it is," he answered.

He led her past the bewildered, terrified sentry on to the grey, dusty highroad. It was the first time that his feet had crossed the threshold.

"I shall watch you till you are out of sight," he said. "Good-by."

"Good-by—and thank you!"

According to his word, he stood where she had left him, his eyes fixed immovably, like those of a bronze statue, on the slight, elastic figure, as it hurried toward the lights of the distant Station. When at last the purple mist had swallowed her from his sight, he looked up toward the heavens.

Just where the mist ended and the clear sky began, the evening star rose in its first splendor and shone through the dry atmosphere, signaling to its fellows that night was come. One by one others followed. As time passed, the moon in a cloud of silver lifted herself in stately progress above the black outline of the jungle and touched with her first beams the filigree minarets of the temple.

Nehal Singh bowed his head in prayer.

"Oh, Lord Brahma, I thank thee!"

A short-lived breath of evening air caught up the passionate murmur of his voice and mingled it with the rustling of the Sacred Tree whose restless, shimmering, silver leaves hung above his head. He understood their whisper as he listened. It was the accents of the god to whom he prayed, and all the poetic mysticism of his nature responded to the call.

"Oh, Lord Brahma, Creator, I thank thee!" he repeated; then turned, and with head still bowed, passed back through the high marble gates.

CHAPTER V
ARCHIBALD TRAVERS PLAYS BRIDGE

The ayah put the last touches to Beatrice Cary's golden hair, drew back a little to judge the general effect, and then handed her mistress the handglass.

"Is that well so, missy?" she asked. "Missy look wonderful to-night—wonderful!"

Beatrice examined herself carefully and critically, without any show of impatience. Only a close observer would have noticed that her eyes had the strained, concentrated look of a person whose thoughts are centered elsewhere than on the immediate subject.

"Yes, that will do," she assented, after a moment. "You have done extra well to-night. You can go."

"Not help missy with dress?"

"No, you can go. I shall only want you again when I come back."

The ayah fidgeted with the garments that lay scattered about the room, but an imperative gesture hastened her exit, and she slipped silently from the room, drawing the curtains after her.

Beatrice watched her departure in the glass, and then, turning in her chair, looked at the languid, exhausted figure upon the couch.

"Now, if you have anything to say, mother, say it," she said. "We are quite alone."

"I have a great deal to say," Mrs. Cary began, in a tone of extreme injury, "and first of all, I must ask you not to interrupt me in the way you did just now before the—the what-do-you-call-it?—the ayah. I can not and will not stand being corrected before my own servants."

"I did not correct you," Beatrice returned coldly. "I stopped you from making disclosures to ears which know enough English to understand more than is good for either of us, and whose discretion is on a par with that of our late friend, Mary Jane. It seems impossible to make you realize that English is not a dead language."

"You are very rude to me!" Mrs. Cary protested, in high, quavering tones that threatened tears. "Very rude! Beatrice, you ought to be ashamed—"

"I am not rude. I am only telling you the simple truth."

"Well, then, you are not respectful."

"Respectful!" The reiteration was accompanied with a laugh which brought into use all the harsh, unpleasing notes in the girl's voice. She turned away from her mother, and with one white elbow resting on the dressing-table, began to play idly with the silver ornaments. "No, I suppose I am not respectful," she went on calmly. "I think we are too intimate for that, mother. We know each other too well, and have spoken about things too plainly. People, I imagine, only retain the respect of their fellow-creatures so long as they keep themselves and their projects a haloed mystery. That isn't our case. There are no haloes or mysteries between us, are there?"

"I'm sure I don't know what you mean," Mrs. Cary declared plaintively. "There are moments, Beatrice, when I think you talk nonsense."

"I am sure you do!" An ironical smile played an instant round the small mouth, then she went on calmly: "Let us put our personal grievances against each other aside, mother. *Revenons a nos moutons.* You were saying, when I interrupted you, that you were afraid of Mr. Travers. Why?"

"Why! You know as well as I do. I recognized him at once, and the sight of his face nearly gave me a heart stroke. Of course you remember him. He gave evidence against your poor, dear father when—"

Beatrice Cary held up her hand.

"That is one of the advantages of having discarded the mystery and halo," she said. "We do not need to go into any details concerning ourselves or the past. I know quite well to what you refer. To be quite honest, I *did* recognize him, only I did not let him see that I did."

"And then you ask why I am afraid!"

"I fail to see what harm he can do us."

"He can tell the truth."

Beatrice Cary rose and began to slip into the white silk dress which hung across the back of her chair.

"The truth!" she said meditatively. "That is something, mother, of which, I fear, you and I will never rid ourselves. It has chased us out of England and out of all possible parts of Europe; and, large though India is, it seems already to have tracked us down. It has a good nose for fugitives, apparently."

Mrs. Cary sat up, mopping her florid face free from tears of irritability.

"You will drive me mad one of these days!" she cried. "You laugh at everything. You laugh even at this, though it concerns our whole future here—"

"Excuse me for interrupting you again. I take the matter very much to heart—so much so that there are moments when I am thoroughly weary of it, and feel inclined to write on a large placard: 'Here standeth Beatrice McConnel, alias Cary, daughter of the—'"

"Be silent!" broke in the elder woman furiously. "Do you really want the whole Station to be taken into our confidence?"

"I am sorry!" with half-sincere, half-mocking contrition. "I am as bad as you are. But, as I say, there are times when I should like to shriek the truth in the world's face, and see what it would do. I don't think anything could be worse than our present life."

"If you did anything of the sort, I should take poison," Mrs. Cary declared.

"No, you wouldn't. We should move on to another continent, and try our luck there, that's all. It's the very futility of truth-telling which prevents me from experimenting in that direction. Perhaps, as you suggest, Mr. Travers will take the task from my shoulders."

Mrs. Cary rose to her feet and came ponderously over to her daughter's side. Her voice, when she spoke, was troubled with genuine emotion.

"Beatrice," she said, "I don't ask respect of you—I don't suppose it would be any sort of good if I did. You haven't any respect in you. But at any rate have some consideration for me. You needn't make my life worse than it is. It's no use your saying to me, 'Give up the money, and hide your head.' I can't. I never could hide my head, and at the bottom I don't believe you could either. It's the way we are made. Ever since I was a little child, and played about in my father's shop, I wanted people to bow down to me and respect me. I meant that one day they should. When I married they did—for a time at least. When the crash came, and—and all the shame, I just ran away from it. I couldn't have done anything else. Ever since then I have been trying to build things up elsewhere, and I had to have money for it. You can't blame me, Beatrice. You aren't any better. You always want to be first in your singing and your painting, you always want the best of what's going. You always want to be admired and successful in everything you do. You take after me in that." A note of curious pride crept into her voice. "So it's just like this, Beatrice—I can't live without position. I may not take poison, but I shall die all the same if I can't play a part in the world. All I ask is that you help me all you can. It's not much. I've been a pretty decent mother to you. You can't say that there was ever a time when I grudged you a pretty frock or a dance—" She stopped in her long speech, yielding to Beatrice's irrepressible gesture of impatience.

"You needn't have gone into so much explanation," the girl said, fastening a small diamond pendant round her white neck. "I know you and I know myself. As to my gratitude, I am fully aware of what I owe you, and am ready to pay. What do you want me to do?"

"Don't go against me."

"I haven't done so yet. I don't mean to. As far as I can recollect, I've pulled us both out of as many scrapes as you have landed us into," Beatrice replied.

"I know. That's why I want you to do your best now."

"To do what?"

"To keep Marut tolerable for us."

"I can't prevent Mr. Travers gossiping if he wants to."

A smile flitted over Mrs. Cary's fat face, robbing it of its good-nature and leaving it merely vulgarly cunning.

"You could if you wanted to."

"How?"

"Oh, you know! You have a way with men. You could shut his mouth."

Beatrice laughed outright.

"There are moments when you betray your origin in the most painful way, mother," she said cruelly. "A remark like that in Mrs. Carmichael's hearing, and we should find Marut too hot for us without any assistance from Mr. Travers."

"I'm sorry," Mrs. Cary apologized humbly. "It slipped out. What I meant was, that I am sure you could manage him. And you know you could, Beatrice."

Beatrice looked at her reflection in the glass. There was little feminine vanity in the glance—rather a cool judging and appraising, untempered with any personal prejudice.

"I suppose I could," she admitted.

"Won't you?"

"Would it make you very happy?"

"It would be my first moment's real peace since I saw Mr. Travers at the garden-party."

"Well, I'll do my best."

"You promise?"

"Yes, I'll promise if you want me to."

Mrs. Cary drew a deep sigh of relief.

"That's one thing about you, you keep your promises, Beatrice," she said.

"It is rather curious, under the circumstances, isn't it?" the younger woman returned, submitting to the mother's grateful embrace with an indifference which seemed to indicate more than an indifference—rather a stoic, smothered antipathy. When it was over, and Mrs. Cary had once more ensconced herself on the lounge, Beatrice shook her shoulders as though thrusting something intensely disagreeable away from her.

"In any case, it may be too late," she said, putting the finishing touches to her toilet. "If Mr. Travers meant to tell, he has probably done so already. I shall be able to judge by Mrs. Carmichael's hand-shake to-night."

"We must hope for the best," returned Mrs. Cary, with pious resignation.

The two women relapsed into silence. Beatrice hovered lightly about the room, collecting her fan, handkerchief and gloves, every now and again casting the same curious, unloving glance at herself in the long mirror. Presently she went to the window and pulled aside the muslin curtain.

"Some one is driving up the avenue," she said. "It's a dog-cart. I wonder who it is."

"A dog-cart!" Mrs. Cary repeated thoughtfully. "Now, who has a dog-cart in Marut? Not many people, I fancy." A dull flush mounted her coarse cheeks. "Why," she exclaimed, "I believe Mr. Travers has!"

Beatrice dropped the curtain back into its place.

"That would be a coincidence, wouldn't it?" she remarked, with a faint irony from which her tone had never been wholly free.

A minute later the ayah entered the room.

"Travers Sahib is here," she announced. "He asks if missy drive with him to the Colonel Sahib in his cart. Travers Sahib waiting."

Beatrice and her mother exchanged glances.

"Very well," Beatrice then said quietly. "Tell Travers Sahib I shall be delighted. Paul need not bring round the carriage."

The ayah retired, and with an undisturbed calm Beatrice proceeded to slip into her evening cloak.

"At any rate, he hasn't spoken yet," she said. "Fate seems to mean well with you, mother."

"It all depends on you, Beatrice," the other returned impressively.

"Do you think so? Well, I have half-an-hour's drive before me—tete-a-tete. I dare say I shall manage. Good night!" She patted her mother lightly on the hand as she passed her on the way to the door.

"Good-by, my dear. Do your best, won't you?"

"Haven't I been brought up to do my best?" Beatrice answered with a laugh.

She hurried on to the verandah which faced out on the drive, the ayah accompanying her with numerous wraps and shawls. Archibald Travers, who had remained seated, greeted her with a cheerful wave of the whip.

"Please excuse my getting down, Miss Cary," he said. "My horse is in a state of mind which does not allow for politeness. Can you trust yourself to his tender care?"

"I am not in the least nervous," she answered, scrambling up to his side, "and a drive through this lovely air is worth a few risks. I was dreading the half-hour alone in our stuffy brougham."

"I'm glad I came, then," he said. "I heard that Mrs. Cary was ill and could not go, but I was not sure whether you would care for it. There, are you tucked in all right? Can we start?"

"Yes, by all means."

He cracked his whip, and immediately the impatient chestnut sprang forward into the darkness. They swayed dangerously through the compound gates on to the broad, straight highroad.

Beatrice laughed with excitement.

"That was splendid!" she exclaimed, pulling her cloak closer round her. "How well you drive!"

"You seem to enjoy danger," he said, with an amused smile.

"Yes, I enjoy it," she answered, more gravely. "It is the only flavoring which I have hitherto discovered in life. The rest is rather insipid, don't you think?"

"You talk like a man," he said.

"I have been brought up to be independent and fight for myself," she returned. "That sort of thing does away with the principal differences between the sexes."

As she spoke they dashed suddenly into an avenue of high trees through whose branches the moonlight played fantastic, uncanny shadows on the white road. Travers' horse shied violently, and for some minutes his work was cut out for him in pacifying the excited animal. When they were once more bowling smoothly over the open plain, he glanced down at the girl beside him.

She was smiling to herself.

"You have nerve!" he remarked admiringly.

"I have lots more when it is wanted," she answered, looking up at him. The light struck full on their faces, and they could read each other's expressions as clearly as if it had been midday.

"How much farther is it at the rate we are going?" she asked.

"Another twenty minutes."

"Another twenty minutes!" she repeated thoughtfully. "That is quite a long time, isn't it?"

He flicked his whip across the horse's ears.

"Yes, and I'm glad," he said. "Otherwise, I shouldn't have seen much of you. I happen to know that I am taking in Miss Caruthers to dinner, and dinner takes up most of the evening at these functions."

"You are taking in Lois Caruthers!" she said, laughing. "I know of some one who will be annoyed."

"Stafford, you mean?"

"And Lois herself."

He joined in her amusement.

"Yes, I suppose so."

"You have a good-natured hostess. I dare say the arrangement could be altered if you wished it."

"But I don't. They happen to be *my* arrangements, you see."

"Oh!" she ejaculated, somewhat taken back.

"On my left there will be Mrs. James, who, as you perhaps know, is stone deaf," he went on calmly. "On Miss Caruthers' right will be Mr. James, who from long custom never opens his mouth except to put something into it. Stafford will be right at the other end of the table."

"You are malicious," she said.

"Not a bit. I only go hard for what I want, that's all." He chuckled to himself and then went on: "I've confided to you my subtle underground plans—why, goodness knows. I'm not usually of a confiding nature. But really, Miss Cary, I feel as though I had known you all my life."

"We have already plotted together," she said. "Possibly that forms some sort of link between us."

He glanced down at her, and this time, as she did not return his gaze, he was free to study her calm, undisturbed profile.

"By Jove!" he exclaimed, half under his breath, "I don't blame the young fool for being taken in."

Her brows contracted sharply.

"Thank you. I suppose that is a compliment."

"It is meant for one. By the way, are you really sure of your success?"

"Perfectly sure."

"That's a good thing. We shall have the laugh over old Stafford and his grandmother's ideas if it comes off. All I fear is that the youth's impressionable mind may lose its impressions as quickly as it receives them."

"I don't think so. He did not seem that sort."

"Besides," added Travers, with a sudden drawl, "your face is not one that a man forgets easily, Miss Cary."

She stirred very slightly in her seat. It was the instinctive movement of a woman bracing herself secretly for a coming shock.

"Really?"

"Yes, really. That was what I meant to tell you the other day, but there was no fitting opportunity. I recognized you at once."

"And I you," she returned.

He whistled.

"So we recognized each other and didn't recognize each other. Rather a queer thing, eh?"

Again there was that scarcely noticeable stiffening of her whole body.

"I see nothing queer about it. We were both taken aback, and after the first shock we realized that to acknowledge a previous meeting was not to either of our advantages. You were ashamed; and I—well, you can guess my reasons."

"By Jove! You know, you really are plucky!" he burst out, with genuine admiration.

"Thank you. You have intimated that to me already, and, as a matter of fact, there is no question of pluck. I'm taking the bull by the horns because I must. Mr. Travers, I can't live in the same place with you and not know if you are going to explode the mine under our feet or not. I may have nerve, but I haven't got nerve enough for that."

"I see. You want to know whether I am going to gossip or hold my tongue. Is that it?"

"Yes, that's it."

"Suppose I gossip?"

"I see no reason why you should be our enemy, so I don't mind admitting to you that it would spoil our plans."

"What may they be?"

"Firstly, to get clear of everything that has happened. We've tried to do that in different places all over Europe, without success. Something or somebody has always cropped up and driven us away. It was just as though every one least concerned in the matter had made up their minds to track us down. At last mother thought of India, and of Marut in particular. My father held a small post somewhere about here before we left for England, and we make out that it is tender associations and all that sort of thing. Of course, we might be found out any day, but perhaps people are not so curious out here, and it gives us a rest."

"Might I ask why you take all this trouble?"

"I was going to tell you. Because my mother wants what she calls position—she wants to mix with the best. We couldn't do that in England, for the reasons I have given you. As for me—I fulfil my destiny. I am seeking a suitable husband."

He drew in his breath in something that was not unlike a gasp.

"My dear Miss Cary, do you know what the world—particularly the woman world—would call you?"

"*Does* call me, you mean? Of course. An adventuress."

"To be quite frank, you've hit it. But I don't. I call you a jolly extraordinary and clever woman."

"Please don't pay me compliments," she said coldly. "My cleverness— if I have any—is not more than that of any hunted animal who seeks cover where best he can. As to my being extraordinary, I do not see that you have any reason to call me so. You might as well say that it is extraordinary when a weed springs up where a weed has been sown—"

"Or a flower," he interposed suavely.

She sank back in her seat, saying nothing. Her silence was a weary sort of protest.

Travers pulled out his watch with his free hand.

"We have only five minutes more," he said. "We are splendidly up to time. I tell you what, Miss Cary—you can eat Colonel Carmichael's dinner in peace." She looked quickly at him. "I mean that I shall hold my tongue. I don't know that I ever intended doing anything else. I am not responsible to society, and in any case, no direct blame for the past can attach itself to you. As it is, after your confidence, I give you my word that I'll do my best to see you through here. You deserve it, and I have always had a sneaking sympathy for the hunted fox and the much-abused weed. You can be quite easy in your mind."

"Thank you," she said without much warmth.

"I have only one condition—" he went on, and then hesitated.

"I was waiting for that," she said.

He laughed good-naturedly.

"You know me very well already."

"I know men," she retorted.

"Well, then, I have a condition. Please don't look upon me as a sort of blackmailer. If you don't choose to agree to the condition, you needn't. I shan't on that account go round gossiping about your affairs. At the same time, I expect you would rather drive a fair and square bargain with me than be in any way in my debt."

"You are quite right," she said quickly.

"My condition is merely this: I want you, if the time and opportunity ever present themselves, to lend me a hand with my plans. I confess privately to you I have one or two irons in the fire up at Marut, and that it is pretty hard work single-handed. You are a clever woman, say what you like, and your help would be invaluable."

"In what way?"

"I will put it as short as possible. You know, Miss Cary, I am not a rich man, but I have got some big ideas and one at least of them requires wealth to be carried out. I have every reason to believe that considerable mineral treasure lies buried under the native Bazaar in Marut, but I can do nothing unless some one comes to my assistance both with authority and money. The Rajah is the very man, if only I can get him interested in my project. Will you help me?"

"As I have gone so far I might as well go on," she assented indifferently.

"Thanks. Then there is something else—I want to marry Lois Caruthers."

Beatrice started and looked up at him as though she thought he might be joking. His face had indeed undergone a change, but there was something stern, resolute, almost brutal in the hard-set profile.

"Indeed? Will that not be more difficult? There is Stafford in the way, and Stafford—"

"Stafford must be cleared out of the way," he interrupted, with a cool decision which his expression partly belied. "I believe she is fond of him and he of her in a Platonic sort of fashion which might lead to marriage and might not. He is not the danger. There is a fellow, Nicholson, though—"

He stopped short and seemed for an instant to be plunged in his own thoughts.

"Who is this Nicholson?" she asked curiously. "I have heard his name constantly since I have been here. People talk of him as though he were a demigod. Why are you afraid of him?"

"Just because of his godlike qualities," Travers explained, with a laugh. "In earlier ages, no doubt, he would have been a god and among the natives he is one. In reality, he is an ordinary mortal blessed with an extraordinary influence. I believe he is a captain in some native regiment on the frontiers and has done grand work there. I heard today that he is coming down to Marut on leave."

"Oh—?"

"He was Lois' old playfellow," Travers added pointedly.

"And so you are afraid of him?"

"All women adore heroes of that type," he remarked without mockery or bitterness, "and when Nicholson appears I have a fair idea that Stafford and I will have to be content with the back seats in Lois' affections. You see, they were great friends, and moreover the Carmichaels have their matrimonial eye on him. So it's now or never as far as I am concerned."

"And Stafford—?"

He looked down at her with a jolly laugh.

"He must find consolation elsewhere. I thought he would do for you, Miss Cary."

"Thanks!"

"Don't be ungrateful. Rich, good position, good family, worthy character, a trifle slow, not to say stupid—what more do you want?"

"You talk as though—"

"—As though he were being given away with a pound of tea? Well, so he is to all intents and purposes. One can do anything with an honest, pig-headed man like that if only one takes him the right way. He would suit you clear down to the ground, and if you will help me I will help you. Is that a bargain?"

They were now in sight of their destination, and he pulled his horse into a walk.

"Well, what do you say, Miss Cary?"

He tried to look into her face, but it was turned resolutely away, and all he could see was a grave profile which might have belonged to a much older woman.

"Well?" he repeated.

They were entering the drive which led up to the brightly lighted bungalow before she answered.

"It's a bargain then," she said. "I promise."

He pressed her hand with his left.

"That's all right," he said cheerily. "You won't find yourself overburdened. The case is just this: we're partners, you and I, with some good cards between us. Just at present it's my call, and your hand goes down. Do you understand?"

"Pretty well," she answered.

They pulled up at the open doorway, and flinging the reins to the waiting syce, Travers sprang to the ground.

"By the way, I believe you go in to dinner with Stafford," he remarked casually as he helped her to alight. "I hope you will get on well together."

CHAPTER VI
BREAKING THE BARRIER

The Colonel's dinner-party was Beatrice's first great triumph in the face of her enemies. They were all there and all armed to the teeth with spite and envy. There was, for instance, Mrs. Berry with her marriageable if somewhat plain daughter, and many more women besides to whom the beautiful girl was of necessity an unforgivable opponent. The more the men laughed at her quick and occasionally rather pointed observations, the more an obvious admiration shone out of their criticisms, the more determined the hatred became. Among themselves they had already fulfilled Travers' prophecy and had christened her "the Adventuress" for no other reason than that she was a woman with the same ambitions as themselves, but better accoutred for success. Truly, she had made no bid for their favor, choosing to stand alone and without their support; but even had she done so it would have been useless. She wore an enemy's color in her face, and keen, pitiless eyes had already probed into the innermost depths of her plans and found them dangerous.

In the middle of the dinner the Colonel broke the news that the whole of the English community had been invited by the Rajah to a reception in the palace grounds. He made the announcement with evident reluctance, and Beatrice was conscious that Stafford, who sat beside her, stiffened and frowned. The sense of opposition and disapproval on the part of the man whom she had set out to conquer put her on her metal, and with the verve and *sang-froid* of a woman too sure of her own power to know fear, she related her adventure in the temple. Her hearers listened, according to their sex, with amusement, curiosity and pious horror. Some were unreservedly delighted, others—such as the Colonel and Stafford—struggled between a certain admiration for her and a decided disapproval of her action and its results. Yet Stafford at least was a soldier before he was a conventionalist, and her bold, well-played comedy in the temple of Vishnu, told simply, but with fire and energy, could not fail to stir to flame the embers of his own daring. From that time he ceased to rivet his attention to the other end of the table, where Lois was sitting, and Beatrice was conscious that she had won the first move in the great game which she had set herself to play. The next day the whole Station was made aware of the startling change in the Rajah's attitude and the means by which it had been brought about, but no one, not even those who were disposed to judge the matter in its most serious light, guessed what passed within the palace previous to the sending out of the now famous invitation. For the greater part of the English community the whole thing was rather a bad joke, with the Rajah for its victim. That a pretty woman should have unbarred the gates which no other force, diplomacy or cunning had been able to stir was a matter for light, somewhat contemptuous laughter. Rajah Nehal Singh was nicknamed the Impressionable Swain. He and Beatrice Cary were linked together either in good-natured chaff or malicious earnest, and curiosity, thanks to the dullness of the season, strained itself in expectation.

Thus, beyond the marble gates the world laughed, and inside Life and Death had faced each other and for a moment hung in the balance.

It was toward the cool of the evening. Behar Asor and the prince paced slowly backward and forward in the chief entrance hall of the palace, plunged in a conversation which was to mark a final stage in their relationship toward each other. Both knew it, and on both faces was written the same determination—a determination curiously tempered and moulded by the character of the man himself. On Behar Asor's furrowed, withered face it was resolve, armed with treachery and all the hundred and one weapons of oriental cunning. Nehal Singh's head was lifted in calm, unshakable confidence. He had no need of weapons. He had seen his destiny, and the obstacle which would be thrown in his path would, with equal certainty, be thrown out of it. He felt himself extraordinarily strong.

His very surroundings seemed to fortify him with their splendor. Other parts of the palace bore the grievous traces of a past devastating race-hatred; crumbling pillars, images whose jeweled eyes had been made dark and lifeless by robber hands; broken pavements, defaced carvings—all these pointed to a period in human life which was gone for ever, a period of mad fanaticism and passionate clinging to the Old in defiance of the New. Here the New was triumphant. Hands still living had raised the mighty golden dome; the fountain whose waters bubbled up from the Sacred Tank within the temple was his own creation. The whole place became a sort of outward and visible sign of the New Life, New Era, which was opening out before him, and the old man at his side was nothing more than a relic, a piece of clinging wreckage. Yesterday he had been a wise man whose judgment and guidance was a thing to be considered.

But between Yesterday and Today there is occasionally a long night in which much may happen. A life may go out, a life may come in; a devil may become a saint, or a saint a devil; a man may swing from one pole of opinion to another, and this last is perhaps the easiest of all. For it does not require much to change a man's standpoint. A very little thing will make him turn on his heel and look at a piece of the landscape which he has hitherto chosen to ignore or despise, and probably acknowledge that it is finer than his hitherto obstinately retained outlook. A very little thing—like Columbus' egg—if one only knew just what it was! The little thing in Nehal Singh's life had been a woman's face. It shone between him and his old gods; it smiled at him from amidst the shadows of his imagination, beckoning him unceasingly to follow. And he was following—with the reckless speed of a man who had been kept inactive too long at the starting point of life.

"I am weary of all that has hitherto been," he told Behar Asor. "My palace has become a prison from which I must free myself. The very air I breathe is heavy with sleep and dreams. It suffocates me. I must have life— here and without."

"I understand thee too well," came the answer from compressed lips. "The curse is on thee. Thou wilt go among my enemies, and it is I, with my mistaken wisdom, who have opened thy path to them. It was I who taught thee their tongue, their knowledge, their law, that when the time came thou shouldst stand before them more than their equal. This is my punishment."

"It is no punishment. It is the will of God."

"The will of God!" The old man threw up his hands with a wild laugh that echoed among the pillars. "It is the will of the devil, who has been my curse and shall be thine! Ay, ay, look not at me! It is true. Thinkest thou that I have brought thee up in solitude without cause? Thinkest thou that I have hidden thee like a miser his treasure, in the dark, unseen places, for a whim? Son, I have suffered as I pray thou mayst not have to suffer, and I have within my heart a serpent of hatred whose sting I would thou couldst feel." He paused, biting his lip as though the pain he described was actual and physical. "Go not among the Unbelievers!" he continued vigorously. "Let not their shadow defile thee! For their breath is poison, and in their eyes is a deadly flame—or if thou goest, let it be with steeled breast and in thy right hand a sword of vengeance!"

"I can not," Nehal Singh answered impatiently. "Nor do I believe what thou sayest. This people is surely brave and good. I know, for I have read—"

"Read!" the old man interrupted, with another burst of stormy laughter. "What is it to read? To see with the eyes and feel with the body—that alone can bring true wisdom. And I have seen and felt! Callest thou a people 'good' who drink our hospitality and spit upon us—who hail us with their unclean right hand and steal our honor with their left?"

Nehal Singh stopped short.

"What meanest thou?" he demanded.

"I have a meaning!" was the stern answer. "I will tell thee now what I have never told thee before—I will tell thee of a young man who, like thyself, was fearless, impetuous, a lover of the new and strange, who went out into the world, and welcomed the White People as a deliverer and friend. I will tell thee how he flung down caste and prejudice to welcome them, drank in their Thought and Culture, trembled on the brink of their Religion. Already the path had been broken for him. His mother's sister had married out of her race—an Englishman—I know not how it came about—and their child followed in her steps. I will tell thee how the young man came to know this cousin and her husband, also an Unbeliever. How often these two became his guests I will not tell thee. He took pleasure in their presence, partly for his mother's sake, partly because the white race had become dear to him. They brought others with them, and among them an English officer. Hear now further.

"This young man had one wife, following the English custom—one wife more beautiful than her sisters, whom he loved as a man loves but once in life. In his madness, in spite of warnings of his priests, he gave her the freedom almost of an English-woman. Wheresoever he went she followed him; with her at his right hand he received his English guests; it was she who sang to them—" He ground his teeth in a sudden outburst of rage. "Mad, mad was I! Mad to trust a woman, and to trust the stranger! Son, the night came when my wife sang no more to me, and the stranger's shadow ceased to darken my threshold. Three years I sought them—three years; then one night she came back to me. He had cast her from him. She lay dead at my feet." His voice shook. "In vain I sought justice. There is no justice for such things among the White People—not for themselves and not for us. I drew my sword and in hatred and scorn as deep as my love and reverence had been high, I slew my way to the false devil who had betrayed me. Him I slew—and his pale wife I—"

"Who was this man?" Nehal Singh asked heavily.

"I know not. His name has passed from me. But the hate remains. For with that act of treachery he drew back the veil from my blind eyes, and I saw that they were all as he—bad, cruel, hypocrites—"

"Not all—not all!" Nehal Singh interrupted. He stopped by the splashing fountain and gazed dreamily into the clear waters. His own face he saw there—and another which was neither bad, cruel, nor hypocritical, but wholly beautiful. "Not all," he repeated. "You judge by one man. There are others, and it is those I will see and know, and—"

"I would rather see thee dead at my feet!"

"My father, I will judge them as I find them,"

Nehal Singh went on imperturbably. "If they be good and noble, I will serve and love them. If they be bad, as thou sayest—then thou shalt live to see me do thy will."

He heard a shrill cry, and his eyes, still fixed on the water, saw a hand that swept upward, the flash of steel falling swiftly through the sunshine. He swung round and tore the dagger from the nerveless hand.

"Thou dost wrong, my father," he said, with unshaken calm. "To learn treachery from treachery is a poor lesson. And thou canst not stay me. What I will do I will do. Do not cross me again."

The old man, who had shrunk back, gasping and staring, against the marble basin, pulled himself painfully upright.

"Ay, I did wrong," he said. "With my old hands I tried to forestall the sword of Fate. For, mark me, the hour will come when thou wilt curse thyself that thou didst stay my knife!"

He tottered slowly away, vanishing like a curious twisted shadow amidst the deeper shadows of the columns.

Nehal Singh watched him till he was out of sight, and then, snapping the dagger across his knee, flung the pieces into the water. They lay there, at the bottom of the marble basin, sparkling and twinkling in the sunshine. When he looked in, trying to conjure up once more the beautiful face, it was always the dagger he saw. It was always the dagger he saw when the memory of that short, violent scene came back to him—and it came back often, springing up out of his subconscious self like an evil, slinking shade that could never be wholly brought to rest. Yet he went on resolutely. One barrier had given way—one more remained, and he flung himself against it with a reckless determination which would have overcome any resistance. But there was none. The old priest who had been his guide and teacher welcomed him as he had always done, seated cross-legged at the edge of the Sacred Tank, motionless, rigid, like some handsome bronze statue of Buddha, whose eyes alone spoke of a fierce flowing life within. He bowed his head once in return to Nehal's greeting, but as he began to speak he interrupted him, and in a low, chanting voice uttered the last words he was ever heard to address to any living creature:

"Speak not to me, Son of the Night and Day, for the Spirit of the Holy Yog is on me, and his tongue speaketh through my lips. Behold, mine eyes see with his into the wells of the future—my heart stands still for fear of the things that are to be. I see a Holy Temple and hear the ring of Accursed Footsteps. I see a young man at daybreak, beautiful, strong and upright, and I see him stand beneath the high sun like a blade of withered grass. I see him go forth in the morning with laughter on his lips, and at nightfall his eyes run blood. A voice calleth him from the thicket, and wheresoever the voice calleth him he goeth. He standeth on the banks of Holy Ganges, and behold! the waters burst from their course and pour westward to the ocean. Behold, then shall he draw his sword against his people, and from that hour he shall serve them and become theirs. Then shall the doors of the temple be closed for ever, and the lips of Vishnu silent. Go forth, son of the Evening and Morning Star! That which is to be shall be till the stream of the Future ceaseth to flow from the mouth of Heaven!"

Nehal Singh listened to this strange, disjointed prophecy in perfect silence, his eyes following the fierce stare of the old Brahman into the oily waters of the Sacred Pool. Amidst the hundred reflections from the temple he seemed to see each separate picture as the monotonous voice called it up before his mind, and always it was his own face which shimmered among the shadowy minarets, and always it was a familiar voice calling him through the ages which whispered to him from the trembling leaves of the Bo-Tree as it hung its branches down to the water's edge.

"Tell me more, for thy words have drawn the veil closer about the future!"

His pleading received no response. The priest remained motionless, passive, indifferent, seemingly plunged in an ecstatic contemplation; and from that moment his lips were closed, and he passed his once loved pupil with eyes that seemed fixed far ahead on a world visible only to himself. Neither in his words or manner had there been any anger or reproach, but a perfect resignation which walled him off from every human emotion, and Nehal Singh went his way, conscious that the world lay before him and that he was free. The great dividing wall had turned to air, and he had passed through, satisfied but not a little troubled, as a man is who finds that he has struck at shadows.

Afterward he told himself that the walls had always been shadows, the links that bound him always mere ghostly hindrances, part of the vague dreams that had filled his life and bound his horizon. Now that was all over. The more perfect reality lay before him and was his. The dim figures of his childhood's imagination gave place to definite forms. And each bore the same face, each face the same grave goodness—that of the woman destined for him by Heaven.

CHAPTER VII
THE SECOND GENERATION

Thus it came to pass that after more than a quarter of a century the gates of the palace were thrown open, and strange feet crossed the threshold in apparent peace and friendship.

A crowd of memories flooded Colonel Carmichael's mind as he followed the guide along the narrow paths. There was a difference between his last entry and this—a difference and an analogy whose bizarre completeness came home to him more vividly with every moment. Then, too, he had been led, but by a dark figure whose flaming torch had sprung through the darkness like an unearthly spirit of destruction. Then, too, he had followed—not, as now, old and saddened—but impetuously, and behind him had raced no crowd of laughing pleasure-seekers, but men whose bloody swords were clasped in hands greedy for the long-deferred vengeance. He remembered clearly what they had felt. For a year they had been held at bay by a skill and cunning which outmatched their most heroic efforts, and now, at last, the hour of victory was theirs. He remembered how the thirst for revenge had died down as they stormed the marble steps. No living being barred their course. Stillness greeted them as they poured into the mighty hall, and a chilly awe sank down upon their red-hot rage as they searched an emptiness which seemed to defy them. It was the Colonel himself, then only a young captain, who had heard the piteous wailing cry issuing from a side apartment. He had rushed in, and there a sight greeted him which engraved itself on his memory for ever. The place was almost in darkness, save that at the far end two torches had been lit on either side of what seemed to be a throne—a beautiful golden chair raised from the floor by ivory steps. Here, too, at first all had seemed death and silence; then the cry had been repeated, and they saw that a tiny child lay between the high carved arms and was watching them with great, beautiful eyes. Around his neck had hung a hastily-written message:

"This is my son, Nehal Singh, whose life and heritage I intrust to my conquerors in the name of justice and mercy."

And he had taken the boy in his arms and borne him thence as tenderly as if he had been his own.

Since then twenty-five years had passed. The throne had been given to the tiny heir under the tutelage of a neighboring prince, and the spirit of forgotten things brooded over the wreck of the tempest that for over a year had raged about Marut. But the Colonel remembered as if it had been but yesterday. Others had forgotten the little child, but, perhaps because he had no children of his own, the memory of the dark baby eyes had never been banished from his mind. He caught himself wondering, not without a touch of emotion, what sort of man had grown out of the minute being he had rescued; but curiously enough—and typically enough of the contrariness of human sympathy—from the moment he caught sight of the tall figure advancing to meet him from the steps of the palace, all kindly, gentle feelings died out of him, and his old prejudice of race awoke. Possibly— nay, certainly—the child had had less need of sympathy than the man, but the Colonel's heart froze toward him, and his formal response to his host's greeting was icy with the unconquerable consciousness of the gulf between them.

Yet, for eyes unblinded by preconceived aversion, Nehal Singh was at that moment good to look upon. He was simply dressed in white, with no jewels save for a great diamond in his turban, and this very simplicity threw into strong relief his unusually well-built figure and the features to whose almost classical perfection was added a strength, a force of intellect which classical beauty is too often denied. Quietly and modestly, conscious of his own worth, ignorant and inexperienced of the world, he was utterly unaware of the stone barrier that his guests presented to his own open-hearted welcome. For him the whole of his past life concentrated itself on this moment when the gates of the Universe rolled back, and he advanced to meet the representatives of its Greatest People. He thought, in the simple, natural egoism of a man who has lived a life cut off from others, that they would understand this and feel with him.

What his own feelings were he hardly knew—perhaps among them, though unrecognized, was the faintest chill of disappointment. He had had no definite expectations, but his imagination had unconsciously been at work, and touched with its illuminating fire the sons of the heroes whose deeds had filled his quiet existence with romance, painting his picture of them with colors which the reality did not justify. Certainly the little Colonel had nothing either romantic or heroic in his appearance, and what was good and kindly in his bronzed face was hidden behind the mask of his racial pride.

His first words were delivered in a harsh voice, which betrayed only too clearly his real feelings, though Nehal Singh recognized nothing but its disagreeableness.

"Rajah Sahib, you have honored us with the wish to become acquainted with the English people dwelling in your State," he began, "and it is therefore my pleasure and duty to present to you the officers of the regiments—" He stumbled awkwardly, the strangeness of the situation, the direct and searching gaze of his host, throwing him completely out of whatever oratory powers he possessed. It was Nehal Singh himself who saved the situation.

"It is my pleasure to receive you," he said, in his slow, painstaking English, "and I am honored by the readiness with which you have complied with my desire to meet the Great People to whom my land owes so much. Though hitherto I have lived apart from them, I am not wholly ignorant of their greatness. I know, for my fathers and my books have shown me, that there is no other nation so powerful nor whose sons are so noble. Therefore I welcome you with all my heart as a brother, and if such entertainment as I have tried to prepare for your pleasure is not to your taste, I pray you to forgive me, for therein am I indeed ignorant."

For a few among the English party his words, spoken slowly and with a simple sincerity, were not without their charm. Yet, little as he knew it, he had succeeded in one short speech in touching two dangerous spots in his relationship to his guests—his ancestry and his equality. But here again his ignorance veiled from him what was written clearly enough on a dozen frozen faces.

"I should be glad to be made personally acquainted with each of your officers," he went on. "For men who serve under one flag should know each other well."

Colonel Carmichael obeyed, thankful for any occupation which saved him the necessity of replying; and one by one the solemn, unmoved faces came under Nehal Singh's eager gaze, bowed, and passed on. Each resented in turn the intense scrutiny of their host, and none guessed its cause. For them it was the insolent stare of a colored man who had ventured to place himself on an equality with themselves. They could not have known that he was seeking familiar features, nor that, as one after another passed on, a cold chill of disappointment was settling on a heart warm with preconceived admiration and respect. They could not have known that his unconscious presumption had hidden a real desire to find among them the hero to whom his man's worship of courage and greatness could have been dedicated. He was too young—and especially too young in worldly wisdom—to realize that the outside man is not of necessity the man himself. He merely felt, as each wooden face confronted his own, that here was surely no Great Man, no Hero. Only when it came to the civilians his eyes rested with some degree of satisfaction on Travers' well-knit figure and fresh-colored face. For the first time during the whole proceedings the prince smiled, and in turn received a smile.

The ladies had by this time arrived, and the presentations continued. There was no change in Nehal Singh's demeanor when he stood before Beatrice Cary—no change, at least, visible to the curious eyes that watched. If there was any hidden meaning in his expression during the brief instant that they looked at each other, only she herself could have read it; and this she apparently did not do, for her face retained its Madonna peace and dignity.

"I think Rajah Sahib and Miss Cary have already met?" remarked Travers, who was acting as master of the ceremonies.

"Yes, we have met," Nehal Singh answered, and passed on.

If any hesitation showed itself in his manner, it was before Lois Caruthers. A swift shade of puzzled surprise clouded his features.

"You have been a long time in India?" he asked, after the first words of introduction. The question sounded as though he merely sought her affirmation to something he already knew.

"Almost all my life, Rajah Sahib," she answered. Possibly it was a natural shyness which made her voice sound troubled and nervous. She seemed to heave a sigh of relief when he once more moved on. Yet he had impressed her agreeably.

"Is he not handsome?" she said in an undertone to her companion, Stafford. "I think he is quite the handsomest man I have seen, and he has the manners of an Englishman. I wonder where he got them from."

"I don't know," Stafford returned. "These people have a wonderful trick of picking up things. At any rate he realizes Miss Cary's curious description—beautiful; though, with Miss Berry, I do not care for the word as applied to a man. He seems a nice sort of fellow, too, quiet and unaffected, and that is more to me than his good looks. It's rather a pity."

"What is a pity?" she asked, surprised.

"Oh, well, that he is what he is. Don't look so pained. It's not only my 'narrow-hearted prejudice,' as you call it. It's more than that. I'm sorry for the man himself. It all confirms my first opinion that it is rather bad luck."

"Why?" she demanded obstinately.

"Don't you understand? If you had seen Webb's face when he talked about 'as a brother a brother,' you would have understood well enough. He has been made a fool of, and sooner or later he will have his eyes roughly opened. As I say, it seems bad luck."

"You mean he would have done better to keep to his old seclusion?" she said thoughtfully.

"That's about it." He smiled down at her, and they suddenly forgot the Rajah in that curious happiness of two beings who need no words to tell them that each is understood by the other, and that a secret current of thought and feeling flows beneath every word and touch. "Come," he went on. "It seems that we are to have the run of the place. Shall we explore?"

She nodded a quick agreement, and they started off, thus following the example of others of the party who had already made use of the Rajah's suggestion that they should visit the chief and most interesting portions of the palace. Nehal Singh himself stood alone, and thankful for his loneliness. For the last ten minutes Colonel Carmichael and he had stood side by side, and found no word to say to each other. The past, which might have been a link, proved itself a barrier which neither could scale, and presently, on some excuse, the Colonel had hurried off to join his wife. As though guided by a sure instinct, Nehal Singh turned in the direction where Beatrice was standing with her mother and Travers. Without hesitation he went up to her.

"I have waited to be your guide," he said. His words sounded amusingly decided and matter-of-course, and a smile of not very sympathetic meaning passed over the faces of those within earshot.

"You can be sure she went a lot further than she cared to say," Mrs. Berry whispered to her daughter. "You can see how everything was made up beforehand. I wonder what she expects to get out of him?"

Though the remark did not reach her, Beatrice's instinct and bitter experience supplied her with a sure key to the look that was exchanged between the two women. She smiled gaily.

"I shall be only too pleased," she said. "What I have seen has made me thirst for more."

"Indeed, Your Highness," Mrs. Cary broke in eagerly. "I must not forget to thank you for the really very kind assistance you lent my reckless daughter the other day. I do not know what would have happened to her if it had not been for you!"

Nehal Singh looked at her with a grave wonder.

"You are her mother—?" he said, and then stopped short. The wonder was reflected so clearly in his tone that an angry flush mounted to Mrs. Cary's fat cheeks.

"I have that honor, Your Highness," she said acidly.

"Mrs. Cary!" Travers called from the flower-bed over which he was leaning. "If the Rajah Sahib can spare you, do come and look at these flowers. They are extraordinary."

With her head in the air, her plumes waving, a picture of ruffled dignity, Mrs. Cary swayed her way in the direction indicated, and Nehal Singh and Beatrice found themselves alone.

"Will you come with me now?" he asked. "I have still so much to show you."

She saw the look of self-satisfied "I-told-you-so" horror written on the faces of Mrs. Berry and her friends, who stood a little farther off whispering and nodding, and if she had felt the slightest hesitation, she hesitated no longer.

"Lead the way, Rajah Sahib," she said coolly. "I follow."

CHAPTER VIII
THE IDEAL

On either side of them tall palm-trees raised their splendid heads high above the shrubs and sweet-smelling plants that clustered like a protecting wall about their feet, and as Beatrice and her companion passed a sharp bend it seemed as though they had been suddenly cut off from the chattering crowd behind them and had entered into a wonderful, silent world in which they were alone.

Was it the beauty of her surroundings, or was it the man beside her, which sent the curious, almost painful emotion through her angry heart? For she was angry—angry with her mother, with herself and him—chiefly with him. He had been too sure. And yet she was flattered. Also, it was a pleasure for the first time to be with some one with whom she could drop her weapons and have no fear. She looked up at him, and found that he was watching her.

"It was not good-by for ever," he said. "We have met again."

Her anger suddenly subsided. His slow English, with its foreign accent, his dark features and native dress reminded her vividly that he was of another (implied, inferior) race, and therefore not to be judged by ordinary standards. She gave herself up to the pleasure of the moment.

"You have overthrown destiny," she said, smiling. "You have made the impossible possible. How was I to know all that when I prophesied we should not meet again?"

"I have not overthrown destiny," he answered. "I have fulfilled it."

"Are you sure of that?"

"Quite sure."

She looked away from him up to the golden dome of the temple which rose before them against the unclouded sky. Because she had thrown down her weapons, and in the irresponsible pleasure of the moment become herself, she acquired a power of penetration and understanding which is denied to those who with their own hearts closed seek to know the hearts of others.

"Do you know," she said suddenly, "when Colonel Carmichael presented himself to you, and all the others, I watched you, and I rather fancy I read something on your face which you didn't want to show. I wonder if I am right."

"It is possible," he answered gravely. "In this last hour I have already begun to regret that I have never studied to control my emotions. I show when I am surprised, disappointed, or—startled. Hitherto, there has been no reason why I should not do so. But now that I am among my equals, it is different."

She bit her lip, not in anger but in an almost pained surprise at this man's ignorance of the world into which he was entering. He was not presuming to place himself on the level with the Englishman; it seemed as if he were inoffensively lifting the Englishman up to himself. She was sorry for him as one is sorry for all kindly fools.

"Tell me what you read!" he begged, after a moment. "Perhaps you will know better than I myself. I am almost sure you will."

"I read disappointment," she answered. "Was that so?"

His brows contracted slightly.

"I *was* disappointed," he admitted, "but that was my own fault. I had never met English people—only heard of them. What I had heard made me imagine things which it seems have no reality."

"Did you expect demigods?" she asked.

"I do not know what I expected—but it was something different. You know the men I have met to-day. Are they all great-hearted and brave?"

She did not laugh at the question, though there was cause enough to have excused it.

"I can not tell you," she answered. "Only circumstances can bring such virtues to light, and hitherto the circumstances have been lacking. All men do not wear their heart on their sleeve," she answered, not without malice.

He nodded.

"I am glad to hear you say that, for no doubt you are right. I am very ignorant, I fear, and was foolish enough to expect heroes to have the face and figure of heroes. It grieved me for a moment to find that I was the tallest and best-looking among them. Now that you have explained, I see that the greatness lies beneath."

This time she laughed, and laughed so heartily that he joined in with her, though he did not know what had caused her amusement. He took pleasure in watching her when she laughed. Her statuesque beauty yielded then to a warm, pulsating life, which transformed her and made her seem to him more human, more attainable. For he had never shaken off the belief that she and a divine agency were closely linked together.

"You must not compare yourself with Englishmen," she said, when she had recovered, "neither in face, nor stature, nor ideals. You must always remember that we are of another race."

"And yet you fulfilled my highest ideal."

"Perhaps I am the exception," she retorted, dangerously near another outburst. "Did all the women this afternoon fulfil your ideal?"

"No!" very decidedly.

"There! You see, then, that I am the exception. Besides, I am not a man. Men require to be differently judged, and we have perhaps other ideals."

"That also is possible," he assented, "and I know that, because the English are such a great people, their ideals must be very high, perhaps higher than mine. Since I am now to go among them, I wish to know what they consider necessary in the character of a great man.".

"That is too hard a question," she said hurriedly. "I can not describe the national ideal to you, because I am too ignorant and have never thought about it. You must ask some one else."

They had come to the end of the path and stood before a square opening, on the other side of which the two massive gopuras of the temple rose in their monumental splendor two hundred feet above them. They were still alone. None of the sightseers seemed to have found the sacred spot, and for a moment she stood still, awed in spite of herself.

"I should be quite content with *your* ideal," he said gently, breaking in upon her admiration. "I feel that it will be the highest."

"You ask of me more than I can answer."

"I beg of you!" he pleaded earnestly. "I have my reasons."

Again she bit her lip. It was too absurd, too ridiculous! That she, of all people, who had seen into the darkest, most sordid depths of the human character, and long since learned to look upon goodness and virtue as exploded myths, should be set to work to draw up an ideal which she did not and could not believe in, seemed a mockery too pitiful for laughter. Yet something—perhaps it was a form of national pride—stung her to the task, moreover stung her to do her best and place beyond the reach of these dark hands a high and splendid figure of English ideals.

To help herself, she sought through the lumber-rooms of her memory, and drew thence a hundred ideas, thoughts and conceptions which had belonged to a short—terribly short—childhood. Like a middle-aged woman who comes suddenly upon a hoard of long since forgotten toys, and feels an emotion half pitying, half regretful, so Beatrice Cary displayed to her companion things that for years had lain forsaken and neglected in the background of her mind. The dust lay thick upon them—and yet they were well enough. They would have been beautiful, had she believed in them, but, like the toys, they had lost the glamour and illusionary light in which her youth and imagination had bathed them.

"Our highest ideal of a man we call a gentleman," she said slowly. "It is a much-abused term, but it can mean a very great deal. What his appearance is does not so much matter—indeed, when one looks into it, it does not matter at all, save that you will find that the ugliest face can often give you an index to a lovely character. The chief thing that we require of him is that he should be above all meanness and pettiness. He must be great-thinking and great-feeling for himself and others, especially for others. You will find that a good man is always thinking or working for those others whose names he may not even know. Whatever power or talent he has—however little it may be—he concentrates on some object which may help them. It is the same with his virtues. He cultivates them because he knows that there is not a high thought, or generous impulse, or noble deed which does not help to lift the standard of the whole world."

"Of what virtues are you speaking?" Nehal Singh interposed.

"Oh, the usual things," she returned, with a note of cynicism breaking through her sham enthusiasm. "Honesty, purity, generosity, loyalty—especially loyalty. I do not think a man who is true to himself, to his word, to his friend, and to his country can ever fall far below the ideal." She took a deep breath. "It is a very poor description that I have given you. I hope you have understood?"

"Yes, I have understood," he answered. "And this man—this gentleman—can be of all nations?"

So deeply ingrained is national prejudice, even in those who profess to regard the whole world with an equally contemptuous eye, that for an instant she hesitated.

"Of course," she said then. "Nationality makes no difference."

They crossed over the broad square, through the gopura, into the inner temple. Nehal Singh, who had sunk into a deep meditation, roused himself and called to her notice many curious and beautiful things which she would otherwise have passed by without interest. Whether it was his loving description, or whether it was because she was calmer, she could not say, but the place impressed her with its stately magnificence as it had not done before.

"The ages seem to hang like ghosts in the atmosphere," she told her companion, in a hushed undertone.

He assented, and the dreamer's look which had haunted his eyes for twenty-five years crept back into its place.

"Who knows what unseen world surrounds us?" he said quietly.

They had already left the first court behind them and passed the Sacred Pool, a placid, untroubled mirror for the overhanging trees and towering minarets. There they had paused a moment, watching their own reflections which the warm evening sunshine cast on to the smooth surface. Then they had moved on, and now stood before the entrance of the Holy of Holies. Beatrice drew back with a gesture of alarm. A tall, white-clad figure had suddenly stepped out of the shadowy portal and stood erect and threatening, one hand raised as though to forbid their entrance. Long afterward, Beatrice remembered the withered face, and always with a shudder of unreasonable terror.

"Do not be afraid," Nehal Singh said. "He defends the entrance against strangers. He will let you pass."

He went up to the old priest and spoke a few words in Hindustani, which Beatrice did not understand. Immediately the Brahman stood aside, and though his stern, piercing gaze never left her face, she felt that by some means or other his animosity had been disarmed.

"What did you say to him?" she asked.

Nehal Singh shook his head.

"One day I will tell you," he answered; and some instinct made her hesitate to press the question further.

Thus they stood once more before the great golden statue, this time side by side. The sanctuary was built in the shape of a half-circle, the high, vaulted roof supported by slender pillars of carved black marble. There was no other attempt at ornamentation. The three-headed figure of the god reigned in the center from a massive altar in solitary splendor, and from a small opening overhead a frail ray of evening light mingled its pale yellow with the brilliant crimson flame of the Sacred Lamp which burnt before the idol, casting an almost unearthly reflection about the passionless chiseled features. In spite of herself, Beatrice felt that the place was charmed, and that the charm was drawing into its ban her very thoughts and emotions. She felt subdued, quieted. It was as she had said—the ages seemed to hover like ghosts about them, and her hard, worldly skepticism could make no stand against the hush and mystery of the past. Here generation after generation, amidst danger, battle and death, men had bowed down and poured out their hottest, most fervent prayers, and their sincerity and faith had sanctified the ground for Christian, Brahman and skeptic alike.

Beatrice looked at the man beside her. She had the feeling that, while she had stood and wondered, he had been praying; and possibly she was right, though he returned her glance immediately.

"This is a holy place," he said. "It is holiest of all for me. Here I have spent my most solemn happy hours; here God spoke direct to me and answered me."

It seemed quite natural that he should speak thus so openly and directly to her of his nearest concerns. The barrier which separated them perhaps, after all, made the intercourse between them easier and less constrained than it would otherwise have been. They had no responsibility toward each other. They lived in different worlds, and if for a moment they exchanged messages, it was only for a moment. When it was over, the dividing sea would once more roll between them, leaving no trace of their brief intercourse.

Remembering all this, she threw off the momentary sense of trouble.

"Tell me how and when that was," she said.

"I can not tell you—not now. One day I will. One day I shall have a great deal to tell you, and you will have a great deal to tell me. You will tell me of your faith. I know nothing of your God. All that has been kept secret from me."

"How do you know I have a God?" she demanded sharply.

They had passed out of the sanctuary and were walking back toward the entrance. He half stopped and looked at her in grave surprise.

"How do I know? How, rather, is it possible that it should be otherwise? You are too good and beautiful not to have learnt at the feet of a great teacher."

His naivete and confidence set her once more in a state between indulgent amusement and anger. Another man she would have laughed at straight in the face, but this simple belief in her goodness threw her out of her usual stride, and in the end she left him without answer, save that which he chose to interpret from her silence.

As they reached the great doorway through the gopura, a tall figure advanced to meet them which Beatrice at once recognized in spite of the gathering twilight. She had been expecting this new-comer for some time, yet his appearance disturbed her as something undesirable.

"There is a man I like," Nehal Singh remarked, with a sudden pleasure. "Is not Travers his name? He disappointed me least of all."

"You have an excellent judgment," Beatrice returned.

If there was an undercurrent of sarcasm in her approval, Nehal Singh did not notice it. He advanced quickly to meet Travers.

"I am glad you have found your way here," he said. "It is the most beautiful part of all, and perhaps I should have acted as guide to my other guests. But my first duty was here." He turned to Beatrice with a grave inclination.

Travers laughed.

"You need be in no alarm, Rajah Sahib," he said. "We have been enjoying ourselves immensely, and no wonder, considering all the glories that have been laid open to us. I have seen much wealth and splendor in India, but not as here. I feel overwhelmed."

"There is still much for you to see," Nehal Singh answered with a proud pleasure.

Other members of the party had by this time joined them, and Beatrice dropped back to her mother's side. The whole thing had been, as Mrs. Berry said, arranged, but not in the way the good lady supposed, and Beatrice's task was at an end.

Travers hastened his step imperceptibly, so that the distance between him and the rest was increased beyond hearing distance.

"Of course," he began, with a frank confidence which fell pleasingly on his companion's ears, "I am a business man, and a great deal of my admiration is from a business standpoint. You will perhaps hardly understand me when I say that my flesh simply creeps when I think of all the wealth that lies here inactive. Wealth is power, Rajah Sahib, and in your hand there lies a power for good or evil which dazzles the senses of a less fortunate man."

Nehal Singh lifted his face thoughtfully toward the evening sky.

"Power for good or evil!" he echoed. "It may be that you are right. But power is a great clumsy giant, who can accomplish nothing without the experienced guiding brain."

"I imagine you have both, Rajah Sahib."

"Not the experience. I have led a life apart. I feel myself helpless before the very thought of any effort in the world. Yet I should be glad to accomplish something—to help even a little in the general progress."

"You will learn easily enough," Travers broke in, with enthusiasm. "It is only necessary to go outside your gates to find a hundred outlets for energy and purpose. If you traveled two days among your people, you would come back knowing very well what awaited your power to accomplish."

"I am glad to hear you say so," Nehal returned, smiling, "for I am ambitious."

"Ambition and power!" exclaimed Travers. "You are indeed to be envied, Rajah Sahib!"

"What would you do in my place?" Nehal asked, after a moment, in a lighter tone, which concealed a real and eager curiosity.

Travers shook his head.

"The greater the power the greater the responsibility," he answered. "I couldn't say on the spur of the moment. If I were given time, no doubt I should be able to tell you."

"I give you till our next meeting, then," Nehal said gravely.

"Our next meeting? I trust, then, Rajah Sahib that you will condescend to be the guest of the English Station?"

Nehal turned his head to hide the flash of boyish satisfaction which shone out of his eyes. It was that he wanted—to go among this people, from their own hearth to judge them, and to probe down into the source of their greatness.

"It would give me much pleasure," he answered quietly.

It was Travers' turn to hide the triumph which the willing acceptance aroused. Nevertheless, his next words were whimsically regretful.

"Unfortunately, we have no place in which to offer you a fitting welcome, Rajah Sahib," he said. "For a long time it has been the ambition of the Station to build some place wherein all such festivities could be properly celebrated. But alas!"—he shrugged his shoulders—"it is the fate of the Anglo-Indian to work for the richness and greatness of his country and himself remain miserably poor."

"How much money would be required?" Nehal Singh asked.

"You will no doubt be amused at the smallness of the sum—a mere four thousand rupees—but it is just so much we have not got."

Nehal Singh smiled.

"Let me at once begin to make use of my power," he said graciously. "It would be a pleasure to me to mark my first meeting with you by the gift of the building you require. I place the matter in your hands, Sahib Travers. For the time being, until I have gained my own experience, yours must be the guiding brain."

The good-looking Englishman appeared to be considerably taken aback—almost distressed.

"You are too generous, Rajah Sahib!" he protested. To himself he commented on the rapidity with which this fellow had picked up the lingo of polite society.

All further conversation was cut short by a cry of admiration from the crowd behind them. They had reached the chief entrance to the palace, and suddenly, as though at a given signal, every outline of the building became marked out by countless points of light which sparkled starlike against the darkening sky. At the same instant, the temple to their left took form in a hundred colors, and a burst of weird music broke on the ears of the wondering spectators. It was a strange and beautiful scene, such as few of them had ever seen. Fairy palaces of fire seemed to hover miraculously in the evening air, and over everything hung the curious, indefinable charm of the mysterious East.

Nehal Singh turned and found Lois Caruthers standing with Stafford a little behind him. Both their names were forgotten, but the dark eager face of the girl attracted him and at the same time puzzled him as something which struck a hitherto unsuspected chord in his innermost self.

"You find it well?" he asked her.

"It is most beautiful," she answered. "It is good of you, Rajah Sahib, to give us so much pleasure."

That was all she said, but among all his memories of that evening she remained prominent, because she had spoken sincerely, warmly, enthusiastically. Others thanked him—the Colonel's little speech at the end was a piece of studied rhetoric, but it left him cold where her thanks had left him warm, almost gratefully so.

On the whole, the first meeting between the English residents of Marut and the young native prince was classified as a success. As they drove through the darkness, the returning guests called terse criticisms to one another which tended to the conclusion that the whole thing had not been at all bad, and that for the circumstances the Rajah was a remarkably well-mannered individual.

Beatrice Cary took no part in the light-hearted exchange. Her mother had gone off with Mrs. Carmichael in her carriage, and Travers having offered to drive her home, she had accepted, and now sat by his side, thoughtful, almost depressed, though she did not own it, even to herself.

Try as she would she could not throw off the constantly recurring memory of her parting with Nehal Singh. She made fun of it and of herself, and yet she could not laugh over it—her power of irresponsible enjoyment had been taken suddenly from her.

"You will not now say that we shall never meet again," he had said, pressing something into her hand. "Now you will never forget," he had added. "It is a talisman of remembrance."

What he had given her she did not know. It lay tightly clutched in the palm of her hand—something hard and cold which she dared not look at.

She had not even been able to remonstrate or thank him. She had been spellbound, hypnotized.

"It really has been splendid!" she heard Travers say in her ear. "Things went just like clockwork. Five minutes' conversation got the whole clubhouse out of him, and what you managed in your quarter of an hour, goodness knows. You are a clever woman and no mistake!"

"Please—don't!" she burst out irritably.

"Hullo! What's the matter? What are you so cross about?"

"I'm not cross—only tired, tired, tired and sick of it all. Do drive on!"

Far behind them a solitary figure stood on the broad steps of the palace, amidst the dying splendors of the evening and gazed in the direction which the merry procession had taken. A long time it had stood there, motionless, passive, the fine husk of the soul which had wandered out into a new world of hope and possibilities following the woman whose hand had flung the gates wide for him to enter in.

Another figure crept out of the shadows and drew near. Twisted and bent, it stood beside the bold, upright form and lifted its face, hate-filled, to the pale light of the stars.

"Nehal Singh, Nehal Singh—oh, my son!"

The prince turned coldly.

"Is it thou? Hast thou a dagger in thy hand?"

"I have no dagger—would to God I had! Nehal Singh, I have seen mine enemy's face."

"How meanest thou? Thy enemy is dead."

"Nevertheless, his face is among the living. As a servant, I crept among the strangers, and saw him straight in the eyes. He has grown younger, but it is he. It is the body of the son, but the soul of his father in his eyes—and, father or son, their blood is poison to me."

Nehal Singh knit his brows.

"Knowest thou his name?"

"Ay, now I know his name. It came back to me when I saw his face. Stafford he was called—Stafford!" He crept closer, his thin hand fell like a vise on Nehal's arm. "Kill him!" he whispered. "Kill him—the son of thy father's betrayer!"

Nehal Singh shook himself free.

"I can not," he answered proudly, and a warm thrill of enthusiasm rang in his voice. "I can not. They are all my brothers. I can not take my brother's blood."

With a moan of anger the twisted figure crept back into the shadow, and once more Nehal Singh stood alone.

Unconsciously he had accepted and proclaimed Beatrice Cary's ideal as his own. The hour of bloodshed was gone, mercy and justice called him in its stead. And in that acceptance of a new era his gaze pierced through the obscurity into a light beyond. The jungle which had bound his life was gone; all hindrances, all gulfs of hatred and revenge, were overthrown and bridged. The world of the Great People stood open to him, and to them he held out the casteless hand of love and fellowship.

CHAPTER IX
CHECKED

Lois and Stafford had arrived at that stage of friendship when conversation becomes unnecessary. They walked side by side through the Colonel's carefully tended garden and were scarcely conscious that they had dropped into a thoughtful silence. Yet, as though in obedience to some unspoken agreement, their footsteps found their way to the ruined bungalow and there paused.

As a look can be more powerfully descriptive than a word, so these shot-riddled walls had their own eloquence. Each shot-hole, each jagged splinter and torn hinge had its own history and added its pathetic detail to the whole picture of that disastrous night when the vengeance of Behar Singh had burst like a hurricane over the defenseless land.

After a moment's hesitation Stafford stepped forward and, pushing aside the heavy festoons of creeper which barred the doorway, passed through into the gloomy interior.

"I should like to see the place from the inside," he explained to Lois, who, with an uncontrollable shudder, had followed him. "One can imagine better then how it all happened."

"I think of it all—often," she answered in a hushed voice, "and every time I seem to see things differently. My poor mother!"

"You never knew her?" he asked.

"No, I was too young—scarcely more than a year old. Yet her loss seems to have overshadowed my whole life."

"Was she like you?"

"Yes, I believe so. She was dark—not so dark as I am—but she was stately and beautiful. So she has always been described to me, and so I always seem to see her."

Stafford turned and looked about him.

"It must be almost as it was then," he said wonderingly, pointing to the rusty truckle-bed in the corner. "And there is the broken over-turned chair! It might have been yesterday."

She nodded.

"So my guardian found it," she said. "It had been my father's bungalow and he never allowed it to be touched. When I came of age I gave it to him. It seemed to belong to him, somehow. They say that it nearly broke his heart when he found that he had come too late to save my father. My father was his dearest, almost his only friend."

"Were they killed at once?" Stafford asked with hesitating curiosity. "I have never known the rights of the case. It has always been a painful subject for me—with you I don't mind."

It was the faintest allusion to a bond between them which both silently recognized, and Lois turned away to hide the signal of happiness which had risen to her cheeks.

"No one knows," she answered. "The bodies were never found. It was part of Behar Singh's cruelty to hide the real fate of his victims. For a long time people used to hope and hope that in some dungeon or prison they would find their friends, but they never did. One can only pray that the end was a mercifully quick one."

"And Behar Singh died in the jungle?"

"So the natives said. No one really knows," she replied.

"I wish he hadn't," Stafford said, his good-natured face darkening. "It seems unfair that he should have caused our people to suffer so much and we have never had the chance to pay back. Whatever made the Government give his son the power, goodness only knows."

"The present Rajah was a baby then," she said in a tone of gentle remonstrance. "It would have been hard to have punished him for the sins of his father."

Nothing appeals to a man more than a woman's undiplomatic tenderness for the whole world. Stafford looked down at Lois with a smile.

"You dear, good-hearted little girl!" he said. "And yet, blood is blood, you know. Somehow, one can't get over it. In spite of his good looks, it always seems to me as though I could see his father's treachery in Nehal Singh's eyes. It made me sick to think that I was enjoying his hospitality—it makes me feel worse that we have to accept the club-house at his hands. Travers behaved pretty badly, according to my ideas."

"It was mostly Miss Cary's doing," Lois objected. She liked Travers, and was inclined to take up the cudgels on his behalf.

Stafford's eyes twinkled. On his side he had the rooted and not unfounded masculine notion that all women are jealous of one another.

"Miss Cary is young and inexperienced and probably did not realize what she was doing," he retorted. "From what she told me, she takes the whole matter as a big joke, and now that the fat is in the fire it's no use enlightening her."

Lois made no immediate answer, though she may have had her doubts on the subject of Beatrice Cary's inexperience.

"The poor Rajah!" she said, after a pause, as Stafford walked curiously about the room. "I could not help being sorry for him. He seemed so eager and enthusiastic and anxious to please us, and we were so cold and ungrateful. Tell me, does it really make so much difference?"

He came back to her side. Something in her voice had touched him and stirred to life a warmth of feeling which was more than that of friendship.

"What makes so much difference?" he asked, smiling down at her small troubled face. "What are you worrying yourself about now?"

"Oh, it has always troubled me," she answered with the impetuosity which characterized her. "I have often worried about it. I mean," she added, as he laughed at her incoherence, "all that race distinction. Does it really mean so much? Will it never be bridged over?"

"Never," he said. "It can't be. It is a justified distinction and to my mind those who ignore it are to be despised."

He had answered her question with only a part seriousness, his whole interest concentrated on the charm of her personality. But for once her gravity resisted the suppressed merriment in his eyes.

"Are the natives, then, so contemptible?" she asked.

"Not exactly contemptible, but inferior. They have not our culture, and whatsoever they borrow from us is only skin-deep. Beneath the varnish they are their elemental selves—lazy, cruel, treacherous and unscrupulous. No, no. Each race must keep to itself. Our strength in India depends on our exclusiveness—upon keeping ourselves apart and above as superior beings. So long as they recognize we *are* superior, so long will they obey us."

"It is superiority, then, which prevents every one except professors from taking any interest in the natives?"

"Possibly," he returned, not quite so much at his ease. "One feels a natural repugnance, you know."

"You would never have anything to do with them?"

"Not if I could help it."

She sighed and turned away as though his gaze troubled her.

"I don't know why—it makes me sad to hear you talk like that," she said. "It seems so terribly hard."

"It *is* hard," he affirmed, following her out of the curious, heavy atmosphere into the evening sunshine. "There are a great many things in life which, as far as we know, are inevitable, so that there is no use in worrying or thinking about them." Her more serious mood had conquered his good spirits, and for a moment he stood at her side looking at the disused bungalow with eyes as thoughtful as her own. "Isn't it strange?" he went on. "Our parents came together from different ends of the earth, doomed to die in the same spot and in the same hour, and we children, far away in England, knowing nothing of each other, have drifted back to the fatal place to find each other there and to—"

"Yes," she said as he hesitated, "it is strange. I could almost think that this bungalow had some mysterious influence over our lives."

He smiled in half confirmation of her fancy.

"It may be. But come! We have had enough gloom for one evening. Let me gather some flowers for you before we go back."

She assented, and they followed the winding paths, stopping here and there to cut down some of the most tempting of Mrs. Carmichael's tenderly loved blossoms and always turning aside when they came in sight of the Colonel's verandah. No word of tenderness had ever passed between them, and yet they were happy to be together. It was as though a bond united them which had grown up, silent and unseen, from the first hour they had met, and in a quiet, peaceful way they knew that it existed and that they loved each other.

From the verandah where she was sewing by the fading light Mrs. Carmichael could watch their appearing and disappearing figures amidst the trees with the satisfaction of a confirmed match-maker. She, too, knew of this bond, and though she was a trifle impatient with the slowness of the development, she was content to bide her time.

"I don't usually pay any attention to Station gossip," she said to her husband, who was trying to read the newly arrived English paper, "but for once in a way I believe there is something in it. According to my experience, they should be engaged in less than a fortnight."

Colonel Carmichael started.

"Who? Lois and Stafford?"

"Yes, of course. Who else? Everybody looks upon it as practically settled. Why do you look like that? You ought to be pleased. You said yourself that you were very fond of Stafford—"

Carmichael made a quick gesture as though to stop the threatening torrent of expostulation. He had turned crimson and his whole manner was marked by an unusual uneasiness.

"Of course, I am fond of Stafford," he began. "I only meant—"

He was saved the trouble of explaining what he did mean by a sudden exclamation from his wife, who had let her work fall to the ground with a start of alarm.

"Good gracious, Mr. Travers!" she cried in her sharp way. "What a fright you gave me! I thought you were a horrible thug or something come to murder us all. There, how do you do!" She gave him her hand. "Will you have a cup of tea? We have just had ours, but if you would, I am quite ready to keep you company. Tea, as you know, is a weakness of mine. That is why my nerves are so bad."

Travers bowed, smiling. He was rather paler than usual and the hand which held a large bouquet of freshly cut flowers trembled as though the shock his sudden appearance had caused Mrs. Carmichael had recoiled on himself.

"Thank you—no," he said. "As a matter of fact, I came to bring these for Miss Caruthers, but as she is not here I should be very grateful if I might have a few words with you alone. I have something of importance, which it would be perhaps better to tell you first."

"Certainly," the Colonel said, clearing his throat and settling himself farther back in his chair. "There is no time like the present."

Travers looked at him in troubled surprise. The elder man's tone and attitude were those of some one confronted with a not unexpected but unpleasant crisis.

"It concerns your ward, Colonel Carmichael," Travers said, taking the chair offered him. "I think you must have known long ago that I cared very dearly for her. I have come now to ask her to be my wife."

He spoke quickly and abruptly, as though to hide a powerful emotion, and there was an instant's uncomfortable silence. Mrs. Carmichael's head was bent over her work. She did not dislike Travers, but this unexpected proposal upset all her plans and though it flattered her pride in Lois, she felt disturbed and thrown out of her course.

"I think you have made a mistake, Mr. Travers," she said at last, as her husband remained obstinately silent. "I have every reason to believe that Lois' heart is given elsewhere. However, we have no right to interfere—Lois must decide for herself. She is her own mistress. What do you say, George, dear?"

The Colonel shifted his position. Evidently he was at a loss to express himself, and his brow remained clouded.

"If it is Lois' wish, I shall put no obstacle in the way of her happiness," he said slowly.

"Have you any personal objection, Colonel?"

"I? O, dear, no!" was the hurried answer.

There was a second silence, in which Mrs. Carmichael and Travers exchanged baffled glances. The Colonel seemed in some unaccountable way to have lost his nerve and, as though he felt and feared the questioning gaze of his wife, he leaned forward so that his face was hidden.

"Personally I have no objection at all," he repeated, as if seeking to gain time. "Like my wife, I had other ideas on the subject, but that has nothing to do with it. At the same time, I feel it—eh—my duty to—eh—tell you before you go further—for your sake, and—eh—every one's sake—certain details concerning Lois which I have not thought necessary to give to the world in general. You understand—I consider it my duty—only fair to yourself and Lois."

"I quite understand," Travers said. He seemed in no way surprised, and his expression was that of a man waiting for the explanation to a problem which had long puzzled him.

"Really, George!" expostulated Mrs. Carmichael, not without indignation, "one would think you were about to disinter the most horrible family skeleton. You are not to be alarmed, Mr. Travers. It is all a little mysterious, perhaps, but nothing to make *such* a fuss about."

The Colonel looked up under the sting of her reproach and tried to smile.

"I dare say my wife is right," he said. "I am rather foolish about the matter—possibly because it is all linked together with a very painful period of my life. Mr. Travers, my dearest friend, Steven Caruthers, had *no* children. The baby girl whom by his will he intrusted to my care was not his child, nor have I ever been able to discover whose child she really was. His will spoke of her as his adopted daughter, who was to bear his name and in fault of any other heir to inherit both his own and his wife's large fortune. More I can not tell you, for I myself do not know more."

He laid an almost timid emphasis on the word "know," as though somewhere at the back of his mind there lurked a suspicion which he dared neither deny nor express openly, and, in spite of his attempt at cheerfulness, his features were still disturbed and gloomy.

"You know one thing more, which you haven't mentioned," Mrs. Carmichael said, "and that is that Lois is of good family on both sides. Steven Caruthers told you so."

"Yes, that's true—I forgot," the Colonel assented. "He assured me that on both sides she was of good, even high birth, and that he had adopted her partly because he had no children of his own and partly because of a debt of gratitude which he owed her father. It does not seem to me that it makes much difference."

"It makes all the difference in the world, George," retorted Mrs. Carmichael, who for some reason or another was considerably put out. "You don't want Mr. Travers to think that Lois was picked up in the street, do you?"

"Of course not," her husband agreed, "but then—" He broke off, and all three relapsed into an awkward silence. Travers was the first to speak. He had been looking out over the garden and had seen Lois' white dress flash through the bushes.

"For my part," he began quietly, "I can not see that what you have told me can have an influence on the matter. I love Lois. That is the chief thing—or rather the chief thing is whether or not she can learn to love me. Whether she is the child of a sweep or a prince, it makes no difference to my feelings toward her."

Mrs. Carmichael held out her hand.

"Well, whatever happens, you are a man before you are a prig," she said, "and that is something to be thankful for in these degenerate days. Why, there is the child herself! Come here, my dear."

Lois came running up the verandah steps with Stafford close behind her. Her eyes were full of laughter and sunshine, and in her hand she held a mass of roses which Stafford had gathered during their ramble.

"Good-evening, Mr. Travers," she exclaimed with pleased surprise, as he rose to greet her. "I did not expect to find you here. How grave you all look! And what lovely flowers!"

Travers considered his bouquet with a rueful smile.

"I brought them from my garden, Miss Caruthers," he said. "They were meant for to-night's festivity. But it seems they have come too late—you are already well supplied."

"Flowers never come too late and one can never have too many of them!" Lois answered gratefully. "Please bring them in here and I will put them in water."

She led the way into the drawing-room and he followed her eagerly. Whether it was the sight of her charm and youth, or the warm greeting which he had read in her eyes, or the satisfied calm on Stafford's face, Travers himself could not have told, but in that moment he lost his usual self-possession. He was white and shaken like a man who sees himself thrust suddenly to the brink of a chasm and knows that he must cross or fall.

"Miss Caruthers!" he said.

She turned quickly from the flowers which she was arranging in a bowl. The smile of pleasure which still lingered about her lips died away as she saw his face.

"Miss Caruthers," he repeated earnestly, "it is perhaps neither wise nor right of me to speak now, but there are moments when anything—even the worst—is better than uncertainty, when a man can bear no more. Forgive me—I am not eloquent and what I have to tell can be encompassed in one word. I love you, Lois. I think you must know it, though you can not know how great my love is. Is there any hope for me?"

She drew her hand gently but firmly from his half-unconscious clasp.

"I am sorry—no," she said.

"Lois—I can't give up hope. Is there some one else?"

She lifted her troubled eyes to his face. He saw in their depths a curious doubt and uncertainty.

"I do not know," she said almost to herself. "I only know that you are not the man."

The blow had calmed him. Like a good general who has suffered a temporary check, he gathered his forces together and prepared an orderly retreat.

"I will not trouble you," he said gently. "I feel now that I did wrong to disturb your peace—God knows I would never willingly cause you an instant's sorrow—but a man who loves as I do must feed himself with hope, however wild and unreasonable. Now I know, and whatever happens—I hope you will be happy—I pray you will be happy. Yes, though I am not given to uttering prayers, I pray, so dear to me is the future which lies before you."

"I am very grateful," she said with bowed head. Something in his broken, disjointed sentences brought the tears to her eyes and made her voice unsteady. She knew he was suffering—she knew why, and her heart went out to him in friendship and womanly pity.

"You need not be grateful," he answered. "It is I who have to be grateful. In spite of it all, you do not know what good you have brought into my life nor how you have unconsciously helped me. I shall never be able to help you as you have helped me—and yet—will you promise me something?"

"Anything in my power," she said faintly.

"It is not much—only this. If the time should ever come when you are in trouble, if you should ever be in need of a true and devoted friend, will you turn to me? Will you let me try to pay my debt of gratitude to you?"

She lifted her head and looked at him with tear-dimmed eyes. Every good woman sympathizes with those whose suffering she has inadvertently caused, and in that moment Lois would have done anything to alleviate Travers' pain.

"If it should ever be necessary, I will turn to you," she said gently. "I promise you."

"Thank you!" he said, and, taking her out-stretched hand, raised it reverently to his lips.

CHAPTER X
AT THE GATES OF A GREAT PEOPLE

Although Travers lost no time in setting to work on the task of calling a new and suitable club-house into existence, he realized immediately that, do what he would, he could not hope for completion before the lapse of a considerable time, and this period of waiting did not suit his plans. Already on the day after the Rajah's reception he had arranged for a return of hospitality which was to take place in his own grounds and to be on an unusually magnificent scale. The European population of Marut shrugged its shoulders as it saw the preparations, and observed that if Travers had been as generous in the first place there would never have been any need to have sought for support from a foreign quarter—at which criticism Travers merely smiled. The club-house was, after all, only a means to a very much more important end of his own.

Rajah Nehal Singh of course accepted the invitation sent him, and scarcely a week passed before the eventful evening arrived toward which more than one looked forward with eager anticipation—not least Mrs. Cary, who saw in every large entertainment a fresh opportunity for Beatrice to carry out her own particular campaign. It was therefore, as Mrs. Cary angrily declared, a fresh dispensation of an unfriendly Providence that on the very same day Beatrice fell ill. What malady had her in its clutches was more than her distracted and aggrieved mother could say. She sat before her writing-table, playing idly with a curiously cut stone, and appeared the picture of health. Yet she was ill—she repeated it obstinately and without variation a dozen times in response to Mrs. Cary's persistent protests.

"You don't *look* ill," Mrs. Cary exclaimed in exasperation as, arrayed in her newest wonder from Paris, she came to say good-by. "I can't think what's the matter with you, and you won't explain. Have you got a pain anywhere?—Have you a headache? For goodness' sake, say something, child!"

Beatrice looked at her mother calmly, and a curious mixture of bitterness and amusement crept into her expression as her eyes wandered over the bulk in mauve satin to the red face with the indignant little eyes.

"What do you want me to say?" she asked. "I can't explain pains I haven't got."

"If you haven't got any pains, then you aren't ill."

Beatrice laughed.

"That shows how ignorant you are of the human constitution, my dear mother," she said. "The worst illnesses are painless—at least, in your sense of the word."

"I am not so ignorant as not to know one thing—and that is you are simply shamming!" burst out the elder woman, with a vicious tug at her straining gloves. "Shamming just to aggravate me, too! You do it to spite me. You are a bad daughter—"

Beatrice turned round so sharply that Mrs. Cary broke off in the middle of her abuse with a gasp.

"I do nothing to aggravate or spite you," Beatrice said, with a calm which her eyes belied. "I have never gone against you in the whole course of my life. What have I done since we have been here but play an obedient fiddle to Mr. Travers' will, in order that your position might not be endangered—"

"*Our* position," interposed Mrs. Cary hurriedly.

"No, *your* position. There may have been a time when I cared, too, but I don't now. I have ceased caring for anything. To suit Mr. Travers, I have fooled, and continue to fool, a man who has never harmed me in his life. I move heaven and earth to come between two people for whom alone in this whole place, I have a glimmer of respect."

"Respect!" jeered Mrs. Cary.

"Yes, respect—not much, I confess, but still enough to have made me leave them alone if I had had the chance. Lois has been kind to me. I happen to know that, little as she likes me, she is about the only one in the Station who keeps her tongue from slander and—the truth. As for John Stafford, if he is a narrow-minded bigot, he is at least a man, and that is something to appreciate."

"That is just what I think!" Mrs. Cary said conciliatingly. "And therefore he is the very husband for you, dear child."

"You think so, not because he is a man, but because he has a position in which it would suit you excellently to have a son-in-law. Well, I have promised to do my best, though I am convinced it is too late."

"There is no official engagement between them," Mrs. Cary said hopefully, "and you know your power, Beaty. He already likes you more than enough, and what with Mr. Travers on the other side—All the same," she continued, becoming suddenly petulant, "it's too bad of you to throw away a chance like this."

Beatrice covered her face with her hand with a gesture of complete weariness.

"I have promised to do my best," she reiterated. "Let me do it my own way. I can not go to-night—I feel I can not. If I went, it would only be a failure. Let me for once be judge of what is best."

Her mother sighed resignedly.

"Very well. I suppose I can't force you. You can be as obstinate as a mule when you choose. I only hope you won't live to regret it. Good night."

This time she did not give her daughter the usual perfunctory and barely tolerated kiss. At the bottom of her torpid, selfish soul she was bitterly hurt and disappointed, as those people always are who have hurt and disappointed others their whole lives, and only a glimmer of hope that Beatrice's determination might have softened made her hesitate at the door and glance back. Beatrice sat just as she had sat the whole evening, in an attitude of moody thought, her fingers still playing with the blood-red ruby, and Mrs. Cary went out, slamming the door violently after her.

In consequence of her long and futile appeal, Mrs. Cary had made herself very late, and when she entered the large marquee which Travers had had erected in his garden she found that all the guests had arrived, including Rajah Nehal Singh himself. He stood facing the entrance, and she felt, with a consoling sense of spiteful triumph, how his glance hurried past her, seeking the figure which no doubt above all else had tempted him thither.

The senior lady, Mrs. Carmichael, was at his side, and as Mrs. Cary in duty bound went up to pay her respects, she added satisfaction to satisfaction by relating loudly that her daughter had a slight headache which she had not thought it worth while to increase by a form of entertainment which, between you and me, dear Mrs. Carmichael, bad taste as it no doubt is, has no attractions for Beatrice. Now, anything outdoor, and nothing will keep her from it! She turned to Stafford, who was standing with Lois close at hand. "That reminds me to tell you, Captain, how tremendously my daughter enjoyed her ride with you yesterday. If you promise not to get conceited, I will tell you what she said."

"I promise!" he said, with a mock gravity which concealed a very real amusement.

"She said that in her opinion there wasn't a better horseman in Marut, and that it was more pleasure to ride with you than any one else. Now, are you keeping your promise?" She tapped him playfully on the arm. Stafford bowed, looking what he felt, hot and uncomfortable. There are some people who have the knack of making others ashamed of them and of themselves. Mrs. Cary was just such a person.

"It was very kind of Miss Cary to say so," Stafford said stiffly. "I am afraid her praise is not justified."

All this time Nehal Singh had been standing at Mrs. Cary's elbow, and she had persistently ignored him. Deeper than her reverence for any form of title was her wounded conviction that he had once laughed at her and made her ridiculous, and to this injury was added the insult that it came from a man whom, as an Englishwoman, she had the privilege of "tolerating." A true parvenu, she had quickly learned to suspect and despise the credentials of other intruders.

He turned away from her and for the first time there was something hesitating and troubled in his manner. Hitherto there had been songs and music for his entertainment; it was now the turn of the Europeans to follow their usual form of pleasure, yet they looked at one another questioningly. It was the custom of the chief guest of the evening to open the dancing, but this could hardly be expected of a native prince who was as yet ignorant of such things and who must still be bound and fettered by caste and religion.

The pause of uncertainty lasted only a moment, but for those at least whose eyes were open, it was a moment symbolical of a great loneliness. In the midst of a gay and crowded world of people, linked together by a common tie of blood, Nehal Singh stood isolated. He did not know it, but it was that loneliness which cast a transitory chill upon his enthusiasm and made him draw himself stiffly upright and face the hundred questioning eyes with a new hauteur. An instant and it was gone—that illuminating flash vanished, like a line drawn across a quicksand, beneath the surface, never to be seen again, perhaps never even to be remembered.

Stafford led Lois out into the center, and one pair after another followed his example. With Travers still at his side, the Rajah drew back from the now crowded floor of dancers, and watched the scene with glistening, eager eyes, happy at last to be in the midst of them—the Great People of the world. It was a brilliant scene, for Travers had spared nothing. The sides of the marquee banked with flowers, the music, the brilliant dresses and uniforms, were all calculated to impress a mind as yet curiously unspoiled by the pomp and magnificence of the East. They impressed Nehal Singh deeply; his mind was filled with a wonder and pleasure which did something toward soothing the first bitter disappointment that the evening had brought him.

But above all else, he wondered at himself and the rapidity of the fate which in two short weeks had swept him out of his solitude into the very vortex of a world unknown to him save through his books. He asked himself what power it was that had flung aside caste, religion, education, like a child's sandcastle before the onrush of a mighty tide. Caste, religion, hatred of the foreigner, these things had been sown deep into him, had been fostered and trained like precious plants, and now they were dead at the first contact with European ideas. They were gone as though they had never been. He had made no resistance. He had drifted with the stream, regardless of the entreating, threatening hands held out to him; yielding to a divine power stronger than himself, stronger far than the implanted principles of his life.

His wonder, though he did not know it, was shared by the Englishman at his side. Travers, accustomed as he was to look upon human theories and principles as buyable and saleable appendages, could not suppress a mild surprise at the rapidity with which this Hindu prince had assimilated the ideas and mental attitude of another hemisphere. Possibly it could be traced back to the parrot-like propensities of all inferior races, but Travers, much as the solution appealed to him, could not accept it. A parrot that assumes with apparent ease the ways of his master within a fortnight, and thereby retains a striking originality of his own, is not an ordinary parrot, and the conviction was dawning on Travers that Nehal Singh was not an ordinary Hindu. The unusual simplicity of his dress, which nevertheless concealed a costly and refined taste, his firm though unpretentious bearing, the energy with which he had overthrown what Travers guessed must have been a fairly violent opposition on the part of his priestly advisers, pointed to a decided, interesting and perhaps, under certain circumstances, dangerous personality. The latter part of this deduction had not as yet struck Travers in its full force, but so much he at least felt that he proceeded to go warily, relying on his diplomacy and still more on a weapon which was not the less effective for being kept, as on this occasion, in the background.

"Rajah Sahib, this is our second meeting," he said, after a few minutes' study of the handsome absorbed face. "I have my answer ready."

Nehal Singh turned at once, as though he had been waiting for Travers to broach the subject.

"You have not forgotten, then?"

"Forgotten? No; it lent itself too easily to my fancy and secret ambition for me to forget. Doubtless, though, my answer will not appeal to you, for it is the answer of a business man with a business hobby of immense proportions and of the earth earthy."

"Nevertheless, tell it to me," Nehal Singh said, looking about him as though seeking a way out of the noise and confusion. "Whatever it is, it will interest me so long as it has one object."

"I venture to think I know that object," was Travers' mental comment as he led the way into the second division of the marquee.

The place had been laid out as a refreshment room, with small, prettily decorated tables, and was for the moment empty, save for a few busy native servants. An electric globe hung from the ceiling, and immediately beneath its brilliant light Travers came to a standstill. He put his hand in his pocket and drew out what seemed to be a jewel-case, which he opened and handed to the Rajah.

"Before I say anything further, I want you to look at that and give me your opinion, Rajah Sahib," he said. "I will then proceed."

Nehal Singh took the small white stone from the case and studied it intently. He held it to the light, and it flashed back at him a hundred brilliant colors. He smiled with the pleasure of a connoisseur.

"It is a diamond," he said, "a beautiful diamond. Though smaller, it must surely equal the one I wear in my turban."

"You confirm my opinion and the opinion of all experts," Travers answered enthusiastically, "and I will confess to you that it is that stone which has prolonged my stay indefinitely at Marut. About a year ago a friend of mine, an engineer, who was engaged on some government work at the river, had occasion to make excavations about a quarter of a mile from the Bazaar. He happened to come across this stone, and being something of an expert, he recognized it—and held his tongue. When he came south again to Madras, he confided hit discovery to me, and, impressed by his story, and the stone, I sent a mining engineer to Marut to make secret investigations. I received his report six months ago."

Nehal Singh replaced the stone slowly in its case.

"What did he say?" he asked.

"He reported that there were sure and certain signs that the whole of the Bazaar is built upon a diamond field of unusual proportions, which, unlike other Indian mining enterprises, was likely to repay, doubly repay, exploitation. I immediately came to Marut, and found that the Bazaar was entirely your property, Rajah Sahib, and that you were not likely to be influenced by any representations. Nevertheless I remained, experimenting and investigating, above all hoping that some chance would lead me in your way. Destiny, as you see, Rajah Sahib, has spoken the approving word."

Nehal Singh sighed as he handed the case back, and the sigh expressed a. rather weary disappointment.

"I have stones enough and wealth enough," he said. "I have no need of more."

"It was not of you I was thinking, Rajah Sahib," Travers returned.

"Of whom, then?"

"Of myself, to some extent, as becomes a business man, but also, and I venture to assert principally, of the general welfare of your country and people."

"I fear I do not understand you."

"And yet, Rajah Sahib, you have read, and have no doubt been able to trace through history the source of prosperity and misfortune among the nations. The curse of India is her overpopulation and the inability of her people to extract from the earth sufficient means for existence. If I may say so, the ordinary native is a dreamer who prefers to starve on a treasure hoard rather than bestir himself to unbury it. Lack of energy, lack of initiative, lack of opportunity, lack also of guides have made your subjects suffering idlers whose very existence is a curse to themselves and an unsolved problem for others. Charity can not help them—that enervating poison has already done enough mischief. You could fling away your whole fortune on your state, and leave it with no improvement. The cure, if cure there be, lies in the awakening of a sense of independence and ambition and self-respect. Only work can do this, only work can transform them from beggars into honorable, self-supporting members of the Empire; and the crying misery of the present time calls upon you, Rajah Sahib, to rouse them to their new task!"

He had spoken with an enthusiasm which grew in measure as he saw its effect upon his hearer. For though he did not immediately respond, Nehal Singh's face had betrayed emotions which a natural dignity was learning to hold back from impulsive expression. He answered at last quietly, but with an irrepressible undercurrent of eagerness.

"You speak convincingly," he said; "and though I fear you overrate the hidden powers of activity in my people, you have made me still more anxious for a direct answer to my question—what would you do in my place?"

"If I had the money and the power, I would sweep the Bazaar, with all its dirt and disease, out of existence," Travers answered energetically. "I would build up a new native quarter outside Marut, and enforce order and cleanliness. Where the present Bazaar stands, I would open out a mine, and with the help of European experts encourage the natives into the subsequent employment which would stand open to them. In a short time a mere military Station would become the center of native industry and commercial prosperity."

A faint skeptical smile played around Nehal Singh's mouth, but his eyes were still profoundly grave.

"If I know my people, I fear they will revolt against such changes," he said. "You have described them as dreamers who prefer starvation to effort—such they are."

"Your influence would be irresistible, Rajah Sahib."

Nehal Singh looked at Travers keenly. For the second time he had been spoken of as a power. Was it perhaps true, as his father had said, and this cool Englishman had said, that the thoughts and actions of more than a million people lay at his command? If so, the twenty-five years of his life had been wasted, and he stood far below the high standard which had been set him. He had wandered aimlessly along a smooth path, cut off from the world, plucking such fruits and flowers as offered themselves within his reach, deaf to the cries of those to whom his highest efforts should have been dedicated. He had dreamed where he should have acted, slept where he should have watched and labored unceasingly, yet it was not too late. He felt how his whole dream-world shivered beneath the convulsions of his awakening energies. The vague, futile, uneasy longings of his immaturity took definite shape. His shackled abilities awaited only the signal to throw off their fetters and in freedom to create good for the whole world.

"You have shown me possibilities of which I never dreamed," he said to Travers. "I must speak to you again, and soon, for if things are as you say, then time enough has been wasted. But not tonight. Tomorrow I will see you—or no, not tomorrow—the day after. I must have time to think."

The waltz had died sentimentally into silence, and he made a gesture indicating that he wished to return to the ball-room. Yet on the threshold he hesitated and drew back.

"The light and confusion trouble me," he said, passing his hand over his eyes, "and my mind is full of new thoughts. If you will permit, I will take my leave. My servants are waiting outside, and if you will carry my thanks to my other hosts, I should prefer to go unnoticed."

"It is as you wish, Rajah Sahib," Travers returned, "It is we who have to thank you for partaking of our poor hospitality."

"You have given me more than hospitality," Nehal Singh interposed. Then he lifted his hand in salute. "In two days I shall expect you."

"In two days."

Travers watched the tall, white-clad figure pass out of the brightly lighted tent into the darkness. From beginning to end, his plans had been crowned with unhoped-for success, and yet he was puzzled.

"I wonder why in two days?" he thought. "Why not tomorrow? I wonder if by any chance—!" He broke off with a smothered laugh. "It is just possible. I'll make sure and send her a line."

Then, as the band began the first bars of a second waltz, he hurried back into the crowded room in time to forestall Stafford at Lois' side.

CHAPTER XI
WITHIN THE GATES

Nehal Singh's servants stood with the horses outside Travers' compound and waited. Their master did not disturb them. Glad as he was to get away from the crowd of strangers and the dazzling lights and colors, it still pleased him to be within hearing of the music which, softened by the distance, exercised a melancholy yet soothing influence upon his disturbed mind. For the dreamy peace had gone for ever—as indeed it must be when the soul of man is roughly shaken into living, pulsating life, and he fevered with a hundred as yet disordered hopes and ambitions. To be a benefactor to his people and to all mankind, to be the first pioneer of his race in the search after civilization and culture—these had been the dreams of his hitherto wasted life, only he had never recognized them, never understood whither the restless impulses were driving him. It had needed the pure soul of a good woman to unlock the best from his own; it had needed the genius of a clear brain to harness the untrained faculties to some definite aim. The soul of a woman had come and had planted upon him the purity of her high ideal; the genius had already shot its first illuminating ray into his darkness. Henceforth the watchword for them all was to be "Forward," and Nehal Singh, standing like a white ghost in the deserted compound, shaken by the force of his own emotions, intoxicated by his own happiness and the shining future which spread itself before his eyes, sent up a prayer such as rarely ascends from earth to Heaven. To whom? Not to Brahma. His mind had burst like a raging tide over the flood-gates of caste and creed and embraced the whole world and the one God who has no name, no creed, no dogma, but whom in that moment he recognized in great thanksgiving as the Universal Father.

Thus far had Nehal Singh traveled in two short weeks—guided by a woman who had no God and a man who had no God save his own ends. But he did not know this. As he began to pace slowly backward and forward, listening to the distant music, he thought of her, and measured himself with her ideal in a humility which did not reject hope. One day he would be able to stand before her and say, "Thus far have I worked and striven for inner worth and for the good of my brothers. I have kept myself pure and honest,

I have cultivated in myself the best I have, and have been inexorable against the evil. Thus much have I attained."

Further than that triumphant moment he did not think, but he thanked God for the ideal which had been set him—the Great People's ideal of a man—and for the afterward which he knew must come.

Thus absorbed in his own reflections, he reached Travers' bungalow, and a ray of light falling across his path, brought him sharply back to the present reality. He looked up and saw that a table had been pulled out on to the verandah, and that four officers sat round it, playing cards by the light of a lamp. At Marut there was always a heavy superfluity of men, and these four, doubtless weary of standing uselessly about, had made good their escape to enjoy themselves in their own way. Nehal Singh hesitated. He felt a strong desire to go up and join them, to learn to know them outside the enervating, leveling atmosphere of social intercourse where each is forced to keep his real individuality hidden behind a wall of phrases. Now, no doubt, they would show themselves openly to him as they were; they would admit him into the circle of their intimate life, and teach him the secret of the greatness which had carried their flag to the four corners of the earth. Yet he hesitated to make his presence known. The study of the four faces, unconscious of his scrutiny, absorbed him.

The two elder men were known to him, although their names were forgotten. Their fair hair, regular, somewhat cold, features led him to suppose that they were brothers. The other two were considerably younger—they seemed to Nehal Singh almost boys, though in all probability they were his own age. One especially interested him. He was a good-looking young fellow, with pleasant if somewhat effeminate features and a healthy skin bronzed with the Indian sun. He sat directly opposite where Nehal Singh stood in the shadow, and when he shifted his cards, as he often did in a restless, uneasy way, he gave the unseen watcher an opportunity to study every line of his set face.

Nehal Singh wondered at his expression. The others were grave with the gravity of indifference, but this boy had his teeth set, and something in his eyes reminded Nehal Singh of a dog he had once seen confronted suddenly with an infuriated rattle-snake. It was the expression of hypnotized fear which held him back from intruding himself upon them, and he was about to retrace his steps quietly when the man who was seated next the balustrade turned and glanced so directly toward him that Nehal Singh thought his presence was discovered. The officer's next words showed, however, that his gaze had passed over Nehal Singh's head to the brightly lighted marquee on the other side of the compound.

"I'm glad to be out of that crush," Captain Webb said, as he lazily gathered up his cards. "Fearfully rotten show I call it—not a pretty girl among the lot, and a heat enough to make the devil envious! I can't think what induced our respected Napoleon to make such a fool of himself."

"Napoleon hasn't made a fool of himself, you can make yourself easy on that score," Saunders retorted. "Napoleon knows on which side of the bread his butter lies, even if you don't. When he dances attendance on any one, you can take it on trust that the butter isn't far off. No, no; I've a great reverence for Nappy's genius."

"It's an infernally undignified proceeding, anyhow," Webb went on. "I'm beginning to see that old Stafford wasn't so far wrong. What do we want with the fellow? All this kowtowing will go to his head and make him as 'uppish' as the rest of 'em. He's conceited enough, already, aping us as though he had been at it all his life."

"That's the mistake we English are always making," grumbled Saunders, as he played out. "We are too familiar. We swallow anything for diplomacy's sake, even if it hasn't got so much as a coating of varnish. We pull these fellows up to our level and pamper them as though they were our equals, and then when they find we won't go the whole hog, they turn nasty and there's the devil to pay. In this case I didn't mind so long as he kept his place, but then that's what they never do. That's our rubber, I think. Shall we stop?"

"I've had enough, anyhow," his vis-a-vis answered. "Add up the dern total, will you, there's a good fellow. I must be getting home. There's that boring parade to-morrow at five again, and I've got a headache that will last me a week, thanks to Nappy's bad champagne. Well, what's the damage?"

The young fellow who had sat with his head bowed over his cards looked up with a sickly smile.

"Yes, what's the damage?" he said. "I can't be bothered—I've lost count. You and I must have done pretty badly, Phipps."

"I dare say we shall survive," his partner rejoined carelessly. "We have lost five rubbers. How does that work out, Webb?"

"I'll trouble you for a hundred each," Webb answered, after a minute's calculation. "Quite a nice, profitable evening for us, eh, Saunders. Thanks, awfully, old fellow." He gathered up the rupees which the boy's partner had pushed toward him. The boy himself sat as though frozen to stone. Only when Saunders gave him a friendly nudge, he started and looked about him as though he had been awakened out of a trance.

"I'm awfully sorry," he stuttered; "you and Webb—would you mind waiting till to-morrow? I'll raise it somehow—I haven't got so much—"

Phipps broke into a laugh.

"You silly young duffer!" he said. "What have you been doing with your pocket money, eh? Been buying too many sweeties?"

The other two men roared, but the boy's features never relaxed.

"I tell you I haven't got so much with me," he mumbled. "I'll bring it to-morrow, I promise."

Webb rose from his chair, stretching himself languidly.

"All right," he agreed. "To-morrow will do. By Jove, what a gorgeous night it is!" He leaned over the balustrade, lifting his aristocratic face to the sky. "Saunders, you don't want to go to bed, you old cormorant. Come on with me, and we'll spend the night hours worthily."

"I'm game!" Saunders rejoined. "That is, if it's anything decent. I'm not going to do any more tar-worshipping, that's certain."

"Don't want you to. I'm going to dress up and have a run around the Bazaar, and if you want a little excitement, you had better do likewise. You see things you don't see in the daytime, I can tell you, and some of the women aren't bad. Come on! We can run round to my diggings and change. Are you coming, Phipps and Geoffries?"

The weedy young man addressed as Phipps rose with alacrity.

"Anything for a change," he said. "Wake up, Innocence!" He brought his hand down with a friendly thump on Geoffries' shoulder, but the boy shook his head.

"No," he said, in the same rough, monotonous voice. "I'm done for to-night. You fellows get on without me."

"As you like. Good night."

"Good night."

The three men went into the bungalow. Gradually their voices died away in the distance, but the boy never moved, never shifted his blank stare from the cards in front of him. It was a curious tableau. In the midst of the darkness it was as though a lime-light had been thrown on to a theatrical representation of despair, while beneath, hidden by the shadow, a lonely spectator, to whom the scene was a horrible revelation, fought out a hard battle between indignation and disbelief.

Throughout the conversation Nehal Singh had stood rigid, his hand clenched on the jeweled hilt of his sword, his eyes riveted on the faces of the four men who were thus unconsciously drawing him into the intimate circle of their life. Much that they said was incomprehensible to him. The references to "Napoleon" and to the unknown individual contemptuously dubbed "the fellow" were not clear, but they left him a gnawing sense of insult and scorn which he could not conquer. The subsequent chink of money changing hands had jarred upon his ears—the final dispute concerning their further pleasure made him sick with disgust. These "gentlemen" sought their amusement in a place where he would have scorned to set his foot.

This fact obliterated for a moment every other consideration. Was it to these that his hero-worship was dedicated? Were these the men from whom he was to learn greatness of thought, heroism of action, purity in life, idealism—these blatant, coarse-worded, coarse-minded cynics to whom duty was a "bore" and pleasure an excuse to plunge into the lowest dregs of existence? In vain his young enthusiasm, his almost passionate desire to honor greatness in others fought his contemptuous conviction of their unworthiness. Gradually, it is true, he grew calmer, and, like a climber who has been flung from a high peak, gathered himself from his fall, ready to climb again. He told himself that as an outsider he did not understand either the words or the actions which he had heard and witnessed, that he judged them by the narrow standard of a life spent cut off from the practical ways of the world. He repeated to himself Beatrice Cary's assurance—"All men do not carry their heart on their sleeve." He told himself that behind the jarring flippancy there still could lurk a hidden depth and greatness. Nevertheless the received impression was stronger than all argument. The climber, apparently unhurt, had sustained a vital injury.

Nehal Singh was about to turn away, desirous only to be alone, when a sound fell on his ears which sent a sudden sharp thrill through his troubled heart. It was a groan, a single, half-smothered groan, breaking through compressed lips by the very force of an overpowering misery. Nehal looked back. The blank stare was gone, the boy lay with his face buried in his arms.

In that moment the dreamer in Nehal died, the man of instant, impulsive action took his place. He hurried up the steps of the verandah and laid his hand on the bowed shoulder.

"You are in trouble," he said. "What is the matter?"

As though he had been struck by a shock of electricity, Geoffries half sprang to his feet, and then, as he saw the dark face so close to his own, he sank back again, speechless and white to the lips. For a moment the two men looked at each other in unbroken silence.

"I am sorry I have startled you," Nehal said at length, "but I could not see you in such distress. I do not know what it is, but if you will confide in me, I may be able to help you."

"Rajah Sahib," stammered the young fellow, in helpless confusion, "if I had known you were there—"

"You would not have revealed your trouble to me?" Nehal finished, with a faint smile. "And that, I think, would have been a pity for us both. If I can help you, perhaps you can help me." He paused and then added slowly: "I have been standing watching you a long time."

"A long time!" A curious fear crept over the boyish face. "You saw us playing, then—and heard what we said?"

"Yes."

"And you wish to help me?"

"If I can."

Geoffries turned his head away, avoiding the direct gaze.

"You are very kind, Rajah Sahib. I'm afraid I'm not to be helped."

The sight of that awkward shame and misery drove all personal grief from Nehal's mind. He drew forward a chair and seated himself opposite his companion, clasping his sinewy, well-shaped hands on the table before him.

"Let us try and put all formalities aside," he said. "If you can treat me as a friend, let nothing prevent you. We are strangers to each other, but then the whole world is stranger to me. Yet I would be glad to help and understand the world, as I would be glad to help and understand you if you will let me."

Geoffries looked shyly at this strange *deus ex machina*, troubled by perplexing considerations. How much had the Rajah heard of the previous conversation, how much had he understood? Above all, what would his comrades say if they found him pouring out his heart to "this fellow," who had been the constant butt for their arrogant contempt? And yet, as often happens, amidst his many friends he was intensely alone. There was no single one to whom he could turn with the burden of his conscience, no one to whom he did not systematically play himself off as something other than he was. And opposite he looked into a face full of grave sympathy, not unshadowed with personal sadness. Yet he hesitated, and Nehal Singh went on thoughtfully:

"There are some things I do not understand," he said. "You were playing some game for money. I have heard of that before, but I do not understand. Are you then, so poor?"

Geoffries laughed miserably.

"I am now," he said.

"Then it *is* money that is the trouble?"

"It always is. At first one plays for the fun of the thing and because—oh, well, one has to, don't you know. Afterward, one plays to get it back."

"But you have not got it back?"

Geoffries shook his head.

"I never do," he said. "I'm a rotter at bridge."

"A hundred rupees!" Nehal went on reflectively. "That was the sum, I think? It is very little—not enough to cause you any trouble."

"Not by itself," Geoffries agreed, with a fresh collapse into his old depression. "But it is the last straw. I'm cut pretty short by the home people, who don't understand, and there are other things—polo ponies, dinner-races, subscriptions—"

"And the Bazaar."

Geoffries caught his breath and glanced across at the stern, unhappy face. He read there in an instant a pitying contempt which at first seemed ridiculous, and then insolent, and then terrible. Boy as he was, there flashed through his easy-going brain some vague unformed recognition of the unshifting national responsibility which weighs upon the shoulders of the greatest and the least. He understood, though not clearly, that he and his three comrades had dragged themselves and their race in the mud at the feet of a foreigner, and with that shock of understanding came the desire to vindicate himself and the uncounted millions who were linked to him.

"You think badly of us, Rajah Sahib," he said fiercely. "Perhaps you have a right to do so from what you have seen; but you have not seen all—no, not nearly all. You've seen us in the soft days when we've nothing to do but drill recruits and while away the time as best we can. Think what the monotony means—day after day the same work, the same faces. Who can blame us if we get slack and ready to do anything for a change? I know some of us are rotters—especially here in Marut. Most of us belong to the British Regiment, and are accustomed to luxury and ease in the old country. I haven't got that excuse—I'm in the Gurkhas—and what I do I do because I *am* a rotter. But there are men who are not. There are men, Rajah Sahib, right up there by the northern provinces, who are made of steel and iron, real men, heroes—"

Nehal Singh leaned forward and caught his companion by the arm.

"Heroes?" he said with passionate earnestness. "Heroes?"

Geoffries nodded. That look of enthusiastic sympathy won his heart and awoke his soldier's slumbering pride.

"I'm no good at explaining," he said, "but I know of things that would stir your blood. For a whole year—my first year—I was up north in a mud fortress where there was only one other European officer. It was Nicholson. You mayn't have heard of him—precious few people have—but up there in that lonely, awful place, with wild hill-tribes about us and a handful of sepoys for our protection, he was a god—yes, a god; for there was not one of us that didn't worship him and honor him. We would have followed him to the mouth of hell. He was young, only six months a captain, and yet there was nothing he didn't seem to know, nothing he couldn't do. Every day he was in the saddle, reconnoitering, visiting the heads of the tribes, making peace, distributing justice. Every day he went out with his life in his hands, and every night he came back, quiet, unpretending, never boasting, never complaining, and yet we knew that somewhere he had risked himself to clear a stone out of our way, to win an enemy over to our side, to confirm a friend in his friendship. Yes, he was a man; and there are others like him. No one hears about them, but they don't care. They go on giving their lives and energy to their work, and never ask for thanks or reward. I—once hoped to be like that; but I came to Marut—and then—" He stumbled and stopped short. "I'm a ranting fool!" he went on angrily. "You won't understand, Rajah Sahib, but I couldn't stand your thinking that they are all like me—"

Nehal Singh rose to his feet.

"Nicholson!" he repeated slowly, as though he had not heard. "I shall remember that name. And there are more like him? That is well." Then he laid his hand on the young officer's shoulder. "I am going to help you," he said. "I am going to save you from whatever trouble you are in, and then you must go back to the frontiers and become a man after the ideal that has been set you. One day you can repay me."

The storm of protest died on Geoffries' lips. Prejudices, the ingrained arrogance of race which scorned to accept friendship at the hands of an inferior, sank to ashes as his eyes met those of this Hindu prince.

"What have I done to deserve your kindness, Rajah Sahib?" he began helplessly, but Nehal Singh cut him smilingly short.

"You have saved me," he said. "To-night my faith hung in the balance. You have given it back to me, and in my turn I will save you and give you back what you have lost. And this shall be a bond between us. You will hear from me to-morrow. Good night."

"Good night, Rajah Sahib—and—thank you." He hesitated, and then went on painfully: "You have shown me that we have behaved like cads. I—am awfully sorry."

He was not referring to the Bazaar, as Nehal supposed.

"The past is over and done with," Nehal Singh answered, "but the future is ours—and the common ideal which we must follow for the common good."

Hugh Geoffries stood a long time after the Rajah had left him, absorbed in wondering speculation. Who was this strange man who a few weeks ago had been but a shadow, and to-day stood in the midst of them, sharing their life and yet curiously alone? He had met other Indian rulers, but they had not been as this man. They had also joined the European life, but they had come as strangers and had remained as strangers. They had learned to assume an outward conformity which this prince had not needed to learn. And yet he stood alone, even among his own people alone. Wherein lay the link, wherein the barrier? Was it caste, religion?

Hugh Geoffries found no answer to these questions. He went home sobered and thoughtful, dimly conscious that he had brushed past the mystery of a great character, whom, in spite of all, he had been forced to reverence.

CHAPTER XII
THE WHITE HAND

It is an old truth that things have their true existence only in ourselves. A picture is perfect, moderate, or indifferent, according to our tastes; an event fortunate or unfortunate according to our character. Thus life, though in reality no more than a pure stream of colorless water, changes its hue the moment it is poured into the waiting pitchers, and becomes turbid, or assumes some lovely color, or retains its first crystal clearness, in measure that the earthenware is of the best or poorest quality.

In Travers' pitcher it had become kaleidoscopic, only saved from dire confusion by one steady, consistent color, which tinged and killed by its brilliancy the hundred other rainbow fragments. Such was life for him — such at least it had become — a gay chaos in which the one important thing was himself; a game, partly instructive, partly amusing, with no rules save that the player is expected to win. Of course, as in all matters, a certain order, or appearance of order, had to be maintained; but Travers believed, and thought every one else believed, that it was a mere "appearance," and that, as in the childish game of "cheating," the card put on the table has not always the face it is affirmed by the player to possess. Doubtless it is sometimes an honest card — Travers himself played honest cards very often — but that is part of the game, part of the cheating, one might be tempted to say.

A suspicious opponent becomes shy of accusing a player who has been able to refute a previous accusation, and those people whose doubts had been aroused by one of Travers' transactions, and had been rash enough to conclude that all Travers' works were "shady," had been badly burned for their presumption. After one indignant vindication of his methods Travers had been allowed to go his way, smiling, unperturbed, with a friendly twinkle in his eye for his detractors which acknowledged a perfect understanding. On the whole he had been successful. A Napoleon of finance, he never burned his bridges. If any of his campaigns failed, as they sometimes did, he had always a safe retreat left open; and if his bridge proved only strong enough to carry himself over, and gave way under his flying followers — well, it was a misfortune which could have been averted if every one had taken as much care of himself as he had done. When well beyond pursuit, he would hold out a helping hand to the survivors, and received therefor as much gratitude as on the other occasions he received abuse. Which filled him with good-natured amusement, the one being as undeserved as the other.

His last enterprise, the Marut Campaign, thanks to a happy constellation of circumstances, promised an unusual degree of success, and his enthusiasm on the subject was not the less real because he kept hidden his usual reserve for unforeseen possibilities. According to the Rajah's invitation, he repaired early on the second day after their momentous conversation to the palace. He was received there by an old servant, who told him that Nehal Singh had gone out riding before sunrise, but was expected to return shortly.

"The Rajah Sahib remembers my coming?" Travers asked.

"Yes, Sahib. The Rajah Sahib commanded that the palace should be at the Sahib's disposal while he waits."

The idea suited Travers excellently. He shook himself free from the obsequious native, who showed very clearly that he would have preferred to have kept on a watchful attendance, and began a languid, indifferent examination of the labyrinth-like passages and deserted halls. But the languidness and indifference were only masks which he chose to assume when too great interest would have thwarted his own schemes. In reality there was not a jewel or ornament which he did not notice and appraise at the correct value. The immensity of the palace's dimensions and its intricate plan made it impossible to obtain a complete survey in so short a time, but at the end of half an hour Travers' original theory was confirmed. Here was a power of wealth lying idle, waiting, as it seemed to his natural egoism, for his hands to put it into action.

In his imagination he saw the jeweled pillars dismantled and the inlaid gold and silver changed into the hard money necessary for his campaign— not without regret. The man of taste suffered not a little at the changed picture, and since there was no immediate call upon his activities, he allowed the man of taste to predominate over the speculator. But the punishment for those who serve God and mammon is inevitable. There comes the moment when the worshiper of mammon hears the voice of God calling him, be it through a beautiful woman, a beautiful poem, a beautiful sculpture, or a simple child, and the soul, God-given, struggles against the bonds that have been laid upon it.

So it was with Travers as he stood there in the Throne Room, gazing thoughtfully out over the gardens to the ornate towers of the temple. He was fully conscious of the dual nature in him, and it gave him a sort of painful pleasure to allow the idealistic side a moment's supremacy, to imagine himself throwing up his plans, and leaving so much loveliness and peace undisturbed. It was a mere game which he played with his own emotions, for it was no longer in his power to throw up anything upon which he had set his mind. Without knowing it, he had become the slave of his own will, a headlong, ruthless will, which saw nothing but the goal, and to whom the lives and happiness of others were no more than obstacles to be thrown indifferently on one side. Yet in this short interval, when that will lay inactively in abeyance, he suffered.

He had lost Lois, among other things, and the loss stung both sides of him. He wanted her because he loved her, and because she had become necessary to his plans. He had wanted her, and in spite of every effort she had seemed to pass out of his reach. Seemed! As he stood there with folded arms, watching the sunlight broaden over the peaceful terraces, it pleased his fancy to imagine that the loss was real and definite, and that he stood willingly on one side, resigning himself to the decree that ordained her happiness. With a stabbing pain came back the memory of their brief interview together. He had talked of praying for her future. Had he been wholly sincere or, as now, only so far as a man is who concentrates his temporary interest upon some sport, only to forget it as soon as it is over? Possibly, nay, certainly. He did not believe in himself—not, at least, in the generous, self-sacrificing side. He called that sort of thing in other people "pose" and in himself a necessary relaxation. For it was one of his maxims that a man may act as heartlessly as he likes, but to be successful he must never let himself grow heartless. From the moment that he ceases to be capable of feeling, he loses touch with the thoughts and sensibilities of others. And his power of feeling "with" others was one of Travers' chief business assets.

It is dangerous, however, to play with emotions that are never to be allowed an active influence. They have a trick of growing by leaps and bounds, and before the will has time to realize that an enemy is at its gates, to fling their whole force against the citadel and overwhelm the dazed defenses. How near Archibald Travers came that morning to yielding to himself he never knew. Lois' happy, thankful face hovered constantly before his eyes. He felt very tender toward her. He felt that he should like to be able to think of her in the keeping of a good man—like Stafford—who, if pig-headed and bigoted, was yet calculated to stick to a woman and make her happy. Looking straight at himself and his past, Travers could not be sure that he would stick to any one. Also there was the Rajah, optimistic, and trusting, so much so that it left an unpleasant taste in the mouth to fool him.

But above all else, there was Lois. Lois recurred to him constantly, overshadowing every other consideration. He thought of her in all her aspects: Lois, the enterprising, the energetic, plucky, daredevil comrade; Lois, the ever-ready, untiring, uncomplaining partner in the hunt, on the tennis-court, in the ball-room; Lois, the woman, with her gentle charm, her tenderness, her frankness, her truth. He bit his lip, turning away from the sunshine with knitted brows and fierce eyes. No, it is no light matter to trifle with the heart, even if it is only one's own. Nor is it wise for a man, set on a cool, calculating task of self-advancement, to call up waters from his hidden wells of tenderness, or to allow a nature strangely susceptible (as even the worst natures are) to the appeal of the good and beautiful to have full play, if only for a brief hour. Another five minutes undisturbed in that splendid hall, with God's divine world before him and the highest, purest art of man about him, and Travers might never have waited to meet Nehal Singh. He might have gone thence, and taken his schemes and plans and ambitions to another sphere of activity. Five minutes! One second is enough to change a dozen destinies. A straw divides an act of heroism from an act of cowardice.

Archibald Travers turned. He had heard no sound and yet he was certain that he was no longer alone, that some one stood behind him and was watching him. For a minute he remained motionless; the bright sunlight had dazzled him and he could only see the shadows in which the back of the chamber was enveloped. Yet the consciousness of another presence continued, and when suddenly a shadow freed itself from the rest and came toward him, he started less with surprise than with a reasonless, nameless alarm. It was a woman's figure which came down toward the golden patch of light in which he stood. He could not see her face for it was completely shrouded in a long oriental veil, but the bowed shoulders, the slow, unsteady step indicated an advanced age or an overpowering physical weakness. She came on without hesitation, passing so close to Travers that she brushed his arm, and reached the hangings before the window. There she paused. Travers passed his hand quickly before his eyes. Her movements had been so quiet, so blindly indifferent to his presence that he could not for the moment free himself from the fancy that he was in the power of an hallucination. Then she lifted her hand, drawing the curtain back, and he uttered an involuntary, half-smothered exclamation. The hand was thin, claw-like, white as though no drop of blood flowed beneath the lifeless skin, and on the fourth finger he saw a plain band of gold.

"Who are you?" Travers demanded. The question had left his lips almost without his knowledge. She turned and looked at him, and in spite of the veil he felt the full intensity of a gaze which seemed to be seeking his very soul. How long they stood there watching each other in breathless silence Travers did not know. Nor did he know why this strange, powerless figure filled him with a sickening repulsion and held him paralyzed so that he could only wait in passive, motionless expectation. Suddenly the hand sank to her side and he shook himself as though he had been awakened from a nightmare.

"Who are you?" he repeated firmly.

"You are not the one I seek," she answered. "Why do you keep me from him? He is mine—my very own. Where is he? I am always seeking for him—but he is like the shadows—he vanishes—with the sunshine. In my dreams I see him—" Her voice, thin and low-pitched, died into silence. She seemed to have shrunk together; she swayed as though she would have fallen, and Travers took an involuntary step toward her.

"You speak English—perfect English," he said. "Who are you? Whom do you seek? Perhaps I can help you—?" His words electrified her. She caught his arm in a grip of iron and drew close to him so that her hot, quickly drawn breath fanned his cheek.

"Help me?" she whispered. "Who can help me? Don't you know that I am dead?"

Travers shuddered; he tried to free himself from the clutch of the white, bloodless hand, but she clung to him desperately, despairingly, while her voice rose in an agonized crescendo.

"Don't you know that I am *dead*?"

Footsteps came hurrying down the corridor. A sudden impulse, a reawakening of the spirit of action and enterprise, which had carried him through his life, bade him grasp her hand and drag from it the loosely fitting ring.

"I will see you again—dead or living, I will help you," he said.

The next instant he drew quickly back. A white-bearded native servant had entered and was moving swiftly with cat-like stealth toward the veiled figure by the window. He was breathless, as though with hard running, and seemed oblivious of Travers' presence until, with an exclamation of relief, he had grasped the unresisting figure by the wrist. Then he turned, salaaming profoundly.

"May the Lord Sahib forgive his servant!" he said with a humility which in Travers' ears rang curiously ironical. "The woman is possessed of a devil who speaketh lies out of her mouth. It would cost thy servant dear if she were found with the Lord Sahib."

Travers assumed an air of indifference.

"Who is she?" he asked carelessly.

"My wife, Lord Sahib. The devil has possessed her these many years."

Travers caught the flash of the cunning, suspicious eyes and knew that the man had lied. But he said nothing, dismissing him and his captive with a gesture. Only for an instant, governed by an irresistible instinct, he glanced over his shoulder. He saw then that the woman's head was turned toward him and that one white hand was raised as though in mingled appeal and imperative command. Travers nodded almost imperceptibly and she disappeared into the shadows of the corridor.

For some minutes Travers remained motionless, then, as though nothing unusual had happened, he resumed his critical survey of the precious stones with which the pillars were adorned, apparently so absorbed that he did not notice the sound of approaching footsteps. Only when he was called by name did he look up with a start of pleased surprise.

"Ah, Your Highness!" he exclaimed.

The young prince stood in the curtained doorway, dressed as though he had just returned from riding. He was dusty and travel-stained and, in spite of his energetic, upright bearing, he looked exhausted. There were heavy lines under the keen eyes, and Travers noticed for the first time that his cheeks were slightly hollow, giving his whole appearance an air of haggard weariness. He lifted his hand in return to Travers' salute, and came forward with a welcoming smile.

"My servants told me I should find you here," he said. "I hope the time of waiting has not been too long?"

"Indeed, no!" Travers returned, as he descended the throne steps. "I have been amusing myself right royally. You have surely the most perfect collection of stones in India."

"They are well enough," Nehal answered, his smile deepening. "Have you been calculating how many rupees they will bring in?"

The remark, which at another time would have called a frank laugh of agreement from Travers, caused him instead a faint feeling of annoyance.

"Perhaps I have," he said, not without a suggestion of bitterness, "but I am still sufficiently alive to beauty to be able to appreciate it apart from its intrinsic value."

Nehal Singh motioned him to take his seat at the low table which a servant had at that moment brought in.

"Forgive me," he said. "I fear my remark hurt you. I thought as a business man you had only one standpoint from which you judged—you told me as much."

"Yes, and I told you the truth," Travers said, after a moment, in which he bent frowningly over his cup of coffee. "I am a business man, Rajah, and for a business man who wants to make any sort of success of his life there must be only one standpoint. If he has another side to his nature, as I have—the purely artistic and emotional side—he must crush it out of sight, if not out of existence, as I do." He looked up with a sudden return of his old tranquil humor. "You must not count it as anything if the beauty of these surroundings for a moment lifted the unpractical side of me uppermost," he said, laughing. "It was purely *pro tem.*, and I am once more my normal, hard-headed self, at your disposal, Rajah."

Nehal Singh nodded absently.

"I believe what you say is true," he said. "A man who goes out into the world and enters into her conflicts must have only one side—the strong, hard, practical side; otherwise he can do nothing, neither for himself nor others. The idea came to me already the other night after I left you."

"Indeed?" Travers murmured. "What made you think of that, Rajah?"

Nehal gave a gesture which seemed to put the question to one side.

"Something I heard—saw," he said. "It does not matter. It made me hesitate. That is all."

"Hesitate?"

"To enter into the conflict. I felt for the moment that I was not fit—that it would overwhelm me. I had made a picture of the world, a picture which after all might not be the true one. I did not believe that I could bear the reality."

He bent his head wearily on his hand, and there followed an instant's silence in which Travers thoughtfully studied his companion. He was wondering what cross-current of influence had flowed into the stream on which he meant to sweep the prince toward his purpose. Any idea of relinquishing his plans had evaporated; the very suggestion of another influence having been sufficient to put him on his mettle and call to life the full energy of his headstrong ambition. He had the tact, however, to remain silent, and to leave Nehal's train of thought uninterrupted. And this required considerable patience and self-control, for the Rajah seemed to forget his existence, and sat staring vacantly in front of him, his head still resting on his hand.

"Yes," he went on suddenly, but without changing his position, "that is what I felt two nights ago. The practical, hard side of me seemed lacking. I felt that I was a dreamer, like the rest of my unfortunate race, and that to enter into battle with the world, as you suggested, could only bring misfortune. I did not realize then that, at whatever cost, it was my duty."

"Duty?"

"Yes. A dreamer has no right to his dreams, be they ever so beautiful, unless he changes them into substance. In my dreams I have loved the world and my fellow-creatures. But what does that avail me if I do nothing for the suffering and sorrow with which the world is filled? I must go out and help. I must put my whole wealth and strength to the task, even if I lose thereby my peace. I must 'sell all that I have.' Is not that the advice your Great Teacher gave to the young man seeking to do his duty?"

Travers started, and then smiled.

"Is there anything you do not know or have not read, Rajah?" he said, with an amused admiration.

"I have read a great deal," was the earnest answer, "but it seems to me as though I had known nothing until yesterday. Yesterday, in an hour, a new world was revealed to me." He leaned forward, extending his hand. "I ask you as a man of honor," he said, "before you show me your plans, before I definitely engage myself in this great work, tell me, do you believe that it will be for my people, what you say? Will it lift them from their misery; will it make them prosperous and happy?"

Travers took the hand in his own. For a moment he studied it intently, curiously, as though it had been the sole topic of their conversation. Then his eyes met those of the Rajah with unflinching calm and decision.

"As far as I can be sure of anything, it will do for your country all that I have said," he answered. And therein he was sincere—as sincere, that is, as a man can be whose retreat is already secured.

With a sigh of relief Nehal Singh drew the table closer.

"Show me your plans," he said.

For three uninterrupted hours the two men sat over the papers which Travers had brought. Now and again he lifted his head and glanced toward the doorway through which the strange apparition had disappeared, half expecting to see once more the white extended hand, half believing that he had been the victim of a delusion, a fantasy born of the mysterious veil with which the whole palace seemed shrouded. Then he glanced at the ring which sparkled on his own finger, and he knew that it was no delusion, but that a corner of the veil lay perhaps within his grasp.

CHAPTER XIII
THE ROAD CLEAR

The English colony heard of the Rajah's project with mingled feelings of amusement and anxiety. As Colonel Carmichael expressed it, it would have been safer to have stirred up a hornet's nest than to attempt any vital reform in the native quarters; and he was firmly convinced that the inhabitants of the Bazaar would cling to their dirt and squalor with the same tenacity with which they clung to their religion. When the first batch of native workers, under the direction of a European overseer, set out on the task of constructing new and sanitary quarters half a mile outside Marut, he announced that it was no more than the calm before the storm, and kept a weather eye open for trouble. But, in spite of these gloomy prognostications, the work proceeded calmly and steadily on its way. The new dwellings were well constructed, broad, clean thoroughfares taking the place of the narrow, dirty passages which had run like an unwholesome labyrinth through the old Bazaar. Water in abundance was laid on from the river. Natives of superior caste, who had proved their capacity for order, were put in charge of the different blocks and made responsible for their condition. Of more value than all this was the energy and willingness with which the people entered into the project. More workers offered themselves than were required, and could only be comforted with the assurance that very soon a new enterprise would be set on foot in which they, too, would find occupation.

A month after the first stone had been laid, Stafford paid a visit of inspection in company with the Rajah and Travers. On his way back he passed the Carys' bungalow, and seeing Beatrice on the verandah, he had ridden up, as he said, to make his salaams. Very little persuasion tempted him into the cool, shady drawing-room. He knew that Lois would be up at the club, and, *faute de mieux*, Beatrice's company was something to be appreciated after a hot and exhausting afternoon. For a rather curious friendship had sprung up between these two. They had nothing in common. His stiffly honest and orthodox character was oil to the water of her outspoken indifference to the usual codes and morals of ordinary society. And yet he liked her, and, strangely enough, he never found that her supercilious criticisms and daring opinions jarred on him. Perhaps it was his honesty which recognized the honesty in her, just as, on the reverse side, the sanctimonious Philistinisms of Maud Berry left him glowing with irritation because his instincts told him that they were not even sincere.

On this particular afternoon he was more than usually glad to have a few minutes' quiet chat with Beatrice. That which he had seen and heard on his four hours' ride had stirred to life a sudden doubt in himself and in his hitherto firmly rooted principles, and, like a great many men, he felt that he could only regain a clear outlook by an exchange of ideas with some second person.

"You know my standpoint pretty well by now," he said, as, seated in a comfortable lounge chair, he watched Beatrice busy over some patterns which she had just received from London. "It isn't your standpoint, of course, and no doubt you would be fully in your right to say, 'I told you so,' when I confess that I am beginning to waver."

"I never say, 'I told you so,'" she returned, smiling. "That is the war-cry of those accustomed to few triumphs."

"Not that by wavering I mean that I am coming round to your opinions," he went on. "On the contrary, nothing on this earth will shake my theory that a mingling of races is an impossibility. They must and will, with few exceptions, remain separate to all eternity, and one or the other must have the upper hand if there is to be any law or order. No, it's not that. It's my self-satisfaction that is beginning to waver."

"You must be more explicit," Beatrice observed.

"I mean, men like myself—in fact, most Englishmen—are pretty well convinced, even when they have the rare tact of keeping it to themselves, that they are the salt of the earth. They may be, as a whole, but there are exceptions all round, which we are inclined to overlook because of the foregone conclusion. It has struck me lately that there are some of us—well, not up to the mark."

"Has this revelation come to you by force of contrast?" she asked. "Haven't you been out with the Rajah?"

He looked at her with the pleasure of a man who has been saved the bother of going into explanatory details.

"Yes, I have," he admitted, "and you are not far wrong when you talk about the force of contrast. You know what I thought of the Rajah. There are any amount of good-looking native princes with nice surface manners— that sort of thing wouldn't impress me. But this man has more than good looks and manners. He is a born leader. You should have seen him this afternoon. There wasn't a thing he overlooked or forgot. Every detail was at his fingers' ends, and he has a fire, an energy, an idealistic belief in himself and in the whole world which fairly sweeps you off your feet. It did me. I believe it did the Colonel, and I know it did the natives. The dust wasn't low enough for them. And it wasn't face worship, either. It came straight from the heart; I could see that they were ready to die for him on the spot, at his mere word."

"What a power!" Beatrice murmured. She had stopped turning over the patterns and was leaning back in her chair, her eyes fixed thoughtfully in front of her.

"Yes, it is a power," he echoed emphatically, "and I wish to goodness we had more men like him on our side. We English take things too lightly— most of us. And in India it is not safe to take things lightly."

He saw that she was about to make some observation, but at that moment Mrs. Cary entered. She had evidently been out in the garden, for she had a bunch of freshly cut flowers in her hand and a girlish muslin hat shaded the fat cheeks flushed with the unusual exertion.

"Ah, there you are, Captain Stafford!" she said, extending her disengaged hand. "Mr. Travers said he was sure you had dropped in, and wouldn't believe it when I told him that I had heard and seen nothing of you. There, come in, Mr. Travers. It's all right."

She smiled at Stafford with a playful significance that seemed to indicate an unspoken comprehension of the situation, but Stafford did not smile back. Like a great many worthy and honest people, he was not gifted with a sense of humor, and the ridiculous, especially if it took a human form, was his abomination. Consequently he disliked Mrs. Cary, though not for the reason which made her unpopular in other quarters.

Travers followed almost immediately on her invitation, like Stafford, bearing the marks of a hard day's work on his unusually pale face.

"I expect Stafford has told you what a time we've been having," he said, in response to Beatrice's greeting. "It's no joke to have aroused an energy like the Rajah's, and I can see myself worked to a shadow. Please forgive my get-up, Miss Cary, but this isn't an official call. I only wanted to fetch Stafford."

"I'm afraid you can't," Mrs. Cary put in. "We have engaged the poor exhausted man to tea, and you are strictly forbidden to worry him with your tiresome business. You can stop, too, if you promise not to bother."

Travers, who had as a rule an equally amiable smile for every one, remained unexpectedly serious.

"I am awfully sorry," he said, hesitating. "Perhaps it would do another time."

"What is it about?" Stafford asked. "Will it take long?"

"As far as I am concerned, only a few minutes."

There was a significance in the tone of Travers' answer which passed unnoticed. Stafford rose lazily to his feet.

"Perhaps you'll give us the run of your garden for just so long, Mrs. Cary?" he said. "I'm not going to let Travers cheat me out of my promised cup of tea. Come on, my dear fellow. I'm ready for the worst."

The two men went down the verandah steps, and Mrs. Cary and her daughter remained alone. Beatrice returned at once to her contemplation of the fashion-plates, her attitude enforcing silence upon the elder woman, who stood by the round polished table nervously arranging the flowers. Evidently she had something to say, but for once had not the courage to say it. At last, with one of those determined gestures with which irresolute people strive to stiffen their wavering wills, she pushed the flowers on one side, and came and sat directly opposite Beatrice.

"Have you got a few minutes to spare?" she asked.

Beatrice looked up, and put the papers aside.

"As many as you like."

Mrs. Cary's eyes sank beneath the direct gaze, and she began to play with the rings that adorned her fat fingers.

"I'm afraid you'll be angry," she said. "If it wasn't for my duty as a mother, I should let you go your own way—as it is, I must just risk it."

"There is no risk," Beatrice returned gravely. "Where duty is concerned, I am all consideration."

"It's about your intimacy with His Highness," Mrs. Cary went on. "I can't help thinking it has gone too far."

"In what way?"

"You ride out with him every morning."

"You said nothing a month ago—when I went out for the first time."

"It was the first time. And I didn't know people would talk."

"Do they talk?"

"Yes. Mrs. Berry told me only this afternoon that she thought it most *infra dig*. She told me as a friend—"

Beatrice laughed.

"Mrs. Berry as a friend is a new departure."

"Never mind. There was something in what she said. She told me it spoiled your chances—with others."

"I dare say she told you that it is very immoral for me to ride out with Captain Stafford?"

Mrs. Cary threw up her head.

"I don't take any notice of that sort of thing. That is only her cattishness, because she wants Stafford for Maud."

"You don't mind about Captain Stafford, then?"

"Goodness, no! Why should I? A man wants to know a girl before—well, before he asks her. I don't see anything in that. But this business with the Rajah is quite different. Of course, I know you are only amusing yourself, but still it lowers your value to be seen so much with a colored man."

"Why should you mind? Surely you can see for yourself that Captain Stafford is to all intents and purposes engaged to Lois?"

"Rubbish! She thinks so, but it's a lukewarm business which could easily be brought to nothing—if you tried. And besides, I don't want you talked about. We have been talked about quite enough."

"Why should people talk?" exclaimed Beatrice, with a sudden change in tone. "What harm do I do? What do they suppose goes on between us?"

Mrs. Cary shrugged her shoulders.

"I'm sure I don't know," she said indifferently.

Beatrice sat back in her chair, for a moment silent. A faint smile moved the corners of her fine mouth.

"I fancy our conversation, if they heard it, would startle the unbearable Marut scandal-mongers," she said. "What do you say to a Bible-class on horseback?"

Mrs. Cary's small round eyes opened wide.

"A Bible-class?" she repeated suspiciously.

Beatrice nodded.

"Yes. I have been teaching him the rudiments of Christianity. It seems you must have neglected my education in that respect, for I have had to burn a good deal of midnight oil to keep pace with the demand upon my knowledge. I tell him it as a story, and he reads it himself afterward. We are halfway through St. John. What are you laughing at?"

The tone of intense irritation pulled Mrs. Cary up short in the midst of a loud fit of laughter.

"I'm sorry, my dear," she apologized, "but you really must admit it's rather funny."

"What is rather funny?"

"Oh, well, you, you know. Fancy you as a missionary! I must tell Mrs. Berry. It will amuse her, and—"

She stopped again, as though she had inadvertently trodden on the tail of a scorpion. She had seen Beatrice angry, but not as now. There was something not unlike desperation in the eyes that were suddenly turned on her.

"You won't tell Mrs. Berry, mother. You will never breathe a word to a single soul of what I have told you. It was very absurd of me to say anything—I don't know what made me. I might have known that you would not understand—but sometimes I forget that 'mother' is not a synonym for everything."

Mrs. Cary smarted under what she felt to be an unjust and uncalled-for attack.

"I don't see what I have done now," she protested indignantly. "What is there to understand that I haven't understood, pray?"

Her daughter got up as though she could no longer bear to remain still, and began to walk restlessly about the room.

"Never mind," she said. "That doesn't matter. What *does* matter is that I will not have the Rajah made a butt for the Station's witticisms. You can say what you like about me—I don't care in the least—but you will leave him alone."

"Dear me, what are you so annoyed about?" Mrs. Cary inquired, with irritating solicitude. "How was I to know you were seriously contemplating the Rajah's conversion? I'm sure it's very nice of you. Child, don't pull all those roses to pieces!"

Beatrice dropped the flowers impatiently.

"It's more likely that he will convert me," she muttered, but the remark fell on unheeding ears.

"I wish you would let me tell Mrs. Berry about it," Mrs. Cary went on. "It might make quite a nice impression, and stop her saying disagreeable things. Of course, if your intimacy with His Highness was due to your desire to bring him to a nice Christian state, it would be quite excusable. I might even ask Mr. Berry for some of those tracts he is always distributing among the natives."

It was Beatrice's turn to laugh. Her laugh had a disagreeable ring.

"For the Rajah? I wonder how he would reconcile them with all I have been telling him about love, and pity, and tolerance? Besides, my dear mother, diplomatist as you are, don't you see that it wouldn't have the least effect? Do you think the most kindly thinking person in this Station would believe for an instant that I would ever convert anyone? Of course I should be seen through at once. They would say—and perfectly correctly, too—that I was just fooling the Rajah for my own purposes."

"What are your purposes?" Mrs. Cary demanded.

Beatrice raised her eyebrows.

"You knew them a month ago."

"Oh, yes; then it was for Mr. Travers' sake. But now—"

"Now things are the same as they were then. I—I can't leave off what I have begun."

She had gone over to the piano and, opening it, sat down and began to play a few disjointed bars. Mrs. Cary, who watched the lovely face with what is sometimes called a mother's pride, and which is sometimes no more than the satisfaction of a merchant with salable goods, saw something which made her sit bolt upright in her comfortable chair. A tear rolled down the smooth cheek turned toward her—a single tear, which splashed on the white hand resting on the keys. That was all, but it was enough. With a jingle of gold bracelets and a rustle of silk, Mrs. Cary struggled to her feet and came and stood by her daughter, her heavy hand clasping her by the shoulder.

"Beaty!" she said stupidly. "Are you—crying?"

Beatrice turned on the music-stool and looked her mother calmly in the face. There was not a trace of emotion in the clear, steady eyes.

"I—crying?" she said. "What should have made you think that? Have you ever seen me cry?"

"No, never. I couldn't understand. You are all right?"

"Perfectly all right, thank you. Hadn't you better see about the tea?"

Mrs. Cary heaved a sigh of relief and satisfaction.

"Of course. How thoughtful you can be, my dear! The gentlemen may be back any moment."

She sailed heavily across the room, on her way passing the glass doors which opened on to the verandah.

"Why!" she exclaimed, stopping short, "if that isn't Captain Stafford mounting his horse! Look, Beaty! And he hasn't even come to say good-by."

Beatrice turned indifferently.

"I expect he has some important business—" she began, and then, as her eyes fell on the man outside swinging himself up into the saddle, she stopped and rose abruptly to her feet. "I have never seen anyone look like that before!" she said, under her breath. "He looks—awful."

Mrs. Cary nodded.

"As though he had seen a ghost," she supplemented unsteadily. "What can have happened?"

The horse's head was jerked around to the compound gates. Amidst a clatter of hoofs and in a cloud of dust Stafford galloped out of sight, not once turning to glance in their direction. The two women stood and stared at each other, even Beatrice for the moment shaken out of her usual self-control by what she had seen. They had no time to make any further observations, for almost immediately Travers came up the steps, his sun-helmet in his hand. Whatever had happened, he at least seemed unmoved. The exceptional pallor of his face had given place to the old healthy glow.

"I have come to drink Stafford's share of the tea as well as my own," he said cheerily. "You see, Mrs. Cary, in spite of your strict injunctions, I have sent the poor fellow flying off on a fresh business matter. He asked me to excuse him, as he was in a great hurry."

"So it seems!" Mrs. Cary observed, rather tartly. "He might at least have stayed to say good-by."

"Oh, well, you know what an impulsive creature he is," Travers apologized. "Besides, I believe he means to drop in later on. Please don't punish me, Mrs. Cary, for his delinquencies."

The suggestion that Stafford might resume his interrupted visit later mollified Mrs. Cary at once.

"No, you shan't suffer," she assured him, with fat motherliness. "I will go and tell the servants about tea at once."

The minute she was out of the room Travers came over to Beatrice's side. A slight change had taken place in his expression. It reminded her involuntarily of that night in the dog-cart when for an instant his passions had forced him to drop the mask.

"You and I have every reason to congratulate each other," he said, in a low voice. "We can now go ahead and win. The road is clear for us both."

"What do you mean—what have you done?"

"Nothing," he answered, as Mrs. Cary reentered. "You will know in a day or two. And then—well, the game will be in our hands, Miss Cary."

Mrs. Cary, who had caught the last remark, looked quickly and suspiciously from one to the other.

"What's that you are talking about?" she demanded. "What game is in your hands, Beaty?"

Travers smiled frankly.

"Miss Cary and I are working out a bridge problem," he explained. "We have just discovered a solution to a difficulty. That's all."

His smile deepened as he glanced across at Beatrice, but there was no response on her grave face. She half turned away from him, and for the first time he thought that the climate was telling on her. She looked white and harassed.

CHAPTER XIV
IN WHICH MANY THINGS ARE BROKEN

"I can't think what is making Captain Stafford so late," Lois said to Mrs. Carmichael, who was, as usual, knitting at some unrecognizable garment destined for a far-off London slum. "I wonder if he has forgotten that to-day is the tournament, and that he promised to fetch me."

"I hardly think he has forgotten the tournament," Travers remarked carelessly. "He was speaking about it to Miss Cary this morning. I expect he will be around soon—and if he fails, will I do instead?"

He looked at her with such a pleasant frankness in his eyes that any awkwardness she might have felt became impossible, and she could only smile back at him, grateful for the unchanged friendship which he had retained for her.

"Of course you will do!" she said gaily. "But I must give him a few minutes' grace. It has only just struck four o'clock."

The Colonel looked around. He had come in five minutes before, hot and tired from a long ride of inspection, and his family, knowing his small peculiarities, had allowed him to get over his first exhaustion undisturbed.

"I shouldn't wait too long, little girl," he said, smiling kindly. "I fancy Stafford is not at all up to the mark. I told him to take a day off if he wanted it."

"Why, when did you see him?" his wife asked.

"This morning, of course, at parade. He struck me then as being rather peculiar."

"Ill?" Lois exclaimed with some alarm. She put her racquet on the table and came and slipped her hand through the Colonel's arm. "You don't think he is ill?" she asked earnestly.

Colonel Carmichael shook his head.

"No," he said, "not exactly ill." He laid his hand gently upon hers, so that she could not draw it back. "Let us go outside and see if he is coming," he went on.

The old man—for sorrow and physical weakness had made him older than his years—led the way on to the verandah, still holding Lois' hand in his own. He could not have explained the indefinable force which drove him out of his wife's presence. His ear shrank from her hard, matter-of-fact voice and undisturbed optimism. She who had never had any mood but the one energetic and untirable one, had no comprehension for the changing shades of his temper—would, indeed, have rather scorned the necessity of understanding them. She did not believe in what she called "vapors," and when they ventured to cross her path she swept them away again—or thought she did—with a none too sparing brush.

Unfortunately, there are some characters who can not overcome depression, be it reasonable or unreasonable, simply because someone else happens to be cheerful. The source of their melancholy lies too deep, and the more hidden it is, the more inexplicable, the harder it is to be overcome. It is as though a chord in their temperament is linked to the future, and vibrates with painful presentiment before that which is to come. Colonel Carmichael was one of these so-called sensitive and moody people—quite unknown to himself. When the cloud hung heavily over his head, he said it was his liver or the heat, and took his cure in the form of solitude, thus escaping his wife's pitiless condemnation. And on this afternoon, yielding to his instinct, he sought to be alone with Lois. Lois never disturbed him or jarred on his worn-out nerves. In spite of her energy and vigor, there was a side of her nature which responded absolutely to his own, and with her he could always be sure of a sympathetic silence, or, what was still more, a gentle sadness which helped him more than any overflow of strident high spirits.

For some little time they stood together arm-in-arm, looking over the garden. The excuse that they were watching for Stafford was no more than an excuse, for from their position the road was completely hidden by the high wall with which the whole compound was surrounded. Through the foliage of the trees the outline of the old bungalow was faintly visible, and thither their earnest contemplation was directed. For both of them it was something more than a ruin, something more than a relic out of the tragic past. It had become, above all for the Colonel, a part of their lives, a piece of inanimate destiny to which they felt themselves tied by all the bonds of possession. It was theirs, and they in turn were possessed by the influence it exercised over their lives. Their dear ones had died within its walls, and some intuition, feeling blindly through the lightless passages of the future, told them that its history was not yet ended.

Colonel Carmichael bent down and looked into Lois' dark face. He had grown to love her as his own child, and the desire to protect and guard her from all misfortune was the one strong link that held him in the world. Life as life had disappointed him, not because he had made a failure out of it, but because success was not what he had supposed it to be. It is very likely that his subsequent indifference to existence, coupled with a far from robust constitution, would have long since cut short his earthly career had it not been for Lois. She held him fast. He flattered himself—as what loving soul does not?—that he was necessary to her, that only his old hand could keep her path clear from thorns and pitfalls. It was the last duty which life had given him to perform, and he clung to it gratefully, never realizing the pathetic truth—the saddest truth of all—that with all our love, all our heartfelt devotion and self-sacrifice, we can no more shield our dear ones from the hand of Fate than we can shield ourselves, and that their salvation, if salvation there be for them, can only come from their own strength.

"What a grave face!" he said, with a lightness he was not feeling. "Why so serious, dear? Has anything gone wrong?"

She shook her head.

"No, nothing whatever; on the contrary, I was thinking how grateful for all my happiness I ought to feel—and do feel. Would you call me an ungrateful, discontented person, Uncle?"

"You? No! What makes you ask?"

"I think I *am* ungrateful, only you don't notice it, because I am not more so than most, and perhaps less than a good many. Everybody has flashes of self-revelation, don't you think, when one sees oneself and the whole world in the true proportions and not as in every-day life. I have just had such a revelation. I was feeling rather annoyed that Captain Stafford should have forgotten the tournament and so make me late; and then you said something about him—you spoke as though he were ill—and the sickening thought flashed through my mind: suppose you—or some one I loved—were taken from me—died? Then things slipped into their right size. The petty woes and grievances which so constantly irritate me became petty. I didn't care in the least about the tennis—I thanked God for you and for your love."

He saw that she was strangely moved. Her voice had a rough, dry sound which he had not heard before, and her brows were knitted in a plucky effort to keep back the tears that some inward pain had driven to her eyes.

"I didn't mean to frighten you, Lois," he said remorsefully. "How was I to know that you were so easily alarmed?"

She pressed his arm with warm affection.

"There is nothing to be regretted," she said. "I ought to be glad that a little thing can stir me—some people need catastrophe. If it had not been for that sudden fear, I might have been bad-tempered and spoiled the day for myself and every one."

"And then you would have had to add it to the long list of days which haunt us in later life," he added almost to himself, "—one of the occasions for happiness which we have wilfully defaced. But there, I think I hear some one coming. It is probably Stafford. Won't you run and meet him?"

She drew her hand quickly from his arm as though in answer to his suggestion, then hesitated and shook her head.

"I think I will wait here with you," she said, looking up at him.

He nodded, and they stood side by side watching the pathway which led around to the highroad beyond the compound. Colonel Carmichael was smiling to himself. His wife's sure conviction that the hour of Lois' union with Stafford was not far off had at last overcome his own inexplicable doubts and objections, and he even considered the possibility with a kind of satisfaction not unmingled with pain. "It is well that she should have a good strong man to protect her," he thought, conscious of age and growing infirmity. Then he looked down at the happy face beside him and his smile lost all trace of bitterness. "She loves him," was the concluding thought that flashed through his mind as Stafford appeared around the corner. He meant to say something in tender jest to her, but the words died on his lips and he felt that the hand upon his arm had tightened. It was the only sign which Lois made that a sudden change had come over her horizon. She said nothing, but in the same moment that the Colonel's eyes rested on her in half tender, half teasing query, she knew instinctively that her happiness had shattered against a rock which, hidden beneath a treacherously calm sea, had struck suddenly at the very foundations of her world.

Stafford was coming toward them slowly, his head bent. It was not his face which, like a bitter frost, froze the overflow of her happy heart to icy fear—for she could not see it. It was his attitude, his movements, above all a terrible return of that presentiment which already once that day had darkened her hopeful, cheery mood. Do what she would, she could not move to meet him. She could only stand there, clinging to her guardian's arm, the smile of welcome stiffening on her pale lips. The Colonel was the first to speak. He held out his disengaged hand with a frank movement of pleasure.

"Glad to see you, Stafford," he said. "I was beginning to think the fever had really got hold of you. What has caused the delay?"

"Delay?" Stafford repeated dully, looking from one to the other.

Travers, who had joined them a moment before, laughed with sincerity.

"My good fellow—surely you have not forgotten?" he said. "You promised to fetch Miss Caruthers for the tournament."

"Ah, the tournament!" Stafford passed his hand quickly across his forehead like a man who has been awakened roughly from a dream. "Of course—the tournament. I am awfully sorry—" He turned to Lois with a curious, awkward gesture. "—I'm afraid I can't come. I—I am not very fit— in fact—" He hesitated and then stopped altogether, looking past her with his brows knitted, his lips compressed as though in an effort to keep back an exclamation of pain.

"You look out of sorts," Travers agreed sympathetically. "Come and take my chair. I'll look after Miss Caruthers—if she will let me."

Lois shook her head. She was watching Stafford's ashy face and there was a pity in her eyes which was deepening every instant to tenderness. All suffering awoke in her an instant response, and this man was dear to her— how dear she only realized now that the lines of pain were on his forehead.

"You are not to bother," she said gently, but with an unmistakable decision. "I can manage quite well by myself. I shall start as soon as I have given Captain Stafford a cup of tea. Sit down—it will do you good."

Stafford made an abrupt gesture of refusal. The movement was almost violent, as though for an instant he had lost hold over himself. Then he pulled himself together, looking her full and steadily in the face.

"It is very good of you," he said, "but indeed I can not wait. I have only come to break a piece of news to you. As—my best friends here, I thought it only right that you should be told first."

Travers rose with a mock alacrity.

"Am I *de trop*, or do I count among the 'best friends'?" he asked.

Stafford nodded, but he did not meet the quizzical eyes which studied his face. He was still looking at Lois.

"Please remain," he said. "I wish you to know—and Miss Cary wishes you to know also."

"Miss Cary?" It was the Colonel's turn to speak. His veined hand rested clenched on the verandah balustrade, and there was a sudden sternness in his attitude and voice which filled the atmosphere with an electric suspense. "What has Miss Cary to do with the matter?"

"Everything. Miss Cary has consented to become my wife."

He was not looking at Lois now, but at the Colonel, and then afterward at Travers. The latter had turned away and was gazing out over the garden, his arms folded over his broad, powerful chest. His silence was pointed, brutally significant. It threatened to force an explanation which each present was ready to give his life to avoid. The Colonel, Mrs. Carmichael, Stafford himself, each thought of Lois in that brief silence, and each after his own character acted in obedience to the instinctive desire to protect and uphold her. No one looked at her. It was as though they were afraid to read a pitiful self-betrayal on her young, mobile features, and with a fierce attempt at composure the Colonel turned to Stafford. He meant to break the icy threatening silence with the first commonplace which occurred to him, and at the bottom of his heart he cursed Travers for his attitude of unconcealed scorn. The next instant, the clumsy words which he had gathered together in his rage and distress were checked by Lois herself. She advanced to Stafford with outstretched hand, her face grave but absolutely composed.

"I congratulate you," she said. "I hope you will be very happy."

That was all, but it sufficed to break the spell which held them bound. The Colonel's commonplace passed unnoticed, and Mrs. Carmichael murmured inaudibly. Only Travers remained silent, immovable.

"Thank you," Stafford said. He had taken Lois' hand without hesitation and the painful uneasiness which had at first marked his manner had given place to a certain grave, decided dignity. "Thank you," he repeated. "I hope we shall be happy. In the meantime, I must ask you to keep our engagement private. My future wife wishes it for the present—only you were to be told. So much I owed to you."

"Yes, you owed us so much," the Colonel said, and there was a faint, irrepressible irony in his tone.

Stafford still held Lois' hand. He seemed to have forgotten that he held it, and when she gently drew it away he started and a wave of dark color mounted to his forehead.

"I must go now," she said. "I shall be late for the tournament, and I am to play with Captain Webb in the doubles. It would not be fair for me to spoil everything. I—I am very glad and grateful that you told us."

Mrs. Carmichael gripped the arms of her chair. She saw more than her husband saw, and there was something in that absolute self-possession which frightened her.

"Please go with Lois, Mr. Travers," she said sharply, recklessly. "I do not want her to go that long way alone. I should worry the whole evening."

"May I, Miss Caruthers?" Travers had turned at last and was looking at her. "You promised me that I might act as substitute. Do you remember?" His tone was low, significant, full of a profound feeling which he knew she would hear and understand.

She took his extended arm and he felt that she clung to him for support.

"Thank you," she said under her breath.

She went with him to the head of the verandah Steps, blindly obeying his strong guidance. Then she saw the Colonel's face and suddenly she laughed lightly, cheerfully, as though nothing in the world had happened, and her eyes flashed with an unconquerable courage.

"You are not to bother," she called back to him. "I shall play up and win. I shall come back with all the prizes."

He nodded. He understood and recognized the fighting spirit, and his admiration kindled and mingled with a biting, cruel grief. He watched her as she walked proudly erect at Travers' side, and his heart ached. He understood what his wife had understood in the first moment and what an hour before would have seemed impossible to them both; he understood that they were helpless, that they could neither protect nor comfort the brave young life which had been confided to their care. Their love, great as it was, lay useless, and his last pride, his last consolation was gone. He threw it to the wrecked lumber on his life's road. He did not hear Stafford's farewell nor his wife's icy response. He stood there with his hand clenched on the balustrade, motionless and wordless, until the evening shadows had crept over the silent garden. In that hour he knew himself to be an old and broken man.

Many miles away a dusty, haggard-faced rider urged his weary horse over the great highroad. Danger lurked in every shadow, but he heeded nothing—was scarcely conscious of what went on about him. He, too, suffered, but no remorse mingled itself with his tight-lipped grief. He had done the right and—according to his code and way of thinking—the only merciful thing.

CHAPTER XV
THE GREAT HEALER

"Yes, it's a fine building," Travers said, looking about him with an expression of satisfaction. "The Rajah hasn't spared the paint in any way. You see, it was all native work, so he killed two birds with one stone—pleased us and gave the aborigines a job. He has gone quite mad on reforms, poor fellow!" He laughed, not in the least contemptuously, but with a faint pity. "And it's all your doing, Miss Beatrice," he went on, turning to her with an elaborate bow. "You should be very proud of your work."

She looked him straight in the face. They were in the new ballroom of the clubhouse which the Rajah of Marut had just opened. In the adjacent tearoom she heard voices raised in gay discussion, but for the moment they were quite alone.

"You give me more credit in the matter than I deserve," she said. "Is that generosity on your part, or—are you shirking your share of the responsibility?"

"I—shirk my share of the responsibility!" he exclaimed with a good-tempered lifting of the eyebrows. "My dear lady, have you ever known me to do such a thing?"

She smiled rather sarcastically.

"No, Mr. Travers, but I own that the idea does not seem to me wholly impossible."

"And even if you were right, why should I in this particular case 'shirk the responsibility,' as you put it? Surely it is not responsibility we have incurred, but gratitude."

She walked by his side over to the open windows which looked out on to the as yet uncultivated and barren gardens.

"The question is this," she said at last: "Does the superficial gratitude of a crowd in any way compensate for the fact that, in order to obtain it, a whole life's happiness has been incidentally sacrificed?"

"I know to whom you are alluding," he said, looking earnestly at her, "although, as a matter of fact, the two things have nothing to do with each other, except in your imagination. You mean Lois. Yes, of course she has had a hard time. Who doesn't? But it's rubbish to talk of a 'life's happiness.' In the first place, there isn't such a thing—nothing lasts so long as a lifetime, I assure you. In the second, Lois has not sustained any real loss—not any which I can not make good to her."

"Do you imagine yourself so all-sufficient?" she asked.

"I have confidence in my own powers," he admitted. "That is the first condition of success. I believe that in a few hours I shall have Lois on the road to recovery."

"I do not in the least understand your methods," Beatrice said, "but they have hitherto been so eminently successful that I suppose I ought not to question them. I hope for the best. I really was rather sorry for Lois—especially as she behaved so well."

"Are you starting a conscience, Miss Beatrice?" Travers asked gaily. "I rather suspect you. It would be such a typically feminine proceeding."

"There you are quite wrong," she answered, with a shade of annoyance in her cool voice. "A conscience is an appendage which I discarded a good many years ago as the luxury of respectability. As you know, and as any woman at the Station would tell you, I am not respectable."

"Whence this anxiety, then?"

"It is purely a practical one. You talk of gratitude—do you really think anyone is grateful to me for—this?" She waved her hand toward the lofty, handsomely decorated room before her. "Why, I doubt if anyone remembers that I had anything to do with it. But every one suspects me of having bewitched Stafford into becoming a deserter—thanks to Mrs. Carmichael's tongue—and every one feels a just and holy indignation. I doubt whether they really care a rap about poor Lois, and indeed I could accuse one or two of a certain satisfaction; but the matter has given them a new whip with which to beat us out of Marut."

"But you will not be beaten out of Marut," Travers said, a smile passing over his fresh face. "You have got a far too firm footing. The woman who has bagged the finest catch in the Station has nothing more to fear."

"You mean Captain Stafford?"

"I do."

"Then, if you have no objection, we will leave that subject alone."

"By all means, if you wish it," he agreed, somewhat taken aback. "But, between friends, you know, one does not need to be so delicate."

Her hands played idly with the handle of her silk parasol.

"It is not a matter of delicacy," she said, "—at least, not altogether. It would be rather silly to begin with that sort of thing at my time of life, wouldn't it? But—you don't know for certain that I shall marry Captain Stafford."

"My dear lady! You have accepted him!" Travers exclaimed.

She looked at him, her clear hazel eyes flashing with momentary fun.

"It is very bad policy to rely upon what a woman says further back than twenty-four hours," she warned him.

For once he remained serious.

"That may be true, but it is sometimes necessary to warn her that first thoughts are best."

"Now, what do you mean?"

He folded his arms over his broad chest.

"Miss Beatrice," he said, appearing to ignore her question, "do you remember some time ago my telling you that we were like two partners at a game of bridge?"

"I remember very well."

"Well, we are still partners, though the game is nearing its end. As a rule I am for straight, aboveboard play, but there are moments when a man is strongly tempted to cheat."

"Haven't we cheated all through?" she inquired, with a one-sided smile.

"By no means. We have finessed, that's all. Just at present I feel impelled to—well, give you a hint under the table."

"Why?"

"Miss Beatrice, more or less I stand in the position of a skilled and rich player who has tempted a less wealthy partner into a doubtful game. If my plans fail, I can look after myself; but I shouldn't like to get you in a mess. If I give you a hint, will you keep counsel?"

"I suppose I must."

"Well, then, it's just this. Your mother has invested the greater part of her money in the Marut Company. I did not want her to—I'll say that for myself—but she has the speculating craze, and nothing would stop her. Of course the mine will be an immense success—but if it isn't, I should like to see you, as my partner, well out of reach of the results."

"Now I understand. Thank you."

"As to the Rajah, I think you had better let him run before things go too far. I'm afraid he has got one or two silly ideas in his head. You had better make your engagement public."

"Thank you." She looked perfectly calm and collected. The red had died out of her cheeks and left them their pale rose, which not even the hottest Indian sun had been able to wither. Still, her tone had something in it which startled even the self-possessed Travers.

"By Jove!" he began, "are you angry—?"

She passed over the question before he had time to finish it.

"I am going into the garden to look for my mother," she said. "The band is just beginning. *Au revoir.*"

Travers watched her curiously and admiringly as she walked across the parquetry flooring to the door. It requires a good deal of self-possession and carriage to walk gracefully under the scrutiny of critical eyes, and this self-possession and carriage were the final clauses to Beatrice's claim to physical perfection. There was a natural dignity in her bearing and an absolute balance in all her movements which Travers had never seen before combined in one woman. At first sight an observer called her pretty, and then, as one by one the perfect details unfolded themselves to a closer criticism, beautiful. He was never disappointed, and even the most carping and envious of Marut's female contingent had failed to find her vulnerable point. So they had turned with more success to her character, and proceeded there with their work of destruction. Her beauty they left unquestioned.

Travers often asked himself—and asked himself especially on this afternoon—why, apart from practical considerations, he had not fallen in love with her instead of Lois. He liked beautiful women, as he liked all beautiful things, and Lois had no real pretensions to beauty. Was it, perhaps, as he had said, that her honesty and genuine heart-goodness had drawn him to her? Of course he had pretended that it was so. He knew that, in company with all true women, she was susceptible to that form of flattery where other compliments merely disgusted, and he had made good use of his knowledge. He had often laughed to himself at the feminine craze for salvaging lost souls, but he had never taken it seriously, not even with Lois. Was there any truth in the assertions that he had made to her, more than he knew? The idea amused him immensely, and also drew his attention back to his previous conversation with Beatrice Cary. He shook his head whimsically in the direction she had taken.

"I don't care what you say," he thought, "you are getting a conscience. Now, I wonder whom you caught it from? Not from me, I'll be bound."

He laughed out loud, and shaking himself up from his half-lounging attitude against the window casement, he proceeded to follow in Beatrice's footsteps. At the door he was met by three men—the Rajah, Stafford, and a new-comer whom he did not recognize and for the moment scarcely noticed. He had a quick and sympathetic intelligence, which was trained to read straight through men's eyes into their minds, and in an instant he had classed and compared, not without a pang of real if very objective regret, the two familiar faces and their expressions. Gloom and sunshine jostled each other.

On the one hand, Nehal Singh had never looked better than he did then. The old film of dreamy contemplation was gone from his eyes, which flashed with energy and purpose; the face was thinner and in places lined; the figure, always upright, had become more muscular. From a merely handsome man he had developed into a striking personality, released from the bonds of an enforced inactivity and an objectless destiny. By just so much Stafford had altered for the worse. His character was too strong and rigid to allow an absolute breakdown. He still carried himself well; to all intents and purposes, as far as his duty was concerned, he was as hard-working and conscientious as he had ever been, but no strength of will had been able to hinder the change in his face and expression. He looked years older. There was grey mixed with the dark brown of his hair; the eyes were hollow and lightless; the cheeks had painfully sunken in. A friend returning after a two months' absence would have said that he had gone through a sharp and very dangerous illness; but Marut, who knew that he had not been ill, wondered exceedingly.

They wondered all the more because, though nothing was known for certain, they suspected a rupture in the relations between Stafford and the Carmichael family, and Beatrice was recognized as the undoubtable cause. Her engagement with Stafford had been kept secret, but the Marut world had its ideas and was puzzled to distraction as to why he seemed to shun her society and had become morose and taciturn. "It is his conscience," said the busybodies, whose inexperience on the subject of conscience excused the mistaken diagnosis. Travers knew better. He felt no sort of regret, but he was rather sorry for Stafford and sometimes Stafford felt his unspoken sympathy and shrank from it.

"We have been looking all over the place for you, Travers," he said, after the first greeting had been exchanged. "Nicholson arrived here last night, and he has already been on a tour of inspection. He wants to know the man who has built the modern settlement."

Travers turned to the new-comer and held out his hand.

"Glad to meet you," he said cordially; "but please don't run off with the idea that I have anything to do with the innovations. I am no more than the artisan. The Rajah is the moving spirit."

Nehal Singh's expression protested.

"If money is the moving power, you may be right," he said; "but if, as I think, the conception is everything, then the credit is wholly yours."

"You have been the energizing spirit," Travers retorted.

"Well, we will divide the honors. And, after all, it does not matter in the least who has done it, so long as it is done."

"Well spoken!" Adam Nicholson said. "If that's your principle, I'm not surprised at the marvels you have brought about."

Nehal Singh turned to the speaker.

"You think the changes are for the good?" he asked eagerly.

"Without a doubt. The new Bazaar is a model for Indian civilization."

"And the mine?"

"Excuse me—is that part of the reform? I understood that it was merely a speculation."

The prince's brows contracted with surprise.

"It is part of the reform. I wish to give my people a settled industry. There is no idea of—personal gain."

"I see. Well, I don't know about that yet. I haven't looked into the matter; I must to-morrow—that is, no, I won't. You know,"—with a movement of good-tempered impatience—"I've been sent here on a rest-cure, and I'm not to bother about anything. Please remind me now and again. I always forget."

Stafford smiled grimly.

"You don't look as though you knew what rest is," he said.

Travers, who stood a little on one side, felt there was some truth in the criticism. During the brief conversation between Nehal Singh and Nicholson he had had ample opportunity to study the two men and to glean the esthetic pleasure which all beauty gave him. Both represented the best type of their respective races, and, curiously enough, this perfection seemed to obliterate the differences. Travers could not help thinking, as he glanced from one to the other, that, had it not been for the dress, it would have been difficult to decide who was the native prince and who the officer. Nehal Singh's high forehead and clean-cut features might have been those of a European, and his complexion, if anything, was fairer than that of the sunburnt man opposite him. It was doubtful, too, which of the two faces was the more striking. Travers felt himself irresistibly drawn to the new-comer. The bold, aquiline nose, the determined mouth under the close-cut moustache, the broad forehead with the white line where the military helmet had protected from the sun, the black hair prematurely sprinkled with grey—these, together with the well-built figure, made him seem worthy of the record of heroism and ability with which his name was associated.

"If you want a rest, your only hope is with the ladies," Travers said, as he turned with Nicholson toward the garden. "They are the only people who haven't got mines and industrial progress on the brain. Are you prepared to be lionized, by the way? We are all so heartily sick of one another that a new arrival is bound to be pursued to death."

"I don't care so long as I get in some decent tennis and polo," Nicholson answered cheerfully. "Not that I've starved in that respect. I got my men up at the Fort into splendid form. We made our net and racquets ourselves, and rolled out some sort of a court. It was immense fun, though the racquets weren't all you might have wished, and the court had a most disconcerting surface." He laughed heartily at his recollections, and Travers laughed with him.

"No wonder the men worshiped you," he said, and then saw that the remark had been a mistake.

"They didn't worship me," was the sharp answer. "That sort of thing is all rubbish. They respected me, and I respected them—that's all."

"It seems to me a good deal," Travers observed.

"It is a good deal, in one sense," Nicholson returned. "It is the only condition under which native and European can work in unity."

Nehal Singh and Stafford were walking a little ahead, and Travers thought he saw the Rajah hesitate as though about to join the conversation. Almost immediately, however, Nicholson changed the subject.

"I've had no time to look up my old friends," he said to Travers. "Perhaps you could tell me something about them. Colonel Carmichael is, of course, still here. I had a few words with him this afternoon. Do you know if that little girl, Lois Caruthers, is with him, or has she gone back to England?"

"No, she is still in Marut."

"That's good. When I was a young lieutenant, she and I were great pals. Of course she is grown-up now, but I always think of her as my wild little comrade who led me into the most hairbreadth adventures." He smiled to himself, and Travers, looking sharply at him, felt that there was a wealth of memories behind the pleasant grey eyes.

"Things change," he said sententiously.

"Do they? Well, perhaps; though the change, I find, lies usually in oneself, and I never change. Is she married?"

"No—not yet."

He saw that Nicholson was on the point of answering, asking another question, and he went on hurriedly:

"She is not here this afternoon. If you are anxious to meet her, how would it be if I ran over to the Colonel's bungalow and persuaded her to come? I dare say I could manage it."

"Excellent, if you wouldn't mind. Or I might go myself. We shall have any amount to say to each other."

There was a scarcely noticeable pause before Travers answered:

"I think it would be better if I went. I know a short cut, and could get there and back with Miss Caruthers in half an hour. Would you mind telling the Colonel what I have done?"

"Certainly. In the meantime, I'll have a talk with the Rajah about this mining business. He seems to have an exceptional individuality, and—"

"Remember the doctor!" Travers warned him.

"Oh, yes, thanks! I forgot again. By the way, when you see Lois—Miss Caruthers—tell her for me, the cathedral still lacks the chief spire, but otherwise is getting on very nicely."

"I'm afraid I don't understand."

"No, but I dare say she will. Good-by."

Travers borrowed a buggy from one of the other guests, and started impetuously on his self-imposed errand. He had lied about the short cut, and about the half-hour. He would have lied up to the hilt if it had been required of him, because his instinct—that instinct which had saved him untold times from blundering—warned him that danger was at hand. It told him that it was now or never, and the realization filled him with a reckless resolve which was ready to ride down all principles and honor. He was still sufficiently master of himself to hide the storm; it showed itself only in so far that, when he stood before Lois, he seemed more moved and agitated than she had ever seen him. She had just returned from a long and lonely ride, and was about to retire to change her white habit, when he came upon her in the entrance hall. Had he not found her himself, she would have refused to see him, for she dreaded his message. She felt that he had come to urge her attendance at the opening ceremony, and old fondness for social pleasures of that kind had given place to dislike. It was the only change that sorrow had wrought upon her character. Otherwise she was the same as she had always been. For one week she had suffered something like despair, and then the brave spirit in her despised itself for its weakness, and set to work on the rebuilding of her life on new foundations. To all appearances, she had succeeded admirably in her task. There was no drooping hopelessness in her attitude toward the world. And if beneath the surface there lay hidden the dangerous flaw of purposelessness, no one knew—at least, so she believed.

To her surprise, Travers made no mention of the subject she dreaded. He took her hand in his, and led her into the shady drawing-room. She made no attempt to protest, nor did she offer him any formal greeting. She was oppressed and hypnotized by the conviction that a crisis was about to break over her head which no power of hers could avert. He did not let her hand go. He still held it between his own as they stood opposite each other, and she felt that he was trembling.

"Lois," he said, "Lois, don't think me mad. There are limits to a man's endurance. I have held out so long that I can hold out no longer. I have come because I must speak to you alone. Will you let me?"

She knew now what was coming, and she made a gentle effort to free herself.

"Mr. Travers, will you think me very conceited if I say that I know what you have come to tell me?" she said, with an earnestness which did not conceal her anxiety. "Will you forgive me if I ask you not to tell me? It would be hard to have to spoil our friendship. It has been a great deal to me."

"Does that mean that you don't care?"

"I did not say that. As proof that I do care I will give you my whole confidence, I will be absolutely honest with you. Will you think me very low-spirited if I tell you that a man still holds a place in my life—a man who cares nothing for me? I ought to forget him—my pride should make it possible, and yet I can not, and somehow I do not think I ever shall."

"Isn't that rather a hard punishment for him, Lois?"

"For him?"

"I, too, will be honest. I know whom you mean and I ask you—does Stafford look a happy man? He looks like a man weighed down by a heavy burden. I believe that burden is the knowledge that he has sinned against you, that in his heedlessness, folly, what you will, he has spoiled your life. Until he feels that you have regained your happiness he will never be able to find his own."

A spasm of pain passed over her face.

"You mean—I stand in his way?"

"I believe so. And I am sure of one thing—for your own sake as well as for his, you must shake off your old affection for him, and how better than through the cultivation of a new and stronger love? My dear little girl, you couldn't pretend that all the happy hours we have spent together count for nothing. You say my friendship has been a great deal to you. What else is friendship but the sanest, most lasting, and noblest part of love? What surer basis was ever the union between a man and woman built upon? I know what you would say—it has come too soon. You have only just pulled yourself up from a hard blow, and you feel that you must have time to right yourself and all the hopes that were bowled over with you. My dear, I understand that—God knows, I understand too well—but have pity on me. Think how I have waited, and how time has drifted on and on for me. Must I wait the best years of my life? Won't you let me add the whole of my love to time's cure for healing the old wound?"

There was no pretense in his pleading, no pretense in the passion with which his voice shook. And because it was genuine, it carried her forward on the wave of powerful feeling toward his will.

"I do care for you," she said, with a strong effort to appear calm. "As a friend you are very dear to me, and you are no doubt right to class friendship so highly. But I can not pretend that I love you. I do not love you. And a woman should love the man she marries."

He let her hands fall.

"And so you are going to let your life remain empty, little woman?"

"Empty?" she echoed.

"Yes, empty. Will it prove the strength of my love for you if I tell you that it has given me the power to look straight into your heart? How many times have I read there the thought: 'Of what use is it all? My life has no object, no end or aim. No one needs me now.' Lois, one man needs you— needs you perhaps as much as he loves you. That man is myself. If you say you have done nothing in the world, look into the soul that I open out to you and to you alone. There is not a generous, honest deed or thought which has not its origin in you. For your sake I have beaten down the devil under my feet—I have tried to live as I meant to live before the time when I, too, found that there was no object in it all, that no one cared whether I was good or bad. This much have you changed in me—it has been your unconscious work. Are you going to leave the task which surely God has left for you to accomplish?"

He had touched the chord in her which could only give one response, and he knew it. There lay the canker which made her energy and cheerfulness a mere task to hide the real disease. Half unconsciously she had loved Stafford and half unconsciously she had built her life upon him. When he had been taken from her, the foundations had been shaken, and she found herself crippled by a horrible sense of emptiness and purposelessness. In England she would have flung herself into some intellectual pursuit, as other women do who have suffered heart shipwreck. But she was in India, and in India intellectual food is scarce. Pleasure is the one serious occupation for the womenkind; and though pleasure may be a good narcotic for some, for Lois it was worse than useless. She needed one being for whom she could bring sacrifices and endless patient devotion, and there was no one. Her two guardians lived for her, and that was not what she hungered after with all the thwarted energy of her soul. She wanted to work for somebody, not to be worked for—and no one needed her, no one except this man. She looked at him. She saw that her long silence was torture to him; she saw that he was suffering genuinely, and her heart went out to him in pity. Pity is a woman's invariable undoing. How many women—sometimes happy, sometimes unhappy, according to the rulings of an inscrutable Fate—have married, partly out of flattered vanity, but chiefly because they are good-hearted, and labor under the mistaken conviction that a man's happiness rests on their decision? And in this particular instance Lois was honestly attached to Travers. She felt that to lose him would be to lose a friend whom she could ill spare. Yet a blind instinct forced her to a last resistance.

"I do not love you," she repeated, almost desperately.

"I do not ask for that now, because I know that it will come. I ask you to be my lifelong friend and helper. Remember your promise, Lois! Has not the time come when we need each other—when no one else is left?" He took her hand again. He felt that she was won.

"If you need me—I care for you enough to try and love you as my husband."

"Thank you, Lois!"

His inborn tact and knowledge of the human character stood him again in good stead. He made no violent demonstration of his triumph and happiness, thus breaking roughly into a region which as yet for him was dangerous ground. As he had done months before, when the road to success had seemed blocked, he lifted her hand reverently and gratefully to his lips.

Thus it was that Captain Adam Nicholson waited patiently but in vain for Travers' return with his old playfellow. As one by one the Rajah's guests took their departure in order to prepare for the evening's festivities, he gave up his last hope.

"I suppose it was too late," he thought ruefully. "Or—she was so young, and it's many years ago—maybe she has forgotten."

It was not till long afterward that he knew how unconsciously his first supposition had brushed past the truth.

CHAPTER XVI
FATE

Travers had correctly described the new Marut club-house as a fine building on which the paint had been laid with a generous hand. The original modest design had been rejected as unworthy, and Nehal Singh had ordered the erection of a miniature copy of his own palace, the ball-room being line for line a reproduction of the Great Hall, save that the decorations, which in the palace were inimitable, had been carried out with dignified simplicity, and that some necessary modernization had been added. Gold and white predominated, where in the original, precious stones glistened; the brackets for the torches were transformed into small artistic lamps which had been ordered from Madras; and from the ceiling a heavy chandelier added brilliancy to the shaded light. The central floor had been left free for dancing, but the slender pillars ranged on either side formed separate little alcoves banked with flowers and plants. It was in one of these refuges from the whirr and confusion of gay dresses and white uniforms that Stafford took up his watch. He had arrived late, thanks to Travers, who had detained him at his bungalow in a long and earnest conversation. The two men had subsequently driven together to the club, and had further been hindered on their way by a curious accident. Just where the road passed an unprotected ravine, a native had sprung out from some bushes and, having waved his arms wildly, disappeared. The horse had immediately taken fright, and for a moment the car and its occupants stood in danger of being flung headlong down the precipice. Stafford's strength and nerve had saved the situation, but the incident had effectually put an end to their conversation, and now for the first time Stafford found himself alone and at liberty to bring some order into his troubled thoughts.

He was not, as Marut supposed, a conscience-stricken man, but a man with a diseased conscience, his sense of duty and responsibility developed to abnormities which left him no clear judgment. He had broken with Lois because he loved her and because there seemed no other way of shielding her from the most terrible blow that could fall upon any human life—judging by the only standard he knew, which was his own. He had asked Beatrice to be his wife because it cut the last link and because he knew—Travers had told him—that the Station had long since coupled their names together in a way that cast a deeper shadow about Beatrice's reputation.

"It's no one's fault, old fellow," Travers had said sympathetically. "You meant no harm, but you were often with her, and that old fiend, Mrs. Cary, has told every one that you 'were as good as—' And then you know what the people are here. When they see that things are at an end between you and Lois they will dig their knives deeper into Miss Cary, without giving her the credit of having won her game. She is fairly at every one's mercy here. I am sorry for Lois, but the other is worse off, according to my lights."

Stafford had said nothing. Goaded by Travers' words and blinded by the catastrophe which had broken upon him, he had acted without thought, without consideration, for the first time in his life obeying the behests of a headlong impulse. He had asked Beatrice to be his wife, and to-night was to put the final seal upon their alliance. Again it was Travers who had spoken the decisive word.

"A secret engagement is a piece of folly," he said, "and Miss Cary is mad to wish it. For your sake as well as hers, everything must be above-board. Or are you shirking?"

Stafford had made a hot retort. It was not in the scope of his character to turn back on a road which he had marked out for himself, and he waited now for Beatrice with the unshaken resolution of a man who believes absolutely in himself and his own code. He waited even with a certain impatience. Shortly before he had seen her standing at the Rajah's side, a fair and beautiful contrast to his eastern splendor, and, somehow, in that moment, he had understood Travers' warning as he had not understood it before. She was to be his wife, she was to bear his name, and it was his duty to protect her if need be from herself. He was about to leave the alcove to go in search of her when she pushed aside the hangings and entered. The suddenness of her appearance and something in her expression startled him. He did not notice how radiantly beautiful she was nor the taste and richness of her dress. He saw only that there was a curious look of pain and fear in her eyes which warmed his friendship and aroused in him afresh the desire to shield her from the malice of the eyes that watched them.

"Have I been a long time coming?" she asked, taking the chair he offered her. "I am so sorry. The Rajah kept me."

Her voice sounded breathless and there was a forced lightness in her tone which did not escape him. He bent a little over her.

"It does not matter," he said. "You look troubled. Is there anything wrong?"

She laughed.

"Nothing."

He hesitated, and then went on slowly:

"There is one matter I want to speak to you about, Beatrice. It is the matter of—our engagement. I think you are wrong to wish it kept secret. I think it can only bring trouble and misunderstanding. Will you not allow me to tell every one?"

The white satin slipper stopped its regular tattoo on the rugged floor. She lifted her face to his and looked him full in the eyes.

"You think it was foolish and unreasonable to wish no one to know? But I had my reasons—very good reasons. I wanted the retreat kept clear for you."

"Retreat—for me?"

"Yes, for you. Captain Stafford, why did you ask me to be your wife?"

He drew himself stiffly erect.

"I told you at the time," he said sternly. "I was quite honest. I told you that the best a man can bring the woman he marries is not in my power to give you. It was—shipwrecked some time ago."

"Not so very long ago," she corrected.

"That does not matter. The point is that I believe it in my power to make you happy—at any rate, it would always be my ambition to see you so; and therein I should no doubt regain a great deal that I have lost—"

"But you do not love me, Captain Stafford?"

"I have just said that I have lost the power of loving."

For a moment she was silent, her jeweled hands resting wearily on the arms of her chair, her eyes sunk to the ground.

"You made me an honorable proposal, Captain Stafford," she said at last. "You are an honorable man and inspire me with the desire to be honorable also. Won't you take back your freedom while there is yet time?"

"No."

"There are others—good women among whom you would find one who would love you as you deserve. I do not love you. All I can bring is a certain respect and friendship—that is all."

"I am grateful for so much," he said. He was thinking of Lois, and his voice sounded hard and compressed.

"If I marry you it will be because I must."

He nodded.

"Yes, I am aware of that."

"Aware of that?" she said, looking up into his haggard face. "How should you be 'aware of that?' Is my private life so public then?"

"You misunderstand me," he said, striving to cover up what he felt to have been a wanton piece of brutality. "I only mean, you must for the same reason that I must—because circumstances have linked us inseparably together, and because—"

He broke off. The tall figure of the Rajah had passed the alcove and he had seen Beatrice sink back in her chair. As the figure moved on she broke into one of her harsh, jarring laughs.

"Good heavens, Captain Stafford," she exclaimed, "your arguments haven't a leg to stand on! What are you marrying me for?"

"I have tried to explain," he said, swinging himself clumsily up to the great lie of his life—"because I need you—and I hope you will come to need me."

"You mean I *do* need you? Well, perhaps I do!" She sprang to her feet and held out her hand to him. "There! I seal the bargain. I warned you but you would not be warned. *Vogue la galere!* Tell the whole world—it is better so."

He took the small firm hand and pressed it. At the same moment he saw the Rajah approaching for a second time.

"I will leave you now," he said in a low, earnest whisper. "I fancy the Rajah wishes to speak with you. It would be a good opportunity to tell him that we are engaged."

She drew back her hand hastily.

"Yes—of course I shall tell him."

Stafford bowed ceremoniously, making way for Nehal Singh. As he did so, he saw Lois enter the hall at Mrs. Carmichael's side. The two women bowed to him, the elder in a way which he had learned to understand. He drew aside out of their path, avoiding the genuine kindness which Lois' eyes expressed for him.

"Pray God you believe the worst of me!" was the thought that flashed through his mind. "Pray God I have taught you to forget!"

Nehal Singh had meanwhile taken Stafford's place at Beatrice's side. As he had entered the alcove she had made an effort to pass out, but her eyes had met his, and the look in them had held her rooted to the ground. The color died and deepened by turns in her cheeks, and the hand that clasped the ivory fan shook as it had never shaken before in the course of a life full of risks and dangers. But then no man had ever looked at her as this man did. She had outstared insolence and snubbed sentimentality. She had never had to face such an honest, pure-hearted worship as this young prince brought and laid silently at her feet. No need for him to tell her that she embodied every virtue and every perfection of which human nature is capable. She knew it, and the knowledge broke the very backbone of her daring and stirred to life in her sickened soul emotions which she could scarcely recognize as her own.

He stood quite close to her, but he did not touch her. In all their acquaintance he had never, except when he had taken her hand in farewell, made any attempt to draw nearer to her than the strictest etiquette allowed. Other men — men whom she hardly knew — had taken the opportunity which a ride or drive offered to kiss her, and had been offended and surprised at her contemptuous rebuff. (What girl in Marut objected to being kissed?) This man had treated her as though she were holy, an object to be respected and protected, not to be handled as a common plaything; and her heart had gone out to him in gratitude and admiration. But tonight his very respect was painful to her. For a moment she would have given the best years of her life to know that he despised her and that all was over between them; and then came the revulsion, the wild longing to hold him to her as though his trust in her were her one salvation.

"Lakshmi!" he said, in a voice broken with feeling. "Lakshmi, you are the most perfect woman God ever sent to earth. Every hour I grow to know you better I feel how pale and empty of all true beauty my life was until you came. How can I thank you for all you have given me?"

"Hush!" she said. "You must not talk to me like that. You must not."

"Why should I not tell you what is true?"

"Because — oh, don't you see?" — she gave a short, unsteady laugh — "we English don't tell people everything that is true. A man does not say that sort of thing to a woman —"

"To one woman!" he said.

"Yes, to one woman, perhaps. But I — I —" She hesitated, the truth struggling feebly to her lips. She felt herself turn sick and faint as she looked into his earnest face. She knew what answer he had ready for her, and though it would have brought the end for which she was praying, she sought with all her strength to keep it back. All the brutality in her character, her indifference to the feelings and opinions of others, failed. She dreaded the change that would come into his eyes; she did not believe that she could bear it. Tomorrow would be time enough. But was it any longer in her power to determine when it would be time enough? There was an expression in Nehal Singh's face which told her that he had already decided, and that the reins had suddenly slipped from her hands into his.

"Rajah—" she began, wildly seeking for some inspiration which would give her back control over herself and him. But the triviality died on her lips as the truth had died. A shrill cry broke above the dying waltz, and the Rajah and Beatrice, startled by its piercing appeal, turned from each other and confronted a catastrophe which overshadowed, and for the moment obliterated, their own threatening fate.

The dancers had already retired to the sitting-out alcoves. Only one figure occupied the floor, and that figure was Stafford's. He was crossing the room and had reached the center when the cry had been uttered. The amazed and startled watchers saw Lois rush toward him and with an incredible strength and rapidity thrust him to one side. A second later—it scarcely seemed a second—the immense golden chandelier crashed with a sound like thunder on to the very spot where he had been standing. A moment's uproar and horrified confusion ensued. The place, plunged in a half-darkness, seemed filled with dust and flying fragments, and people hurrying backward and forward, scarcely knowing what had happened or what had been the extent of the accident. Stafford's voice was the first to bring reassurance to the startled crowd.

"It's all right!" he shouted. "We are both safe, thank God!"

They saw that he was deadly pale, though otherwise calm and collected. In the first moment of alarm he had instinctively caught Lois in his arms, as though to shield her from some fresh danger, but immediately afterward he had let her go, and she stood apart amidst the debris of the wrecked chandelier, trembling slightly, but firmly refusing all assistance.

"I owe my life to you," Stafford said to her, with awkward gratitude.

"You do not need to thank me," she answered at once. "I did what any one else would have done in my place. I saw it coming."

"How did it happen?" The question came from Nehal Singh, who had forced his way to her side. "I can not understand how such an accident was possible."

There was an anxiety in his manner which seemed to increase during Lois' brief hesitation.

"I hardly like to say," she said at last, in a troubled voice. "I could not believe my eyes, and even now it seems like a dream. Or a shadow might have deceived me. I don't know—"

"Please tell me what you saw, or thought you saw!" the Rajah begged earnestly.

"I seemed to see the chandelier being lowered," she said, with an irrepressible shudder, "and then from a dark hole in the ceiling a hand appeared—a black hand with a knife—"

One of the women moaned, and there was afterward a silence in which a wave of formless fear surged over the closed circle. The men exchanged questioning glances, to which no one had an answer.

"That's just the way," Beatrice heard some one behind her say. "We dance on the crust of a volcano or under a threatening avalanche. Sooner or later the one gives way or the other falls. There is no real safety from these devils."

Meanwhile Nehal Singh had approached the wreckage and was examining the crown, to which a piece of gilded rope and chain were still attached. One or two of the men were engaged in stamping out the candles, which still sputtered feebly on the floor. The rest stood about uncomfortably, hypnotized by an indefinable alarm.

"I fear you did not dream, Miss Caruthers," the Rajah said at last. "The rope has been cut—the chain unlinked. Some wicked harm was intended to us all."

"Not to us all," Stafford observed coolly. "I think you will admit, Rajah, that whoever the murderer was, he would have chosen a more advantageous moment if he had intended general damage. My life was the one aimed at, and I am all the more convinced that I am right, because this is the third time within twenty-four hours that I have escaped by a miracle from accidents which were not accidental."

The Rajah started sharply around.

"How?—what do you mean?" he demanded.

"Yesterday my boat on the river was plugged. To-day a native tried to frighten my horse over the ravine. This"—pointing to the chandelier—"is the third attempt."

"Do you know of any one who could have a grudge against you?"

"No."

"Or against—your family?"

There was a slight hesitation in Stafford's manner. He frowned as a man does who has been pressed with an unpleasant question.

"That is more possible," he admitted.

Nehal Singh made no further remark. He stood staring straight ahead into the half-darkness, and every eye in that uneasy assembly fixed itself on his face, as though striving to read from his expression the conclusion to which his mind was groping. For his exclamation after Stafford's first announcement had betrayed that a sudden suspicion had flashed before him, and they waited for him to take them into his confidence. But they waited in vain. He seemed to have forgotten their existence, and the silence grew tense and painful. All at once, Mrs. Berry, who was clinging to her husband's arm, uttered a scream, which acted like a shock of electricity on the overstrained nerves of those who stood about her.

"Look! Look!" she cried. "Miss Caruthers is on fire! Oh, help! Help!"

She turned and rushed like a frightened sheep to the back of the hall, crying incoherent warnings to those who tried to bar her headlong flight. It was a catastrophe upon catastrophe. How it happened no one knew— possibly some half-extinct candle had done the work. In an instant Lois' white silk dress had become a sheet of flame which mounted with furious rapidity to her horror-stricken face. In such disasters it is only the question of a fraction of a second as to who recovers his wits first. Almost on the top of Mrs. Berry's heedless scream Beatrice had sprung toward the doomed girl—with what intention she hardly knew—but before she was in reach of danger Adam Nicholson thrust her to one side and, folding Lois in his arms, flung her to the ground.

"A rug—a shawl—anything!" he shouted.

Mrs. Carmichael tore the long wrap from her shoulders, and a dozen willing hands lent what assistance first occurred to them. But Nicholson fought his enemy alone.

"Stand back!" he commanded. "Stand back!"

They obeyed him instinctively, and stood helpless, watching the short, desperate struggle between life and death. Scarcely a moment elapsed before the flames died down—one last tight drawing together of Mrs. Carmichael's wrap, and they were extinct. Nicholson stumbled to his feet, the frail, unconscious burden in his arms.

"Please make way," he said. "I do not think she is badly hurt, but she must be taken home at once. Stafford, go and see if the carriage is there."

His own face was singed, and one of his hands badly burnt, but he did not seem to notice his own injuries. Colonel Carmichael, who had entered the hall with him at the moment of the accident, helped to clear the road. His features in the half-light were grey with the fear of those last few moments.

"You have saved our little girl!" he said brokenly to Nicholson. "You have saved her life. God bless you for it, Adam!"

"That's all right," was the cheerful answer. "You know, Colonel, Lois and I were always helping each other out of scrapes, and I expect it was my turn." He looked down at the pale face against his shoulder, and there was an unconscious tenderness in his expression which touched the shaken old man's heart.

"She will be glad to hear it was you, Adam," he said. "You were always her favorite."

They had reached the great doors, which the Rajah himself had flung wide open, when Travers sprang up the steps to meet them. He was dishevelled, breathless, and exhausted as though with hard running, and his eyes, as they flashed from one to the other of the little procession, were those of a madman.

"What has happened?" he demanded frantically. "I was outside with Webb. What has happened?—Oh!" He caught sight of Lois in Nicholson's arms, and his cry was high and hysterical, like a frightened woman's.

Stafford seized him by the shoulder and dragged him back into the now empty hall.

"Control yourself!" he said roughly. "Don't behave like a fool. She is all right, but they won't want you interfering, especially if you can't keep your head."

"They won't want me!" Travers exclaimed, staring at him. He then broke into a discordant laugh. "Why, my good Stafford, they'll have to have me, whether they want me or no. Lois is mine—mine, I tell you; and that fellow, Nicholson, had better look to himself—"

"You are beside yourself, Travers. Nicholson saved her life. What do you mean by saying she is yours?"

"She is to be my wife. Who can have more right to her than I have?"

The two men stared at each other through the semi-darkness. One by one the lights at the side of the hall were extinguished by the softly-moving servants. The hushed voices of the departing guests died away in the distance.

"Your wife!" Stafford repeated slowly. "Since when is that, Travers?"

"Since this afternoon. Let me pass!"

Stafford made no effort to detain him. He stood on one side, and Travers hurried down the steps. A minute later he was driving his trap down the avenue at a pace which boded danger for himself and for any who dared to cross his path.

CHAPTER XVII
FALSE LIGHT

The way to the new Bazaar lay to the right of the mine through a forest clearing, and was one of Marut's most beautiful roads. Of late, increased traffic had held the English pleasure-seekers from their once favorite haunt, and in this early evening hour the bullock wagons had not as yet begun their journeyings to and from the residential quarter to the Bazaar, and the road was pleasantly quiet and peaceful. Hitherto Beatrice had kept her thoroughbred at a constant and exhausting canter, but here, against her resolution, she pulled up to a walk and let the cool scented air from the pines blow gently and caressingly against her hot cheeks.

"This is one of the moments which Fate herself can not take from us," she said to her companion. "It is perhaps a very brief moment, but it is unclouded. We are just glad and happy to be alive in such a lovely world, and all the outward circumstances which make our lot hard and bitter are forgotten. Great and little worries are put on one side, and we can feel like children to whom the past and future is nothing and the present everything."

"I know what you mean," Nehal Singh answered, "and the hours spent with you are always those which no one can ever take from me."

She bent over her horse and stroked the glossy coat with her gloved hand. Then she remembered that she would never ride him again, and the thought pained her. It was *his* horse, and this was their last ride together, though he did not know it. She was going to tell the truth—or something like the truth—now. No, not now—later on, when they turned homeward. Then she would tell him, and it would be well over. But there was no hurry. All that was still in the future. The moment was hers—a happy moment full of unalloyed charm such as she had never known in her barren, profitless life. She was not going to throw it away unless he forced her, and hitherto he had made no attempt to lead the conversation out of the usual channels.

It was the first time that they were alone together since the eventful evening at the club, and in the intervening week enough had happened to give them food for intercourse. By mutual consent, the accident of the chandelier was not touched upon. Nehal Singh, though promising to investigate the matter thoroughly, had shown a distress out of proportion to his responsibility, and it was understood that for some reason or another, the subject was painful to him. On the other hand, he had shown a lively and warm-hearted interest in Lois' recovery. She had sustained little more than a severe shock, and he had been constant in his attentions, as though striving to atone for an injury he had unwittingly done her. The accident had also served to deepen his interest in Adam Nicholson.

"That is a man!" he had said to Beatrice, as they had spoken of his presence of mind, and his enthusiasm had rung like a last echo of his old boyishness. "I can not understand why Travers seems to dislike him so."

Beatrice had made no reply. She had her own ideas on the matter, having a quick eye for expressions, and she knew that the news of Lois' engagement had been a shock both to Nicholson and to the Carmichaels. Travers was one of those men whom the world receives with open arms in society, but repudiates at the entrance to the family circle; and of this fact Travers himself was bitterly conscious. And, on the other hand, there was Nicholson, the accepted and cherished friend, to whom the world looked with unreserved respect and deserved admiration. It was not altogether surprising that the two men had little in common, and on Travers' side there was added a certain amount of satisfied spite. His instinct told him that he had won Lois at the critical moment, and that another twenty-four hours would have seen her safe under the reawakening influence of an old, only half-forgotten friendship; and Nicholson, too, felt dimly that a cunning and none too scrupulous hand had shattered a secret hope that he had cherished from his first year in India. Altogether, there was a stiffness between them which the world was quick to recognize without understanding. But Beatrice had made her observations, and, as it has been said, had come to a definite conclusion. Her interest in Lois was now thoroughly aroused, and the vision of a dark, suffering little face against a white pillow recurred to her as she walked her horse beside Nehal Singh's. As they passed out of the wood, her companion lifted his whip and pointed in front of them.

"Look!" he said.

She raised her hand to the rim of her helmet, shading her eyes from the dazzling sun, and gazed in the direction which he indicated.

"Why!" she exclaimed, smiling, "a model world, Rajah!"

"Yes," he answered, "that is what I have tried to make it. I do not think plague or disease will ever find firm foothold here, and one day my people will learn to do for themselves what I do for them. They are as yet no more than children who have to be taught what is good and bad. There is the chief overseer."

A respectable looking Hindu, who stood at the door of his hut, salaamed profoundly. It was as though he had given some secret signal, for in an instant the broad street was alive with dark, scantily clad figures, who bowed themselves to the dust and raised cries of welcome as the Rajah and his companion picked their way among them. It was a picturesque scene, not without its pathos; for their joy was sincere and their respect heartfelt. Beatrice glanced at Nehal Singh. A flush had crept up under his dark skin, and his eyes shone with suppressed enthusiasm.

"Is their homage so precious to you?" she asked.

"It is a sign that I have power over them," he answered, "and that is precious to me. Without power I could not do anything. They believe that I am God-sent, and so they obey blindly. Otherwise, these changes would have been impossible." He paused, smiling to himself; then, with a new amusement in his dark eyes, he looked at Beatrice. "My people are not fond of an over-abundance of clothing," he observed. "Do you consider a change in that respect essential?"

Beatrice stared at him, and then, seeing that he was laughing, she laughed with him.

"Certainly not! If the poor wretches knew what we poor Europeans have to suffer with our artificial over-abundance, their obedience would stop short at such a request. What made you think of such a thing?"

"It was Mr. Berry who spoke to me about it. He said I ought to insist on them having what he called decent attire. It seems he had been using his influence in vain, and was very unhappy about it. He said as much that— that trousers were the first and most necessary step toward salvation." He looked quickly at her to see if she was offended at his outspokenness, but she only laughed.

"Poor Mr. Berry is a Philistine," she said. "He can't help thinking absurdities of that sort."

"Would you mind telling me what you mean by a Philistine?" he asked.

"A Philistine is a person who sees everything in its wrong proportions," she answered. "He mistakes the essential for the unessential, and *vice versa*. He can never recognize the beauty in art or nature, because he can never get any further than the unpleasant details. One might call him a mental earth-worm who has only the smallest possible outlook. Mr. Berry, for instance, has never, I feel sure, felt the charm of India and its people. He is always too overpowered by the fact that the clothing is too scanty for his idea of decency. You must not take him as an example of European taste, although you will find only too many like him."

"I am glad to have your reassurance," Nehal Singh replied. "Mr. Berry angered me, and I can well understand that he has no influence among my people. They are very innocent in their way, and they can not understand where the wickedness lies. Nor do I wish them to understand. It does not seem to me necessary." His mouth settled in a new and rather stern line. "I shall order Mr. Berry to leave them in peace."

She smiled at this little outburst of autocracy.

"You do not wish your people to become Christians?" she asked.

"I shall not interfere in their religion," was the quick answer—"or, at any rate, I shall force nothing. If my people believe truly and earnestly in their gods, I shall not destroy their belief, for then they will believe in nothing. And the belief is everything. As for me"—his voice sank and grew suddenly gentler—"I am different. I have been led by a light which I must follow."

After a moment's thoughtful silence he changed the subject and began pointing out to her the improvements he had brought about in the native dwellings. Even Beatrice, who had seen little of the old conditions, felt that the change was almost incredible. A conservative, indolent and superstitious people had within a few months been transferred from loathsome dirt and squalor into a "model village" such as an English workman might have envied. Nehal Singh showed her the houses at the end of the Bazaar which belonged to the chief men, or those responsible to him for the cleanliness and order of the community. Small, prettily planted gardens separated one low dwelling from the other, and each bore its stamp of individuality, as though the owner had tried by some new and quaint device to outdo his neighbor.

"Of course," Nehal Singh explained to her, as they turned homeward, "there are men with whom nothing can be done. They have spent their lives as beggars, and can not work now even if they would. For such I have made provision, although they, too, have been given small tasks to keep them from appearing beggars. But they are the last of their kind. There shall in future be no idlers in Marut. From thenceforward every man shall work honestly and faithfully for his daily bread, and I will see that he has no need to starve. The mine will employ the strongest, and then, later, Travers and I intend to revive the various industries suited to the people's taste and talent."

"You have already done a great deal," she said, moved to real admiration. "I tremble to think what it has cost you." As she spoke, the hidden irony in her casually spoken words came home to her, and she felt the old fear clutch at her heart.

"I have given the best I have—myself," he answered gravely. "Of material wealth I have only retained what is beautiful; for beauty must not be sold to be given as bread among the poor. That would be a crime—as though one would sell Heaven for earth. Travers wished me to sell the old jeweled statues and relics, but I would not. They belong to my people, and one day, when they have learned to see and understand, they will thank me that I have kept the splendors intact for them."

"You are wise," she said thoughtfully—"wiser than Travers and many others."

"In my first enthusiasm, I meant to sell everything, and live as the poorest of them all," he went on; "but I soon saw that that was wrong. The man into whose hands wealth is given has a great task set him. He has a power denied to others. He can collect and preserve all that is beautiful in art and nature—not for himself, but for those who otherwise would never see anything but what is poor and squalid and commonplace. True, he must also strive to alleviate the sufferings of their bodies, so that their minds may be free to enjoy; but he must not sacrifice the higher for the lower task— that would surely be the work of what you call a Philistine. And his higher task is to feed their souls with all that is lovely and stainless. Has not the Master said, 'A man shall not live by bread alone'? Is it not true? And again, I have read: 'What profiteth it a man if he gain the whole world and lose his own soul?' And is not the man who sits, fed and clothed, in a low, flat, level world of mud-huts in danger, of forgetting that there were ever such wonders as the minarets of a high, Heaven-aspiring temple? Will he not grow to think that there is nothing more beautiful than a mud-hut, nothing more to be desired than his daily bread? I have thought of all this, and I have preserved my palace and everything that it contains. I have preserved it for my people. It shall be for them a goal and encouragement, a voice speaking to them day by day from the high towers: 'See what the hands of thy fathers have created! Thou people in the low dwellings, arise and do greater things still, for the great and beautiful is nearest God'!"

He stopped abruptly, shaken by his own passionate enthusiasm. His fine head raised, his eyes flashing, his hand extended, he could have stood for the statue of some inspired prophet.

"You are a modern Buddha," she said, smiling faintly. Inwardly she was comparing him to Mr. Berry—Mr. Berry, whose highest ideal in life was to bring everything down to a nice, shabby, orthodox level.

Nehal Singh's hand dropped to his side and he looked at her earnestly.

"That is what they say," he answered. "My people say that I am the tenth Avatar. But I am not. I am only a man—scarcely so much. A few months ago

I was no more than a beggar in the Bazaar, an idler and a dreamer. If I have thrown aside my false dreams and come out as an untried worker into the light of truth, it is because I have been led by God—through you."

Every trace of color fled from her face, and the clear eyes which met his from beneath the broad helmet distended as though at some sudden shock. In the course of their earnest but impersonal conversation she had almost forgotten what was to come. This was the end of the ride, this was the to-morrow, the inevitable to-morrow of those who procrastinate with the inevitable.

"I—I have done nothing," she said, striving to hush down the rising tide of suffocating emotion.

"Yes, it is nothing. I know it is nothing, but it may still become something," he answered. "Or is it not already something? Is it not something that you have led me to the feet of the Great Teacher? Is it not something that I am awake and standing on the threshold of a new Earth and Heaven, as yet blinded by the light, but with every day gaining courage and strength to go forward? Do not say that this is nothing—you to whom I owe all that I am and ever shall be!"

She threw back her fair head. Now was the time to call to her aid all her cynicism, all the shallow, heartless skepticism which had hitherto ruled her character. Now was the time to laugh and to throw into this man's face what she had been glad and satisfied to throw into the faces of a dozen other men—the biting acid of her mockery. But she could not laugh—she could not laugh at this man. Her tongue cleaved to the roof of her mouth, her throat seemed thick with a suffocating dust, so that she could make no sound.

"God forgive me if I have boasted of my own progress," he went on earnestly. "I know too well how much of the long road I have still to travel. It could not be otherwise. I can not reach in a few months what men have attained who have always lived in the light of truth. But I have hope. I carry in my heart your image and the ideal you have set me—the ideal of your race."

Then speech was given her.

"Cast that ideal out!" she said wildly and recklessly. "It is too low for you. You have passed it. You never needed it. Choose your own ideal, and forget me—forget us all. We can teach you nothing." She caught her breath as though she would have called back her own words. They were not the words she had meant to speak. They did not sound like her own. They had been put in her mouth by a force within her whose existence had been revealed to her, as a hidden volcanic mountain is revealed, by a sudden fierce upheaval, which threw off all the old rubbish loading the surface of her nature. It was only a momentary upheaval. The next minute she was trying to save herself behind the old flippant subterfuges. "I am talking nonsense!" she exclaimed, with a short angry laugh.

"Then it is not true what you said?" He had urged his horse close to hers, and she could almost feel the intensity with which his eyes were fixed upon her face. That gaze stifled her laughter, drove her deeper into the danger she was striving to escape.

"Yes, it is true!" she answered between her teeth.

His strong hand rested upon hers and held it with a gentleness which paralyzed her strength.

"If it is true, then the time has come!" he said. "The hour has struck which God ordained for us both. Beatrice, I may tell you now what you have surely known since the day we stood together before the altar—I love you. You are the first and last woman in my world." His voice pierced through to her senses through waves of roaring, confusing sound. Her heart beat till it became unbearable torture. "Do you remember that second evening?" he went on. "The priest tried to stop you at the gate of the sanctuary, but I spoke to him, and he let you pass. You asked me what I had said, but I would not tell you—not then. Now I may: 'This is the woman whom God has given me—'"

She flung his hand violently from her.

"You must not say that!" she cried, with desperate resolution. "You must not say that sort of thing—to me."

"Why should I not? I love you."

"You must not love me. I—I am to be Captain Stafford's wife."

"Beatrice!" His cry of incredulous pain drove her to frantic measures.

"It is true. I swear it."

Then it was all over. He made no protest. He rode by her side as though he had been turned to stone, rigidly upright, his hand hanging lifeless at his side, his face expressionless. She felt that she had struck right at his life's vitality—that she had killed him. Yet it was not remorse that blinded her till the white road became a shimmering blur—it was a frightful personal pain which was hers and hers alone. Neither spoke. They passed a crowd of natives returning to the Bazaar. They salaamed, but Nehal Singh made no response, as was his wont. He did not seem to see them. Mechanically he guided his horse through the bowing crowd. The silence became unbearable.

She had flippantly told herself that as long as he did not make a "scene" she would be satisfied. He had not made a "scene." From the moment that she had made her final declaration he had not spoken, and now she was praying that he would say something to her—anything, she did not care what, only not that terrible accusatory silence. At last, in desperation, she began to make it up with him as she had planned—in an incoherent, helpless way.

"I have hurt you," she stammered. "Forgive me—I did not mean to. It has all been a cruel mistake. I looked upon you as a friend. How could I tell that you meant more than that? If I have deceived you, I can only ask you with all my heart to forgive me."

He turned his head and looked at her. His eyes were dull and clouded, as though a film had been drawn across them.

"Not you have deceived me," he answered quietly. "I have deceived myself. I thought I was following a great God-sent light. It was nothing more than a firefly glittering through my darkness. You are not to blame."

He was already casting contempt at the influence which she had exercised over him; he was cutting himself free from her—as she had desired, as was inevitable. Yet, with a foolish, senseless anger, she sought to draw him back to her and hold him, if only by the reverence for what had been.

"Do not despise our friendship!" she pleaded. "If it has not been what you thought it was, has it any the less opened the gates of Heaven and earth, as you said? What I have given you is good—the very best I had to give. The ideal was a high one. I helped you toward it with my friendship. Is it bad because it was only friendship—because it couldn't be more than that? You do not know," she went on, with a forced attempt to appear cheerful and matter-of-fact, "you do not know how much your trust and confidence has been to me. I have been so proud to help you. If I had ever thought it would come to this—I would have stopped long ago."

So she lied, clinging to his respect as though it had been her salvation. And he believed her. His face relaxed, and for the first time she saw clearly what he was enduring.

"I do not despise our—friendship, even though it must end here," he said. "What you have given me I shall always keep—always. I shall not turn back because I must go on alone. Your image shall still guide me in my life. It is not less pure and noble because I can not ever call it my own." She heard his voice break, but he went on quietly and gently: "I pray you may be happy with the man you love."

She had conquered. She had kept her place in his life at the same time that she was thrusting him out of her own. He would continue undeterred along the road on to which she had tempted him—perhaps to his destruction—believing in her, trusting in her as no other being had ever done or would do. This much she had snatched from the wreckage.

They did not speak again until they reached her bungalow. Then he dismounted and, quietly motioning the syce to one side, helped her to the ground.

"It is for the last time," he said. "Good-by, Lakshmi!"

"Good-by!"

She could not lift her eyes to his face, but from the top of the steps she was tempted to look back. He stood where she had left him, his hand resting on her saddle, his head bent, and there was something in his attitude which sent her hurrying into the house without a second glance.

She found her mother waiting for her in her room, whither she fled to be alone and undisturbed to fight and stamp out the pain that was aching in her heart. Mrs. Cary, wonderfully curled and powdered, received her daughter with unusual rapture.

"My dear!" she exclaimed, kissing Beatrice on both cheeks, "I am so glad you have come back early! Captain Stafford is here, and has something for you—I shouldn't be surprised if it was a ring, you lucky child! Did I not tell you he was the very husband for you? He has been telling me all about Lois and Travers. Everybody is quite pleased about it. Now hurry up and make yourself pretty. Why, what's the matter? You look so—so queer!"

Beatrice pushed past her mother and, going to the table, flung herself down as though exhausted.

"It's nothing," she muttered. "Tell—John I can't see him. I'm tired—ill—anything you like."

"Beaty, I won't do anything of the sort. What has happened? Is it that horrid Rajah? Did you tell him?"

"Yes."

"And he made a scene, my poor Beaty?"

"No."

"Can't you answer me properly? Tell me what happened."

"He asked me to marry him."

Mrs. Cary first gasped, and then burst into a loud, cackling laugh.

"He asked you to marry him! That colored man! I hope you laughed in his face?"

Beatrice turned, one clenched hand resting on the table.

"No," she said, "I did not laugh—there was nothing to laugh at. I have kept my promise to you." Then, unexpectedly she buried her face in her arms and burst into tears.

Mrs. Cary stood there thunderstruck, her mouth open, her eyes wide with alarm. For one moment she was incapable of reasoning out this catastrophe. She had never seen Beatrice cry—her tears, because of their rarity, were as terrible as a man's, and could not be explained away by nerves or fatigue. This was something else. Mrs. Cary crossed the room. She laid a fat, trembling hand on her daughter's shoulder.

"Beaty, what's the matter?" she asked uneasily. "What is it? Are you ill?—or—or—Beaty!"—a light dawning across her dull face—"good heavens! you don't love that man?" There was no answer. After a long moment, Mrs. Cary's hand fell to her side. "You couldn't!" she muttered. "It wouldn't do. Think of what people would say! Our position!" Still no answer. She turned and stumbled toward the door. "I will tell the captain—you are ill," she said.

Beatrice did not move.

BOOK II

CHAPTER I
BUILDING THE CATHEDRAL

The pretty little drawing-room was already in half darkness. Travers went to the window and, leaning his shoulder lazily against the casement, began to sort out and open the letters that had been lying on the tea-table waiting for him.

"One from the Colonel, Lois," he said, after a moment's perusal. "No news in particular. He is down with a touch of fever, and the whole regiment is camping out without him. Stafford's marriage still hanging fire. Silly girl! What's she waiting for, in the name of conscience?"

Lois looked up from her duties at the table.

"They have been engaged over a year," she said.

"As long as we have been engaged and married," he answered with an affectionate smile. "How long is that, little woman? About eighteen months, eh? They don't either of them seem in much of a hurry."

He went on reading, only stretching out his hand mechanically as she brought him his second cup of tea. Lois remained at his side, her eyes fixed thoughtfully, almost hungrily, on the torn envelope which lay on the floor at his feet.

"Why did you call Beatrice Cary a silly girl?" she asked at last. "It never struck me that she was silly."

"She wasn't, but she will be if she doesn't hold Stafford fast."

A shadow passed over the face still turned to the floor.

"Is Stafford—so—so desirable?"

"His money is, dear child, and the Carys may need money in the near future."

"I thought they were rich?"

"Their money is in the mine."

"But the mine is to be successful?"

He smiled in good-natured amusement at her persistency.

"Have you ever heard of a mine that wasn't to be successful? If you wait a moment, I will tell you the latest news. Here's a note from the Rajah."

He tore open the large square envelope, and went on reading with the same idle interest. "There's been an accident with the blasting," he observed casually. "Five men killed. Our native friend is, of course, in a fever. Has pensioned all the families. I don't know where he will land us with his extravagances. We shall want all the money we can get for repairing the damage. Philanthropy is becoming a sort of disease with him. Fortunately, I am not bitten so far." He laughed, and threw the letter to one side. "I expect I shall have to run up north to put things straight."

"Hasn't the mine brought in enough?" Lois answered innocently.

"Enough?" He looked at her with a twinkle in his bright eyes. "Dear girl, it hasn't paid so much as a quarter of its expenses."

"But will it ever?"

"Heaven knows—or perhaps even Heaven does not. I'm sure I don't."

"You talk so calmly about it!" she exclaimed, aghast. "Surely you are heavily involved—and not only you, but the Rajah and the people in Marut?"

He patted her on the cheek.

"Don't worry on that score," he assured her. "Besides, it's not my way to sit down and cry over what can't be helped. I dare say I shall pull through somehow."

"Yes, *you*, perhaps."

He changed color slightly under the challenge in her eyes, but his expression remained unruffled.

"You are not exactly a very trusting wife, are you, Lois? It comes of letting a woman have a look into business. Never mind, we won't argue the subject all over again. I know what you think of me. There, good-by. I must be off again. Nicholson will be around shortly. I told him he would find me at home."

"Had you not better wait for him, then?"

"Oh, no. I only told him I should be at home as a sort of *façon de parler*. He only comes when he thinks I am there—admirable person—and I know you like to have old friends about. Good-by, dear."

"Good-by." She accepted his kiss listlessly, and when he had gone went back to the window.

The window had become Lois Travers' vantage-point of life. From thence she could overlook the bustling Madras square into which four streets poured their unending stream, and build her fancies about each one of the atoms as they passed unconsciously beneath her gaze. Some of the faces were well known to her. They always passed at the time when she took her sewing and sat by the window, pretending to work by the fading glow of evening light, and about each she wove a simple little story, always, or nearly always, happy. She imagined the men returning from business to their homes. If there was ever a cloud upon their brow, she smiled to think how the trouble would be brushed away by loving hands; if their step were more than usually light and elastic, her own heart grew lighter with the thought that they were hurrying back to the source of their happiness.

Lois lived on the real or imagined joys of others. She clung to her air castles in which her unknown heroes lived, building them more beautifully, fitting them out with more perfect content, as her own brick dwelling grew darker and more desolate. She felt that if ever she let go her hold on them she would lose faith in human happiness, and thus in life itself. For between Lois Travers the woman and Lois Travers the light-hearted, high-spirited girl there stretched a year's gulf. Marriage had been to her what it is more or less to all women—a Rubicon, a Book of Revelations in which girlish ideals are rarely realized, sometimes modified, more often destroyed.

Clever and pliable women, women with the "art of living" do not allow their hearts to be broken in the latter event, supposing them to have relaxed their cleverness so far as to have had ideals at all; but Lois was not clever or pliable, and her ideals had been destroyed. She had loved John Stafford, and in some inexplicable way he had failed her. She had given her life into Travers' hands in the belief that he needed her for his progress, and that in helping him her idle powers of love and devotion would not be wasted. Too late she realized—what no woman ever realizes until it *is* too late—that the man who needs a woman for his salvation is already far beyond her help.

Beneath Lois' light-heartedness and love of gaiety there lurked a spirit of Puritanism which had drawn her to Stafford, and now brought her into violent conflict with Travers' fundamental frivolity. In the first month of their marriage she had had to admit that she had reached the bottom of his character, and found nothing there—not so much as a deeply planted vice.

He had pretended a depth of feeling which was only in part sincere, and he was too lazy to keep up a pretense when his chief object was gained. He really cared for Lois, but he had wilfully exaggerated the role she played in his life. Always good-natured and kindly, he never allowed her to ruffle or anger him. She had never seen him rough or cruel to any human being, and all these superficial virtues forced her farther from him.

A few significant incidents had revealed to her that his good nature covered a cold-blooded indifference where his own interests were vitally concerned. His apparent pliability hid a dexterity which evaded every recognized principle. In vain she exerted the influence with which he had pretended to invest her. The first effort proved that it had never really existed. It was no more in his life than the valuable ornament on his mantel-shelf—a thing to be dusted, preserved, and admired in leisure hours, never set to serious use. This last discovery, made shortly after their arrival in Madras, had broken her. From that moment she had felt herself crippled. Her life became a blank, colorless waste, all the more terrible because of the mirages with which it was lighted. The world saw the mirages: the good-looking, genial-tempered husband; the well-furnished house; all the outward symptoms of an irrefutably satisfactory and successful life.

Only one person perhaps saw deeper, and that was Nicholson. He had been ordered for a year to Madras, and thus it came about that they often met. Travers' first dislike for the officer had evaporated, and he seemed rather to insist on an increase of their intimacy, inviting Nicholson constantly to the house. And in those long evening visits Nicholson had seen what others did not see and what Lois kept hidden in her own heart. For she had told no one that the mirages were no more than mirages—that her life still lacked all the vital elements of reality and sincerity. She was proud, and not even the people in dear old Marut suspected that she was stifling in the hot Madras air and in the unhealthy atmosphere of small lies and loose principles in which Travers was so thoroughly at home. Only Nicholson's sensitive temperament felt what others neither heard nor saw.

So a year had passed, and every evening Lois sat by the window, watching the busy crowd, and building up their lives as she had once dreamed of building up her own. She scarcely thought of herself. Memories are dangerous. The present was too real to be considered, and the future too blank and hopeless.

The darkness increased. Twilight yielded to nightfall, and the yellow lights sprang up in the shops opposite her window. She heard the door open, but did not turn, thinking it was her husband unexpectedly returned.

"Shall I light the lamp?" she asked.

It was not Travers who answered. A familiar voice struck on her ears, like the memories, ringing out a dangerous response from her tired soul.

"Forgive me, Mrs. Travers. I met your husband this afternoon, and he told me to drop in unannounced, as he would be alone. It seems the other way about. I am very sorry to seem so rude."

Lois rose quickly to her feet. She saw Nicholson standing in the doorway, tall, upright, his face hidden by the shadow.

"I won't disturb you," he added, after a moment's hesitation.

The tone of formality hurt her. With a return of her old impulsiveness, she began searching for the matches.

"You are not disturbing me," she said. "On the contrary, I—was expecting you. Archibald told me you were coming, but I forgot to light up. I was twilight-dreaming, if there is such a term."

She laughed with a forced cheerfulness, and he made no answer. The little red-shaded lamp gave her some trouble, and when she looked up she saw that he was standing opposite her, the light falling on a broad scar across his forehead.

"How the burn shows to-night!" she exclaimed involuntarily. "Will you never lose it?"

"Never," he answered. "I do not want to. When I am depressed, I look at it, and remember that I have done one thing worth doing in my life."

"I don't know," she returned. "You have done more useful things than that."

"Not to my mind."

"Well, but to mine. There, when I have pulled the curtains and put the lamp just at your elbow, you could almost imagine yourself back in England, couldn't you? Imagine the street outside as a bit of London. There could hardly be more noise. The idea may refresh you. You look so tired."

He seated himself in the comfortable wicker chair by the table and looked about him with a faint smile of content.

"Yes," he said, "it is homely, isn't it? The red light, and the pretty little room, and you sitting there working. It might be a corner of the old country—or of Marut. Your study was just like this, I remember."

"Yes, I copied it. It made me feel less lonely. Only I flatter myself that it is tidier here than it used to be in the old days."

He laughed, and the laughter sent the light shining in his eyes.

"Rather! When I first joined I had the chemical craze on, do you remember? I thought I was going to discover some wonderful new gunpowder, and we used to experiment together in your room. The business came to an untimely end when I blew off part of the ceiling—"

"And some of my eyebrows!" she interposed merrily.

"Yes, of course. I don't know which disaster upset Mrs. Carmichael most, good soul. After that I forget what craze came about, but we always had a new one on the list, hadn't we?"

She nodded, her head once more bent over her work.

"None of them lasted," she said. "Crazes never do."

There was a moment's silence. Their little burst of gay recollections was over, and the restraint had regained its old ascendancy over them. Unknown to her, Nicholson was watching his companion with keen, anxious eyes.

"You look pale and tired," he said gently. "Madras is getting too much for you. When is Travers going to take you for a change?"

"I don't know. Not just now. Besides, I am happier here. I like the noise and bustle."

"You used not to. You were all for outdoor sports and beautiful scenery."

"Yes, but now it is different. I could not stand the quiet. I must have noise to distract me—I mean, I have grown so accustomed to it."

"Yes," he said slowly, "one grows accustomed to it." Then, presently, he added, in another tone: "At any rate, my term in Madras is at an end. I return to Marut next week."

She started. The start was almost a violent one, and her hands fell limply in her lap.

"You are going back to Marut?" she said. "For ever?"

He smiled, but his eyes avoided hers.

"Not for ever, I hope. I am sick of pen-work, and want to get back to the front among my men. There is a company of sepoys to be stationed at Marut, and they have given me the command. It's a good post, though of course I would rather be at the frontier, where there's something doing. At any rate, I must get away from Madras as soon as possible."

"Yes," she said absently, "no doubt it is best."

She went on stitching as though nothing had happened, but her hands trembled, and once she threw back her head as though fighting down a strong emotion. But he had ceased to watch her. He was leaning a little forward, one elbow resting on his knee, his eyes fixed steadfastly in front of him.

"Can I be the bearer of any messages?" he asked at last.

"No, thank you. I write regularly. Or—yes, you might tell them that you left me well and happy. That will please them. Will you be so kind?"

"Will it be kind to give a message which is not quite true?—I mean," he added hastily, "you do not seem strong."

"Oh, I am strong enough. I do not think I shall ever be ill."

Another long and painful silence intervened. There was no sound, save Lois' thread as it was drawn through the thick material. Nicholson drew out his watch.

"You mustn't think me rude, Mrs. Travers," he said, with an abrupt return to his old formality, "but I have any amount of work to do before I leave, and among other things I wanted to see your husband on business. He told me the other day that he had some shares in the Marut Company going, and said if I would care for them—"

Her work dropped from her hand to the floor. She stared at him with a face whiter than the linen she had been stitching.

"But you are not going to buy them?" she asked sharply. Something in her tone forced him to meet her eyes.

"Oh, I don't know. Why not? I'm a poor business man, and your husband always seems to come off well in his ventures. Without being in the least a speculator, I should be glad to make a little money." He smiled. "I have another craze on, you see—a gun this time—and it requires capital to complete. So I thought—"

She leaned forward. One small hand lay clenched on the table between them, and there was a force and energy in her attitude which arrested his startled attention.

"I think you are mistaken, Captain Nicholson," she said. "My husband has no shares to sell."

"But yesterday he told me that he had!"

"Yes, yesterday, no doubt. But he heard to-day from the Rajah. I think, if you do not mind waiting, he will tell you himself that what I say is true."

For a second they looked straight at each other without speaking. Neither was conscious of any clear thought, but both knew that in that breathing space they had exchanged a signal from those hidden chambers which men unlock only in brief moments of silent crisis. The crisis had come in spite of a year's defiant struggle. It had broken down the barrier of trivial commonplaces behind which they had always sought shelter; it had rushed over them in a flash, like a sudden tidal wave, scorning their painfully erected defenses, driving them helplessly before it. It had no apparent cause, save that in that moment of alarm she had looked at him with her soul unguarded, and he, overwhelmed by that silent revelation, had allowed his own sternly repressed secret to flash back its breathless message. Nicholson was the first to regain his self-control. He bent down and, picking up her work, restored it gently to her hands.

"You must go on with your sewing," he said. "I like seeing you work. It completes the picture of a—home—"

"Yes," she interrupted, in a rough, broken voice. "It is a perfect picture, is it not? Just so, as it is—only, of course—" she laughed as he had never heard her laugh before—"of course it's only a tableau—it isn't real."

Once more her head was bent over her work. He saw how with every stitch she was fighting stubbornly for calm—fighting with all the dogged desperation of a high-minded woman who sees herself trembling at the edge of a bottomless abyss. He knew now for certain that her apparent happiness was a sham and an heroic lie—that she knew what he knew of Travers' outside life, and suffered with the intensity which honor must suffer when linked with dishonor. He saw, with a soldier's instinctive admiration, that she was holding her ground against the fierce and unexpected attack of an overwhelming enemy, and that he, who had his own battle to fight, must hold out to her a helping, strengthening comrade's hand.

"Lois!" he said quietly. "Lois!"

She went on working. The name had been a test of her strength, and she had borne it. He knew that he could go on with what he had to say.

"Lois, we had our young enthusiasms in those old days—crazes, we will call them—and of course, like all young enthusiasms, they are gone for ever. But there were other things. Sometimes we used to talk very seriously about life, do you remember? I dare say we talked nonsense for the greater part—we were very young—but we were intensely serious. We told each other what we thought life was, and what we intended to make of it. It was then we had the idea of the cathedral."

She looked up earnestly at him.

"The cathedral? Haven't you forgotten?"

"No. I never forgot it."

"I thought you had. It is all such a long time ago. When I read about you in the papers, and heard of all the wonders you had done, I was sure you must have forgotten the chatter of your fifteen-year-old playfellow. A man who spends his day as you did, in the saddle, and the night in long, anxious watches, does not have time for such ideas as we cultivated in those days."

"You are wrong, Lois. The idea is everything. It is the mainspring of a man's life. If I did anything wonderful, as you say, it was for the sake of the cathedral. There was, for instance, one night which I remember very well. A whole tribe had risen. Half my men were down with fever, and I felt—well, pretty bad. I was a bit delirious, I fancy, and in delirium very often the foundations of a man's character come uppermost. The cathedral was always in my mind. I saw your half, and it was getting on splendidly. That goaded me. I felt I had to go on, too. So I pulled myself together and went ahead. We pulled through somehow, and I have always felt that in that night I laid the chief stone."

The burning tears sprang to her eyes.

"So all that splendid work was done for the sake of our cathedral?"

"Partly, but not in the first place. Do you remember of what use our cathedral was to be in the world? It wasn't merely to be a monument to our own glory—it was to be a sheltering place for others, an example to them, an inspiration. You said once, very rightly, that if every here and there a human being made a cathedral out of his life, other people would soon get ashamed of their mud-huts, and pull them down. They would try to build cathedrals on a bigger and nobler scale than the first one, and probably would succeed. Thus the work would go on from one generation to another. It was an idea worthy to form the foundations of a man's ambition. I made it mine, as I knew you had made it yours. It strengthened me to think that every decent action was a fresh stone to the building which in the end would stand perfect—not to my glory, but to the glory of the whole human race." He smiled, though his eyes remained serious. "As an Englishman, I can not help wishing that cathedrals should be most plentiful on English soil."

"Do you really think that one small human life can make so much difference?" she asked, rather bitterly. "I used to think so, in my self-important days, but I am beginning to believe that our little individual efforts are hopelessly lost in a sea of rubbish."

"Our youthful conceit is more justifiable than such self-disparagement," he answered. "I often think that humility—at any rate a certain kind—is a questionable virtue. In lessening our own value, we lessen our own responsibility, and our responsibility is tremendous. One life can make the difference of a cathedral spire in a town of low-built huts or of a snow mountain in an ugly plain. I am sure of it—and so are you. So is everybody who thinks about it. But people do not think. It is sometimes much more convenient to believe that one is too insignificant to have any responsibility. But to my mind there is not a vagabond in the street who is not directly helping on our national decay, and who might not be building up the Empire." He leaned toward her, lowering his voice. "You know I am not just talking, Lois. It is my life's principle which I lay before you—mine and yours. How long is it since we have spoken of these things? Ten years. Since then we have been building steadily at our cathedral. We must go on."

"How can we?" she answered wearily. "It is not our cathedral any more. I thought you had forgotten, and—"

"My first day in Marut I sent a message to you—a little in fun, but with an earnest purpose. I wanted to see if you had forgotten, and I wanted you to know that I had remembered. I told you that the cathedral still lacked its chief spire."

"I never got the message. It was that day Archibald asked me to be his wife. When did you send the letter?"

"It was not a letter but a verbal message, by Travers."

"That afternoon?"

"Yes, that afternoon."

She covered her face with her hand.

"He—he must have forgotten," she said at last.

"Yes, he must have forgotten," he agreed quietly.

There was a long silence. She remained motionless, but he heard her breath being drawn in quick, painful gasps. The battle for them both was at its height. He bent forward and took the hand that lay clenched in her lap gently in his own.

"Dear little Lois, dear little comrade! We are like two architects, you and I. We were very young when we set out on our great task, and no doubt we have made many blunders. In the beginning we each hoped secretly that the time would come when we should be able to crown our work hand in hand. It was that I was thinking of when I sent my message. Well, things have turned out differently—perhaps through our own fault. But the cathedral must go on. Instead of one spire, as we had hoped, there will be two spires. You will build yours, I mine. They will be far apart, and so we of necessity must be apart, too. But the cathedral will go on; and in the end—who knows?—it may be more perfect than as we saw it in our first great plan."

"But we might have built together, Adam!"

"Yes. We might even build together now—but then it would no longer be a cathedral. It would be a mud hovel like the rest. And that would be wrong—wrong to the world and wrong to ourselves. Have you understood what I mean?"

He waited patiently, his hand still clasping hers. One single piteous tear rolled down her cheek, but that was all, and when she looked up at him her eyes were calm and steadfast.

"I understand quite well what you mean," she said, "and I know that you are right. God bless and help you."

"And you, Lois."

They exchanged a firm pressure. Then Nicholson rose.

"I must be going," he said. "Will you tell Travers that I shall be around at the office to-morrow morning? If by any chance he has any shares going, I should be obliged if he would allot them to me."

Lois rose also. Her face was turned toward the door.

"If you wait one moment, you will see him yourself," she said. "I think I hear him coming upstairs."

She was right. The next minute the door opened quickly and Travers entered. Evidently something unusual had happened. In one hand he held an open telegram. His face was crimson with excitement and his lips parted as if with a hasty announcement. But as he saw the two standing at the table watching him, he stopped short, looking from one to the other with a flash of amused curiosity in his eyes.

"Hullo, you both here?" he said cheerfully. "How cozy you look. See here, Lois, I've just had a telegram from the Rajah. He wants me to come at once. Can you be ready to start in three days?"

"For Marut?" A rush of color filled her pale cheeks.

"Yes, of course. By the bye, Nicholson, that's your destination, isn't it? We might travel together."

"I think not," was the quiet answer. "I have orders to start next week."

"Well, there's no great hurry for us, I expect. Our friend, Nehal, is of an excitable disposition. I hope you haven't had to wait long for me, Nicholson. You said you had some business you wanted to talk over with me."

"Yes, it was about those shares. But if you are busy—"

"Oh, that's all right. It won't take more than a few minutes to settle. How much do you want to invest? I tell you, my dear fellow, it's a splendid thing, and—"

He was unexpectedly interrupted. He had taken out a heavy pocket-book and was busily looking through some papers, when Lois laid her hand on his.

"I think Captain Nicholson is under a misapprehension, Archibald," she said, in a low voice. "He said you had some shares to sell him, but I remembered what you said about the mine, and I told him that there must be some mistake. I was quite right, wasn't I?"

Every word she had spoken sounded emphasized as though she were striving to convey a double meaning, and the second in which husband and wife looked at each other was to the puzzled witness a painful eternity. With a strong perceptible effort, Travers turned away.

"So my wife has broken the news to you?" he said, smiling. "Yes, I'm awfully sorry. Everything good gets snapped up so confoundedly quickly. Better luck next time. I was quite dreading disappointing you, but Lois, as usual, has taken my disagreeable task from me." He patted the hand which still rested on his own. "Stay and have a little dinner with us," he added cordially, as Nicholson prepared to take his leave. "I'd like to make up to you with a little of my best Cliquot."

Nicholson shook his head. The impression that he stood before a veiled and unpleasant comedy increased his desire to get away.

"Thanks, I'm afraid I can't," he said. "I have work to do. Good night."

"Good night. To our next meeting in Marut!" The two men shook hands.

"Good night, Mrs. Travers. You will be able to be your own messenger now," Nicholson said.

She met his glance with quiet courage.

"They will be able to see with their own eyes that things are going well with me," she answered simply.

When the door closed upon Nicholson's tall form she went back to her husband's side. He was busy consulting time-tables, and hardly seemed aware of her approach. Only when she touched him on the arm did he look up.

"Well, what is it?"

"I want to know if you are angry?"

"What about?"

"The shares—and Captain Nicholson. I felt it was wrong to deceive him. He is not rich, and you told me that the mine was a failure."

"Of course, you have every reason, no doubt, to consider your friend before your husband," he said with a sudden outburst which he instantly regretted. He had encouraged—nay, forced—her intimacy with Nicholson. With what purpose? He himself hardly knew. Perhaps somewhere at the bottom of him he was beginning to dread the honesty of her character as an unspoken reproach. If she were less perfect in her conduct, his own life would have seemed less blamable. Or perhaps his motives had been more generous. He knew he had nothing to give her—and Nicholson was a good fellow. At any rate, it was a mistake to have betrayed even a moment's irritation. She had shrunk back from him, but he put his hand on her shoulder and kissed her. "There! Of course I am not angry. You've lost me a few hundreds, but you're worth it, and I dare say it was all for the best. Run and write a note to the Colonel and say we are coming, there's a good little woman!"

Lois turned wearily away. He had not understood her. She considered him more than she had considered Nicholson. She had wanted to save him from what she felt was a mean and treacherous step. But he had not been able to understand. Nor could she have explained. Between certain characters all real communication is an impossibility, and words no more than sounds.

CHAPTER II
CATASTROPHE

The tea-room, usually the most animated portion of the Marut club-house, had lost its cheerful appearance. The comfortable chairs had been cleared on one side and replaced by a long green baize table littered with papers; the doors leading on to the verandah were closed, and a stifling atmosphere bore down upon the five occupants who were ranged about the table in various attitudes of listless exhaustion.

"I can't think what we have been called here for," Mrs. Cary protested loudly; "and from the way we have been locked in, we might be in a state of siege. I know I shall faint in a minute. Beatrice, pass me my salts, child."

Her daughter obeyed mechanically, without moving her eyes, which were fixed in front of her. Colonel Carmichael, who was seated at the far end of the table, opposite the Rajah, smiled good-naturedly.

"If *you* feel yourself justified in grumbling, what about me, Mrs. Cary?" he said. "You at least are a share-holder, and I suppose there are some formalities to be gone through, but what I have to do with the business I can not imagine."

"Business!" groaned Mrs. Berry from his right. "That's the silliest part of it all! What's the good of getting me to talk business? I don't understand business; I never did, and never shall. Why doesn't Mr. Travers come? I'm sure I have been waiting quite ten minutes."

"Perhaps the Rajah can give us a clue to the mystery," the Colonel suggested. "Rajah, don't you think the ladies could be allowed their liberty? I can not think that their presence is so essential."

Nehal Singh looked up. From the moment he had exchanged nothing more than a brief salutation with the four Europeans, he had sat with his head bent over some papers, reading, or pretending to read. The months had brought a new expression to his face. Pain had cut her lines into the broad forehead; anxiety met the Colonel's questioning gaze from eyes which had once flashed happy confidence and enthusiasm.

"I am afraid I can give you no answer, Colonel Carmichael," he said quietly. "Since Mr. Travers has returned to Marut all control over affairs has passed out of my hands into his. For some reason, I have been kept in ignorance as to the progress of events, and I wait here to-day with you as completely in the dark as any one. No doubt he will be here in a few minutes."

"With good news, I hope," Mrs. Cary sighed. "I also am no sort of a business woman, but I understand enough to know that if one invests money in an honest concern one gets interest sooner or later. And so far the Marut Company hasn't paid me a penny piece."

Nehal Singh started slightly, and his glance wandered to the red face of the speaker with an expression that was akin to fear.

"An honest concern!" he repeated. "Do you mean that—that it is not honest?"

Mrs. Cary beamed with recovered equanimity.

"Good gracious! How could you suppose I should mean such a horrid thing, dear Prince! Of course everything to which you put your hand is hall-marked. Otherwise I should never have dreamed of investing my money in the Marut Company."

There was a silence. The Colonel drummed with his fingers on the table, watching the native sentry who passed stolidly backward and forward in front of the closed windows. Mrs. Cary fanned herself and exchanged whispered comments with Mrs. Berry on the opposite side. Beatrice remained motionless. From the beginning of the meeting she had once raised her eyes—on Nehal Singh's entry—and then it had been for no more than a second. That second had been enough. She had seen his face. She had seen—and it was not her imagination, but a real and bitter irony— that of all the people in the room she alone had been the object of his quiet greeting. She knew then—for her eyes had not lost their keenness—that the eighteen months in which they had scarcely met had made no difference to him. He still reverenced and loved her. For him she was still "Lakshmi," the goddess of beauty and perfection; for him she was still the ideal, the woman of goodness and truth and purity. Her victory over him had been complete, eternal. She had betrayed him and retained him. Of all her triumphs over men and circumstances this was the most perfect. Yet she sat there, white and still, not lifting her eyes from the table, and seemingly unconscious of all that went on about her.

Presently a carriage drove up the avenue. They heard Travers' voice giving some orders, and a moment later he himself entered, followed by a Mr. Medway, his chief mining engineer. He closed the door and with a grave bow took his place at the table. He seemed indifferent to or unaware of the curious and somewhat anxious glances which were turned toward him. There was something in his appearance which cast an unpleasant chill over every one of the little assembly. Even the Colonel, though an outsider, felt himself disagreeably impressed by Travers' new bearing, and the good-natured banter which he had held in readiness for the new arrival died away on his lips as he responded to the cold, formal bow. For some minutes no one spoke. Travers was busy arranging some papers which he had brought with him, and only when he had laid these out to his satisfaction did he rise to address the meeting. He held himself stiffly erect, his fingers resting lightly on the table, his pale face turned toward the window as though he wished to avoid addressing any one directly. The usual geniality was lacking in his composed features.

"Colonel Carmichael and honorable share-holders in the Marut Diamond Company," he began, "you are no doubt wondering why I have called this private meeting. I do so because you are the chief partakers in the concern, and because, as my friends, I wish to offer you an explanation which I do not feel bound to offer to the other share-holders within and without Marut. This excuse does not hold good for you, Colonel Carmichael, and you must feel I am encroaching heavily on your valuable time. Nevertheless, I assure you that your presence will assist me considerably in my difficult task."

"I am sure I shall be delighted to do anything in my power," Colonel Carmichael responded, "but I fear my knowledge of intricate business details is not such as to make it of the slightest use to you."

"The business is not intricate," Travers went on. "Nor do I propose drawing out this meeting to any tiring length. The heat must be very trying for the ladies present, but my wish to keep what passes between us, at any rate for the time being, entirely secret, makes it essential to sit in closed rooms. I will be as brief as possible. Two years ago the Marut Diamond Company first came into existence under the protection of our friend, Rajah Nehal Singh. For some time previous to this event it had been my great ambition to open out a diamond field in which, thanks to favorable reports, I sincerely believed. My position, however, and above all my lack of personal means, made the scheme an impossibility so far as I was concerned. Chance brought me the pleasure and misfortune of making your acquaintance, Rajah. I say 'misfortune,' because, as events have turned, I can not but feel that my casual observations led you to enter into an enterprise before which another man, if I may say so, with more experience and less impulse, would have hesitated.

"Your generosity and enthusiasm brought my half-conceived plans into a reality almost before I had any clear idea as to whither we were all drifting. You will remember, Mrs. Cary, I did my best to dissuade you from any rash investment; and even there, as director of the company, I felt that I was not acting with entire loyalty to the man who had put me into that position. The responsibility of the whole matter rested heavily on my shoulders, and grew still heavier as the circle of share-holders without Marut increased. I felt that, should my first hopes prove unfounded, my friends and many others would suffer losses which they could ill afford to bear. Ladies and gentlemen, it is my painful duty to tell you that the dreaded collapse has come. Mr. Medway, here, the company's chief engineer and mining expert, informed me yesterday that any continuation of the works was useless and a mere waste of the share-holders' money. I therefore beg to announce to you that the Marut Diamond Company Mine is definitely closed."

The Colonel clenched his teeth half-way through the first oath he had ever allowed himself in the presence of ladies. He was not an unusually egoistical man, but his first thought was one of unutterable gratitude that in the moment of strong temptation his wife had held an obstinate hand on the purse-strings.

The first person to speak was Mrs. Cary. She leaned half-way across the table.

"And my money?" she said thickly and unsteadily. "Where's my money? Where's my money? Tell me that!"

Travers shrugged his shoulders.

"I fear it has gone the way of mine and of the other share-holders'," he said. "Nor can I hold out any hopes of its coming back. The expenses of the mine have been terribly heavy, the workmen have been extremely well paid—extremely well paid." There was a distinct note of reproach in his voice, though he looked at no one.

Mrs. Cary sat down in her seat. It was a pitiful and almost terrible sight to see her, all the florid, vulgar ostentation and sleek content dashed out of her, leaving her with pasty cheeks and horror-stricken, staring eyes to face the ruined future. Mrs. Berry burst into ever-ready tears.

"Oh!" she sobbed. "What will my husband say! I told him it was such a good thing—it isn't my fault. What will he say!"

The sharp, wailing tones broke through Mrs. Cary's momentary paralysis. She sat up and brought her fat clenched fist down with a bang upon the table.

"You!" she half screamed at the Rajah. "You—you black swindler—you thief—it's you who have done it—you who have ruined us all with your wicked schemes. You baited us with this clubhouse—you pretended you wanted to do us such a lot of good, didn't you? And all the time you meant to feather your own nest with diamonds and the Lord knows what. Give us back our money, you heathen swindler! For you aren't a Christian! You pretended that, too, just as a blind—"

Her flow of frightful coarse invectives came to an abrupt end. Colonel Carmichael, who knew now why his presence had been required, leaned forward and pushed her firmly down in her seat.

"For Heaven's sake, Mrs. Cary, hold your tongue!" he expostulated, in a rapid, emphatic undertone. "You don't know what you are saying. You are not in England. A little more of that sort of thing, and our lives aren't worth an hour's purchase."

"I don't care," she retorted, with all the headlong brutality of her origin. "It's true what I say! It's true!"

"It is true." The interruption came from the Rajah himself. He had risen and stood before them, very pale, but calm and composed, his eyes fixed with haggard resolution on the furious face of his accuser. "It is true. I am a swindler. I have ruined you all. Why should you believe it was done unwittingly? Yet that is true also. I, like my poor friend here whom I used as my tool, believed that I was doing the best for you all. But I have ruined you. I have done worse than that—I have ruined my country, my people. You have friends who will help you in your distress, but who will help my people? I pulled them out of their miserable homes only to cast them into deeper misery. I have taken their pitiful savings, meaning, without the use of charity, to increase them tenfold. I have taken everything from them. I gave a hope, and have left them with a deeper despair. Not all my wealth— and not a stone, not a farthing piece shall be held back from your and their just claims upon me—will fill up the ruin of those I wished so well. It is true—I stand before you all a dishonored man."

There was a moment's petrified silence. Even Mrs. Cary's coarse nature stood baffled before this pitiless, dignified self-accusal. Nor could the Colonel find a word to say. He had been ready—knowing the native character—to defend Mrs. Cary from the stroke of a revenging dagger. His half-outstretched arm sank powerless before the stroke of these few words, spoken with a calm which thinly covered a chaos of remorse and broken-hearted grief.

"I have a question I should like to ask you, Mr. Travers."

There was a general uneasy start. Each shook off his brooding considerations and turned with surprise to this unexpected speaker. It was Beatrice, hitherto silent and apparently unmoved, who leaned across to Travers. He himself felt the blood rise to his face. In his absorbed state he had not noticed her presence, and now that he met her cold eyes a curious discomfort crept over him—a discomfort that was nearly fear.

"I will answer your question to the best of my ability," he said quietly.

"The Rajah has spoken of you as his tool, and I think from your tone that you think yourself aggrieved. In what way have you suffered? What is your share of the losses?"

"I have lost all I have."

"All you have, no doubt. But your wife is very rich, and I believe has grown richer within the last year. I am anxious to know if you intend to follow the Rajah's generous example and meet your liabilities with her fortune."

The Colonel, who had been staring vacantly at her, gave a start of recollection.

"Yes!" he exclaimed energetically. "The settlement and Lois' own money—what's become of it all? Has that gone, too?"

"Of course not." Travers' hand tightened instinctively upon the arm of his chair. "I should never have dreamed of touching what was my wife's personal property. Nor do I intend to do so now. I am no more than the manager of the company—I am not responsible for its liabilities. Miss Cary's suggestion is beside the mark, and I warn her, for her own advantage"—there was a somewhat unpleasant note of warning in his rough voice—"not to pursue her questions further."

Beatrice rose to her feet. She was calm and, save for the vivid color in her cheeks, betrayed at first little of the seething storm of indignation which rose gradually above the barriers of her self-control. She did not look at the Rajah. She stared straight into Travers' face, and once she pointed at him.

"You have been good enough to threaten me," she said. "It would be best for you to know at once that your threats are quite useless. There is nothing you can say about me which I am not ready to say myself—and there is nothing you can do which will prevent me from revealing the true facts of this case. You have feathered your nest, Mr. Travers. That is what you told me to do, and now I understand what you meant. You saw this ruin coming at the very time that you were encouraging every one to partake further of the company's future success. You honored me, as a sort of accomplice, with a private piece of advice. Thank God, I did not take it, for then I should have been your debtor.

"As it is, I owe you absolutely nothing—not even the wealthy husband you promised me. There is a bottom to my depths. And even if I did owe you something, I should not hesitate to speak. You can call me a traitor if you like—I don't care. I am that—and I have been far worse than that to a man who did not deserve it—and I have, anyhow, not much reputation to lose. Besides, you have stood by without a word and let an innocent man bear your burden, and for that alone you have no right to claim loyalty from another."

She turned for the first time to Nehal Singh, and met his gaze boldly and recklessly. "Do not stand there and call yourself a dishonored man!" she exclaimed with increasing force. "You are not dishonored. Do not call Mr. Travers your 'tool.' He is not your tool, and never has been. You are his tool,—his and mine!" She paused, catching her breath as she saw him wince. Then she went on: "Don't burden yourself with the consciences of us all, for we have not got any; and what has been done we have done knowingly and wilfully. Do you remember that evening when you found me in the temple? You thought it was—chance—or—or the hand of God. Why, Mr. Travers hired one of your old servants to slip me through by the secret path, and I had on my prettiest frock and my prettiest smile and my prettiest ways—as I told them all afterward at a dinner-party—pious goodness, with a relieving touch of the devil—just to tempt you out of your cloister and make you do what we wanted.

"You followed like a lamb. It took five minutes to wheedle the club-house out of you—five minutes, I think you told me, Mr. Travers?—and the other things went just as smoothly. Do you remember that ride we had together after Mr. Travers' dance? He had broached the subject of the mine, but the next day something or other seemed to have shaken your implicit belief in our integrity and general holiness. At any rate, you asked me for my advice—my honest advice. I gave it you. I told you to go ahead—that Mr. Travers was an angel of goodness and perfection. That was what he suggested I should say, in a note he had sent me an hour before. So you went ahead. You did the dirty work for him, and took his responsibility upon your shoulders. You have ruined a few of us incidentally, but above all things you have ruined yourself and your people. Mr. Travers is unharmed. He has his wife's money."

She paused to gather her strength for a final effort. "So much for Mr. Travers' and my partnership. I did my share of the work to shield myself and my mother from a trouble which must now go its way. But after that,

I played my own game. I did not want to lose you—even though I knew quite well that you cared for me, and that I should never marry you. Months before I had made up my mind to marry a man with a high position and money. It was just a game I was playing with you. Even when you forced things to a head, I kept it up. I pretended innocency and high motives—because I wanted to feel you at my apron-strings always. We all treated you more or less badly, but I was the worst. I fooled you—for—for—"

"For what?"

His voice burst from him, harsh and terrible as though it had been torn from the bottom of a tortured soul.

"For the fun of the thing."

Among the seven present there was no movement, no sound. Scarcely one seemed to breathe or be alive except the woman who stood there, her breast heaving, a twisted smile of wild self-mockery on her ashy lips.

Nehal Singh turned and went to the door. There he stopped and looked back at her and the little group of which she formed the central figure. Then he made a gesture—one single gesture. He raised his hand high above his head and brought it down, palm downward. In that movement there was a contempt, a scorn, a bitterness so profound that it seemed to mingle with a terrible pity; but above all there was a final severing, a breaking of the last link which bound them. The next minute the door closed behind him.

How long the silence that followed lasted no one knew. It was broken by Mrs. Cary, who flung herself face downward on the table, and burst into wild, uncontrollable sobs.

"Oh, Beaty!" she moaned. "Our reputations—our good name! How could you have told such wicked stories about yourself and poor Mr. Travers! How could you!"

Colonel Carmichael shook his head. He was overwhelmed by a cross-current of conflicting emotions to which he could give no name.

"True or not true, your—eh—statement has got us into a pretty mess, Miss Cary," he said. "You have played with fire. Pray Heaven that it has not set light to Marut!"

She turned and looked at him. In that pale face upon which had sunk the light of a sudden peace the Colonel read something which sent his blunt instinct searching wildly for a solution.

"I did what I had to do, Colonel Carmichael," she said. "Come, mother, we must go home."

CHAPTER III
A FAREWELL

John Stafford sat at his table by the open door which looked on to the garden. The room behind him was bare of all graceful or even tasteful ornament—a few native weapons, captured probably during small frontier wars, hung on the wall, but nothing else relieved its blank, whitewashed monotony. The one photograph of his father which had once been fastened above the mantelpiece had been taken down months before and the hole made by the nail carefully and methodically filled and painted over. The room typified the man in its painful order, its painful whitewashed cleanliness, its rigid plainness. But the garden was the symbol of the hidden possibility in him, the corner of warm, impulsive feeling which the world had never seen. The roses grew up to the very steps of the verandah; they had been trained to clamber over the trellis-work as though seeking to gain entrance to his room; they spread themselves in rich, glowing variety over the little patch of ground, and one of their number, the most lovely and fullest blown, hung her heavy head in splendid isolation from the vase upon his table.

He looked at the rose and he looked at the garden, on which lay the first clear rays of the rising sun. In him stirred a rare wistfulness, a rare melancholy. For to him all the gentler, softer forms of sorrow were rare. In the last year he had suffered, but in his own way—rigidly, coldly, unbendingly. His lips, even in the loneliness of his own room, had always been tight closed over the smothered exclamation of pain. He had gone on steadily and conscientiously with his work. He had never for one moment "given way to himself," as he expressed it. But this morning he was in the power of that strange "atmosphere"—call it what you will—which we feel when still only half awake, and which, independent of all outward circumstances, destines our day's mood of cheerfulness or depression. Strangely enough, he had made no struggle against it—he had yielded to it with a sense of inevitableness.

The inevitable compassed him about and numbed his stern, merciless system of self-repression. Fate, irresistible and unchangeable, obscured the clear path of duty which he had marked out for himself, and held him for the moment her passive victim. It was no idle fancy. He was not a man in whose thought-world fancy played any part. Nor was it the gloomy impression which a lonely twilight might have stamped upon a mind already burdened with a heavy weight of trouble. The young day spread her halo of pure sunshine over a world of color; the red rose upon his table bowed her head toward him in the perfection of a mature beauty which as yet hid no warning of decay. But in the sunshine he saw the shadow; the daylight foretold the night; his eyes saw the withered petals of the rose strewn before him. In vain he had striven to see beyond the night to the as inevitable to-morrow; in vain he had pictured the rose which his careful hand would bring to replace her dead sister. The future was a blank dead wall whose heights his foresight could not scale.

Before him on the table lay a closed and sealed envelope. It contained his will, which half an hour before he had signed in the presence of two comrades. He wondered what the world would say when it was opened— and when it would be opened.

Presently the curtains behind him were pushed quietly on one side. He did not turn around. He supposed it was his native servant with the cup of coffee which formed his early morning refreshment; but the soft step across the uncarpeted floor, the rustle of a woman's dress startled him from his illusion. He turned and sprang to his feet.

"Beatrice!" he exclaimed.

She came toward him with outstretched hand.

"May I speak with you for a few minutes, John?" she asked.

His first impulse to protest against her reckless disregard of propriety died away on his lips. Something on her white earnest face touched him— all the more perhaps because it linked itself with his own mood. He brought a chair—his own, for the room boasted of but one.

"Are you angry?" she asked again, looking up at him.

"At your coming? No. At another time I might have warned you that it was not wise, but I feel sure you would not have run so much risk without a serious and adequate reason."

She nodded.

"Yes, I have a very serious reason," she said. "Have you time to spare?"

"All the morning."

"Were you on duty last night?"

"For the best part."

"Is that why you look so tired and ill?"

He smiled faintly.

"I might reply with a *tu quoque*. But that doesn't matter. You have some trouble to tell me. What has happened?"

"You have heard nothing?"

"Nothing whatever." He drew a stool toward him and seated himself at her side. "You know, I am not a person to whom gossip drifts quickly."

"It's not gossip—it's truth. The Marut Diamond Company is closed— for good and all."

"You mean—it has gone smash?"

"Completely—and we with it."

He sat silent for a moment, his head resting thoughtfully on his hand.

"I suppose it had to come," he said at last. "Somehow, it always seemed to me that the concern was doomed. The foundations weren't honest. The Rajah was more or less beguiled into it—" He broke off, turning crimson with vexation. "I beg your pardon, Beatrice. I forgot that that was one of your—escapades."

She looked at him steadily, and he was struck and again strangely moved by her pale beauty. He had never seen her so gentle, so free from her cold and mocking gaiety.

"You must not apologize. And do not smooth over a mean, low trick with the name of an escapade. It was not an escapade, for an escapade is the overflow of high and reckless spirits, and what I did was done in cold blood and with a purpose. I have come to tell you about that purpose."

He could not repress a movement of surprise.

"Surely you have something more serious on your mind than that? If, as you say, your—your financial position has been rendered precarious by this failure of the Marut Company, would it not be advisable to hurry on our marriage at once? Of course, in the meanwhile, if I can do anything to help your mother—"

She touched him gently on the arm.

"I told you I had come on a serious matter," she said. "Won't you let me tell you what it is?"

"Of course, Beatrice, of course. Only I thought that was the serious matter."

"It is perhaps for my mother, but not for me. Things have changed their value in my life. Just now I feel there is only one thing that has any value at all, and that is freedom."

"From what? I do not understand. Do you mean from debt?"

She smiled sadly.

"Yes, from debt. John, I want to ask you an honest question honestly. Why did you ask me to become your wife?"

He moved uneasily.

"Why do you ask? Surely we understand each other."

"We did, perhaps, but I have told you that things have changed. Won't you answer me?"

"I asked you—because I wished you to be my wife," he returned stubbornly.

"John, isn't that rather a lame equivocation?"

He stared at her with heavy, troubled eyes.

"Yes, it was. But the truth might hurt you, Beatrice."

"No, it wouldn't. Nothing can hurt so much in the end as lies and humbug."

"Well, then, I asked you to become my wife because I believed that my conduct had put you into a wrong and painful situation in the eyes of the world."

"Nothing else?"

"I wished to prove to Lois that I could never be her husband."

"You were afraid that she would see through your pretense to your unchanged affection for her?"

He started.

"Beatrice, how do you know?"

"Look in your own glass, John. Yours isn't the face of a man who has shaken off an old attachment."

He rose and stood with his back half turned to her, playing idly with the papers on the table.

"You are partly right," he said, after a moment's silence, "but not quite. I have more on my shoulders than that; I have a heavy responsibility—a debt to pay."

"You, too?" she asked, with a return of the half-melancholy, half-bitter smile. "Have you also a debt?"

"Not of my making," was the answer. The voice rang suddenly stern and harsh, and Beatrice saw him look up suddenly, as though instinctively seeking something on the wall. "Beatrice, you must know that my actions are dictated by motives which I can not for many reasons give to the world. For one thing, I have given my promise; for another, my own judgment tells me that it is better for every one that I should be silent. But I am free to say this much to you—I am not a dishonorable man who has played lightly with the affections of an innocent girl. I have acted toward Lois as I believe will be for her ultimate happiness—I have shielded her from a misfortune, a punishment I might say, which would have fallen unjustly on her shoulders. I have taken a burden upon my shoulders because I love her—and I have the right to love her—but chiefly because it is my duty to do so. Where there is sin, Beatrice, there must also be atonement, otherwise its consequences can never be wiped out. I have chosen to atone."

Beatrice made no attempt to question him. Her eyes fell thoughtfully on the gaunt face, and for the first time she appreciated to the full what was great and generous in the nature she had condemned all too often as narrow and unbending. Whatever else he was, this man was no Pharisee. If he was narrow, he allowed himself no license; if unbending, he was at least least of all relenting toward his own conduct. She pitied him and she respected him, even though she could not understand his motives nor guess the weight of the responsibility which he had taken upon himself.

"I can not reproach you with deception," she said at last. "You never pretended that you loved me, and on my side I think the matter was pretty clear. I intended to marry you for your position. Afterward money added a further incentive. I saw the loss of our own fortune coming. Travers warned me on the same day that we became engaged."

A dark flood of indignant blood rushed to Stafford's forehead.

"The man is an unscrupulous adventurer—no doubt he has safeguarded his own interest carefully enough," he exclaimed bitterly.

"You are quite right. His wife has all the money, and he has taken care that it should be well tied up and out of reach. That is what my father did."

He turned to her again.

"Your father?"

"Yes, my father," she repeated, meeting his eyes gravely and unflinchingly. "He tried to do what Travers did. But he wasn't quite so clever. He ran too close to the wind, as he said himself, and they put him in prison. He died there."

He stood looking at her with a new interest. He too, was beginning to understand. The bitter line about the mouth was not the expression of a hard, unfeeling heart after all, then, and the sharp, mocking laugh which had jarred so often on his ears was not the echo of a shallow, worthless character? They were no more than the deep wounds left after a rough battle with a world that knows no pity for those branded with inherited shame and dishonor. He had misjudged her. There were unlimited possibilities of nobility and goodness in the beautiful face lifted to his. But he said nothing of the thoughts that flashed through his mind. In moments of crisis we always speak of what is least important.

"And you managed to keep it a secret in Marut?" he asked.

"Yes, it was a marvel, wasn't it?" —her eyes brightening with a spark of the old fun. "We lived in a constant state of alarms and excursions. But Mr. Travers did what he could. He knew all about it, and he helped us."

"On conditions, no doubt?"

"Of course, on conditions. But he said, quite truthfully, that he had no idea of blackmailing me. It was just a fair bargain between us." She paused a little before she went on: "Now, you understand what brought us to Marut, and what made you such a desirable catch. We wanted to get clear away from the past and build up a new life. But we couldn't. One can't build up anything on a lie."

"That is true," he returned sternly, "and yet this is hardly a time for you to talk of your failure. From the moment that you are my wife—"

"But, John, that's what I never shall be." She laughed wearily. "Do you think a clever woman would own up to an unpleasant past to the man she wanted to marry? And if you want to hear more detestable things about me, ask the Colonel, ask Mrs. Berry, ask the Rajah. They know all about me, for I told them yesterday. You don't need to look so white and haggard. I am not going to marry you. That is what I came to say. And I wanted to explain everything, and to ask you, if you can, to forgive me all the trouble I have brought upon you." She rose, and held out her hand to him. "Will you shake hands, John?"

He stood motionless by the table, watching her with a last stirring of the old distrust.

"I do not understand you," he said bluntly, and in truth he did not. This pale-faced woman with the earnest eyes deep underlined with the marks of sleepless nights was a riddle which his stiff, conventional imagination could not solve.

"Is it necessary that you should understand?" she answered. "I have not asked you to explain why, still loving her, you threw Lois over. I believe that you had some grave reason. It could not be graver than mine for doing what I am doing."

"Then you mean that—it is entirely over between us?"

"Yes, it is over between us. Your sense of justice will not have to undergo the ordeal of forcing your sense of honor to link itself with dishonor. To your credit, I believe you would have married me, John, and I am grateful. But there's an end of it. I have come to say good-by. I suppose it is absurd, but I wish we could remain friends."

This time he took her hand in his. Now that the artificial union between them was done away with, their real friendship for each other came back and took its rightful place in their lives.

"Why shouldn't we, Beatrice?" he said. "Heaven knows, we both have need of friends."

"It is a strange thing," she continued thoughtfully, "that, though you are so completely my opposite, I have always liked you. Even when you most jarred upon me with your prunes-and-prisms morality, I was never able quite to close my heart. I wonder why?"

He could not repress a faint amusement at the flash of her old self.

"It has been the same with me," he said. "Even when you trod on all my principles at once, I haven't been able to smother a sort of shamefaced respect for you. You always seemed more worthy of respect than—well, some of the others."

"I suppose it is our sincerity," she said. "You are sincere in your goodness, and I, paradoxical as it sounds, in my badness."

"I think not," he answered, looking her gravely in the face. "I think it is because the hidden best in both of us recognized each other and held out the hand of friendship almost without our knowing."

She smiled, but he saw a light sparkle in her eyes.

"Oh, practical John, you are making fast progress in the soul's world! Who has taught you?"

He turned away from her back to the table and stood there gazing out over the garden.

"No one. It is a mood I have on today which makes me see clearer than I have done before. Go now—if any one saw you here, you know what Marut would say."

"Yes, I know Marut very well by now. Not that it much matters. Good-by. Please—I found my way alone; I can find the way out."

She had reached the door before he stopped her.

"Beatrice!"

She turned.

"What is it?"

"I have a favor to ask of you—or rather, I have a trust to put in your hands. It is in a sort of way the seal upon our good understanding. There is no one else whom I could trust so much."

She came back to his side. A new color was in her cheeks. Her eyes looked less tired, less hopeless.

"A trust? That would make life worth living."

He took up the packet on the table and gave it to her.

"That is my will. I made it afresh last night. It was witnessed this morning. In it I have made you my executrix, with half my estate. The other half I have left to Lois."

"Now you must leave it all to her," she said.

"No, I wish it to remain as it is. Besides—" He broke off hurriedly, as though seeking to avoid an unpleasant train of thought. "Beatrice, the world won't understand that will. Lois won't, and I pray, for the sake of her happiness, that she may never have to—but if the time comes when this must be put into action, I want you to give her a message from me. Will you?"

"Of course I will. But"—she faced him with a sudden inspired appeal—"must you wait until you are dead to speak to her? Would it not be better to go to her now with your message? I do not know what has come between you both, but I know this much—all forms of pretense are fatal—"

He stopped her with a gesture of decision.

"No," he said. "The secret must remain secret. It has overshadowed my life. It has laden me with a burden of responsibility and shame which I have determined to share with no one. I have taken it upon my shoulders, and I shall carry it to the end. Tell Lois that I have never once swerved in my love for her. Ask her to trust me and think kindly of me. It is not I who have sinned against her—"

"Sinned against her! Who has sinned against her? Do you mean me?"

"No, not you. You also have been sinned against. I also." He sighed wearily. "When I look about me, it seems as though not one of us has not in turn sinned and been sinned against. It is an endless chain of the wrong we do one another."

She laughed, and for the first time there rang in her voice a note of the old harshness.

"Look at me, John. There is no turn and turn about with me. From the beginning I have tricked and lied and fought my way through life. I didn't care whom I hurt so long as I got through. I sinned. Who has sinned against me?"

"One person at least," he answered significantly.

She caught her breath, and the hand that passed hastily across her forehead trembled.

"Even if it were true what you say," she said, half inaudibly, "it does not alter the fact that we must atone for what has been done."

"It is the justice of the world," he assented. "We must make good the harm we do and the harm that has been done us." He threw back his shoulders with a movement of energetic protest. "Do not let us waste time talking. We can not help each other. All I ask is—do not forget my message."

She looked at him, strangely moved.

"You talk as though you were going to die to-night," she said.

"I talk as a man does whom death has already tapped on the shoulder more than once of late," he answered, with grim humor. "Good-by, Beatrice."

"Good-by."

He pushed his writing-table to one side so that she could pass out on to the verandah.

"Do not come with me farther," she said. "The carriage is waiting outside. I would rather go alone."

He stood and watched her as she passed lightly and quickly among the rose-bushes. It was as though he were trying to engrave upon his mind the memory of a lovely picture that he was never to see again,—as though he were bidding her a final farewell. Twice she turned and glanced back at him. Was it with the same intent, guided by the same strange foreboding?

She disappeared, and the voice of a native orderly who had entered the room unheard recalled him to the reality.

"A letter for you, Captain Sahib," the man said, saluting.

Stafford took the sealed envelope and, tearing it open, ran hastily over the contents. It was from the Colonel. The subscription, as usual since the rupture in their relations, was cold and formal.

"I should be glad to see you at once," Colonel Carmichael had written. "Events occurred yesterday which I have not as yet been able to discuss with you, but which I fear are likely to have the most serious consequences. In the present weakened condition of our garrison, we can afford to run no risks. Nicholson is with me here. Your presence would simplify matters as regards forming our plans for the future."

Stafford turned to the waiting soldier.

"Present my compliments to the Colonel Sahib," he said. "I shall be with him immediately."

CHAPTER IV
STAFFORD INTERVENES

The threatening cloud which had loomed up on the horizon had acted wonders on Colonel Carmichael's constitution. At the last meeting of the Marut Diamond Company he had looked like a man whose days on the active service list were numbered. Ill-health, disappointment, and a natural pessimism had apparently left an indelible trace upon him, and Mrs. Carmichael's prophetic eye saw them both established in Cheltenham or Bath, relegated to the Empire's lumber-room—unless something happened. The something had happened. The one sound which had the power to rouse him had broken like a clap of unheralded thunder upon his ears. It was the call of danger, the war-note which had brought back to him the springtime of his youth and strength.

Stafford found him restlessly pacing backward and forward in his narrow workroom, deep in conversation with Nicholson, who stood at the table, his head bent over a map of Marut. Both men were in uniform, and it seemed to Stafford that Colonel Carmichael listened to the click of his own spurs with the pleasure of a young lieutenant. It was no longer the sound of weary routine. It was the herald of clashing sabres and the champing of impatient horses awaiting the charge; it was an echo of past warlike days which were to come again. He stood still as Stafford entered, and a flash of satisfaction passed over his face.

"I'm glad you have come," he said. "Whatever is to be done must be done at once. I suppose you know nothing?"

"Nothing," Stafford answered. "Your note was the first intimation I have received that there was anything amiss."

Colonel Carmichael grunted angrily.

"Of course you know nothing," he said, resuming his restless march about the room. "Nor did I—nor did any one. Heaven and earth, I'm beginning to think there's something wrong in our theory that whatever is going on under our noses must be too insignificant to be noticed! There, Nicholson, hurry up and tell him what you know."

Nicholson stood upright, and folding the map put it in his pocket.

"I was in the New Bazaar last night," he began curtly. "I go there regularly, as you know, disguised as one thing or another, just for the sake of having a look at the people when they don't know they are being watched. Last night there was no one there—not so much as a child or a woman. The place was dead. I admit that I was not particularly startled. I knew that there was a great festival at hand. Pilgrims have been streaming in for days past, and it was quite conceivable that some ceremony was taking place in the temple. Curiosity fortunately led me to investigate further. Myself disguised as a traveling fakir, I made my way to the Rajah's palace gates. Already on the road I was joined by a hurrying stream of men and women, principally men. My suspicions were aroused. I knew from experience that it was not a usual crowd of pilgrims. Every man was armed, not only with knives, but guns and revolvers. Some of them were undoubtedly deserted sepoys who had stolen their weapons. Moreover, they exchanged a signal which I recognized and, in order to escape detection, imitated. It was the signal which in past generations revealed one member of the Thug fraternity to another."

"Thugs!" exclaimed Stafford, with a faintly skeptical smile.

"Do not misunderstand me," Nicholson said. "I am not going to recall to your minds the nursery horrors with which our ayahs regaled our childish imaginations. I will only emphasize one fact. The Thugs were not and are not merely a band of murderous and treacherous robbers. They belong to the priesthood, they are the deputed servants of the goddess Kali, and their task is the extermination of the enemy—of the foreigner, that is to say—in this case, of ourselves."

Stafford glanced at the Colonel. The latter's face was set and grave.

"I do not for a moment suggest that the crowd with which I traveled were Thugs," Nicholson continued. "I know that they were not. But they had adopted the Thug sign because they had adopted the Thug mission. Not, however, till we had passed the gates and reached the palace did I realize the gravity of the situation. The Rajah stood on the great steps, surrounded by a body-guard of torch-bearers. He was dressed in full native costume, a blaze of gems, and wearing the royal insignia. The expression on his face was something I shall not easily forget, and at the time it was inexplicable to me. I can not describe it. I can only say that I was instantly reminded of Milton's fallen Satan as he stands above his followers, superb, dauntless, but tortured by hatred, contempt and God knows what strange minglings of remorse and anger. He greeted the crowd with the sign of death. His first words revealed to me that his allegiance to us was at an end, and that he meant to follow in his father's bloody footsteps."

Stafford stretched out his hand, catching hold of the back of a chair as if seeking support.

"Go on!" he said sharply.

"I have very little more to say. I did not wait, for I had heard enough to know that Marut was in instant danger. I made my escape as best I could, but in order to avoid notice I had to resort to circuitous paths, and only reached here this morning."

Colonel Carmichael brought his hand down angrily upon the table.

"To think that the scoundrel should have been pretending friendship all the time that he was preparing to murder us!" he exclaimed. "This comes of trusting a native!"

"Excuse me, Colonel," Nicholson answered, with emphasis. "I have every reason to believe that until yesterday Nehal Singh was our sincere ally."

"You mean to say that he stamped an armed crowd out of the earth in half an hour?"

"No. That armed crowd was the silent work of years. It was the tool which has been held ready for a long time—but not by Nehal Singh—"

"By whom, then, in the name of all—"

Nicholson drew out an old and faded photograph and handed it to the Colonel.

"Do you recognize that face?" he asked.

"Certainly I do. It is the Rajah's father—Behar Singh. How did you come by this?"

"It belonged to my father. He gave it me, and I kept it as a curiosity. Colonel, I saw that man last night at the Rajah's side."

The photograph fluttered from the Colonel's powerless fingers. He looked at Nicholson, and there flashed into his old eyes a terrible primitive passion of revenge and hatred.

"My God! He is alive—and I never knew!"

"He is alive, Colonel. And I believe that, hidden from us all, he has been working steadily and stealthily at the task which saw its completion last night. So long as Nehal Singh stood on our side he could do nothing. The people believe Nehal to be an incarnation of Vishnu, and they will only follow where he leads. Behar knew that—probably he himself had fostered the idea. He guessed, probably, that one day Nehal Singh would turn from us. He waited. Last night I saw a face of devilish triumph which told its own tale. He had not waited in vain."

Colonel Carmichael turned to Stafford and held out his hand. For the first time old friendship shone out of his eyes mingled with a fire of thirsty revenge.

"You and I have a debt to pay before we die, Stafford," he said.

Stafford's hand touched his coldly and powerlessly.

"I have nothing against the Rajah," he said hoarsely. "I can not carry out a revenge against the son—"

Colonel Carmichael interrupted him with a hard laugh.

"They are all of a piece," he said. "Say what you will, Nicholson, Nehal Singh is a traitor. We were fools to trust him. We are always fools when we do not treat a native as a dangerous animal. They murder us for our silly, sentimental confidence."

Nicholson bent down and, picking up the photograph, replaced it in his pocket.

"Do you think so, Colonel?" he said significantly. "From, my experience I have learned that you can always trust a native. You can treat him as your friend and equal so long as the inequality is there and obvious to him. I mean, so long as in everything—in generosity, in courage, and in honor—he realizes that you are his superior."

Colonel Carmichael's face darkened with anger.

"Do you mean, perhaps, that—that we are not all that?" he demanded.

"Surely not all of us. How many men think that any sort of conduct is good enough to show a native? What did Behar Singh see of our honor? He was our friend until an Englishman who had eaten and drunk his hospitality repaid him by a dishonorable theft. What has Nehal Singh seen of our superiority? In spite of his father's influence, he came to us prejudiced in our favor. He saw heroes in us all, and he trusted himself blindly in our hands. What has been the consequence? Look at yesterday's scene, as you have described it to me, Colonel. His best friend had proved himself a mean and treacherous swindler. The woman whom as I judge he regarded as a saint—forgive me, Stafford, I must be honest—no more than a heartless flirt, who had led him on from one folly to another for the sake of a little excitement—"

"Rubbish!" Colonel Carmichael burst out. "What are exceptions in a whole race?"

"In a strange country no one is an exception, Colonel. One coward, one thief, one drunkard is quite enough to cast the blackest slur upon the whole nation in the eyes of another race. As sincerely as he believed yesterday that we were all heroes, as sincerely Nehal Singh believes to-day that there isn't an honest man among us."

This time Colonel Carmichael made no answer. He went over to the window and stood there frowning obstinately out over the neglected garden. His eyes fell on the ruined bungalow, and he called Nicholson to his side.

"Look at that!" he said. "In that place Behar Singh murdered my best and only friend, Steven Caruthers. I have not forgotten and I can not forget. It has branded every native for me as a murderer. No doubt this proves your argument. From the first I shrank from all contact with the present Rajah. I distrusted him, and it is obvious now that my distrust was well founded. What do you say, Stafford? You, too, were against having anything to do with him."

To his surprise and annoyance, Stafford did not respond. He stood there with his hands clasping the back of the chair, his brows knitted in painful thought.

"Come, Stafford, what have you to say?" the Colonel repeated impatiently.

"I think there is a good deal in what Nicholson says," Stafford answered, speaking as though he had only just heard that he was being addressed. "The Rajah has not been well treated. He has a right to feel bitter. And he seemed a fine sort of man. Without prejudice, Colonel, one can not withhold a certain admiration for him. He has behaved better than some of us."

Colonel Carmichael frowned, but his sense of justice forced him to a reluctant admission.

"Yes, he has a few showy virtues. Yesterday, for instance. Under the circumstances, he behaved like a gentleman and a man of honor. Before nightfall the English share-holders in the mine got their money back in gems and rupees—he must have pulled the palace to pieces. In fact, everything might have gone off smoothly if it hadn't been for that—that—" He coughed and glanced at Stafford, not without a touch of malicious satisfaction.

"You are alluding to Miss Cary, Colonel," Stafford said, returning his glance with dignity, "and you are at liberty to say what you like, for I have no longer the right to champion her. At her request, our engagement is at an end. But as her friend I can not refrain from saying this much—she has not spared herself, and, God knows, she also has not been treated well."

What memories passed before the Colonel's mind as he stood there gazing absently in front of him! Recollections of mean and envious criticisms, ugly underhand slanders, petty intrigue, his own shame-faced patronage! And then the vision of a lovely, white-faced woman making her desperate self-accusal, and of a terrible, vulgar mother trying to hold her back with threats and pleadings! He turned at last to the two men, his own face red and troubled.

"I apologize," he said. "I apologize all around. I seem to have been insulting everybody in turn. I dare say you are all right. The Rajah may be ill-used and Miss Cary well-meaning. I don't know. And what on earth does it matter? The fat is in the fire, and here we stand chattering like old women about how it got there. Something must be done. The regiment is a day's march from here, and with a company of your Gurkhas, Nicholson, we shan't do much—scarcely hold out if they dare attack us."

"They will dare," Nicholson answered. "So much I know for certain, and it will probably be to-night. I can vouch for my men, and we must do our best until help comes. But—" He paused rather significantly.

"But what, man? Don't you think it will come in time? I have already telegraphed. They will be here in twenty-four hours. Surely we can manage so long."

"Colonel, if you had seen what I saw last night, you would not count much on help. It isn't the rising of a few unarmed men. It is the revolt of a fanatic, warlike nation led by a man. They call him God. His godhead does not matter to us. As a god we have no need to fear him; but as a man and a born leader of men, with hatred and revenge as an incentive, armed with unlimited power, he is an enemy not to be held at bay by a handful of Gurkhas and not to be conquered by a regiment."

His words had their quiet, fatal significance. Colonel Carmichael and Stafford looked at each other. Hitherto they had faced the situation coolly enough, with their eternal national optimism and self-confidence. This man had wrenched down the veil, and they stood before a chasm to which there seemed no shore, no bottom. It was the end, and they knew it.

"You mean, then, that it is all over?" the Colonel said casually. "You know more than either of us. You ought to be able to tell."

"Yes, Colonel, I should judge that it was all over, unless a miracle happens."

"We might fight our way through."

"On my way early this morning the roads were already guarded. They did not recognize me, otherwise I should not be here."

"And the women?"

All three men had grown cool and indifferent. Death had stepped in, and from that moment it was not seemly to show either trouble or excitement.

"According to my idea, the women had better be lodged here in your bungalow," Nicholson said. "The surrounding walls make it a good place of defense. The barracks are too open."

The Colonel nodded. Quite unconsciously he was letting the reins of command slip into the younger and stronger hands.

"They must be brought over at once," he assented. "Thank Heaven most of them have gone to the hills. Mrs. Berry and that—that other woman had better not be told what's up. They will only make a fuss. My wife will understand—and Lois will be all right. We must get hold of Travers, if it is only for her sake. It would serve him right if we left him to his fate."

Stafford took a step forward.

"I have a suggestion to make, Colonel," he said.

Colonel Carmichael looked at him. Throughout the interview Stafford had acted and spoken like a man who is weighed down by a burden of terrible doubt and perplexity. He alone of the three men had shown the first sign of emotion, and emotion in the face of death was for the Colonel no better than fear. His face hardened.

"Well," he said, "what is it?"

"Rajah Nehal Singh is not a barbarian," Stafford began. "I believe he would listen to reason if one of us could get hold of him. He seems to have his country's welfare at heart, and if it was explained to what horrible bloodshed he was leading it—"

"There must be no cringing!" Colonel Carmichael interrupted sharply.

"It will not be a case of cringing. We could simply put the matter before him."

"There is something in what Stafford says," Nicholson agreed. "From what I know of the Rajah, he seems both reasonable and humane. He may have yielded to his father's importunities in a fit of anger, and is perhaps already wishing himself well out of the mess. For the women's sake, Colonel, we ought to have a shot—and not all for the women's sake, either. Heaven knows what this business will cost England if it comes to a head!"

Colonel Carmichael bit his lip impatiently. He did not recognize his own motives of desiring a last hand-to-hand struggle. They were those of an old man who sees Cheltenham and stagnation looming in the distance and prays for death. But his common sense conquered the selfish promptings.

"Who would be likely to undertake the mission with any hope of success?" he asked.

"Nehal Singh and I were, toward the end, rather more than friendly," Nicholson began. "I believe he entertained a real liking for me—"

"If any one goes, I must!" The interruption came from Stafford. His head was raised. He faced the two men with a stern determination. "No, Nicholson; I know all you want to say. I have no sort of sympathy with the natives—I haven't your power over them. But this is different. I have a power. I may have. Let me go. If I fail, then you can try."

"By the time you have failed it will be too late," Nicholson returned. He was watching Stafford with almost pitying curiosity. His keen instinct penetrated the man's strained and nervous bearing to some conflict which seemed to have had its birth with the first mention of Nehal Singh's name.

"It will not be too late," Stafford answered persistently. "I ask for an hour, Colonel. In an hour I shall know—whether—whether I have the power."

"Captain Stafford, are you mad!" the Colonel said sternly. "This is not a time for experiments."

"I ask for an hour," Stafford repeated, and there was an emphasis and earnestness in his voice which cut short Colonel Carmichael's angry sarcasm. "At the end of that time Nicholson can do what he likes. I am not mad. I beg of you to ask no questions. I can not answer them. I can only tell you that I have a great responsibility—toward you all and toward another."

Colonel Carmichael was silent for a moment. Stafford's manner awed and troubled him in spite of himself.

"Very well," he said at last. "I give you an hour. During that time we will make preparations for the worst." He took out his watch. "It is now eleven. At twelve the matter passes into Nicholson's hands."

Stafford saluted.

"I understand, Colonel."

Nicholson accompanied him toward the door.

"God-speed!" he said simply. Stafford hesitated, his heavy eyes resting on the fine face of his brother-officer with an almost passionate gratitude.

"Thank you, Nicholson, thank you. God help me to do what is right!"

He turned and hurried from the room.

CHAPTER V
MURDER

Archibald Travers stood in his favorite attitude by the window, his shoulder propped against the casement, his arms folded, a smile of good-natured amusement on his healthy face.

"My dear child," he protested, "what earthly interest can it have for you to know the pros and cons of the business? You wouldn't understand, and that small head would ache for a week afterward. Be content with the outline of the thing. Of course it has all been frightfully unfortunate. But the Rajah wasn't to be held back. He believed the mine was going to be the making of Marut—and for a matter of fact so did I at first, otherwise I shouldn't have put all my money in it. The fellow had an enthusiasm and confidence which fairly carried us off our feet. Well, it's done, and it's no use crying about it. The best thing we can do is to clear out of Marut as fast as we can. People are bound to be disagreeable about it."

"The Carys are ruined too?" she asked.

"Oh, I don't know—they have lost a bit, I suppose." His voice sounded unpleasant. "At any rate, I'll say that for them—they behaved as people of their extraction would behave. First the mother poured out a torrent of abuse over the poor Rajah which would have been the envy of a fish-wife, and then the daughter turned on me." He laughed. "It was a most powerful scene of feminine hysterics. I was glad that you were not there."

Lois sat silent, her head resting on her hand, her eyes fixed thoughtfully on the table.

"And what are we going to do?" she asked at last. "You take the matter so easily, but if we are really ruined—"

He laid his hand affectionately on her shoulder.

"*I* am ruined, Lois. I did not say that you were. Even with your rather low opinion of me, you could hardly have supposed that I would touch your money. You are well enough off to do what you like. As for me—" he squared his shoulders—"I feel quite capable of starting things all over again."

His tone touched her. She looked up, and her face softened. There was nothing that could have made her happier than to have discovered in her husband some elements of courage and sincerity.

"Of course, Archibald, whatever is mine is yours," she said. "You must have known that."

"My dear generous little woman!" He bent over her and kissed her, apparently unconscious that she instinctively drew back from his caress. "If you really will help me, no doubt I shall build things up again in no time, and this one blunder won't count for much. You are a worthy comrade for a man."

Perhaps he had accepted her offer too quickly, perhaps his tone jarred on her as too elated, too satisfied. She got up, pushing her letters quickly to one side.

"You really wish us to start for Madras to-night?"

"Yes, if you can manage it. It is important that I should get back as soon as possible, and the business here is finished."

"Very well. I will pack up as much as I can. The rest must be sent on afterward."

He let her reach the door before he stopped her again.

"By the way, Lois, there is one thing I must ask you. I do not wish you to have any further intercourse with that Beatrice Cary. She is not a person with whom I should wish my wife to associate. You were right about her—she is a bad, unscrupulous woman."

With her hand on the curtain she turned and looked back at him. A cloud of curious distrust passed over her pale face.

"I never said that she was bad or unscrupulous. I do not believe that she is. You say that now, but it was not your old opinion."

"I suppose it is possible to see people in different and less agreeable lights?" he retorted sharply.

"Only too possible. But as she was never a friend of mine, and we are leaving within the next few hours, the injunction to avoid her is unnecessary." She paused as though listening. "I hear some one talking to the syce," she went on hurriedly. "It sounds like Captain Stafford's voice. Archibald"—she turned and came quickly to his side—"please let me out of the verandah. I don't want to meet him."

He caught her by the wrist and pushed her back. The movement was brutal, unlike his usual gentleness, and she saw by the expression of his face that for the moment he had lost all consciousness of what he was doing.

"I don't want to see him either. Go and tell him that I am not at home— that I have started for Madras—quick! Don't stand there staring."

His extraordinary excitement, apparently unreasonable and entirely opposed to his calm, easy-going habits, had the effect of setting fire to her dormant suspicion. She wrenched herself free.

"I am not going to tell him a lie," she said firmly.

"Lois, you are a little fool! Do as I tell you. It isn't a lie—only a piece of conventional humbug which everybody understands. There, please!" His tone of entreaty was more disagreeable to her than his roughness. All the pride and rigidity of her Puritan temperament was up in arms against the indefinable something which it had long ago recognized and despised.

"It is not conventional humbug," she retorted—"not in this case. You are lying because you are afraid, because you have a reason for not seeing Captain Stafford which you won't tell me."

He had not time to answer. The curtains were pushed on one side, and Stafford entered hurriedly. He was covered with dust and looked haggard and exhausted. He did not seem to see Lois, though she stood immediately in front of him. His eyes passed over her head to Travers.

"I am sorry to come in unannounced," he said, without giving either an opportunity to speak, "but your servant was making difficulties, and I have not a minute to lose. I have galloped every inch of the way here from the Colonel's bungalow. I must speak to you at once, Travers, alone."

Lois went toward the door. As she passed him she saw him look at her for the first time. And she went her way blinded with tears that had no cause save in the stern, unhappy face which had flashed its message to her. For she knew that his glance had been a message; that he had tried to explain, and that she had not understood. The curtain fell behind her, and Stafford crossed the room to Travers' side.

"You have heard what has happened?" he demanded.

Travers had resumed his old attitude of indifference. Only his eyes betrayed the uneasiness which he was really feeling.

"Do you mean the Rajah? No, I haven't heard anything, but if he is making himself a nuisance, I am not surprised. I expected it."

"Don't talk like that!" Stafford exclaimed, bringing his clenched hand down on the table. "How dare you! Have you no sense of responsibility? For you it was no more than a doubtful speculation, and you took care that there were no risks; but for Marut it means—Heaven knows what it means!"

"Nothing!" returned Travers coolly. "Nothing to get heated about. The Rajah feels sore, no doubt, but that will pass. And that is not my fault. It would have been all right if Miss Cary had not—well, made such a fool of herself, and incidentally of us all."

Stafford gazed steadily at the man who smiled at him. He could not understand a character so absolutely without all moral foundations.

"You are no doubt preparing to start for Madras?" he asked, controlling his voice with a strong effort.

"Certainly. There is nothing more to be done here."

"Let me tell you that you are not likely to leave Marut alive."

Travers laughed.

"Nonsense, my dear Captain! I am not to be frightened with nursery tales."

"It is not a nursery tale. I give you my word of honor that before nightfall we shall be overwhelmed by a force a hundred times larger than anything we can bring on the field for weeks to come."

Travers shifted his position carelessly. Stafford had not succeeded in frightening him. He did not believe in native rebellions. What he had seen of the Hindu character convinced him of its fundamental cowardice and incapability for independent action.

"A few blank cartridges will bring the Rajah very quickly to his senses," he assured Stafford, with perfect good-humor. "We have nothing to be afraid of in that quarter."

"You really think that?" Stafford demanded significantly. "Knowing what you know, you think we have no cause to fear him?"

Travers changed color. The uneasy flicker in his eyes returned.

"What on earth do you mean?"

"You know very well. You know whom we shall be fighting against."

"Of course—a headlong, inexperienced Hindu prince—"

"You are choosing to have a very short memory. Nehal Singh is more than that."

Travers stood upright. The healthy glow had died out of his cheeks.

"Look here, Stafford," he said roughly, "what is it you want? I can see you want something."

"Yes. Give me back my promise. I can not keep it any longer."

"Do you think I extort promises that I don't want kept? Are you in earnest?"

"Yes, terribly in earnest. Look the thing in the face, Travers. Our lives, and, what is far more, the lives of our women and Heaven knows how many of our countrymen, hang in the balance. If you don't believe me, ask Nicholson."

"I shall believe what I like!" Travers began to pace backward and forward, his mind busy with lightning calculations. Before nightfall they would be out of Marut. Stafford was exaggerating the danger, perhaps for his own purposes. The whole thing was nonsense.

"I keep you to your promise," he said obstinately.

Stafford lifted his head. The man's natural reserve and conventionalism were borne down by the sense of his helplessness. He was fighting against a giant of egoism, as it seemed to him, of gross and criminal stupidity, for the lives of untold hundreds.

"You can not realize what you are doing," he said. "It is our one hope of holding the Rajah's hand, and with every moment the danger is increasing. As I came along the road I passed crowds of natives on the way to the palace. Most of them were men from your mine, Travers, and they had an ugly look. They did not touch me, it is true, but I believe they are only waiting for Nehal Singh's order, and then it will be too late. Travers, we must do everything in our power to prevent him giving that order. I have promised Colonel Carmichael to do what I could. At twelve I must be back, or—"

Travers swung around. His face was livid.

"You told him—?"

"No, but I must. I can not keep my promise. You must set me free. I gave it you because you told me that I was not concerned. Now I am concerned, I dare not keep silence."

"My dear fellow, you must—that is, if you are a man of honor."

"Of what use is the secret to you?"

"That is my affair. There was a time when you were anxious enough to keep it."

"It was for Lois' sake. The two things were bound up together. She can not be spared any longer."

"You think not? I am of another opinion. I put my wife's peace of mind higher than your old-maidish alarms." Travers faced his companion with the assurance of a man who feels that he has the whip-hand. His experience taught him that a man of certain orthodox principles has a very limited sphere of action. He runs in herds with hundreds of other men of the same mould, and under given circumstances has only one course of conduct open to him. Had Travers been in Stafford's place, no one living could have told what he would do. But Stafford had no choice—at least, so Travers judged.

"You are one of honor's Pharisees, my dear fellow," he said frankly. "You can't get out of your promise, and you know it. You cling to the letter of the law. It is your way. You had better go back to the Colonel and tell him to manage the Rajah in his own style."

The clock on the table chimed the half-hour. It was ten minutes' full gallop back to the Colonel's bungalow. Stafford set his teeth in a white heat of despair.

"If you have no consideration for the Station, for your own wife, for your own country, at least consider yourself!" he exclaimed. "Are you blind to the danger? We have scarcely fifty men, and up there are thousands quietly waiting for the Rajah's signal. You must have seen them with your own eyes pouring through—"

"I saw any amount of dirty pilgrims, and got out of the way as fast as I could," was Travers' smiling retort.

Stafford stood baffled and helpless. For the first time he was able to recognize and appreciate a certain type of Englishman to which he himself to some extent belonged—an arrogant ignoramus who, encamped behind his wall of superiority, fears nothing because he sees nothing, and sees nothing because outside the walls there can not possibly be anything worth looking at. Nicholson had torn down Stafford's imagined security, and he stood aghast at his old insolent self-confidence as reflected in Travers' smiling face.

"To be quite honest with you," the latter went on, after a moment's pause, "I have very little faith in our dreadful danger. Admitted that I led the Rajah on a more than doubtful speculation, admitted that Miss Cary went further than she need have done, it is still most unlikely that his injured feelings are going to lead him to such a desperate step as to enter into conflict with the whole Empire. Believe me, Stafford, the idea is ridiculous, and I have not the least intention of throwing up my own hard-won security—"

It was a bad slip, and he knew it. Stafford, who had stood with his face half averted, in an attitude of irresolution, swung round.

"Your security?" he echoed.

Travers shrugged his shoulders. He had made a mistake, but he saw no reason to be afraid of Stafford or of any one in Marut.

"I said 'my security,'" he repeated.

Stafford clenched his fists. The expression on his gaunt, rugged face showed that he had understood the full import of Travers' words.

"You blackguard!" he said under his breath.

Travers turned scarlet.

"Mind yourself, Captain Stafford. You may find yourself outside the door quicker than you care for it!"

"You blackguard!" Stafford repeated furiously. "I haven't a better name for you. You have simply humbugged me with your lies about Lois and your devotion to her—"

Travers strode at him.

"How dare you!"

"Don't bluster, Travers! It can't hide what I see. You married Lois for her money—"

"Hold your infernal tongue!"

"And now you are afraid. Well, you shall have some cause." He picked up his helmet, which lay on the table. "I gave you my promise because you assured me it was for Lois' happiness, and I believed you. According to my ideas, both of them were better left in ignorance. I did not know that you had your own motives—silly fool that I am!" He turned to hurry from the room. Travers barred his way.

"What are you going to do?"

"I shall tell the Colonel the truth!"

"It will break his heart."

"I do not believe it. Out of the way, Travers!"

"And then?"

"Rajah Nehal Singh shall be told."

"Have you considered the consequences?"

"I have."

"Lois will be ruined!"

"*You* will be ruined. Lois will have my protection, thank God!"

The two men faced each other an instant in silence. Travers' face betrayed a curious complex emotion of desperation and shame. He had been called a blackguard, and the word had stung like the cut of a horse-whip. He had never believed it possible that any man should have the right to use such a term—to him, the embodiment of geniality, good-humor and good-nature. He did not believe even now that any one had the right. He was not an unprincipled man—not in the sense that he had ever consciously done wrong. He did not know what wrong was—his one conception being an act putting him within reach of the law; and of such an indiscretion he had never been guilty. Throughout his scheming he had always pictured himself as a complaisant Napoleon of finance, combining business with pleasure. His conduct toward Lois had been based on this standpoint. He was genuinely fond of her, and is there any law forbidding a man to lay firm hold upon his wife's money? Yet Stafford had called him a blackguard, and Stafford was the world—the world of respectability of which Travers had believed himself a gifted member. For the moment the incomprehensible insult was more to him than the coming danger to which his plans were put.

"You look at me as though I had committed a crime!" he exclaimed, in a tone of injured protest.

"You have," Stafford answered steadily. "You have fooled me, playing on my prejudices, and God knows what other weaknesses. I won't say anything of that. I deserve my share of blame. But you have tricked and deceived a woman. You have deceived an honorable man into a dishonorable venture. You have brought disaster on your own country. You are no more than a common adventurer. You are the parasite to whom we owe all our misfortunes, and—"

"Stafford, take care!"

"Out of the way! I am going to put an end to it all!"

Travers flung the excited man back. Shame is a dangerous poison in the blood of base natures. It is merely the precursor to a state of absolute license where self-control, self-respect are flung to the winds and the devil is set free to work his full, unchecked will. Travers glared at Stafford, hating his upright bearing, his upright indignation with a violence to which murder would have been the only true expression.

"You are not going till I have your promise to hold your tongue!" he said between his teeth.

Stafford flung the other's detaining hand from him. Freed from his laming diseased conscience, and roused to activity, he acted like a man of lightning determination and iron will.

"That you will never have, and you are a scoundrel to ask for it. As you like—there are other exits than the door." He swung round and made for the open window.

Travers did not stop him. He stood rooted to the spot, his hand on the revolver which he carried at his side. The revolver had not been meant for Stafford. Travers' quick eyes had caught sight of something creeping slowly and stealthily up the verandah steps. He had seen the flash of a knife, and a cry of warning had rushed to his lips. The cry was never uttered. Devil and angel fought their last battle over Travers' drifting, rudderless nature. The word "scoundrel" had been the devil's winning cast.

"Go, then, and be damned to you!" Travers shrieked.

He saw Stafford reach the verandah steps. The stalwart khaki-clad figure was photographed on his reeling brain. He heard the clank of a sword against the first stone step. He tried to cry out—afterward he tried to believe that he had cried out—but it was too late. The hidden something which had crouched behind the heavy creepers sprang up—for a short second seemed to tower above the unconscious officer—then a gleam of light flashed down with the black hand. Stafford flung up his arms, swung around, and fell face downward on the verandah. There was a short, stifled groan, and then— and then only—Travers fired.

CHAPTER VI
CLEARING AWAY THE RUBBISH

All the night following the momentous meeting of the Marut Diamond Company Mrs. Cary had kept to her room, the door locked against her daughter, and had sobbed and wailed in a manner befitting the victim of a hard and undeserved fate.

But in reality hers was the rage of a clumsy workman who has cut himself with his own tools. Her own child, her partner and co-worker, had upset the erection of years. She saw themselves cast out of Marut; she saw the desolate wandering over the earth's surface, this time without the consolation and protection of wealth. For she knew that Beatrice's confession was to go further. Beatrice had made the announcement of her plans quietly but firmly as they had driven home from the club-house.

"To-morrow everybody shall know everything there is to know," she had said, and had remained obdurate to all her mother's commands and pleadings. "I do consider you. I consider you even now. I mean to save you and myself. But this time it must be in another way. Your scheming has only brought us into deeper trouble. We must start afresh."

"But how? But how?" her mother had said, wringing her hands in uncontrolled despair. "Where are we to start? How are we ever going to make people believe in us, now we have no money?"

"It does not matter what people believe," Beatrice had replied. "With our money and our lies we have been building mud-hovels, and now we are going to build palaces. That's all that matters."

Mrs. Cary had not understood. She thought Beatrice had gone mad, and knowing that with madness, reasoning is in vain, she shut herself up in her room, pulled down the blinds, and believed by this ostrich-like proceeding that she could keep off the inevitable moment when they would have to be pulled up again and the cold, pitiless reality faced.

But Beatrice went her way undeterred. From Stafford's bungalow she drove to the Travers'. The place was little more than an ill-cared-for shanty, the garden overgrown with weeds, the rooms damp, ill-aired and badly furnished, its reputation for misfortune phenomenal. Travers had taken it as the only bungalow to be had for such a short period as he intended to stay in Marut, and Lois had made no objection. Her energy and determined striving after everything that was graceful and beautiful was systematically crushed out of sight. She never protested, never laid any difficulties in Travers' path. She seemed to shrink into herself and live an invisible life of her own, leaving him to go his way. She could not help him. She could build up nothing on a character whose foundations were of shifting sand.

And never had she been more fully convinced of her own powerlessness and of his absolute independence than after their brief and stormy interview before Stafford's entry. She had felt how for a moment their two diametrically opposed natures had faced each other. She had felt a brief joyful satisfaction in at last coming to a hand-to-hand struggle with him; but then, as usual, with a smile and an easy word he had eluded her. So it had always been—so it would always be. Too late she realized that she had thrown away her life upon a man who had no need of her devotion. Too late she realized that all sacrifices are wasted unless the ennobling of the sacrificer's character be considered. For true happiness, true content and goodness can not be given. They must be self-won, or they are no more than hothouse plants which shrivel together in the cold blast of an east wind. Lois had sacrificed herself to bring true happiness and content and goodness into Travers' life, and had failed. She had failed all the more signally because she had never loved him. She had loved Stafford—extraordinary and terrible as it seemed to her, she still loved him. She could not root him out of her life, and though his image was overshadowed by a greater and more noble figure he retained his place.

The glance they had exchanged had pierced down to the very center of her being, and if it had revealed nothing to her it had also revealed everything. For she knew now that the strange bond which had linked them together from the beginning united them still. Some reckless and unscrupulous hand had sundered them outwardly, and her instinct, guided by a hundred significant incidents, told her whose hand it had been. She fled to her little gloomy sitting-room, with its worn-out, tasteless furniture and drab walls, and fought her sorrow and despair single-handed and in her own way. She had a man's dislike for tears—though, being a woman, they came all too easily to her—and she fought against them now with all the strength at her command, with all the pluck which in happier days had made her so splendid a partner in a "losing game." She had made a disastrous mistake in her life, but it was not too late.

The cathedral should go on in its unseen growth, and every conquered tear, every brave smile was a fresh stone bringing it nearer to perfection. God be thanked for the fetishes with which the less fortunate of us are still allowed to adorn the barren walls of our life! The cathedral, the imaginary "sheltering-place for others," was Lois' fetish, and the thought of it and of the strong-faced man with whom she worked in spiritual partnership was a deep, inspiring consolation. It stood at her right hand and helped partly to overthrow the weight of dread and evil presentiment which had borne down upon her all too sensitive and superstitious temperament as she had left her husband and Stafford alone.

Thus it was that, when the curtains of her room were suddenly parted and Beatrice stood on the threshold, she could face the new-comer with a calm if grave demeanor. She remembered her husband's last injunctions, but it was too late; and moreover, there was an expression on Beatrice's face which told her that the visit was no ordinary one. A woman's instinct is her spiritual hand feeling through the darkness to another's soul. Beatrice and Lois watched each other without smile or greeting. They forgot the outward formalities of life in the suddenly aroused interest which they found in each other, in the consciousness that in this, their first meeting alone, they were to become closely united.

They were indeed striking contrasts. At no time had they seemed more so than now, as they stood there silently facing each other—Beatrice, tall, fair with the wonderful Madonna beauty; Lois, small and dark, the quick and fiery temperament flashing to meet the other's dignity and apparent calm. And yet at no time had the barrier between them been so insignificant, so slight. Beatrice advanced slowly from the door, where she had first hesitated.

"May I speak with you, Mrs. Travers?" she asked.

Lois nodded, mechanically holding out her hand. Her eyes were riveted on the other's grave face, drinking in with a real admiration a loveliness from which the old marring lines of mockery and cynicism had been swept away.

"Won't you sit down?" she said gently. "You look tired and pale."

Beatrice seemed not to hear. She took the outstretched hand between both her own. Her head was a little bent, and as she looked full into Lois' face her expression softened and saddened.

"You, too, are unhappy!" she said.

Lois made no answer. She was overwhelmed by the directness of the statement, but still more by the change in Beatrice's voice. It sounded low and unsteady, as though a storm of feeling lay close beneath the surface. "Do you wonder how I know?" Beatrice went on, after an instant's pause.

"I don't know," Lois answered, "and for the moment we won't talk about such things. I can't bear to see you look so—so ill. You must sit there and let me get you something to drink. Have you walked?"

Beatrice yielded this time to the kindly persuasion. She sank down in the proffered chair, but she retained Lois' hand.

"No, I drove. But I am tired. It was not easy work getting through the crowd. They did not seem to want to let me pass. Once or twice I thought they were going to attack me."

Lois laughed.

"They are only pilgrims. They come every year, and are quite harmless. Hark at them now! There must be a band of them going past. Would you like to watch from the verandah? It is really amusing—"

"No, no; this is not the time for amusement. I have something else to do. Mrs. Travers, you are very kind to me. You have the right to hate me."

"I—hate you? Why should I, Beatrice?"

"You call me Beatrice. But we have never been friends."

"Not till now."

"Do you think we are going to be?"

Lois drew up a stool and seated herself at Beatrice's side. Something in the other's firm, gentle hold and in the low voice made her heart ache.

"I don't know. I feel as though we were already."

"Don't feel that, because it is not possible. Mrs. Travers, do you know who it was who came between you and John Stafford?" Lois' head sank. "I see that you do. Yes, I did my best. I wanted his position—and money. Are you still my friend?"

Lois met the grave, questioning eyes with a sudden energy.

"Yes. That is all over and past. I like you now. I liked you the moment you entered the room. You seemed different."

Beatrice smiled faintly.

"And you, too, are different from any one I have ever known. Another woman would not have been able to forgive as you have done. I have spoiled your life. I can see that."

Lois pressed her hand.

"Hush! You must not say so. I am married—"

"Lois, I have spoiled your life. I have come here to tell you the truth, and you also must be truthful. For pity's sake, let us put lies and humbug on one side. I am sick of them!" For a moment she seemed to fight desperately with herself, and then she went on more quietly: "I have spoiled your life. I have spoiled the life of a man who trusted me. I have spoiled my own. That is what I have done in the twenty-five years given me to work in. I have lied and cheated my way through. And this is the end—miserable bankruptcy."

"Yes," Lois said, nodding. "I heard about it."

"About what? Has your husband told you?"

"The Marut Company has failed."

Beatrice sat silent a moment. Her free hand supported the firmly moulded chin, her eyes were fixed thoughtfully in front of her.

"I did not mean that sort of bankruptcy," she said at last. "That doesn't count, Lois. I used to think it meant the worst sort of misfortune, but it doesn't. The inner bankruptcy is worse. The loss of self-respect, of honor, of the trust of those one—cares for—" Again the low voice trembled dangerously, but she went on: "Don't commiserate with me, kind-hearted little woman. I don't need your pity—now. Bankruptcy isn't so bad. It is better than living on false credit. When the crash is over, one picks oneself up again. Hope is eternal, and on the ruins—"

"One can build cathedrals," Lois interposed dreamily.

"Yes, or palaces. But first the old rubbish must be cleared away. One must pay one's debts. I have very many to pay. First to you, Lois—"

"Don't! I have told you that that is all over."

"—and then to Captain Stafford. Lois, I did want to take him away from you, but I never succeeded. It was something else that did it—something which I have never understood."

"But which my husband knows?"

Beatrice nodded. She was not there to spare Lois or herself. She was there to tell the truth.

"Yes, he knows. But it is a mystery which we shall never penetrate. At any rate, I have set Captain Stafford free."

Lois said nothing. Her thoughts were busy trying to piece together the secret. With every moment distrust and suspicion were taking stronger hold upon her.

"Lois," Beatrice went on, "that is the least of it all. The worst of all is that I can not pay my debts alone. I must go on ruining others. I must ruin you."

Lois stiffened. She sat upright, as though preparing herself for a shock which she dimly anticipated.

"Tell me what you mean," she said.

"You remember it was I who tempted Rajah Nehal Singh into forming the Marut Company—"

"That is not what you want to say. It was my husband's scheme."

"Very well, it was our scheme, if you like. At any rate, the whole responsibility rests—or should rest—upon our shoulders. We have ruined him, and we have ruined hundreds of others. It is only fair that we should bear our share of the calamity."

"And haven't we done so? You have lost all your money. That is punishment enough. And Archie, too—" She paused, a fierce note of defiance ringing out with her last words. Beatrice made no answer, and the two women looked at each other in significant silence. "You don't mean that—that it was—dishonest?"

"I have no doubt Mr. Travers believed the mine was going to be a success. But it has failed, and the whole burden of the failure rests upon others, not upon him."

"My husband is ruined, too. All his money is gone."

"Yours remains."

"Yes, but—" She stammered and broke off helplessly.

Beatrice said nothing more. She saw the process of rapid thought on her companion's working face. She knew there was no need to explain further the careful precautions which Travers had made for his own safety. She knew that for his wife there was only one action possible. Lois rose to her feet.

"You must forgive me," she said, a new and dangerous light in her dark eyes. "I am very slow and stupid about business matters, but I understand what you have been trying to say to me. You have pointed out a duty to me which otherwise, in my ignorance, I might have overlooked. My husband has incurred responsibilities which must be met—if not by him, at any rate by me. No third person shall take his share of the burden—certainly not the Rajah, who was no more than the tool which my husband used. I would be glad if you would let every one know that of course my money will go toward refunding those whom the failure of the mine has injured."

Beatrice rose also. She put her two hands on Lois' shoulders.

"You needn't do it," she said. "The money is yours. It is a thing that is done every day. The world won't say much if you stick to what is yours."

"It is not mine. My husband's responsibilities are my responsibilities." She paused, and then went on quietly: "Thank you for explaining to me. I should never have understood myself, and Archie—no doubt dreads having to tell me that of course my money must go, too." She looked Beatrice full in the face, and they understood each other. There are some lies which a loyal woman must carry with her to the grave. Beatrice bent and kissed the cold face.

"You do right," she said. "I knew you would. That is why I came to you. I have helped to bring down all this misfortune on Marut. I have helped to lower us all in the eyes of those—those who used and ought to look up to us. Now you are going to lift us out of the mire—Lois, what was that?"

The two women clung to each other. Hitherto there had been no sound in the adjoining room save the regular rise and fall of two voices. Now the startled listeners heard the report of a revolver, followed by a sudden, absolute silence. Lois shook herself free from Beatrice's instinctive clutch.

"It is in my husband's room!" she said hoarsely. "Stay here! I will go—"

She hurried across the room and, thrusting open a curtained door, disappeared. The next instant Beatrice heard a cry which overcame every hesitation. Horror and despair called her in that sound, and the next moment she followed Lois' footsteps. She did not know what she expected to see. Afterward she believed that at the back of her mind there had been some thought of suicide. But it was not Travers' head that she saw pillowed against Lois' knee. Travers stood on the verandah, the smoking pistol still in his hand, his face livid and damp with fear. At his feet his wife was bending over the body of a man whom Beatrice recognized with a shock of pain.

"What has happened?" she asked breathlessly. "What has happened?"

Travers turned and stared at her. His eyes were glazed, and for the moment he did not seem to know who she was.

"Captain Stafford has—been murdered!" he stammered. "He was going down the steps when a native attacked him. I—fired, but it was too late. Oh, thank God! Here is Colonel Carmichael!"

True enough, it was the Colonel himself who sprang up the verandah steps. From beyond the ill-kept garden they heard the tramp of men and a low, continuous sound, like the threatening moan of the wind. On the verandah reigned a complete and awestruck silence. Colonel Carmichael bent over the unconscious man.

"This is the beginning," he said somberly. "How did it happen?"

"A native must have been lying in wait for him," Travers answered. "He struck at him with this." He held out a three-inch blade in a hand which shook like a child's. "I tried to save him, but I couldn't. The man escaped, though I think I hit him."

The Colonel knelt down by Lois' side, and drawing out his brandy-flask tried to force a few drops between the purple lips.

"We were expecting him every minute," he said, "but we couldn't wait. The danger was too pressing. Here, man—it's all right. Look up."

Captain Stafford's heavy eyelids had wavered. The Colonel shifted him into a higher position, his head still resting against Lois' knee. When the dying eyes opened they fell straight on the sweet dark face bent over him in loving pity.

"Lois!" he whispered faintly. "Lois—my—kiss me!"

Lois looked up at her husband. He nodded without meeting her eyes. Her lips rested on the chilly forehead.

"Dear John!"

"Lois—you—tell the Rajah——" He struggled fiercely for breath and his raised hand pointed piteously at Travers. "Tell him—not—his own"— The words died into a choked silence.

"Brandy—here! He's trying to say something. What is it, man?"

Stafford turned with a last effort, his lips parted. A second time he pointed with a desperate insistency at Travers—then with a sudden quick-drawn sigh he sank back, his face against Lois' shoulder. Colonel Carmichael, who knew death too well, rose heavily to his feet.

"It's all over," he said. "We can do nothing more for him, and we must leave him. Come, Lois."

His stern command roused her from her stupor of half-incredulous sorrow. Gently she laid the lifeless head upon the cushions which Beatrice had brought, and crossed the hands over the quiet breast. This time she fought in vain against the blinding tears. They fell on the face of the dead man, and, moved by an irresistible impulse, she bent once more and kissed him.

"God bless you, John!" Then she rose and faced her husband. "I can not help it," she said. "He is dead."

Travers said nothing. He was clinging to the verandah, and his face was grey. Outside the noise and confusion had increased. They could hear yells and imprecations, and a stone whizzed through the trees, falling a few feet short of where the little party stood. Colonel Carmichael shook Travers by the arm.

"Don't stand there like that!" he said, his voice rough with contempt. "It can't be helped, and I dare say we shan't any of us be much better off by to-morrow. I have a patrol outside waiting to take the ladies over to my bungalow. Mrs. Cary and Mrs. Berry are already there. There isn't a moment to be lost. Rouse yourself and look to Lois. I will escort Miss Cary." He turned to Beatrice with a stiff bow. "The enemy must at least find us united."

"The enemy!" exclaimed Beatrice sharply.

"The Rajah is our enemy," was the bitter answer. "You and Travers best know why."

The two women exchanged one brief glance. Lois crossed the intervening space and took her husband's arm.

"Archibald," she said, slowly and emphatically, "if this trouble has anything to do with the mine, it would be well to let the Rajah know that we also take our share. There must be no suspicion that—that we have not acted honorably or have shirked our responsibilities."

He stared at her with dull, listless eyes.

"What do you mean, Lois? He knows I haven't a brass cent."

"But I have. And of course my money must go to refund those whom you have unintentionally ruined."

That roused him. He flung her on one side, with a desperate, goaded curse.

"Your money! How dare you! It's not your money. Half of it is mine. I settled it on you."

"If it is yours, I will give it back to you. You will use it as I say. If not, I shall use it for you."

Colonel Carmichael had reached the garden. He turned now, and there was a gleam of satisfaction in his eyes.

"That's spoken like an honorable woman, Lois!" he said. "God bless you for it. But it's too late. Nicholson has already gone to Nehal Singh. If he fails, there won't be any time to explain. Come on, or we shall have to fight our way through."

He hurried on through the garden, Beatrice at his side. Husband and wife stood an instant alone, the body of poor Stafford between them. Lois' face was grave and contemptuous.

"I do not know what you have done," she said—"I do not understand what part you played in John's life or in mine, nor how far you are innocent or guilty of bringing about all this misfortune—but I know this much—we shall take our share of trouble."

"Lois, you are my wife! You have no right to go against me."

"I have the right where my honor—where your honor—is concerned. I have the right to refuse to commit an act of gross injustice." She glanced down once more at the quiet face of the man who had held so persistently upon her life and heart, and her firmly compressed lips trembled. "Oh, Archie, was it worth while—just for a little bit of gain? Was it worth while? We might all have been so happy!"

He said nothing. His rage had sunk into a sullen, dogged defiance. The roar of voices beyond the compound suddenly subsided. They heard the Colonel's voice issuing a sharp command and the thud of grounded rifles.

"We must go," she said.

He followed her down the steps, his face painfully averted from the figure that lay motionless upon the ground. The world is but a reflection of ourselves. The sunshine is sad or joyful according to our moods. We read threats and promises in the smiles of others as our own heart is hopeful or distrusting. And for Travers, with the bloodstained hand, the poor lifeless body of his enemy had become the towering shadow of an approaching Nemesis.

CHAPTER VII
IN THE TEMPLE OF VISHNU

Nicholson rode his horse slowly through the crowd of dark, threatening faces. He did not hurry or show any sign of impatience, anger or fear. In his left hand he carried a riding-whip, but he made no use of it except as an encouragement to his well-trained charger, whose nose and broad breast forced a passage, like a ship through the waves of a turbulent sea, and otherwise he was absolutely unarmed. A spectator ignorant of the truth might have taken him for an officer riding out on some ordinary duty, so little did the weight and seriousness of his real errand appear written on the strong face beneath the shadow of the helmet.

There was no opposition to his progress. His keen eyes noticed as he passed out of the residential quarter that, on the contrary, the crowd formed a sort of disordered escort which surged restlessly but silently about him. One man even laid hold upon his hanging bridle and led the horse through the less dense passages; but the action was not a friendly one, and though no threats were uttered, Nicholson read a passionate bitterness and distrust upon the faces that thrust themselves across his path or sprang up unexpectedly at his knee. For the most part they were men well known to him by sight. They belonged to working caste whose circles had supplied Nehal Singh with his best workmen, though here and there Nicholson caught sight of the turbaned head of a small merchant or the naked body of a yogi.

It was a significant fact that the worst of Marut's population—the beggars, thieves and vagrants—was mostly lacking. These men were the hope upon which Nehal Singh had built his Utopia, the industrious, intelligent minority, and these were they whom he was now calling about him by the power of personality and superstition. Nicholson knew enough of the Hindu character to be well aware that it was not the loss of employment nor of their small savings which had brought them together and put their knives in their hands ready to strike. The Hindu accepts misfortune with the languid stoicism of the fatalist; injury and wrong rarely rouse him, especially, as in this case, when it comes too indirectly for him to trace the real injurer. But to touch his religion is to touch the innermost sanctuary of his being, where are stored the hidden fires of fanatic energy, hatred and reckless courage. And Nehal Singh was their religion, their Messiah, the Avatar for whose coming their whole nation waited. Hitherto he had led them in peace, and they had followed, though other influences had been at work.

Even in this moment he still controlled them. Nicholson felt that a strong unseen hand held the crowd in that strange silence beneath which rumbled and groaned the growing storm. He had seen dark hands finger the unsheathed knives; he had seen them reluctantly fall away. The hour had not yet come. Nehal Singh waited. For what? For him? The idea seemed absurd, and yet, as Nicholson felt himself being swept on, it took stronger hold upon his mind and his faint hope of success revived. He believed that, once face to face with the prince, he would be able to check the headlong disaster which was bearing down upon them all. They had been friends in a curious unacknowledged way. Nehal Singh would listen to him. He would be made to understand that one adventurer and one heartless woman do not make a nation; that the injury done him was far from irreparable.

A low exclamation close at hand roused him from his rapid considerations. He saw that the man who had hold of his horse's bridle had turned and with one outstretched hand was pointing over the heads of the crowd.

"Look, Sahib, look!"

Nicholson glanced in the direction indicated. They were passing the site of the old Bazaar, now a black, scarred waste of machinery and disembowelled earth over which brooded a death-like quiet. Nicholson remembered vividly the day he had ridden there at Nehal Singh's side. A breathless, eager humanity had worked and slaved beneath the scorching sun, redoubling every effort as the fine commanding presence of the young ruler appeared among them. Then the clank of busy machinery had mingled with the shouted orders of the English overseers, and Nehal Singh had turned to him with a grave pride and happiness.

"See what your people have taught my people," he said. "They have taught them to seek their bread from the earth and to leave their dreams. This is only the beginning. The time shall come when they shall stand shoulder to shoulder with their white brethren!"

How had the over-sanguine prophecy been fulfilled! The native at Nicholson's side pointed a finger of scorn and anger at the silent, ruined waste.

"Devil—English devil!" he said laconically, and continued on his way.

Nicholson's lips tightened. His own words came back to him with a new significance: "In a strange country no one is an exception." This Travers, this one unscrupulous fortune-hunter, heedless of everything save his own advancement, had branded them all. He had undone, with the help of a heedless woman, the work of generations of heroic, honest labor. Truly the chain of individual responsibility is a long one!

Nicholson had left Colonel Carmichael's bungalow at twelve o'clock. The increasing crowd and Stafford's prolonged absence had urged him to instant and independent action. In the best of cases, he had little faith in the brother-officer's secret mission. Stafford was not the man to exert any influence over the native mind. He was the type of the capable and well-meaning English officer who, excellent leader in his own country, is of small use when face to face with Indian problems of character and prejudice. Nicholson had judged himself the better advocate, and having obtained the Colonel's reluctant permission, he had at once started for the royal palace. But his progress had been painfully slow, and he had made no effort to hurry.

Any sign of anxiety or excitement would have looked like fear to the suspicious, hate-filled eyes of the men who swarmed about him, and whatever else happened, they should not see an Englishman afraid. The knowledge that he rode there alone, the representative of his nation, added a greater dignity, a greater firmness to his already calm and upright bearing. It was no new situation for him—it is never an exceptional situation in a country where Englishmen are always in the minority—and it inspired him, as it had always done since his earliest lieutenant days. He knew that as he acted, looked, and spoke, so would the image of his country be stamped upon the minds of a hundred thousand and their children's children. There was no vanity, no self-importance in this conception of his duty. It was a stern, unbending acceptance of his responsibility; and as in the lonely fort upon the frontier where he had dominated, unaided, month after month, over wild, antagonistic races, so now, unarmed and unprotected, he dominated over the fanatic rabble by the pure force of a complete personality. He was to all intents and purposes their prisoner, but he rode there as their conqueror; and that most splendid triumph of all triumphs—the unseen victory of will over will—filled him with a new confidence and hope.

Yet it was three o'clock before he reached the palace gates. It seemed to him that they had deterred his progress for some unknown purpose, and the thought of those he had left behind caused him profound uneasiness. Native treachery was proverbial, and no doubt Nehal Singh felt himself justified in any conduct that seemed wise to him. In any case, there was no return. The crowd in front of Nicholson sank back like a receding tide as he rode through the open gates and then closed in behind, following in one dense stream as he proceeded slowly up the splendid avenue. He felt now that he was in the hands of destiny. Through the trees he caught sight of the palace steps where Nehal Singh had stood the night before. No living soul moved. The whole world seemed to have concentrated itself behind him, a grim and silent force which was sweeping him onward—to what end he could not tell.

Suddenly the native who still held his horse's bridle lifted his hand as he had done before and pointed ahead.

"Look, Sahib!" he cried. "Look!"

Nicholson made no sign. He retained his easy attitude, one hand loosely holding the reins, the other with the riding-whip resting negligently on his hip. There was no change in his bronzed face: his eyes took in the scene which an abrupt turn in the road revealed to him with a steadfast calm, though his pulses had begun to beat furiously. It was as though a painter with two strokes of a mighty brush had smeared the square before the temple with a great moving stain. Only one narrow white line reached up to the temple doorway. On either side, right up to the gopuras and stretching far away down the branching paths, a living mass stood and waited, their faces turned toward him. Pilgrims they might have been, but he saw in the foremost row men with their dark hands clasped over the muzzles of their rifles, and every here and there the sunlight flashed back a reflection from the cold steel at their sides. They made no sound as he rode between them; only a soft shuffling behind him told him that the human wall was closing in. He did not turn. His eyes passed calmly over the watching faces, and the hands that played at their dagger-hilts fell away as though the piercing gaze had paralyzed them. Thus he reached the temple, where he dismounted.

No one had told him, but he well understood that this was his destination, and with a firm step passed into the inner court. For an instant the sudden change from brilliant daylight to an almost complete darkness dazzled him. He saw nothing but a moving shadow intermingled with points of fire that glowed steadily in two long rows up to the altar, where fell a single ray of golden sunshine. Helmet in hand, he moved slowly forward, every nerve strung taut with suspense. As his eyes grew accustomed to the curious half-light, he saw that the unreal shadows were men grouped on either side behind rows of torch-bearers. The red flare fell on their fixed, unmoved faces, and threw weird shadows backward and forward among the massive pillars whose capitals faded into the intensified gloom overhead. There was no other movement, no other sound save Nicholson's own footsteps, which echoed loud and threatening in that petrified silence. On the altar itself a Holy Lamp burned steadily, and behind, half obliterated by a lonely, upright figure, the great three-headed god stretched out ghost-like arms into the sunshine that descended in a narrow ladder of pure light to mingle with the altar fire.

Nicholson moved on. At the altar steps he came to a halt and waited. The figure did not stir nor seem to be aware of his presence. A torch-bearer knelt on the lower step, and the fiery deflection threw into plastic relief the set and pitiless features beneath the jeweled turban. Gone was the old simplicity. The hands that lay clasped one upon the other on the splendid scimitar were loaded with gems, and from the turban a single diamond sparkled starlike in the changing light. A splendid and romantic figure, truly; harmonizing with and dominating over the mysterious background. But it was not the splendor, nor even the stern tragedy written on the worn and haggard face, which caused Nicholson to feel a cold hand grasp at his bold self-confidence. It was the sudden intuitive realization that here the battle began. He was no longer the master personality towering over a hydra-headed multitude. Here it was a man against a man, will against will, despair against despair.

"Hail, Rajah Sahib!" he said in Hindustani. "Hail!"

His voice had echoed into silence before Nehal Singh moved. Then he lifted his hand in greeting.

"Hail, Englishman!"

"You know me," Nicholson went on, drawing nearer. "I am Nicholson, Captain Nicholson of the—Gurkhas."

"I do not know you." There was a pitiless finality in the few words and in the gesture which accompanied them.

Nicholson lifted his head to the light.

"Nehal Singh, you lie. I was and am your friend."

He heard a stir behind him, and his instinct, doubly sharpened, felt how a dozen hands had flown to their weapons. Then again there was silence. His eyes had not flinched in their challenge.

"I have no friends among traitors and cowards."

The insult left Nicholson calm. Something in the tone in which the words were uttered, something that rang more like a broken-hearted despair than contempt, touched him profoundly.

"Thou hast the power to say so, Rajah," he answered quietly. "I am alone and unarmed."

The reproach went home to its mark. He saw the Rajah's hand tighten on the sword-hilt and a deeper shadow pass over the handsome features.

"Thou art right," Nehal Singh said. "I have misused my power, and that I will not do. Whilst thou art here thou needst fear neither insult nor danger."

"I fear neither," was the answer. A bitter, scornful smile lifted the corners of the set lips.

"So thou sayest." Then, with a gesture of impatience, he went on: "Thou hast sought me here, and it is well. I also have sought thee, for I have a message that thou shalt carry from me to thy people. Wilt thou bear it?"

"Bear it thyself, Rajah, to the people with whom thou hast lived in honor and friendship."

"In deceit and treachery!" Nehal Singh retorted, frowning. "But enough of that. Wilt thou bear my message?"

"If it must be—yes."

"It must be. Tell them first that every bond that linked us is broken. Tell them not to count on what has been. What has been is not forgotten, but it is written on my heart in fire and blood—it has crossed out love and respect, pity and mercy."

"Rajah—"

"Hear me to the end, Englishman! I am not here to waste words with thee—henceforward my acts shall be my words. But thou shalt not go back and say that it is ambition or a mean revenge which has drawn my sword from its sheath. It is not that." He paused, and the hand which he had raised to cut short Nicholson's interruption sank slowly back upon his sword-hilt. Then he went on, and his low-pitched voice penetrated into the farthest corner of the silent temple: "Sahib, I loved thy people. I loved them for their past, for their courage, their justice, their greatness. In my boy's mind they were the heroes of the world, and as such I worshiped them. No poison could kill my love—it seemed a part of me, the innermost part of my soul—and when for the first time I stood before them, face to face, it was as though I lived, as though I had awakened from a dream. Be patient, Englishman, for you of all others must understand that there is for me no turning back, no yielding. Great love is sister to a greater hate, respect to scorn. I came among you, inexperienced save in dreams, a believing boy—fool if you will, whose folly received its punishment. The outside of the platter was fair enough to have deceived those wiser than I, Sahib. There were lovely women with the faces of angels, and tall men, honest-eyed and brave-tongued. But the outside was a lie—a lie!" He lifted his hand again in a sudden storm of tortured passion. "The women are wantons—the men tricksters—"

"Rajah!" The stern warning passed, but not unheeded.

"Thou art hurt and stung," Nehal said, in a low, shaken voice. "The truth wounds thee! For me—it was death." He hesitated again, fighting for his self-control. "Sahib, great things are expected of a great people. Others may cheat and swindle, others may lie and blaspheme with God's holy secrets, others may seek their pleasures in the earth's mire, but *they* must stand apart. They must bear forward the banner of righteousness, or their greatness is no more than an empty sound—a bubble which the first bold enemy may prick. Perchance I blinded myself wilfully, perchance I stopped my ears. The platter was fair to my eyes, the falsehood rang like truth. Now I know. I know that the past is all that is left you—you are a fair seeming behind which decay and corruption. Were I another, I would take my broken faith to the darkest corner of the jungle and eat out my life in despair and sorrow. But I have another task before me—my duty to my people."

"And that duty, Rajah—?"

"A great people must rule mine," was the high answer. "I thought you a great people, and I used my strength, my wealth and influence to further your power. But you are not worthy. Who are you that dare to assume authority over millions—you who can not rule yourselves, you who idle away your lives in folly and self-seeking? Well may you crown yourselves with the laurels which your fathers won! You have none of your own—and see to it that those faded emblems from a high past are not snatched from your palsied fingers. I at least have flung from me a yoke which I despise. Parasites shall not feast upon my country!"

A low murmur arose from the serried ranks and grew and deepened as Nicholson retorted passionately:

"Thou canst not measure thyself against an Empire!"

"Empire against Empire!"

"Marut is no Empire!"

"All India shall answer me!"

At another moment Nicholson might have smiled at so vain a boast, but it did not seem to him vain as he faced that towering figure. There was destiny written in the blazing eyes. So might a prophet have called upon his nation—so might a nation, inspired by an absolute belief, have answered him as this swaying crowd answered—with wild, triumphant shouts.

"We follow thee, Anointed One! Lead us, for thou art Vishnu, thou art God!"

"Thou hearest!" Nehal Singh said, turning to Nicholson.

"I hear," the Englishman answered significantly. "And I know, as thou knowest, that it is a lie. Thou art not God. Thou art a Christian."

"No longer. How shall I believe in a God whose disciples mock His commandments?" His voice became inaudible in the suddenly increased confusion.

The next instant, the torch-bearers, who guarded the open space around the two men, were thrust violently on one side, and with a wild scream, which rang high above the uproar, a half-naked figure rushed up the steps and with outspread arms stood like an evil phantom at Nehal's side.

"He is dead!" he shrieked. "He is dead! I killed him—my knife it was that killed him—the son of the Devil Stafford is dead—my enemy is dead!" He swung around toward the light, his arms still raised and Nicholson recognized, with a start of repulsion, Behar Singh's triumphant, distorted features. "Kill!" he shrieked again. "Kill them all, son—son—of—the—so is my revenge—". The harsh, grating voice cracked like a steel blade that has been snapped in half. For a breathing space Behar Singh stood there, drawn to his full height; then he reeled and rolled with a heavy thud to the lowest step, where he lay motionless, his grinning face frozen into a look of diabolical joy. A slow oozing stream of blood crept over the white marble to Nicholson's feet. The voices died into silence. Nicholson and Nehal Singh faced each other over the dead body.

"Thou seest," Nehal Singh said. "There is no turning back."

"No, there is no turning back." The Englishman drew himself upright. The light of unchangeable resolution illuminated his face and made him, unarmed and dressed in the rigid simplicity of his uniform, a fine and impressive contrast to the brilliant bearing of his opponent. "Not that"— pointing to Behar Singh and speaking in clear, energetic English—"not that has made retreat impossible. It was already impossible before. Nehal Singh, I came here to plead with you. I respected you and pitied you too much to allow you to bring disaster upon yourself without an effort to save you. You say you came among us inexperienced save in dreams. It is true. Only a dreamer could have hoped to find perfection. We are a great people, Rajah; we have always been great, and we shall always be.

"And if there be corruption among us, it shall be weeded out. In times of peace, vice and folly grow fast. Scoundrels, idlers, boasters and fools grow side by side with prosperity; they are the weeds which spring up on an over-cultivated soil. But war is the uprooting time of corruption, it is the harvest-time of what is best and noblest in a people. And that time has come. You, like your father, have learned to despise and hate us. Perhaps you are right. You have mingled with the scum which rises to the surface of still waters. The scum shall be cleared away, and if it costs us the lives of our greatest, it will not be at too high a price. We as well as you need the bitter lesson which only disaster can teach us. We shall see our weakness face to face, we shall root out our weeds and start afresh. You and the whole world shall see that the soil is still rich with honor."

A change so rapid that it was scarcely noticeable passed over the Hindu's face. It would have been a flash of hope but for the contradiction of the scornfully curved lips.

"My belief is dead, Sahib."

"It must live again."

"Would to God that were possible!" Suddenly he leaned forward and spoke hurriedly and in English. "Captain Nicholson, there shall be no treachery. This is not a mutiny as in the past—it is war. And war is between men. See that—your women are brought into safety. I give you till midnight."

"They can not go alone."

Nehal Singh laughed sneeringly.

"It is not your lives that I seek. Go with your women. No harm shall be done you. Make good your escape, for I swear that after midnight I shall lead my people against their enemies, and he who falls into their hands need not hope for mercy."

"And I also swear an oath, Rajah Nehal Singh! Not one of us will leave Marut. The men will remain at their posts, and the women will stand by them."

"You are throwing away your lives."

"They will not be thrown away. They will prove at least that I have not boasted."

For an instant the two men watched each other in momentous silence, as two wrestlers each seeking to measure the other's strength. Then Nehal Singh raised his hand in dismissal.

"It is well, Englishman. If you have not indeed boasted, we shall meet again."

"We shall meet again, Rajah Sahib."

Nicholson swung round on his heel. The crowd behind him fell back, and with a rapid step, neither glancing to the right nor left, he strode out of the temple into the fading sunshine. His horse was still held in waiting, and he mounted instantly. Erect in his saddle, he faced the frowning multitude, then rode forward, as he had come, without haste, holding their passions in check by his own high, fearless bearing.

The highroad was empty as he passed through the gates. The enemy lay behind. He set spurs to his horse and galloped headlong toward Marut.

CHAPTER VIII
FACE TO FACE

Mrs. Carmichael turned up the light with a steady hand. Her gaunt, harsh features were expressionless.

"Well, what news, Captain Nicholson?" she said. "You can say it outright. I am not afraid." She turned as she spoke and looked around her. "Are your nerves strong enough, Mrs. Berry? If not, pull yourself together. We can only die once, and there's nothing to whimper about."

Mrs. Berry, who sat cowering in the corner of the sofa, lifted her grey face. The clumsy lips tried to move, but no sound came forth except an inarticulate murmur. Mrs. Carmichael shrugged her shoulders as one does at an irresponsible child. "Well?" she repeated.

Nicholson came farther into the room, so that he stood within the circle of lamp-light. In a rapid glance he had taken in the occupants, and their attitudes were to him what symptoms are to a quick-sighted doctor. Mrs. Cary sat in an arm-chair, bolt upright, her hands clasped before her, her small eyes fixed straight ahead. Beatrice stood at her side, almost in an attitude of protection, pale, but otherwise calm and apparently indifferent. As he had entered, Lois had been preparing some food at a side table. She now came closer, and her dark, serious eyes rested penetratingly on his face, so that he felt that, even if he had thought of deceiving them as to the true state of affairs, it would have been in vain as far as she was concerned. As for Mrs. Carmichael, she stood in her favorite position—her arms akimbo, her chin tilted at an angle which lent her whole expression something bulldog and defiant. The atmosphere of danger with which the little drawing-room was filled acted differently upon each temperament, but upon this typical soldier's wife the effect was to arouse in her all the primitive passions, the fighting instinct, the love of struggle against heavy odds.

"Come!" she exclaimed, as Nicholson still remained silent. "Do you think, because one or two of us are a bit 'nervy', that we are really afraid? Not in the least. For my part, if I've got to die, I shall take good care that one or two of those black heathen come with me!" She flung open a drawer, and, taking out a revolver, thumped it energetically upon the table. "Now then, Captain!"

"My dear lady, I never doubted your courage," Nicholson answered, "and my news is not so hopeless as you suppose. I spoke with Nehal Singh." He saw Beatrice start and glance in his direction with an expression of sudden suspense in her fine eyes. "What he said left me no option. There could be no idea of coming to terms. At the same time it seems that he has no desire for a general massacre. His sole ambition is to drive us out of the country. He has given us till midnight to escape—those who want to."

"Does he think we are going to be got rid of as easily as that?" Mrs. Carmichael broke in. "Do you think that I have forgotten those months when George was fighting around Marut? Do you think I have forgotten all the fine fellows that laid down their lives to take the place and put an end to the disgrace of being held at bay by a horde of heathen? And now we are to run away like sheep? Not if George listens to me!"

"You need have no fear," Nicholson answered. "Not a man of us is going to leave Marut alive. But you ladies—"

"Well, what about us 'ladies'?" in a tone as though the description had been an insult.

"I have just told you—Nehal Singh gives you till midnight to get away."

Mrs. Carmichael snapped her lips together in a straight, uncompromising line.

"Very much obliged to His Highness, I'm sure, but I stay with the regiment," she said.

Nicholson could not repress a smile at this description of her husband, but there was something more than amusement in his brightening eyes.

"Thank you, Mrs. Carmichael, I knew that would be your answer. But it is my duty to ask the others—to give them their choice. There is little hope for those who remain." He could not bring himself to turn to the cowering figure upon the sofa. There is a shame which is not personal, and he was passionately ashamed for that quivering bulk of fear, for that greedy hope which he felt rather than saw creep up into the livid face. He looked at Lois. Her head was lifted and the fiery enthusiasm which spoke out of every line of the small dark face transformed her from a saddened woman back to the girl who never played a losing game but she won it, point by point, by pluck and daring.

"If I shan't be a bother, I wish to stay with you all," she said with studied simplicity. But her tone was eloquent.

"A brave comrade is always welcome," he answered. "Your husband—" He hesitated, and then concluded in a low voice: "Your husband offered to go with you. He is waiting outside with the horses." He avoided her eyes, but her tone betrayed to him the pain that he had unwillingly caused her.

"Please tell Archie that I will not let him sacrifice himself for me. I know that he will wish to remain, and I, too, wish to remain. We are all English, and who knows how little or how much we are all to blame for this disaster? We must share it together."

Something like a sigh of relief passed Nicholson's compressed lips, but he said nothing. In duty bound, he dared not offer encouragement nor plead for the fulfillment of his hopes. With mixed feelings he turned to Beatrice. Possessed as he now was of all the details of her conduct, he could not but lay at her door the consequences of a frivolous and heartless action. But her pitiless self-denunciation at the meeting, her present quiet and dignity, subdued in him all scorn and anger. Courage saluted courage as their eyes met.

"And you, Miss Cary?"

"Lois has already answered for me," she said. "If there was any justice in this world, I alone should suffer; but one can never suffer alone, it seems. The least I can do is to stand by you all." Her tone revealed all the remorse and suffering of which human nature is capable. It stirred in him a sudden impulsive pity. He crossed the room with outstretched hand.

"You are a brave woman."

She smiled bitterly, but the color rushed to her cheeks.

"Thank you. You have paid me the only compliment for which I care. But it is a small thing to take one's punishment without crying. After all, death isn't the worst."

She saw him glance doubtfully at her mother, and she bent down to the frozen face, speaking now gently but distinctly, as though to a suffering invalid whose ears had been dulled with pain.

"Mother, what do you want to do? There is still time—and Captain Nicholson says there is no hope for those who remain. You must not be influenced by my choice."

Mrs. Cary looked up into her daughter's face with a perplexed frown. She seemed scarcely to have heard what had been said to her, not even to have been aware that any escape was possible. She felt for Beatrice's hand, and taking it in her own, stroked it with pathetic helplessness.

"A bad mother!" she said absently. "Well, perhaps I was. Yes, no doubt—and you think so, too, though you never said anything. It was always position I wanted. Now it's all gone. What is it, dear? Why do you look at me like that? I haven't said what I oughtn't, have I?"

"No, no. Only Captain Nicholson wants to know—will you stay or go? We could get some of the servants to go with you. You will be safe then."

Mrs. Cary shook her head.

"Are you—what are you going to do?"

A childish smile twisted the heavy face.

"I'd like to stay with you, Beaty. We have always stuck together, haven't we?" She lay back with her head against Beatrice's shoulder. "You always were so clever, Beaty. I'm sure it will be all right. You'll see your poor mother through." The eyelids sank; she dropped into a drowse of complete mental and physical breakdown, and for a moment no one spoke. Mrs. Carmichael had shifted from her defiant attitude, and her hard, set face expressed a grim satisfaction not unmixed with pity.

"Now, Mrs. Berry, what about you?" she said. "Captain Nicholson has wasted enough time with you women. You must make up your mind—if you've got one," she concluded, in a smothered undertone.

Mrs. Berry drew herself up from her cowering position. Her teeth were still chattering with terror, but Nicholson saw that the crisis of panic was over. There was a curious look of obstinate resolve on the usually weak and silly face.

"If all the men are remaining, I suppose my husband remains, too?" she asked.

"Yes; he is helping Colonel Carmichael with the defenses."

Wonderful indeed are the *volte-faces* of which a character is capable! Nicholson, to whom human nature was a book of revelations, watched with a sense almost of awe this mean, petty and brainless woman, who a moment before had been whimpering with fear, smooth out her skirts and arrange her hair as though death were not sitting at her elbow.

"I am sure," she said, in a sharp voice which still trembled, "I can do what Mrs. Cary can do. I shall stay—please tell Percy so, with my love. And I should like to see him if possible before the end."

Nicholson bowed to her, and for the first time in their acquaintance the salute had a genuine significance.

"I am proud to have such countrywomen!" he said, and then added in a low tone as he passed Lois: "The cathedral is nearly finished."

She nodded.

"It could not have been better finished," she said bravely. "And you see I was right—when there is a noble building in the midst of them, people grow ashamed of their mud-huts. They pull them down and begin their own cathedrals—even when it is too late."

His eyes wandered instinctively toward the woman on the couch.

"Yes, you were quite right." He went to the curtained doorway, where he found Mrs. Carmichael waiting for him, a quaint figure enough with her sleeves rolled back, her skirts tucked up above her ankles, the revolver stuck brigand-wise in her belt.

"I'm coming with you," she said coolly. "I can shoot as straight as most of you, and a good deal better than George. I might be of some use."

"You would be of use anywhere," he returned sincerely, "but, if I may say so, you will be of more use here. Your courage will help the others. As for us, we have fifty of my Gurkhas, and they will do all that can be done. I will let you know what is happening. At present you are safest here."

She sighed.

"Very well. And if any one is hurt, send him around. I have plenty of bandages."

"Yes, of course."

It was a merely formal offer and acceptance. Both knew that it would be scarcely worth while to bandage men already in their full health and strength marked out for death. Nicholson went out, closing the door after him, and once more an absolute stoic silence fell upon the little company. In moments of crisis, it is the strict adherence to the habits of a lifetime which keeps the mind clear and the nerve firm. Lois went on quietly preparing some sandwiches, which in all probability would never be eaten, and Mrs. Carmichael resigned martial occupation for the cutting-out of a baby's pinafore for an East-end child whom she had under her special patronage. But her mind was active and, stern, self-opinionated martinet that she was, she could not altogether crush the regrets that swarmed up in this last reckoning up of her life's activity. Better had her charity and interest been centered on the dirty little children whom she had indignantly tolerated on her compound! Better for them all would it have been had each one of them sought to win the love and respect of the subject race! Then, perhaps, they would not have been deserted in this last hour of peril.

Mrs. Carmichael glanced at Beatrice Cary with a fresh pricking of conscience. What, after all, had she done to deserve the chief condemnation? She had played with fire. Had they not all played with fire? She had looked upon a native as a toy fit to play with, to break and throw away. Did they not all, behind their seeming tolerance and Christian principles, hide an equal depreciation? Was she even as bad as some? How many men revealed to their syces their darkest moods, their lowest passions? How many women were to their ayahs subjects for contemptuous Bazaar gossip. They were all to blame, and this was the harvest, the punishment for the neglect of a heavy responsibility. The thought that she had been unjust was iron through Mrs. Carmichael's soul, for above all things she prided herself on her fairness. She pushed her work away and went over to Beatrice's side. Mrs. Cary's head still rested against the aching shoulder, and Mrs. Carmichael made a sign to let her improvize a cushion substitute. Beatrice shook her head.

"No, thank you," she whispered, glancing down at the flushed, sleeping face. "We have done each other so little real service that I am glad to be able to do even this much. I don't suppose it will be for long. How quiet everything is!"

Mrs. Carmichael looked at the clock on the writing-table.

"It is not yet midnight," she said. "Probably the Rajah is keeping his promise." Her expression relaxed a little. "Don't tire yourself," she added bruskly to Mrs. Berry, who had been fanning the unconscious woman's face with an improvized paper fan. "I don't think she feels the heat."

The missionary's wife continued her good work with redoubled energy. It was perhaps one of the few really unselfish things which she had ever done in the course of a pious but fundamentally selfish life, and it gave her pleasure and courage. The knowledge that some one was weaker than herself and needed her was new strength to her new-born heroism.

"It is so frightfully hot," she said half apologetically. "Why isn't the punkah-man at work?"

"The 'punkah-man' has bolted with the rest of them," Mrs. Carmichael answered. "I dare say I could work it, though I have never tried."

"It is hardly worth while to begin now," Beatrice observed, and this simple acknowledgment that the end was at hand received no contradiction.

Once again the silence was unbroken, save for the soft swish of the fan and Mrs. Cary's heavy, irregular breathing. Yet the five women who in the full swing of their life had been diametrically opposed to one another were now united in a common sympathy. Death, far more than a leveler of class, is the melting-pot into which are thrown all antagonisms, all violent discords of character. The one great fact overshadows everything, and the petty stumbling-blocks of daily life are forgotten. More than that still—it is the supreme moment in man's existence when the innermost treasures or unsuspected hells are revealed beyond all denial. And in these five women, hidden in two cases at least beneath a mass of meanness, selfishness and indifference, there lay an unusual power of self-sacrifice and pity. Death was drawing near to them all, and their one thought was how to make his coming easier for the other. When the silence grew unbearable, it was Mrs. Carmichael who had the courage to break it with a trivial criticism respecting the manner in which Lois was making the sandwiches.

"You should put the butter on before you cut them," she said tartly, "and as little as possible. I'm quite sure it has gone rancid, and then George won't touch them. He is so fussy about the butter."

Mrs. Berry looked up. The perspiration of physical fear stood on her cold forehead, but her roused will-power fought heroically and conquered.

"And, please, would you mind making one or two without butter?" she said. "Percy says all Indian butter is bad. Of course, it's only an idea of his, but men are such faddy creatures, don't you think?"

"They wouldn't be men if they weren't—" Mrs. Carmichael had begun, when she broke off, and the scissors that had been snipping their way steadily through the rough linen jagged and dropped on the table. She picked them up immediately and went on with an impatient exclamation at her own carelessness. But the involuntary start had coincided with a loud report from outside in the darkness, and a smothered scream.

Lois put down her knife.

"Won't you come and help me?" she said to Beatrice. "Your mother will not notice that you have gone."

Beatrice nodded, and letting the heavy head sink back among the cushions, came over to Lois' side.

"How brave you are!" she said in a whisper. "You seem so cool and collected, just as though you believed your sandwiches would ever be eaten!"

"I am not braver than you are. Look how steady your hand is—much steadier than mine."

Beatrice held out her white hand and studied it thoughtfully.

"I am not afraid," she said, "but not because I am brave. There is no room for fear, that is all." She paused an instant, and then suddenly the hand fell on Lois'. The two women looked at each other. "Lois, I am so sorry."

"For me?"

"For you and every one. I have hurt so many. It has all been my fault. I would give ten lives if I had them to see the harm undone. But that isn't possible. Oh, Lois, there is surely nothing worse than helpless remorse!"

The hand within her own tightened in its clasp.

"Is it ever helpless, though?"

"I can't give the dead life—I can't give back a man's faith, can I?"

The light of understanding deepened in Lois' eyes.

"Beatrice—I believe I know!"

"Yes, I see you do. Do you despise me? What does it matter if you do? It has been my fear of the world and its opinion that helped to lead me wrong. Isn't it a just punishment? I have ruined both our lives. Lois, I couldn't help hearing what Captain Nicholson said to you. It explained what you said to me about building on the ruins of the past. That was what he did—he built a beautiful palace on me—and I wrecked it. I failed him."

"Have you really failed him?"

"Lois, I don't know—I am beginning to believe not. But it is too late. I meant to clear away the rubbish—and build. But there is no time."

"You have done your best."

"Oh, if I could only save him, Lois! He was the first man I had ever met whom I trusted, the first to trust me. I owe him everything, the little that is good in me. It had to come to life when he believed in it so implicitly. And he owes me ruin, outward and inward ruin."

Lois made no answer. With a warm, impulsive gesture she put her arms about the taller woman's neck and, drawing the beautiful face down to her own, kissed her. Beatrice responded, and thus a friendship was sealed—not for life but for death, whose grim cordon was with every moment being drawn closer about them.

The sound of firing had now grown incessant. One report followed another at swift, irregular intervals, and each sounded like a clap of thunder in the silent room. Mrs. Cary stirred uneasily in her sleep, a low, scarcely audible groan escaped the parted lips, as though even in her dreams she was being pursued by fear's pitiless phantom. Her self-appointed nurse continued to fan her with the energy of despair, the poor livid face twitching at every fresh threatening sound. Mrs. Carmichael still pretended to be absorbed in her pinafore, but the revolver lay on the table, ready to hand, and there was a look in the steady eyes which boded ill for the first enemy who should confront her. Lois and Beatrice continued their fruitless task.

A woman's courage is the supreme victory of mind over matter. It is no easy thing for a hero to sit still and helpless while death rattles his bullet fingers against the walls and screams in voices of hate and fury from a distance which every minute diminishes. For a woman burdened with the disability of a high-strung nervous system, it is a martyrdom. Yet these women, brought up on the froth of an enervating, pleasure-seeking society, held out—held out with a martyr's courage and constancy—against the torture of inactivity, of an imagination which penetrated the sheltering walls out into the night where fifty men writhed in a death-struggle with hundreds—saw every bleeding wound, heard every smothered moan of pain, felt already the cold iron pierce their own breasts. The hours passed, and they did not yield. They had ceased from their incongruous tasks, and stood and waited, wordless and tearless.

As the first grey lights of dawn crept into the stifling room they heard footsteps hurrying across the adjacent room, and each drew herself upright to meet the end. Mrs. Carmichael's hand tightened over the revolver, but it was only Mr. Berry who entered. The little missionary, a shy, society-shunning man, noted for doing more harm than good among the natives by his zealous bigotry and ignorance of their prejudices, stood revealed in a new light. His face was grimed with dirt and powder, his clothes disordered, his weak eyes bright with the fire of battle.

"Do not be afraid," he said quickly. "There is no immediate danger. I have only been sent to warn you to be ready to leave the bungalow. The front wall is shot-riddled, and the place may become indefensible at any moment. When that time comes, you must slip out to the old bungalow. Nicholson believes he can hold out there."

"My husband—?" interrupted Mrs. Carmichael.

"Your husband is safe. In fact, all three were well when I left. If I wasn't against such things, I should say it was a splendid fight—and every man a hero. The Rajah—"

"The Rajah—?"

Mr. Berry looked in stern surprise at the pale face of the speaker.

"The Rajah has a charmed life," he said somberly. "He is always in the front of his men—we can recognize him by his dress and figure—he is always within range, but we can't hit him. Not that I ought to wish his death, though it's our only chance." He put his hands distractedly to his head. "Heaven knows, it's too hard for a Christian man! Every time I see an enemy fall, I rejoice—and then I remember that it is my brother—" He stopped, the expression on his face of profound trouble giving way to active alarm. "Hush! Some one is coming!"

A second time the door opened, and Travers rushed in. Lois saw his face, and something in her recoiled in sick disgust. Fear, an almost imbecilic fear, was written on the wide-open, staring eyes, and the hand that held the revolver trembled like that of an old man.

"Quick—out by the back way!" he stammered incoherently. "I will lock the door—so. That will keep them off a minute. They are bound to look for us here first. Nicholson is retiring with his men—they are going to have a try to bring down the Rajah. It's our one chance. It may frighten the devils— they think he's a god. I believe he is, curse him!" All the time, he had been piling furniture against the door with a mad and feverish energy. "Help me! Help me!" he screamed. "Why don't you help? Do you want to be killed like sheep?"

Lois drew him back by the arm.

"You are wasting time," she said firmly. "Come with us! Why, you are hurt!"

He looked at the thin stream which trickled down the soiled white of his coat. A silly smile flickered over his big face.

"Oh, yes, a scratch. I hardly feel it. It isn't anything. It can't be anything. There's nothing vital thereabouts, is there, Berry?"

The missionary shrugged his shoulders. He had flung open the glass doors which led on to the verandah, and the brightening dawn flooded in upon them.

"Come and help me carry this poor lady," he said. "We have not a minute to lose."

Travers tried to obey, but he had no strength, and the other thrust him impatiently on one side.

"Mrs. Carmichael, you are a strong woman," he appealed. Between them they managed to bring Mrs. Cary's heavy, unconscious frame down the steps. It was a nerve-trying task, for their progress was of necessity a slow one, and the sound of the desperate fighting seemed to surround them on every side. It was with a feeling of intense relief that the little party saw Nicholson appear from amidst the trees and run toward them.

"That's right!" he cried. "Only be quick! They are at us on all sides now, but my men are keeping them off until you are out of the bungalow. The old ruin at the back of the garden is our last stand. Carmichael is there already with a detachment, and is keeping off a rear attack. I shall remain here."

"Alone?" Berry asked anxiously.

"Yes. I believe they will ransack the bungalow first. When they come, the Rajah is sure to be at their head, and—well, it's going to be diamond cut diamond between us two when we meet. I know the beggars and their superstition. If I get in the first shot, they will bolt. If *he* does—"

"You are going to shoot him down like a rat in a trap!" Beatrice burst out passionately.

The others had already hurried on. With a gentle force he urged her to follow them.

"Or be shot down myself," he said. "Leave me to do my duty as I think best."

She met his grave eyes defiantly, but perhaps some instinct told her that he was risking his life for a poor chance—for their last chance, for without a word she turned away, apparently in the direction which her companions had already taken.

As soon as she was out of sight, Nicholson recharged his smoking revolver, and stood there quietly waiting. His trained ear heard the firing in front of the bungalow cease. He knew then that his men were retiring to join Colonel Carmichael, and that he stood alone, the last barrier between death and those he loved. The sound of triumphant shouting drew nearer; he heard the wrenching and tearing of doors crashing down before an impetuous onslaught, the cling of steel, a howl of sudden satisfaction. His hand tightened upon his revolver; he stood ready to meet his enemy single-handed, to fight out the duel between man and man. But no one came. A bewildering silence had followed upon the last bloodthirsty cry. It was as though the hand of death had fallen and with one annihilating blow beaten down the approaching horde in the high tide of their victory. But of the two this strange stillness was the more terrible. It penetrated to the little waiting group in the old bungalow and filled them with the chill horror of the unknown. Something had happened—that they felt.

Lois crept to the doorway and peered out into the gathering daylight. Here and there, half hidden behind the shelter of the trees, she could see the khaki-clad figures of the Gurkhas, some kneeling, some standing, their rifles raised to their dark faces, waiting like statues for the enemy that never came. A dead, petrified world, the only living thing the sunshine, which played in peaceful indifference upon the scene of an old and a new tragedy! Lois thought of her mother. By the power of an overwrought imagination she looked back through a quarter of a century to a day of which this present was a strange and horrible repetition. For a moment she lived her mother's life, lived through the hours of torturing doubt and fear, and when a stifled cry called her back to the reality and forced her to turn from the sunlight to the dark room, it was as though the dead had risen, as though her dreams had taken substance. She saw pale faces staring at her; she saw on the rusty truckle-bed a figure which rose up and held out frantic, desperate arms toward her. But it was no dream—no phantom. Mrs. Cary, wild-eyed and distraught, struggled to rise to her feet and come toward her.

"Where is Beatrice?" she cried hysterically. "Where is Beatrice? I dreamed she was dead!—It isn't true! Say it isn't true!"

Lois hurried back. In the confusion of their retreat she had lost sight of Beatrice, and now a cold fear froze her blood. She called her name, adding her voice to the half-delirious mother's appeal; but there was no answer, and as she prepared to leave the shelter of the bungalow to go in search of the lost girl, a pair of strong hands grasped her by the shoulders and forced her back.

"Lois, stand back! They are coming!"

Colonel Carmichael thrust her behind him, and an instant later she heard the report of his revolver. There was no answering volley. A dark, scantily-clad figure sprang through the trees, waving one hand as though in imperative appeal.

"Don't fire—don't fire! It's me!"

The Colonel's still smoking revolver sank, and the supposed native swayed toward him, only to sink a few yards farther on to the ground. Carmichael ran to his side and lifted the fainting head against his shoulder.

"Good God, Geoffries! Don't say I've hit you! How on earth was I to know!"

"That's all right, Colonel. Only winded—don't you know—never hurried so much in life. Have been in the midst of the beggars—just managed to slip through. O Lor', give me something to drink, will you?" Colonel Carmichael put his flask to the parched and broken lips. "Thanks, that's better. We got your message, and are coming on like fun. The regiment's only an hour off. You never saw Saunders in such a fluster—it's his first big job, you know." He took another deep draft, and wiped his mouth with the corner of his ragged tunic. "I say—don't look at me, Miss Lois. I'm not fit to be seen." He laughed hoarsely. "These clothes weren't made in Bond Street, and Webb assured me that the fewer I had the more genuine I looked. I say, Colonel, this is a lively business!"

Colonel Carmichael nodded as he helped the gasping and exhausted man into the bungalow.

"Too lively to be talked about," he said. "I doubt if the regiment isn't going to add itself to the general disaster."

"Oh, rot!" was the young officer's forgetful lapse into disrespect. "The regiment will do for the beggars all right. They didn't expect us so soon, I fancy. Just listen! I believe I've frightened them away already. There isn't a sound."

Colonel Carmichael lifted his head. True enough, no living thing seemed to move. A profound hush hung in the air, broken only by Mrs. Cary's pitiful meanings.

"Oh, Beatrice, Beatrice, where are you?"

Geoffries turned his stained face to the Colonel's.

"Beatrice! That's Miss Cary, isn't it? Anything happened to her?"

Colonel Carmichael shrugged his shoulders with the impatience of a man whose nerves are overstrained by anxiety.

"I don't know—we've lost her," he said. "We must do something at once. Heaven alone knows what has happened."

No one indeed knew what had happened—not even the lonely man who waited, revolver in hand, for the final encounter on whose issue hung the fortunes of them all.

Only one knew, and that was Beatrice herself as she stood before the shattered doorway of the Colonel's drawing-room, amidst the debris of wrecked, shot-riddled furniture, face to face with Nehal Singh.

CHAPTER IX
HALF-LIGHT

Once before she had placed herself in his path, trusting to her skill, her daring, above all, her beauty. With laughter in her heart and cold-blooded coquetry she had chosen out the spot before the altar where the sunlight struck burnished gold from her waving hair and lent deeper, softening shades to her eyes. With cruel satisfaction, not unmixed with admiration, she had seen her power successful and the awe-struck wonder and veneration creep into his face. In the silence and peace of the temple she had plunged reckless hands into the woven threads of his life. Amidst the shriek of war, face to face with death, she sought to save him. It was another woman who stood opposite the yielding, cracking door, past whose head a half-spent bullet spat its way, burying itself in the wall behind her,—another woman, disheveled, forgetful of her wan beauty, trusting to no power but that which her heart gave her to face the man she had betrayed and ruined. Yet both in an instantaneous flash remembered that first meeting. The drawn sword sank, point downward. He stood motionless in the shattered doorway, holding out a hand which commanded, and obtained, a petrified, waiting silence from the armed horde whose faces glared hatred and the lust of slaughter in the narrow space behind. Whatever had been his resolution, whatever the detestation and contempt which had filled him, all sank now into an ocean of reborn pain.

"Why are you here?" he asked sternly. "Why have you not fled?"

"We are all here," she answered. "None of us has fled. Did you not know that?"

He looked about him. A flash of scorn rekindled in his somber eyes.

"You are alone. Have they deserted you?"

"They do not know that I am here. I crept back of my own free will—to speak with you, Nehal."

Both hands clasped upon his sword-hilt, erect, a proud figure of misfortune, he stood there and studied her, half-wonderingly, half-contemptuously. The restless forces at his back were forgotten. They were no more to him than the pawns with which his will played life and death. He was their god and their faith. They waited for his word to sweep out of his path the white-faced Englishwoman who held him checked in the full course of his victory. But he did not speak to them, but to her, in a low voice in which scorn still trembled.

"You are here, no doubt, to intercede for those others—or for yourself. You see, I have learned something in these two years. It is useless. No one can stop me now."

"No one?"

He smiled, and for the first time she saw a sneer disfigure his lips.

"Not even you, Miss Cary. You have done a great deal with me—enough perhaps to justify your wildest hopes—but you have touched the limits of your powers and of my gullibility. Or did you think there were no limits?"

"I do not recognize you when you talk like that!" she exclaimed.

"That is surprising, seeing that you have made me what I am," he answered. Then he made a quick gesture of apology. "Forgive me, that sounded like a reproach or a complaint. I make neither. That is not my purpose."

"And yet you have the right," she said, drawing a deep breath, "you have every right, Nehal. It does not matter what the others did to you. I know that does not count an atom in comparison to my responsibilities. You trusted me as you trusted no one else, and I deceived you. So you have the right to hate me as you hate no one else. And yet—is it not something, does it not mitigate my fault a little, that I deceived myself far, far more than I ever deceived you?" He raised his eyebrows. There was mockery in the movement, and she went on, desperately resolute: "I played at loving you, Nehal. I played a comedy with you for my own purposes. And one day it ceased to be a comedy. I did not know it. I did not know what was driving me to tell the truth, and reveal myself to you in the ugliest light I could. I only knew it was something in me stronger than any other impulse of my life. I know what it is now, and you must know, too. Can't you understand? If it had been no more than a comedy, you must have found me out— months ago. But you never found me out. It was *I* who told you what I had done and who I was—"

"Why did you tell me?" He took an involuntary step toward her. Something in his face relaxed beneath the force of an uncontrollable emotion. He was asking a question which had hammered at the gates of his mind day after day and in every waking hour. "Why?" he repeated.

"I have told you—because I had to. I had to speak the truth. I couldn't build up my new life on an old lie. You had to know. I had won your love by a trick. I had to show you the lowest and worst part of myself before the best in me could grow—the best in me, which is yours."

"You are raving!"

"I am not raving. You must see I am not. Look at me. I am calmer than you, though I face certain death. I knew when I came here that the chances were I should be killed before I even saw you, but I had to risk that. I had to win your trust back somehow, honestly and fairly. I can not live without your trust."

"Beatrice!" The name escaped him almost without his knowledge. He saw tears spring to her eyes.

"It is true. Your love and your trust have become my life. Then I was unworthy of both. I tried to make myself worthy. I did what I could. I told you the truth—I threw away the only thing that mattered to me. I could not hold your love any longer by a lie—I loved you too much!"

For that moment the passionate energy of her words, the sincerity and eloquence of her glance, swept back every thought of suspicion. He stood stupefied, almost overwhelmed. Mechanically his lips formed themselves to a few broken sentences.

"You can not know what you are saying. You are beside yourself. Once, in my ignorance, I believed it possible, but now I know that it could never be. Your race despises mine—"

"I do not care what you are nor to whom you belong!" she broke in, exulting. "You are the man who taught me to believe that there is something in this world that is good, that is worthy of veneration; who awoke in me what little good I have. I love you. If I could win you back—"

"What then?"

"I would follow you to the world's end!"

"As my wife?"

"As your wife!"

He held out his arms toward her, impulse rising like the sun high and splendid above the mists of distrust. It was an instant's forgetfulness, which passed as rapidly as it had come. His arms sank heavily to his side.

"Have you thought what that means? If you go with me, you must leave your people for ever."

"I would follow you gladly."

He shook his head.

"You do not understand. You must leave them now—now when I go against them."

"No!" she broke in roughly. "You can't, Nehal, you can't. You have the right to be bitter and angry; you have not the right to commit a crime. And it would be a crime. You are plunging thousands into bloodshed and ruin—" He lifted his hand, and the expression in his eyes checked her.

"So it is, after all, a bargain that you offer me!" he said. "You are trying to save them. You offer a high price, but I am not a merchant. I can not buy you, Beatrice."

"It is not a bargain!" For the first time she faltered, taken aback by the pitiless logic of his words. "Can't you see that? Can't you see that, however much I loved you, I could not act otherwise than implore you to turn back from a step that means destruction for those bound to me by blood and country? Could I do less?"

"No," he said slowly.

She held out her hands to him.

"Oh, Nehal, turn back while there is yet time! For my sake, for yours, for us all, turn back from a bloody, cruel revenge. The power is yours. Be generous. If we have wronged you, we have suffered and are ready to atone. *I* am ready to atone. I *can* atone, because I love you. I have spoken the truth to you. I have laid my soul bare to you as I have done to no other being. Won't you trust me?"

His eyes met hers with a somber, hopeless significance which cut her to the heart.

"I can't," he said. "I can't. That is what you have taught me—to distrust you—and every one."

She stood silent now, paralyzed by the finality of his words and gesture. It was as though the shadow of her heartless folly had risen before her and become an iron wall of unrelenting, measured retribution against which she beat herself in vain. He lifted his head higher, seeming to gather together his shaken powers of self-control.

"I can not trust you," he said again, "nor can I turn back. But there is one thing from the past which can not be changed. I love you. It seems that must remain through all my life. And because of that love I must save you from the death that awaits your countrymen." He smiled in faint self-contempt. "It is not for your sake that I shall save you; it is because I am too great a coward, and can not face the thought that anything so horrible should come near you." He turned to two native soldiers behind him and gave an order. When he faced Beatrice again he saw that she held a revolver in her hand.

"You do not understand," she said. "You say you mean to save me, but that is not in your power. It is in your power to save us all, but not one alone. I know what my people have resolved to do. There are weak, frightened women among them, but not one of them will fall into your hands alive. Whatever happens, I shall share their fate."

Though her tone was quiet and free from all bravado, he knew that she was not boasting. He knew, too, that she was desperate.

"You can not force me to kill you," he said sternly.

"I think it possible," she answered. She was breathing quickly, and her eyes were bright with a reckless, feverish excitement. But the hand that held the revolver pointed at the men behind him was steady—steadier than his own.

Nehal Singh motioned back the two natives who had advanced at his order.

"You play a dangerous game," he said, "and, as before, your strength lies in my weakness—in my folly. But this time you can not win. My word is given—to my people."

"I shall not plead with you," she returned steadily, "and you may be sure I shall not waver. I am not afraid to die. I had hoped to atone for all the wrong that has been done you with my love for you, Nehal. I had hoped that then you would turn away from this madness and become once more our friend. To this end I have not hesitated to trample on my dignity and pride. I have not spared myself. But you will not listen, you are determined to go on, and I"—she caught her breath sharply—"surely you can understand? I love you, and you have made yourself the enemy of my country. Death is the easiest, the kindest solution to it all."

Nehal Singh's brows knitted themselves in the anguish of a man who finds himself thwarted by his own nature. He tried not to believe her, and indeed, in all her words, though they had rung like music, his ear, tuned to suspicion, had heard the mocking undercurrent of laughter. She had laughed at him secretly through all those months when he had offered up to her the incense of an absolute faith, an unshared devotion. Even now she might be laughing at him, playing on that in him which nothing could destroy or conceal—his love for her. And yet—! Behind him he heard the uneasy stir of impatient feet, the hushed clash of arms. He stood between her and a certain, terrible death. One word from him, and it would be over— his path clear. But he could not speak that word. Treacherous and cruel as she had been, the halo of her first glory still hung about her. He saw her as he had first seen her—the golden image of pure womanhood—and, strange, unreasoning contradiction of the human heart, beneath the ashes of his old faith a new fire had kindled and with every moment burned more brightly. Unquenchable trust fought out a death struggle with distrust, and in that conflict her words recurred to him with poignant significance: "Death is the easiest, the kindest solution to it all." For him also there seemed no other escape. He pointed to the revolver.

"For whom is that?" he asked.

"I do not know—but I will make them kill me."

"Why do you not shoot me, then?" he demanded, between despair and bitterness. "That would save you all. If I fell, they would turn and fly. They think I am Vishnu. Haven't you thought of that? I am in your power. Why don't you make yourself the benefactress of your country? Why don't you shoot her enemy?"

She made no answer, but her eyes met his steadily and calmly. He turned away, groaning. In vain he fought against it, in vain stung himself to action by the memory of all that she had done to him. His love remained triumphant. In that supreme moment his faith burst through the darkness, and again he believed in her, believed in her against reason, against the world, against the ineffaceable past, and against himself. And it was too late. He no longer stood alone. His word was given.

"Have pity on me!" he said, once more facing her. "Let me save you!"

"I should despise myself, and you would despise me—even more than you do now. I can not do less than share the fate of those whose lives my folly has jeopardized."

"At least go back to them—do not stay here. Beatrice, for God's sake!—I can not turn back. You have made me suffer enough—." He stood before her now as an incoherent pleader, and her heart burned with an exultation in which the thought of life and death played no part. She knew that he still loved her. It seemed for the moment all that mattered.

"I can not," she said.

"Beatrice, do not deceive yourself. Though my life is nothing to me— though I would give it a dozen times to save you—I can not do otherwise than go on. I may be weak, but I shall be stronger than my weakness. My word is given!"

He spoke with the tempestuous energy of despair. The minutes were passing with terrible swiftness, and any moment the sea behind him might burst its dam and sweep her and him to destruction. Already in the distance he heard the dull clamour of voices raised in angry remonstrance at the delay. Only those immediately about him were held in awed silence by the power of his personality. Again Beatrice shook her head. She stood in the doorway which opened out into the garden where the besieged had taken refuge. There was no other way. He advanced toward her. Instantly she raised her revolver and pointed it at the first man behind him.

"If I fire," she said, "not even you will be able to hold them back."

It seemed to her that she stood like a frail wall between two overwhelming forces—on the one side, Nehal with his thousands; on the other, Nicholson—alone, truly, but armed with a set and pitiless resolve. A single sentence, which had fallen upon her ears months before, rose now out of an ocean of half-forgotten memories: "Nicholson is the best shot in India," some one had said: "he never misses." And still Nehal advanced. His jaws were locked, his eyes had a red fire in them. She knew then that the hour of hesitation was over, and that in that desperate struggle she had indeed lost. Uncontrollable words of warning rushed to her lips.

"Nehal—turn back! Turn back!"

He did not understand her. He thought she was still pleading with him.

"I can not—God have pity on us both!"

Then she too set her lips. She could not betray the last hope of that heroic handful of men and women behind her. He must go to his death—and she to hers. She fired,—whether with success or not, she never knew. In that same instant another sound broke upon their ears—the sound of distant firing, the rattle of drums and the high clear call of a trumpet. Nehal Singh swung around. She caught a glimpse of his face through the smoke, and she saw something written there which she could not understand. She only knew that his features seemed to bear a new familiarity, as though a mask had been torn from them, revealing the face of another man, of a man whom she had seen before, when and where she could not tell. She had no time to analyze her emotions nor the sense of violent shock which passed over her. She heard Nehal Singh giving sharp, rapid orders in Hindustani. The room emptied. She saw him follow the retreating natives. At the door he turned and looked back at her. At no time had his love for her revealed itself more clearly than in that last glance.

"The English regiment has come to help you," he said. "Fate has intervened between us this time. May we never meet again!"

He passed out through the shattered doorway, but she stood where he had left her, motionless, almost unconscious. It was thus Nicholson and the Colonel found her when, a moment later, they entered the room by the verandah. Colonel Carmichael's passionate reproaches died away as he saw her face.

"You must not stop here," he said. "You have frightened us all terribly. The regiment has come and is attacking. There will be some desperate fighting. We must all stick together."

She caught Nicholson's eyes resting on her. She thought she read pity and sympathy in their steady depths, and wondered if he guessed what she had tried to do. But he said nothing, and she followed the two men blindly and indifferently back to the bungalow.

CHAPTER X
TRAVERS

They had no light. They talked in whispers, and now and again, when the darkness grew too oppressive, they stretched out groping hands and touched each other. They did this without explanation. Though none complained or spoke of fear, each needed the consolation of the other's company, and a touch was worth more than words. Mrs. Cary alone needed nothing. She lay on the rough truckle-bed and slept. Thus she had been for a week—a whole week of nerve-wrecking struggle against odds which marked hope as vain. Bullets had beaten like rain upon the walls about her, the moaning of wounded men on the other side of the hastily constructed partition mingled unceasingly with the cries of the ever-nearing enemy. And she had lain there quiet and indifferent. Martins, the regiment's doctor, had looked in once at her and had shaken his head. "In all probability she will never wake," he had said. "Perhaps it is the kindest thing that could happen to her." And then he had gone his way to those who needed him more.

Mrs. Berry knelt by the bedside. Her hands were folded. She had been praying, but exhaustion had overcome her, and her quiet, peaceful breathing contrasted strangely with the other sounds that filled the bungalow. Mrs. Carmichael and Beatrice sat huddled close together, listening. They could do nothing—not even help the wounded men who lay so close to them. Everything was in pitch darkness, and no lights were allowed. They could not go out and help in the stern, relentless struggle that was going on about them. They bore the woman's harder lot of waiting, inactive, powerless, fighting the harder battle against uncertainty and all the horrors of the imagination.

"I am sorry the regiment has come," Mrs. Carmichael whispered. "There is no doubt they will be massacred with the rest of us. What are a few hundreds against thousands? It is a pity. They are such fine fellows."

Her rough, tired voice had a ring of unconquerable pride in it. She was thinking of the gallant charge her husband's men had made only two weeks before; how they had broken through the wall of the enemy, and, cheering, had rushed to meet the besieged garrison. That had been a moment of rejoicing, transitory and deceptive. Then the wall closed in about them again, and they knew that they were trapped.

"Perhaps we can hold out till help comes," Beatrice said.

She tried not to be indifferent. For the sake of her companions she would gladly have felt some desire for life, but in truth it had no value for her. She could think of nothing but the evil she had done and of the atonement that had been denied her. It was to no purpose that she worked unceasingly for the wounded. The sense of responsibility never left her. Each moan, each death-sigh brought the same meaning to her ear: "You have helped to do this—this is your work."

"No help will come," Mrs. Carmichael said, shaking her head at the darkness. "When a whole province rises as this has done, it takes months to organize a sufficient force, and we shan't last out many days. I wonder what people in England are saying. How well I can see them over their breakfast cups! Oh, dear, I mustn't think of breakfast cups, or I shall lose my nerve." She laughed under her breath, and there was a long silence.

Presently the door of the bungalow opened, letting in a stream of moonlight. It was closed instantly, and soft footfalls came over the boarded floor.

"Who is it?" Mrs. Carmichael whispered.

"I—Lois," was the answer. The new-comer crept down by Beatrice's side and leaned her head against the warm shoulder. "I am so tired," she said faintly. "I have been with Archibald. He has been moaning so. Mr. Berry says he is afraid mortification has set in. It is terrible."

"Poor little woman!" Beatrice put her arm about the slender figure and drew her closer. "Lay your head on my lap and sleep a little. You can do no good just now."

"Thank you. I will, if you don't mind. You will wake me if anything happens, won't you?"

"Yes, I promise." It gave Beatrice a sense of comfort to have Lois near her. Very gently she passed her hand over the aching forehead, and presently Lois fell into a sleep of absolute exhaustion.

By mutual consent, Mrs. Carmichael and Beatrice ceased to talk, but when suddenly there was a movement close to them, and a dim light flashed over the partition, they exchanged a glance of meaning.

"That is my husband," Mrs. Carmichael whispered. "Something is going to happen. Listen!"

She was not wrong in her supposition. The Colonel had entered the next room, followed by Nicholson and Saunders, and had closed the door carefully after him. All three men carried lanterns. They glanced instinctively at the wooden partition which divided them from the four women, but Carmichael shook his head.

"It's all right," he said. "They must be fast asleep, poor souls. Let's have a look at these fellows." He went over to a huddled-up figure lying in the shadow. The corner of a military cloak had been thrown over the face. He drew it on one side and then let it drop. "Gone!" he said laconically. He passed on to the next. There were in all three men ranged against the wall. Two of them were dead. "Martins told me they couldn't last," Colonel Carmichael muttered. "It is better for them. They are out of it a little sooner, that's all." The third man was Travers. He lay on his back, his face turned slightly toward the wall, his eyes closed. He seemed asleep. The Colonel nodded somberly. "Another ten hours," he calculated.

He came back to the table, where the others waited, and drew out a paper from his pocket.

"Give me your light a moment, Nicholson," he said.

No one spoke while he examined the list before him. All around them was a curious hush—a new thing in their struggle, and one that seemed surcharged with calamity. After a moment Colonel Carmichael looked up. He was many years the senior of his companions, but just then there seemed no difference in years between them. They were three wan, haggard men, weakened with hunger, exhausted with sleepless watching. That week had killed the youth in two of them.

"Geoffries has just given me this," Carmichael said. "It is a list of our provisions. We have enough food, but there is no fresh water. The enemy has cut off the supply. We could not expect them to do otherwise." He waited, and then, as neither spoke, he went on: "I have spoken with the others. You know, gentlemen, we can not go on another twenty-four hours without water. We have made a good fight for it, but this is the end. We must look the fact in the face."

"Surely they must know at headquarters what a state we are in—" Saunders began.

The Colonel shrugged his shoulders.

"No doubt they know, but they can not help in time. This is not a petty frontier business. It is something worse—a rising with a leader. A rising with a leader is a lengthy business to tackle, and it requires its victims. In this case we are the victims." He smiled grimly. "We have only one thing left to do—make a dash for it while we have the strength. You must know as well as I do that there is scarcely anything worth calling a hope, but it's a more agreeable way of dying than being starved out like rats and then butchered like sheep. I know these devils." He glanced around the shadowy room with a curious light in his eyes. "My best friend was murdered in this room," he added. "Personally, I prefer a fair fight in the open."

"When do you propose to make the start, Colonel?" Nicholson asked.

"Within an hour. The night favors us. The women must be kept in the center as much as possible. I have given Geoffries special charge over them. They will be told at the last moment. There is no use in spoiling what little rest they have had." He drew out a pencil and began to scribble a despatch on the back of an old letter. "I advise you gentlemen to do likewise," he said. "Very often a piece of paper gets through where a man can not, and it is our bounden duty to supply the morning periodicals with as much news as possible."

For some minutes there was no sound save that of the pencils scrawling the last messages of men with the seal of death already stamped upon their foreheads. All three had forgotten Travers, and yet from the moment they had begun to speak he had been awake and listening. He sat up now, leaning upon his elbow.

"Nicholson!" he said faintly.

Nicholson turned and came to his side.

"Hullo!" he said. "Awake, are you? How are you?"

Travers made no immediate answer; he took Nicholson's hand in a feverish clasp and drew him nearer.

"I am in great pain," he said. "You don't need to pretend. I know. The fear of death has been on me all day. Just now I am not afraid. Is there no hope?"

"You mean—for us? None."

Travers nodded.

"I heard you talking, but I wanted to make sure. It has all been my fault—every bit of it. It's decent of you not to make me feel it more. You are not to blame—her. You know I tempted her, I made her help me. She isn't responsible. At any rate, she made a clean breast of it—that's something to her credit. I didn't want to—I never meant to. I am not the sort that repents. But this last week you have been so decent, and Lois such a plucky little soul—she ought to hate me—and perhaps she does—but she has done her best. Nicholson, are you listening? Can you hear what I say? It's so damned hard for me to talk."

"I can hear," Nicholson said kindly. "Don't worry about what can't be helped." In spite of everything, he pitied the man, and his tone showed it.

Travers lifted himself higher, clinging to the other's shoulder. His voice began to come in rough, uneven jerks.

"But it can be helped—it must be helped! Don't you see—I came between you and Lois purposely. From the first moment you spoke of her I knew that you loved her—and I wanted her. I never gave your message. I didn't dare. You are the sort of man a woman cares for—a woman like Lois. I couldn't risk it. But now—well, I'm done, and afterward she will be free—"

Nicholson drew back stiffly.

"You are talking nonsense," he said, in a colder tone. "No one wants you to die—and in any case, you know very well we have no chance of getting through this alive."

Travers seized his arm. His eyes shone with a painful excitement.

"Yes—yes!" he stammered. "You have a chance—a sure hope. I can save you; I can—atone. That's what I want. Only you must help me. I am a dying man. I want you to bring me to the Rajah—at once. Only five minutes with him—that will be enough. Then he will let you go—he must!"

Nicholson freed himself resolutely from the clinging hands.

"You exaggerate your power," he said, "and, besides, what you ask is an impossibility."

He turned away, but Travers caught his arm and held him with a frantic, desperate strength.

"Then if you will not help me—send Miss Cary to me," he pleaded. "I must speak to her."

Nicholson looked down into the dying face with a new interest. He had no suspicion of the burden with which Travers' soul was laden, and yet he was conscious now that the matter was urgent and of an importance which he could not estimate.

"I will tell her," he said. "Stay quiet a minute. We have no time to lose."

Travers nodded and fell back on to his rough couch. His eyes closed and he seemed to sleep, but as Beatrice knelt down by his side he roused himself and looked at her with the intensity of a man who has gathered his last strength for a last great purpose.

"I am dying," he whispered thickly; "I know it and I don't care. I am past caring. But before I die I want to atone; I want, if I can, to save Lois. I care for her in my poor way, and I would like her to be happy. Are you listening?"

"I am listening," Beatrice answered gravely. "Do you think I could close my ears when you speak of atonement?"

He clutched her hand.

"You would be glad to atone for all the mischief we have done?"

"I would give my life."

"Is the Colonel there? I can't see clearly. Colonel, I want you to hear what I have to say."

Colonel Carmichael turned.

"This is no time," he said sternly, "and it is too late for atonement. Our account with this world is closed."

"It need not be. Colonel—in the name of those whose lives lie in your hands, I beg of you to listen to me."

There was a moment's hesitating silence. Travers' glazed eyes were fixed on the elder man's face with a hypnotizing power. The Colonel drew nearer—reluctantly knelt down.

"Be quick then!" he said.

Travers nodded. His head was thrown back against Beatrice's shoulder. With fumbling, trembling fingers he drew a plain gold ring from his pocket and thrust it into the Colonel's hand.

"Look at that!" he whispered. "Look at the inscription."

Carmichael turned to the feeble light. No one spoke or moved. They watched him and waited with a reasonless, breathless suspense.

"My God!" he whispered, "How did you come by this?"

Travers drew himself upright. The shadows of death were banished in that last moment; his voice was clear and steady as he answered.

"Listen," he said. "I will tell you—and then act before it is too late!"

CHAPTER XI
IN THE HOUR OF NEED

Nehal Singh pulled aside the curtains over the window and stepped out on to the balcony. The air in the great silent room behind him stifled him, and even the night breeze, as it touched his cheeks, seemed to burn with fever. He stood there motionless, his arms folded, gazing fixedly into the half-darkness. A pale, watery moonlight cast an unearthly shimmer over the shadowy world before him, brightened every here and there by the will-o'-the-wisp fire points which marked the presence of the camped thousands waiting silently for his word. Only one spot—it seemed like a black stain—remained in absolute gloom, and it was thither the Rajah's eyes were turned. Every night he had come to the same place to watch it. Every night he had tortured himself with the thought of all it contained.

For he knew now, with the clear certainty of a man who has searched down to the bottom of his soul, that in that silent area his whole life, his one hope of happiness was bound up, and waited, with those who were fighting stubbornly, heroically, against the end—its destruction beneath his own sword. He was fighting against himself. With his own hands he was tearing down that which seemed an inseparable, incorporate part of himself. Anger and contempt were dead. In their place the old love had rekindled and grown brighter before the sight of a courage, dignified and silent, which had held back the tide of furious fanaticism and thwarted his own despair. He had seen, with eyes which burned with an indescribable emotion, a regiment of wearied, weakened men, led by a man he had once despised, burst through the densest squares of his own soldiers; he had heard their cheers as they had clasped hands with the defenders; he had looked aghast into his own heart, afire with admiration, aching with a strange, broken-hearted gratitude to God who had made such men. It was in vain that, lashing himself with the knowledge of his own weakness and of his disloyalty to those who followed him, he had flung himself against the defenses of the little garrison.

Day after day they drove him back, fighting hand to hand in the earthworks they had thrown up in a few hours of miraculous labor. He fought against them like a man possessed of an unquenchable hatred; but at night, when he was at last alone, he had slipped out on to his balcony and held out his hands toward them in an unspeakable wordless greeting. Once more they had become for him the world's Great People, the giants of his boyhood's imagination, the heroes of his man's ideal. At the point of the sword they had proved the truth of Nicholson's proud boast, and hour by hour the man who had turned from them in a moment of bitter disillusion saw the temple he had once built to their honor rise from its ashes in new and greater splendor.

Thus two weeks had passed, and to-night was to see the end. Nehal knew that, brave though they were, they could do no more. They had no water, and his forces hugged them in on every side. One last attack and it would be over—Marut would be cleared from the enemy, his victory complete. His victory! It was his own ruin he was preparing, the certain destruction of that which seemed linked invisibly but surely to his own fate. And, knowing that, he knew also that there was no turning back for him, no retreat. His word was given. His people, the people who claimed him by the right of blood, clamored for him to lead them as he had sworn. It made no difference if on the path he had chosen he trampled on every hope, every wish, every rooted instinct. There was no turning back. He knew it—the knowledge that his own words bound him came to him with pitiless finality as he stood there watching the silent, lightless stretch which was soon to be the scene of a last tragic struggle; and if indeed there are such things as tears of blood, they rose to his eyes now.

With lips compressed in an agony he could neither analyze nor conquer, he turned slowly back into the dimly lighted room. Two torches burned on either side of the throne and threw unsteady shadows among the glittering pillars. They lit up his face and revealed it as that of a man who has cast his youth behind him for ever. Only a few months had passed since he had sat there with Travers in the full noon of his hope and enthusiasm. He remembered the scene with a clearness which was a fresh torture. The hopes that had been built up in that hour lay shattered, the woman for whom they had been built was lost. He thought of her now as he always thought of her, as he knew he would think of her to the end. For this love, save that it had grown and deepened into a wider understanding, had remained unchanged. As there had been cowards and tricksters among his heroes, so in that one woman evil and good had stood side by side and fought out their battle. And the good had won—had won because he alone of all men had believed in it. He believed in it still—in the same measure as he had learned to love her—with a deeper understanding of temptation and failure. It was the one triumph in the midst of seeming ruin, the one firm rock in the raging torrent of his fate, beaten as it was between the contending streams of desire and duty. She was indeed lost to him, but not as in the first hour of his shaken trust. He had regained his memory of her as a good woman, striving upward and onward; and already he had invested her with the glory of those whom death has already claimed from us.

Nehal Singh started from his painful reverie, conscious that some one had entered the room and was watching him. He turned and saw his chief captain standing respectfully before him, and, though it was a man he liked and trusted, it seemed to him that the gaunt, soldierly figure had taken on the form of an ugly, threatening destiny.

"All is ready, Great Prince," the native said, salaaming. "Every man is at his post. We do but await thy orders."

Nehal did not answer. His hands clasped and unclasped themselves in the last agony of hesitation. The moment had come, the inevitable and irretrievable moment which had loomed so long upon his horizon. Even now he hardly knew what it was to bring him. The forces warring in his blood were locked in a death struggle. At last he nodded and his lips moved.

"It is well. In half an hour—I will come to them. In half an hour—the attack will begin."

"Sahib—is it good to wait? The dawn cometh, and with the dawn—"

Nehal Singh lifted his hand peremptorily.

"In half an hour," he repeated.

The man salaamed and was gone. Nehal Singh stood there like a pillar of stone. It was over. In half an hour! And yet, at the bottom of his heart, he knew that he had delayed—purposely, but to no end but his own increased suffering. With a sigh of impatience he turned, and in the same instant became once more aware that he was not alone.

For a moment he perceived nothing save the shadows and the unsteady flickering of the yellow torchlight. Then his vision cleared and he saw and understood, and an exclamation burst from his horrified lips. It was a woman who stood out against the darkness, her body clothed in rags, the hair, grey and thin, hanging unkempt about her shoulders, the face turned to his that of some being risen from a tomb. There seemed to be no flesh upon the high cheek-bones nor upon the hands that were stretched toward him; only the eyes were alive with an unquenchable fire which burned upon him with a power that was unearthly. She staggered a few steps and then sank slowly to his feet, her hands still outstretched. He knelt down and supported the sinking head upon his shoulder.

"Who art thou?" he whispered in Hindustani. "Where hast thou come from? Tell me thy history."

A look of intense pain passed over her features. Slowly and with a great effort her lips parted.

"I am English—let me speak in English. I have only a few minutes—I am dying."

He looked about him, seeking something with which to moisten her dry lips, but she clung to him with an incredible strength.

"No, no, I must speak with you. Up to now I have lived in an awful nightmare—amidst ghastly phantoms who pursued and tortured me. But when I heard your voice—when I heard you give that order, I awoke. The dreams vanished, I heard and understood—and remembered!" She drew herself upright and, for a moment spoke with a penetrating clearness. "Not in half an hour—never! Withdraw that order! If you go against them you are accursed. Lay down your arms! You must—you know you must! You dare not—" She clung to his arm and her eyes seemed to burn their way into his very soul. "I tell you—to turn traitor is to inherit an endless hell—"

"A traitor!" he echoed. Something clutched at his heart, a sort of numb suspense which became electrified as he saw a new expression flash into her face.

"Yes, a traitor!" she whispered. "That was what I was. I was English—yes, English in spite of all, but in my bitterness I turned from my people. I let myself be taken alive. I would not share the fate of those who had once been dear to me. My whole life has been the punishment. They tortured me and then came the dreams—the awful, hideous dreams. I was always looking for you, always calling for you. And they laughed and mocked at me. Only one man did not laugh—" her voice grew doubtful and hesitating, as though she were groping in the shadows of her memory. "He did not laugh. He promised to help me but he never came again—and I died—yes, I died—but I saw your face, I heard your voice—and I came back from death—to save you!" Once more her vision cleared and her voice grew steadier. "Go back to them! They are your friends. If you do not go, you will break your heart—as mine is broken. Swear to me—you must, because—"

He bent closer to her to catch every sound that fell from her lips. His pulses were beating with a suffocating violence. Somewhere a veil was lifting. It was as if the sunlight were at last breaking through a mist of strange dreams, strange longings, strange forebodings. The confused voices that had called to him throughout his life grew clearer.

"Because—?" he whispered.

But she did not answer. Her head was thrown back. Her open eyes were fixed intently on his face. Suddenly she smiled. It was a smile that chilled his blood with its hideous distortion. And yet behind it lurked the possibility of a long-lost beauty and sweetness.

"Steven!" she whispered. "Steven!"

Closer and closer she drew his face to hers. Her icy lips rested on his cheek. Pity and a strange, as yet unformed, foreboding made him accept that dying caress and speak to her with an urgent, pleading gentleness.

"You have something to tell me," he murmured, "something I must know. Tell me before it is too late."

But her eyes had closed and she did not answer him.

"Rouse yourself!" he insisted. "Rouse yourself!" It seemed to him that she smiled. Her face had undergone a change. It was younger, and in the flickering light his imagination brightened it with the glories whose dim traces still touched the haggard, emaciated features. One last time her eyes opened and she looked at him. The frenzy of despair was gone. He felt that she was looking beyond him to a future he could not see.

"Go back!" she whispered. "Go back!"

He pressed her to him, seeking to pour something of his own seething vitality into her dying frame. With her life the threads of his fate seemed to be slipping through his fingers.

"Help me!" he implored. "Do not leave me!"

But he knew that she would never answer. She lay heavy in his arms, and the hand that clasped his relaxed and fell with a soft thud upon the marble. He rose to his feet and stood looking down upon her. It was not the first time he had seen death. In these last weeks he had met it in all its most hideous, most revolting forms; but none had moved him, awed him as this did. He knew that she had once been beautiful. Who had made her suffer till only a shadow of that beauty remained? What had she endured? Who was she? What did she know of him? Why did she call him by a name which rang in his ears with a vague familiarity? What was it in her poor dead face which stirred in him a memory which had no date nor place in his life?

Outside he heard the uneasy stirring of the thousands who awaited him. He looked up and through the open windows, saw the camp-fires and that one dark spot which was to be swept clear of all but death. What had she said? "Go back! Lay down your arms! You must—you know you must! To turn traitor is to inherit an endless hell!" A traitor? A traitor to whom—to what? To some blind instinct that had called him in those English voices, that had beaten out an answering cry of thankfulness from his heart when their cheers proclaimed his own defeat?

A soft step roused him from his troubled thoughts. He looked up and saw a servant standing in the curtained doorway. The man's eyes were fixed on the outstretched figure at Nehal's feet, and there was an expression on the dark face so full of fear and horror that the Rajah involuntarily drew back.

"Who was this woman?" he demanded. "Whence comes she?"

"Lord Sahib, she was a mad-woman whom the Lord Behar Singh kept out of mercy. She must have escaped her prison. More I know not."

The man was trembling as though in the shadows there lurked a hidden threatening danger, and Nehal turned aside with a gesture of desperate impatience.

"Why hast thou come before the time?" he asked.

"Lord Sahib, outside there are two English prisoners. They demand to be brought before thee. What is thy will?"

"Bring them hither."

Nehal Singh stood where the bowing servant left him, at the side of the poor dead woman, his hands crossed upon his sword-hilt, his eyes fixed on the parted curtains. There he waited, motionless, passive, as a man waits who knows that he has become the tool of Destiny.

A moment later, Beatrice stood before him.

CHAPTER XII
HIS OWN PEOPLE

She was not alone, but in that first moment he saw nothing but her face. It seemed to him that the whole world was blotted out and that only she remained, grave, fearless, supreme in her wan beauty, a tragic figure glorified by a light of unconquerable resolution. He looked at her but he did not greet her; no muscle of his set and ashy features betrayed the thrill of passionate recognition which had passed like a line of fire through his veins. To move was to awake from a dream to a hideous, terrible reality.

She came slowly toward him. The thin wrap about her head slipped back and he saw the light flash on to the fair disheveled hair. His eyes were dazzled, but it seemed to him that there were grey threads where once had been untarnished gold. Yet he could not and would not speak, and she came on till she stood opposite him, the dead woman lying there between them. Then for the first time she lowered her eyes and he awoke with a start of agonizing pain.

"Why have you come?" he said. "Have you come to plead again? Have you come to torture me again? Was not that once enough? In a few minutes I shall sweep your people to destruction. Shall I save you? — is that what you have come to tell me?"

He waited for her answer, his teeth clenched, his brows knitted in the old terrible struggle. All his energy, all his determination sank paralyzed before her and before his love, and yet he knew he must go on — go on with the destruction of himself, of her, of all that was dearest to him.

She knelt down and touched the dead face with her white hand, closing the glazed, staring eyes with a curious tenderness and pity. There was no surprise or horror in her expression as she at last rose and faced him — rather a mysterious knowledge which held him bound in wordless expectation.

"I have come to tell you that woman's history, Steven Caruthers," she said. "I have not come to plead with you but to tell you the truth — to lay before you the two paths between which you must choose once and for all. Will you listen to me?"

"Beatrice!" he stammered. "Why have you given me a name which is not mine—which *she* gave me with her last breath? What do you know that you have risked your life—"

"It was no risk," she said. "My life was forfeited and it was our last hope. Oh, if I can turn you from all this ruin, then I shall have atoned for the evil I have done you!"

The note of mingled entreaty, despair and hope stirred him to the depths of his being, but he made no response. He could only point to the white face and repeat the question which had beaten in pitiless reiteration against his tortured brain.

"Who was she?"

"She was your mother."

"And I—?"

It was not Beatrice who this time answered. A figure stepped forward out of the shadows and faced the Rajah. It was Carmichael, pale, deeply moved, but erect and steadfast. His eyes were fixed on Nehal's features with a curious, hungry eagerness which changed as he spoke into a growing recognition.

"Let me tell you," he said. "I will be brief, for every minute is precious and full of danger for us all. This poor woman was Margaret Caruthers, the wife of my dearest friend, and your mother. Until an hour ago I believed that she had been butchered with her husband and with all those others who paid the penalty of one man's sin. No doubt you know why your supposed father, Behar Singh, rose against us?"

"His honor—his wife had been stolen from him by a treacherous Englishman," Nehal answered hoarsely.

"Yes, by Stafford, John Stafford's father. The issue of that act of infidelity was a child, Lois, who afterward was adopted by Caruthers, partly out of friendship for Stafford, partly because he had no children of his own. So much, at least, I surmise. I surmise, too, that that adoption cost him his wife's love and trust. Perhaps, ignorant of the child's real parentage, she believed the worst, perhaps there were other causes—be it as it may, in the hour of catastrophe she refused to share the general fate. She chose to throw herself upon the mercy of her mother's people."

"Her mother's people!" Nehal echoed blankly.

"There was native blood in her veins. It was on that account that Behar Singh spared her. She bitterly learned to regret her change of allegiance. She was kept close prisoner, and six months after the murder of her husband she bore him a son—you—Steven Caruthers. Behar Singh, himself without an heir, took the child from her, and from that hour the unfortunate woman became insane. Long years she was kept a secret and wretched captive, and then one day she escaped, and in her wanderings met a man—an Englishman who was then your friend."

"Travers!" Nehal exclaimed.

"Yes, Travers. By means of bribes and threats he obtained her whole history, partly from her own lips, partly from her gaolers. But he told no one of his discovery."

"Why not? How dared he keep silence?"

"It is very simple. He wished to marry my ward, Lois Caruthers, and he wished to have her money. As I have said, Caruthers had adopted her when her mother, the Reni Ona, returned to her own people, and had made her his heir in the case that he should have no children of his own. Had your existence been known Lois would have been penniless. Travers knew this and kept his secret from every one save Stafford."

"Why did he tell Stafford?"

"He had to. Stafford and Lois loved each other—with a love which was all too natural and explicable in the light of our present knowledge. It was necessary that he should be made aware that marriage between them was impossible—that they were, in fact, the children of the same father."

"Stafford kept silence—"

"He had promised. And, moreover, he believed it kinder to hide the truth from Lois. Only at the last he determined to speak at all costs. But it was too late. You know—he was murdered on the steps of Travers' house."

Nehal Singh nodded. An even deadlier pallor crept over his features.

"I know," he said. "It was Behar Singh's last vengeance. God knows, my hands are clean."

"That I know. You are your father's son."

"And the proof of all this?"

"This ring. Take it. It was your mother's. Travers gave it to me when he made his confession. He took it from the poor mad woman at their first meeting. Look at the inscription. It bears your mother's and father's names."

"And Travers—?" The Rajah lifted his hand in a stern, threatening gesture.

"—is dead," was the grave answer. "He died an hour ago, in his wife's arms."

For a moment a profound hush hung over the great, dimly lighted hall. The Rajah knelt down by his mother's side and gently replaced the ring upon the thin lifeless finger.

"She called herself a traitor," he said, half to himself. "A traitor to whom—to what?"

"To the strong white blood that was in her veins. In her bitterness at the real or imagined wrongs that had been done her, she turned away from the people to whom she belonged, to whom she was bound by all the ties of love and upbringing. She disobeyed the voice of her instinct. And you, her son, you, too, have been bitter; you, too, must listen to the call of the two races to whom you are linked. Whom will you obey? You stand at the cross-ways where you must choose—where we must either part or join hands for good and all. The road back to us is open, is still open. That is the message of peace which we have risked our lives to bring you. Rajah, Steven Caruthers—for so I now call you—I plead with you—I may plead with you, for in this hour at least I can not look upon you as an adversary, but as the son of this unfortunate woman—above all, of my friend. I plead with you the more because I owe you years of friendship. I am not the least to blame that you fell away from us in resentment and bitterness. I could have shielded you from the inevitable pitfalls that beset your path, but—God forgive me!—my prejudice blinded me and I held back. It was I who carried you away from the palace on that night when you were left, a helpless child, to the mercy of Behar Singh's enemies. Then I had pity enough—but years after I held back the hand of friendship which I might have offered you. Well, I am punished, twice punished, for my prejudice and blindness. Is it too late for me to make my reparation?"

He held out his hand and there was a silence of tense expectation. The Rajah's head was bowed. He did not seem to see the Colonel's movement.

"You can not think I am pleading with you to save our lives," Carmichael went on with grave dignity. "We have fought for them. An hour ago we were prepared to lay them down without complaint. We are not the less prepared now. It is not for us I am speaking, but for you. Your day as Rajah is over—

your claim to rule in India void. I offer you instead your father's name, your father's people, your father's heritage. The other road—well, you have trodden it, you know it. You must choose. Your mother chose—twenty-five years ago, in the same hour of crisis, blinded by the same bitterness. She chose to tear the bonds of love and duty; she ignored the true voice of her instinct. It broke her heart. The same crisis stands to-night before you, her son. What will you do—Steven Caruthers?"

The Rajah lifted his head. The struggle was written in his dark, sunken eyes and on the compressed lips.

"I can not desert them," he said wearily. "They trust me—my people trust me."

"Who are your people?" was the swift question. "You must choose."

Again the same silence, the same waiting while the hand of fate seemed to hover above them in the darkness. Beatrice left her place at the dead woman's side. With a firm, proud step she came to the Rajah and took his hand in both her own. He started at her touch, and for a long minute his gaze seemed to sink itself in hers, but she never wavered. When she spoke an immeasurable tenderness rang in her voice, a boundless understanding and sympathy.

"Steven—have you forgotten? Long ago in the old temple? Don't you remember what you told me then—how you loved and admired us? You called us the world's Great People, and when you spoke of our heroes there was something in your voice which thrilled me. Was it only your books, was it your teachers—Behar Singh—who made you feel as you did? When you came among us, what led you? The face of a woman? Was it only that? Or was it something more?—the call of a great, wonderful instinct?"

His eyes were riveted on her face, but for that moment he did not see her. He did not see the tears that glistened on her cheeks. He was looking straight through the long vista of the past, right back to the first hours of his memory, when he had wandered alone amidst strange faces, a ruler in a palace which had never ceased to be his prison, an exile whose home lay only in strange, fantastic dreams. And in this final moment he seemed to stand high above the past, and ever swifter and surer to trace through every incident of his life one same guiding power. Through the snares of Behar Singh's hate-filled temptations it had led onward; it had borne him to the temple—to the feet of the woman he was to love through every torture of bitter deception; it had swept him on a wave of impulse beyond his prison walls out into a world which he at last hailed as his; and now, in the hour of fiercest despair, of deepest loss, it was drawing him surely and swiftly homeward. The past vanished. He saw again the face lifted to his—he saw the tears—the Colonel's hand outstretched, waiting to clasp his own. He heard the title that she gave him as a man hears a long-forgotten watchword.

"You are English, Steven. You are English—you belong to us!"

He unfastened the sword at his side. For a moment he held it as though in farewell. But there was no grief on his face as he laid the jeweled weapon in the Colonel's hand.

"I have chosen," he said. "I can not go against my people."

CHAPTER XIII
ENVOI

With the surrender of one man the great Marut rising came to an end. It had been built up by him and on him, and with him it collapsed. As the news reached the armed thousands encamped about the ruined Station, consternation fell upon them. There was no attempt at organization or resistance. They believed simply that Heaven had turned against them and Vishnu joined hands with the Englishman, and they waited to hear no more. What had seemed an overwhelming force melted away as though it had been a shadow, and in the jungle, slinking along the lightless highways, or huddling in the lonely hovels outside Marut, the remnant of Behar Singh's great army hid from the hand of the destroyer. They had followed their god, and their god had deserted them. All hope was lost, and with the fatalism of their race they flung their weapons from them as they fled.

Pending the decision of the Government, Nehal Singh, now Steven Caruthers, was held prisoner in the club-house he had built two years before. Part of the returned regiment was encamped about the surrounding gardens, in order to prevent all attempt at rescue, but the precaution was a mere formality. Visitors came constantly. There was not a man in all the Station who was not anxious to help bury the past and to hold out the hand of friendship to one whom at the bottom of their hearts they had once wronged and slighted. Among them Carmichael and Nicholson were the chief. They passed many hours of each day with him, and worked steadily and enthusiastically for his pardon and release. He was touched and grateful, but beneath his gratitude there still lurked the demon of unrest. She had not come—the one being for whom he waited—she had sent no word. He knew that her mother lay dying—above all things he knew that on the great day of the attack she had stood resolutely between him and death—but nothing, no explanation or assurance, calmed the hidden trouble of his mind. After all, it had been pity—or remorse—not love.

Thus three weeks passed. The Colonel had spent the day with him discussing the future, arranging for the transference of Lois' fortune into his unwilling hands, and now, toward nightfall, he was once more alone, wearied in body and soul. For the first time since his surrender his sense of quiet and release from an immense burden was gone. He was still alone. He felt now that he would always be alone, for there was but one who could fill the blank in his life. And she had not come. He did not and could not blame her. Who was he that a woman should join her lot to his? An Englishman truly, but one over whose birth and youth there hung a shadow, perhaps a curse such as had darkened his mother's life and the life of all those in whose veins there flows an alien blood. She must not even think that any link from the past bound her. She must be free—quite free to choose. Wearily he seated himself at his table and took his pen.

"You have been the great guiding light of my life," he wrote to her. "You will always be, because I can not learn to forget. But for you it would be easier and better to forget. You will be happier—" And then he heard the door open, and she stood before him. The words that he had meant to write rushed to his lips, but no further. Moved by a common impulse, they advanced to meet each other, and the next moment she was in his arms. Neither spoke. It seemed as though, once face to face, there could be no doubts, no misunderstandings between them. Their love was wordless, but it had spoken in a silence more eloquent, more complete than words could ever have been.

"I could not come before," she said, after a little. "I could not leave her. She was only at peace when I held her hand. She was very happy at the last—now it is all over."

He held her closer to him, and she clung to him, not sadly or wearily, but like a strong woman who had fought and won the thing she fought for.

"It was Fate after all," he said, under his breath. "She meant us for each other."

She looked up at him. Though suffering, physical and mental, had drawn its ineffaceable lines upon her face, it had also added to her beauty the charm of strength and experience.

"I knew long ago that it was Fate," she answered. "Do you remember that first evening? You told me that people do not drift aimlessly into each other's lives. Even then, against my will, I felt that it was true. Afterward I was sure. I had entered into your life in a moment of frivolous recklessness, but you had entered into mine with another purpose, and I could not rid myself of you. Your hold upon me was strong. It grew stronger, do what I would, and the farce became deadly earnest."

"For me it was always deadly earnest," he said. "When I first saw you standing before the idol, it was as though a wall which had surrounded my life had been overthrown, and that you had come to be my guide and comrade in a new and unknown world."

"And then I failed you."

His eyes met hers thoughtfully.

"Did you? Now I look back, I am not sure. I had to believe you when you said you had deceived me and played with me. I had to force myself to despise you. Yet, when you confronted me in the bungalow, I felt suddenly that you needed to explain nothing. I understood."

"Did you understand that I had only deceived myself? I told myself that it was a farce played at your expense. But—Heaven knows—I believe it ceased to be a farce from the first hour I saw you. You believed in me so. No one had believed in me before—I had never believed in myself or in man, or in God, either. But I had to believe in you, and afterward—the rest came." She drew herself upright and looked him full in the dark eyes. "Steven, do you trust me?" He nodded. "As you did on that day when you told me that you owed me all that you were and ever would be?"

"As then, Beatrice."

She smiled gravely.

"You do right to trust me. You have made me worthy of your trust."

He put his arm about her shoulder, and led her gently on to the verandah. The night had fallen dark and starless. Through the black veil they saw the gleam of bivouac fires and heard the voices of men calling to one another, and the clatter of piled arms. They remained silent, after the storm and stress of the past, content to be together and at peace. They knew that the long night was over and that the dawn had broken.

When the Colonel entered they did not hear him, and without speaking he turned back and closed the door after him. In his hand he held a telegram ordering the deposition of Nehal Singh, Rajah of Marut, and the recognition, pardon and release of one Steven Caruthers, Englishman. But he crept away with the long-hoped-for message.

"Time enough," he thought. "They are happy."

And if beneath his heartfelt rejoicing there lurked the shadow of bitterness, who shall blame him? There was one dearer to him than his own child could have been, for whose wounded heart there seemed as yet no balsam. And yet, unknown to him, for her also the dawn was breaking. For even as he crept away with knitted brows, sharing her burden with her by the power of love and sympathy, she held in her hands the first herald of a happier future.

"What you have told me I accept—for now," Adam Nicholson had written. "You are wise to travel with the Carmichaels. It will do you good. I, who was prepared to wait my whole life for you, can have patience for a little longer. I know that you suffer and as yet I may not help you. Your pride separates us, but your pride is a little thing compared to my love. What is your birth or parentage to me? You say it would overshadow my whole life, darken my career? It might try. That would be one thing more to fight against. We have come to India to sweep away its prejudices; let us first sweep away our own. We have come to bring freedom; let us first make ourselves free. It will be a good battle, but it will not darken my life, Lois. Do you think opposition and struggle could darken my life? Surely you know me better. Do but stand at my side, and there will be no darkness. I am not a boy. I am a man who sees before him long years of labor, and who needs the one woman who can help him. Is our cathedral forgotten? I do not believe it. You are not the woman to forget. The time is not far off when we will crown our cathedral hand in hand. Only when your love dies can the barrier between us become insurmountable. If your love lives, then, as surely as there is a God in Heaven, I will come and fetch you, Lois—my wife."

And the tears that filled her eyes as she read the boldly written words were no longer the tears of grief. Her love for him had been the rock upon which her life was built. It was imperishable. She knew thus that she would not have long to wait until his coming.